LONGING

In the smoldering wake of the Civil War, the monumental story of beautiful, courageous Kitty Wright continues. Caught in the violent passions and mounting turmoil of a war-torn nation, she keeps body and soul alive with longing—longing for Travis Coltrane, the handsome cavalry officer who has given her a son, but has yet to make her his wife.

LUST

Determined at any cost to save her family's plantation from ruthless carpetbaggers, Kitty marries the wealthy, sadistic Corey McRae, suffering his depraved desires and the hostility of an entire town while consumed with a burning hunger for one man.

LOVE

Kept from fulfilling her destiny by cruel twists of fate—as the man she loves marches south with General Sherman—Kitty Wright battles other men's arms, waiting, longing, fighting for the day when Travis Coltrane will clasp her in his arms again, and claim her as his own . . . forever!

Other Avon Books by
Patricia Hagan

LOVE AND WAR 47704 $2.50

AVON
PUBLISHERS OF BARD, CAMELOT AND DISCUS BOOKS

THE RAGING HEARTS is an original publication of Avon Books. This work has never before appeared in book form.

AVON BOOKS
A division of
The Hearst Corporation
959 Eighth Avenue
New York, New York 10019

Published by arrangement with the author.
Library of Congress Catalog Card Number: 79-52068
ISBN: 0-380-46201-x

First Avon Printing, October, 1979

Printed in the U.S.A.

For my son, Don Blandon Walker

"I am tired and sick of war. Its glory is all moonshine. It is only those who have neither fired a shot nor heard the shrieks and groans of the wounded who cry aloud for blood, more vengeance, more desolation. War is hell."

—William Tecumseh Sherman
General—U. S. Army
(1820–1891)

"I am a good old rebel—
Yes; that's just what I am—
And for this land of freedom
I do not give a dam'.
I'm glad I fit agin 'em,
And I only wish we'd won;
And I don't ax no pardon
For anything I've done."

A Good Old Rebel
Innes Randolph
(1837–1887)

THE RAGING HEARTS

Chapter One

THE warm breath of spring that whispered across the Southland in 1865 held no sweetness in its scent. The lingering odor of the sulphuric smell of war permeated every soul. Waves of rainbow-hued flowers no longer danced in the wind upon a carpet of green, for the terrain was gutted and blackened by the footsteps and fires of war. Few trees dared to bud into new life, as most stood stark and naked against the sky, grim sentinels to remind every living thing of the tortured years of civil strife as North and South had clashed head-on.

Dead. A proud Southland was defeated and lay lifeless among the ruins. Those who survived grieved painfully for the hundreds of thousands of brave men who gave their lives in vain to preserve the world they staunchly believed in.

Kitty Wright was one of those who mourned. The lavender eyes she wearily opened on that chilly March morning no longer sparkled. Now they were dim, gaunt, reflections of her own four years in hell. At 17, before it all began, she had been the most lovely and sought after maiden in all of eastern North Carolina. At 21, she felt very old and very tired. The beauty was still there, but shadowed by grief and despair. Her face reflected the agonizing memories that were forever branded upon her soul.

On this chilly March morning, a mist crept up from the swamplands behind what had once been her home. Rubbing her arms to warm them, she blinked sleepily, wondering where Travis and Sam had gone so early. It had been late when they reached this place, making camp in the thicket to avoid being seen by stray Confederate soldiers. Exhausted, they had fallen on their tattered blankets, and, during the night, Travis had drawn her to him.

The thought of Travis warmed her now. Once, she had loathed him, despised him, even wished him dead. Now, she knew she loved him as she could love no other man. She had only to close her eyes to conjure a picture of the ruggedly handsome cavalryman, his body lean and hard and muscular, his eyes a smoky gray that could shine with mirth or smolder with lust.

While she had known his tenderness, Kitty had also known his harshness, especially during their early times together, when she had been his prisoner-of-war. He had not raped her. No, Travis Coltrane was not a man to force a woman. He knew other ways, ways to make a woman weep with desire, pleading for fulfillment. This was what Travis had done to Kitty, and she had despised him for it.

The sound of metal scraping against earth made her scramble to her feet and peer out of the scrub brush. There, across the field, on the little knoll she had told them about, the two men heaved their shovels. They were digging a grave for her beloved father. That little hilltop had been John Wright's favorite spot on earth. It was there, beneath the pecan trees, that he could sit and survey all his land. It was only fitting that he stay there until Judgment Day.

John Wright had loved his land, though it had not been a prosperous farm. A man of strong convictions, he did not believe in holding souls in bondage. He freed the slaves that had belonged to his father, and there had never been enough money to hire labor to work the lands. So they had been poor, John Wright, his wife, Lena, and the daughter John had adored.

It was with unrelenting horror that Kitty recalled the night when vigilantes had caught her father helping runaway slaves. The hooded men had beaten him so mercilessly that he lost the sight of one eye. For months he was a broken spirit, having lost all will to live. But when war broke out, John Wright took his old hound dog and left to join the Yankee Army.

His move had left Kitty confused and sick at heart, torn between love for him and loyalty to her homeland. And there had been Nathan Collins, the handsome son of the richest plantation owner in all Wayne County, who was courting her. She had fancied herself in love with Nathan, so she stayed near home and worked in a way hospital with old Doc Musgrave, who had taught her medicine.

Early in the war, Kitty had been taken prisoner by a cruel slave-driver who had once been overseer on the Collins plantation. Luke Tate assaulted her brutally and held her captive while he foraged the countryside, plundering and murdering with his men. He took great satisfaction in keeping Kitty prisoner. She was beautiful, and he gloried in making the high-spirited woman submit to his cravings.

It had been Travis Coltrane who rescued her from Luke Tate.

The fighting was terrible, and men were dying by the hundreds on both sides. General Johnston called for his Confederate forces to retreat. But Nathan took Kitty and said they were not going with the other Rebels. He was taking her to Richmond to try and escape the final battles. Realizing he was a coward, she had turned against him. But he forced her to start off with him. Then they encountered her father, who demanded to know where Nathan was taking his daughter. Kitty lied, not wanting to see the two fight. She told her father she was leaving of her own will. As John Wright turned to leave, Nathan shot him in the back.

Travis and Sam had come upon them as her father lay dying in her arms, and Travis avenged John Wright by killing Nathan.

And Kitty had learned in the last moments of John Wright's life that Nathan had ridden with the hooded vigilantes when her father was so cruelly beaten. Whatever love she had ever felt for Nathan Collins fled forever.

"Kitty."

She looked up to see Travis staring down at her, warmth and compassion in those smoky gray eyes. She could only stare at him, her thoughts still whirling.

He knelt in front of her, his voice soft. "We're ready, Kitty. The grave is dug, right where you wanted it. And last night, while you slept, Sam looked around and found some scrap boards from the farmhouse that weren't completely burned. He's made a coffin. We couldn't just lay your father in the ground."

"That was kind of Sam," she murmured. "I think Poppa would like being buried in a box made from the house he loved. Oh Travis, he did love this land." Her eyes swept the now gaunt fields.

Travis' eyes followed her gaze. "I imagine it was pretty—once."

"Everything around us was pretty—once," she said, her voice thick. "Now it's ugly, like the people who walk upon it."

He placed gentle hands on her waist and drew her to her feet. "Soon it will all be over. The South is beaten. Once the Rebels admit that and surrender, we can all start making new lives."

"What about the pain that comes from *remembering*? Can't you see, Travis? I hate *both* sides. Everyone! I hate the North for destroying the South, and I hate my Southern neighbors for what they did to my father. Look at this land. Look at the rubble where the farmhouse and the barn once stood. *They* did that, our good neighbors, because they wanted to vent their rage against my father for joining the Yankees. Wasn't there enough burning and destruction without them attacking my father? And what about me? I did my part for the South! And now this land is mine—but they destroyed it. I hate them all! I hope they suffer as much as—"

"Kitty, Kitty, get hold of yourself." He shook her gently. Folding her against his chest, he murmured against her soft, golden-red hair. "The time for hatred is past. It has to be. This land will prosper again. I promise you that. For now, we have to bury our dead, in reverence and in love. Now is not the time for your heart to be filled with hate. Do you think your father would have wanted you to feel this way?"

"No," she whispered. "Poppa would not want me to hate at all. Let's put him to rest. His suffering is over. Ours is only beginning, or so I fear."

They walked silently to the little sloping hill. Kitty stared down at the gaping hole. She bit down on her lower lip, tasting blood, determined not to cry. Poppa wouldn't want her to cry. He would want her to be strong. He would want her to hold up her head and go on. And this she vowed silently to do, her body starting to tremble with determination.

Travis and Sam had gone into the woods and returned with the crude wooden coffin. They struggled with the weight, positioning it slowly above the grave, then slowly lowering it. Then they stepped back, hands folded in front of them, and Sam said gruffly, "He deserves to have a preacher here. John Wright was one of the finest, bravest, most God-fearing men I ever knew."

"No preacher would stop running from the Yankees long enough to conduct a funeral," Kitty snapped, "much less to pray over the body of a man everyone here considered a traitor. And he was ten times the man any of them were."

"Amen to that!" Sam cried, then, lowering his voice reverently, said, "I've seen John Wright hold a dying soldier in his arms and comfort him along the road to eternity. And maybe that boy would be a'screaming in pain, and with the pure fright of dying. John Wright could talk him into being calm, coax him into praying for his soul with the last breath he drew in this world. And that soldier would die with a smile on his lips. A fine man, John Wright was, and if ever a man was fit to walk through the gates of heaven, it's him."

"I don't think a preacher could have done a better job," Travis said, nodding.

Kitty swayed, feeling dizzy. This could not be happening. The man she adored could not be down there in that hole in the ground, inside that pieced-together wooden box. Sam was straightening, picking up his shovel. With slow, methodical movements, he began to scoop at the mound of dirt beside the grave, dropping clods down into the hole. And as the first thuds hit, the finality of the sound made Kitty gasp and knot her fist against her parted lips to stifle the scream that fought to escape. Travis saw and reached to pull her tightly against his chest.

"I loved him, too," he whispered.

Blinking back the tears, she raised her face to the sky. Taking a deep breath, she began to sing the words to an old hymn her father had taught her as a child, "Rock of ages, cleft for me . . ."

Sam sang along with her, shoveling the dirt in faster.

Travis stood silent, a grim, set look to his face. He was not a religious man, certainly not one given to the singing of hymns. He didn't know the words, anyway. But he cared. He hoped Kitty understood that.

When the grave was completely covered, Sam told her that her father's old dog, shot as he leaped to protect his master, would be buried beside him. "I figure John would have wanted it that way."

Kitty closed her eyes tightly, teeth gritting, as the horrible scene flashed before her once again. Killer, the seemingly lifeless old hound dog, leaping with fangs bared, his body arched in mid air, snarling as he hurtled himself toward the man who had just shot his master in the back. The second blast from Nathan's gun had killed the dog instantly. There was not a sound as the animal crumpled beside his master.

"Yes," Kitty whispered. "Killer was with him all through the war."

Sam nodded firmly. "That old dog would march right into battle like he wasn't scared at all. Balls a'flying all around, men screaming, but as long as John kept a'going, Killer was right alongside him."

Kitty turned away, walking slowly across the rutted field, stumbling now and then, her eyes blinded by tears. She stopped suddenly, trying to focus her vision. Bending down, she touched the tiny green vine that was fighting its way out of the starving earth. Was it possible? It was! It was! And she could see another . . . and another. The scuppernong vines that Poppa had planted so many years ago. He had said scuppernong would thrive in this soil because it was sandy. And he had talked about how tobacco would be king one day, saying she should one day turn the land to tobacco. She got to her feet, smiling, lifting her face to the sun just now breaking through the early morning mist. There was life here, after all. The Southland was not really dead, and surely not the Wright farm.

"As long as a man's got land, he's never really poor," Poppa had said. "I'd rather have my land than all the gold on earth, because you know it's going to be there tomorrow. Don't ever sell this land, Kitty, girl. Never sell the Wright land."

And she had promised him. The land was hers now, for as far as she could see.

She had not heard him walking behind her, nor heard him call to her. Feeling the strong arms slipping about her waist was the first she knew that Travis was there. "I know you're upset, sweetheart, but we need to be moving on. Sam and me need to join back up with our men. I need to find you a room at the hotel. The town is going to be full of Union soldiers, swarming around, and I want you in a safe place."

Kitty wiped at the perspiration on her brow. She was dirty, grimy. The ragged Confederate uniform she had taken from a dead soldier was now bloodstained and stiff with soil from her work in the field hospital. A strand of hair tumbled forward, and she pushed it back from her eyes, seeing that it, too, was stained with blood. How long since she had bathed? She could not remember.

"Kitty, Kitty." Travis was gently shaking her, turning her around to face him, his hand cupping her chin. "I've been talking to you, but you don't hear me. Are you in shock over all that's happened? I know it's been terrible, darling, but you're a strong woman. I know *how* strong, remember? Because we have been through hell, together."

"Yes." Her voice was barely audible. "We have been through hell. It's over now."

"Well, it's almost over. A few more months, that's all the war can last. Then it's a new beginning for us."

She stared up into his handsome face. This man could warm any woman's heart with just a smile. And he was looking at her now as though he wanted to touch those warm lips against hers. His head moved, lowering, but she stepped backward. It was not proper. Not here, now, moments after her father's burial.

She turned from him.

"Kitty."

She turned to stare at him. They had not talked much since he had loomed up out of the swamps at Bentonville in time to avenge her father's death. Kitty had been too anguished. Now, standing only a few feet away from the man she had alternately desired and despised, she felt suddenly shy.

"Kitty. We have to talk. You may not feel it's the time, but we have to. As I said, I think you realize by now that I do care for you."

Kitty stared at him, thinking once again how beautiful his eyes were—not blue, not black, but a blending that became the color of steel. Now they looked warm, loving, but once they had mirrored anger, disgust, even hatred. His hair was the color of the raven's wing, shining black, and he had a firm set to his jaw. His lips were smooth, the bow even. Now she saw a muscle tense. He stood before her, waiting for her to speak, the Union cavalry uniform as dirty and blood-splotched as the clothes she wore.

"I remember an afternoon on a windswept hilltop outside of Richmond," she said. "Poppa and I were sitting on the hilltop talking, happy to be together after so long. And then you came along, saying you had to talk to Poppa about the new orders you had just received from General Grant. You made me leave, saying I couldn't be trusted, since my heart belonged to the Confederacy. I was angry, and I left and went back to the little shack where I was staying in the Yankee camp. And you followed me there, grabbing me and forcing me to submit to you."

"Kitty, I didn't force you," he protested, taking a step towards her, but she held up her hands. "I might have made you want me, but I did *not* force you."

"Your words were: 'I'm the way I am, and I'll never change, but I *do* give a damn about you.' Well, Travis, I'm the way *I* am, and *I'll* never change, but I do give a damn about you." She smiled sadly. "I remember something else about that day, after we made love so sweetly and tenderly. Even though there were times you abused me after you rescued me from Luke Tate, times that I hated you and could have killed you with my bare hands—on that afternoon, I loved you with all my heart. And then I slept in your arms, and I awoke later to find you gone. I went to search for you, and I found you with another woman."

"Kitty"—he gestured helplessly; "that was planned. As cruel as it sounds, it was all set up on purpose. I had to anger you enough to make you leave our camp. I knew what our orders were. I knew you would want to go along, not only because you wanted to be with your father, but because you and I knew at last that we loved each other. Having you see me with that woman was the one way I could send you away from danger."

"My father slipped into Goldsboro to tell me these things. He said you set the whole thing up. But I felt like such a fool. I look back now and think of the way Nathan used me, and then you, and I don't think I can ever trust another man. Poppa was the only man who never deceived me or hurt me."

The steel-gray eyes that had gazed at her so warmly turned cold. "Can you say *you* never deceived *me*, Kitty? Remember after I rescued you from Luke Tate, and you tricked me into believing you could be trusted, made me think you loved me? I let my guard down, and it almost got me killed. In fact, the ball intended for me hit another soldier and sent him to his grave.

And you ran away with a Rebel soldier and never looked back."

"I did look back," she cried, her body trembling as the memories took over. "When I thought you were dead, it hurt me terribly. But you did use me, Travis. Remember how you scorned me? You said it was beneath you to force yourself upon any woman. You made me feel like dirt, Travis, remember? I had every reason to hate you. You wouldn't set me free then, or send me back to my own people. You kept me with you, dragging me through the battlefields. You gave me no other choice. I could not stay with you, not with the humiliation you offered me."

She turned her face away, unable to meet his angry gaze. "I remember the times in your arms, when you made love to me. No, you never forced me to submit, did you? But you knew a hundred ways to make my body scream, ways to make me tremble with desire, my blood turn to fire. Never had I envisioned such joy, and I thought it had to be love. Later, I felt used."

"I never meant to make you feel that way." He stepped forward and put his arms around her, pulling her to his strong chest. She could feel the pounding of his heart. "You had your painful memories to bear, but so did I. I learned early that a woman can't be trusted, and every time I came close to giving you my heart, you showed me you were like all the others. I wanted to give you a chance. I want to give you another now. Damn it, Kitty, I'm asking you to give both of us a chance at a future together. Maybe this isn't the time or the place, with the Union troops marching over your homelands, and your father hardly cold in his grave. But the future is actually the present, when you stop and think about it, no matter what the circumstances. This is here and now, and I'm telling you that I love you, that I want you, and that I want us to have a life together."

Their eyes met and held, each searching the other for some reason for confidence.

"I love you, Kitty. I think I loved you from that first moment. And when we made love that first time, it was like nothing I had ever experienced before. You were in my blood, and for a long time I hated you for it. I had vowed that never again would a woman possess my heart to trample upon it. Yet, you, who were promised to an enemy soldier, you took my heart and made it your prisoner."

"I *know* about your past," she confessed. "I know about your mother. I know about the other woman in your life who used you. Sam told me. He thought I had a right to know. He saw what was happening between us, and he loved us both enough that he wanted to help us get together. But now I wonder if you could ever trust me, Travis. Perhaps your wounds are too deep."

"My mother didn't actually betray me, Kitty." His voice was bitter. He held her tightly, and she could feel his warm breath on her face. "She betrayed my father. He killed her and then himself, leaving me and my sister behind. I had that grief to bear. Then I went through the horror of having my sister kidnapped by slave traders who sold her into a life of hell as a captive prostitute. She could not endure it, and she killed herself. That was why I joined the Union army when the war broke out, even though I was a Southerner. I would give my life to help stop the enslavement of human beings.

"In my agony and loneliness, I turned to a woman of the streets, who found pleasure in any man's arms. True, I have bitter memories of some women, but you're different. I've seen you work as hard to save the life of a Union soldier as you would for a Confederate. I've seen you stand up under pressures that would have made another woman faint. You're strong. You're also the most hellish woman I've ever tried to contend with. But you've a way about you that goes deeper than beauty—and God, you're beautiful! I want a future with you, Kitty Wright. I want to forget the past and build all my tomorrows with you."

She drew in her breath in wonder. Then she reached out to trail gentle fingertips down his stubbled face. "Oh, Travis, there's so much pain to forget."

"We can overshadow that with happiness."

"Yes, yes, we can." Their lips met, and they melted together. Gently he pulled her down to her knees and they sank to the ground. Then they were lying side by side, and he was slowly unbuttoning her shirt. She could feel the hardness of his manhood throbbing against her thigh, the pulsating strength that told her he wanted her.

"How I have dreamed of this, darling," he murmured.

And so they soared together, climbing to the sun, drifting among the clouds, dancing in the wind, and finally floating back to earth.

For a moment, neither moved or spoke. They savored their closeness. Then Travis raised his head to gaze down upon her with a strange coldness in his gray eyes. "I love you, Kitty, but heed me well. I give you my heart, and if you ever trample upon it and deceive me, you will rue the day we met. For I will have my revenge, be assured."

A chill moved through her. He frightened her. Travis could be kind and loving, but he could also be absolutely ruthless. And this was the side of him that she feared, for when he was truly riled, he was a dangerous man.

"Be good to me, Kitty, and I will worship you. But do me wrong, and you will suffer. This I swear."

"I . . . I don't think I like being threatened." Her voice was braver than she felt. But she was not about to be intimidated. "And if you think I'm one of those dizzy women who will be content to sit in the parlor and tat and embroider and make idle chatter with other scatterbrained females, you are wrong, sir. Nor will I be content to sit at home and have a baby every year, while you have adventure and excitement. I have a spirit of my own. It is a free spirit, and no man will ever possess me completely."

He laughed then, that smug laugh that she had always hated. It was infuriating, as though he knew he possessed the upper hand and only humored her when she talked independence. "I already do possess you, little one, and don't you forget it. Now enough of this grim talk. We must leave here and go to Goldsboro and find a room for you while Sam and I rejoin our men. There will be time later to talk about what to do with you."

He got to his feet, straightening his uniform. She scrambled up to put her clothes in order. "What do you mean, 'talk about what to do with' me? I know what I'm going to do, Travis. I'm going to farm this land. The scuppernong vines are coming up. You should see them!" Her voice trembled with excitement. "I might make enough from the crop this year to pay for repairing my father's bee hives. Then, from the honey, I can save money to think about planting tobacco next year. Poppa said this land is good for tobacco. I can find a job in town to tide me over till I can get on my feet. Maybe I can even get a loan at the bank to build a small farmhouse."

He whirled around, eyes wide. "Are you crazy, woman? You talk nonsense. We don't know yet what the impact of the North's victory will be upon the South. Your land may be taken from you. Have you thought about that?"

Her chin jutted upwards in the stubborn gesture that told Travis there was no point in trying to argue with her now. But she would see, he thought wearily. War changes everything, and life as she had known it would never return.

"We'll talk later," he said, forcing a smile and holding out his hands to her. "It's enough for now to know that we have an understanding, Kitty. I love you, and you say you love me. For now, that's enough to build on."

She took his hand and returned his smile. "You'll see, Travis Coltrane." She was bubbling with enthusiasm as they made their way out of the woods. "This farm will one day be the most prosperous in all of Wayne County. It will be a fine place to raise a family."

"Kitty, I don't . . ." He had stopped walking and stood staring down at her, searching her eyes, seeing such a happy glow there that he could not go on. He could not tell her that her dreams would not come true. He could not tell her that it was not his intention to settle in North Carolina. His home was the Louisiana bayou, and it was there he wanted to take her. He would have to tell her these things later.

"Later," he said gruffly, tugging at her hand to pull her along to where Sam Bucher waited on the other side of the field. "Later, I will tell you, Kitty. For now, there are things to be done."

And she squeezed his hand, confident in their love, sure that only joy and happiness lay ahead. She did not see the shadows in Travis Coltrane's eyes.

Chapter Two

IT had been General William T. Sherman's plan from the time he left Savannah, Georgia, to have all available men and armies of the North meet at Goldsboro, North Carolina, which was the most important rail supply center for the Confederate armies around Richmond. General Joseph E. Johnston, with his Army of Tennessee, had not been sure of Sherman's route until after he had left Fayetteville, North Carolina. It had appeared that Sherman was heading for Raleigh, but when his left wing made a right turn along the Goldsboro road, just ten miles out of Fayetteville, his plan became clear.

General Johnston had called on Generals Bragg, Hardee, and Hampton to join him in a surprise attack on Sherman's left wing before Sherman could consolidate all his armies in Goldsboro. These three small Confederate armies numbered only 20,000 men. They knew that their only chance to destroy Sherman's larger army would be a surprise attack on the flank of a divided army. In all, Sherman had 60,000 men, divided into three sections—left and right wings, and middle army.

Johnston chose to attack the extreme left wing of Sherman's army approaching from Fayetteville in the west, thinking this the weakest and most spread out segment of the armies. So he hurried from Smithfield, where he had been concentrating men and supplies to cut Sherman off, reaching Bentonville almost a day ahead of Sherman.

For three days the battle raged, from March 19 to March 21, 1865. More than 100,000 troops were involved. The first day's battle was won by the Confederates, but the second and third days were lost as the South suffered heavy casualties. General Johnston had not figured that Sherman's middle army was so close behind his advance guard, enabling him to reinforce his men quickly. Thus, the tide turned against the South. Casualty records reported 2,825 Confederate soldiers killed, wounded, or missing. There were 1,646 Federal casualties.

Johnston retreated northward over Mill Creek towards Smithfield during the night of the third day of battle, and Sherman was content to let him go, for most of his men were weary after their seven-week march of 430 miles from Savannah to Goldsboro.

As Kitty Wright, Travis Coltrane, and Sam Bucher made their way into town, they passed many of Sherman's men camped along the road.

"Where'd you pick up that pretty Southern belle?" a bedraggled soldier called to Travis, recognizing him. "Is that what you were a'doing while we were fighting our butts off?"

Travis ignored him. Kitty, sitting behind him on the horse, put her arms about his waist a little bit tighter. The looks the men gave her were frightening. Travis sensed as much and said, "Don't worry. I'll make sure you're safe, Kitty. They won't bother you."

"What about the other women in Goldsboro?" she asked worriedly, turning her face as a soldier made an obscene gesture. "Everyone has heard that your General Sherman allows all kinds of horrors—killing, burning, and rape."

"It's been a long war, Kitty. The men are tired, and

they're ready to go home. They are only trying to punish the South for dragging out the damn war, and starting it as well."

She straightened. "And what about you, Travis? Have you gone about the countryside looting and murdering and raping to punish the South?"

"No," he said quietly. "I've killed, yes. So many I lost count. I never stole anything unless it meant the difference in my starving or not. As for rape, no, I never had to rape any woman."

She bristled angrily, and he chuckled. "Now, now, Kitty, you're letting your jealousy show, along with your Southern pride. If you're going to be the woman of a Union cavalryman, you're going to have to get over some of both."

"I'll never give up my Southern pride. This is my country. These are my people."

"Your father was killed by one of your people," he reminded her tartly. "Not by one of mine."

Closing her eyes, she waited for the wave of bitterness to pass. "Nathan Collins was not typical of the gentle Southern people. He was a scoundrel and a traitor, and I never want to hear his name again."

"I imagine you will, though. It's likely that deserters hiding in the bushes saw what happened, and you can be sure they'll spread the word. Nathan Collins will be a hero in these parts, if the people here hated your father the way I think they did. And you talk of staying and rebuilding his farm," he snorted.

"Of course I'm going to stay and rebuild the farm," she flared, her violet eyes flashing. "It's my land. I promised my father I would never give it up. One day it will be the finest farm in all of Wayne County. I'll make it a tribute to my father. I'll never let people forget what a fine man he truly was."

She felt him sigh, saw the slight shaking of his head.

"Don't you believe me, Travis? Can't you see why it's so important to me to make that land prosper? It was my father's dream, and I owe it to his memory to make that dream come true. If you loved him as you say you did, then you share that dream also."

He took a deep breath. "Kitty, the only dream I have right now is to see this war officially end, and then I want to make you my wife. I want us to make a life together, wherever we can find peace. Now, can't you share my dream?"

For some reason, she was frightened. "Where do you propose to find this peace, Travis?"

"Well, not here in Wayne County on land that belonged to a man everyone hated, that's for sure. You want your neighbors to burn you out again? And how do you think they'd take to a Yankee soldier coming in to settle on that land? They'll hate you as much as they hated your father. You would be asking for trouble, Kitty, and you would never know any peace. No, darling, it would be far better for you and me to go far away from here, to forget the pain of the past and look to the future. I had planned to talk about this later, but you brought it up, and I can't stand to hear you talk on and on about the rosy world ahead on your father's farmland. There will never be anything here but trouble."

"I'll never leave," she cried, leaning back, away from him. "You can't make me, Travis."

He reined the horse to a stop, motioning to Sam to keep going. They were in a bend on the road, with thickets on each side. No one was about. Travis got down out of the saddle, then reached to put firm hands about Kitty's waist and pull her down beside him.

"Yes, I can make you leave, my darling," he whispered, pulling her close. She struggled against his chest. "I can make you leave because you love me as I love you, and you know it is meant for us to be together. You are going to go with me now, and I think we should be married for decency's sake." He smiled, eyes twinkling.

"Marry you?" she gasped. "Right now? And do what, Travis Coltrane? The war isn't over yet. What am I supposed to do in the meantime?"

"You're coming with me as I march with General Sherman," he said, as though it were quite simple. "We have hospital wagons, too, you know. I can see that you are assigned to ride with them. When the war is officially over, and I am discharged, we'll go home to Louisiana. Oh, Kitty, wait till you see the bayou country there! It's beautiful, like God spent extra time there so it would be special."

"You are out of your mind!" She pushed him away, trembling. "Travis, you know how I feel about Poppa's land. How could I just walk away from it? You ask if I love you, and I tell you I do. You claim to love me, yet you propose to take me a million miles away to a strange country, away from everything I have ever known."

"We'll make a new life together, Kitty. We'll have our own family, and we won't think about the past."

Why wasn't he taking her seriously? "I won't leave here, Travis. And if you love me as you say you do, you won't ask me to go. You will stay here with me and help me make that land prosper. We have our future right here."

His eyes were no longer shining. "Kitty, you are tired, and so am I. You've been through quite an ordeal in the past day. You lost your father. You realized what a scoundrel Nathan really was. I don't think now is the time for planning. Suppose we go on our way. Once we get to Goldsboro, we can spend time talking. If we keep on this way, we are only going to hurt each other, saying things we may regret."

Suddenly she threw herself into his arms, hugging

him tightly. This man had saved her life many times, seen her through much anguish. She loved him with all her heart. With tear-streaked face, she lifted her lips for his kiss. His hands squeezed her against him, closer.

"Well, well, how sweet the spoils of war."

They sprang apart, jerking their heads about to see two soldiers on foot, both grinning. The one who had spoken saluted. "Captain Coltrane, you sure don't waste any time. Where'd you find the little filly? She looks so willing, too. Hell, we found us a woman last night, and it took three of us to hold her down so we could take turns. It was worth it, though. Some of these Southern women got some sweet ass."

Travis' fist went crashing into his mouth, sending him sprawling to the ground. His companion started to move closer, in defense, but Travis had his side arm out. "Now let me tell you bastards a thing or two," he snarled as the man on the ground raised his head dizzily, blood pouring from his mouth. "This is Miss Kitty Wright, and she is the woman I plan to marry. So you spread the word that she is to be treated with absolute respect. Any man who offends her will answer to me. And as for the other women in town, I'd better not hear of any more violations. Is that clear?"

"Yes sir," the man still standing said, helping his friend to his feet. He was trembling with anger but knew better than to cross Travis Coltrane.

The two moved on. Travis got on his horse and helped Kitty up behind him. They rode along in silence. Rounding a hilltop to find Sam waiting, he called out "We've been asked to camp outside town while General Schofield makes ready a welcome."

"Did he have any resistance in Goldsboro?" Kitty asked worriedly. "Was there much fighting?"

"None at all," Sam told her. "General Johnston had ordered every available soldier in eastern North

Carolina to join him in his stand against Sherman at Bentonville, so all Schofield had to do was march straight in from New Bern. The word from town is that everything is peaceful."

"No rape? No senseless killing?" Kitty cried. "And you say this General Schofield is a *Yankee*? Are you sure?"

Sam looked at Travis. Travis sighed. "Kitty, that's enough. Your beloved Rebels have done some murdering and raping of their own. Neither side can boast of many angels in this war. You've known for quite a while now that it was inevitable the Union Army would march into Goldsboro. So you can stop acting so shocked."

"What happened to General Bragg?" Kitty asked Sam, ignoring Travis. "He was to stand against Schofield below Kinston at Southwest Creek."

Sam and Travis exchanged looks, then Travis laughed. "Now, how did you learn so much? That kind of information is generally known only by high-ranking officers."

"I overheard many high-ranking officers talking in the Goldsboro hospital when they came in for treatment. Well, go on. Tell me what happened to General Bragg."

"He engaged and delayed Schofield where you say he did, and I hear he captured about fifteen hundred men. But he also lost a good bit of soldiers himself. When he heard about Sherman moving so fast towards Goldsboro, he went back there, and they had already set up breastworks—"

"I know about those," Kitty said, nodding anxiously. "And what happened then? They were quite extensive—"

"He never got a chance to use them. Sherman was on his tail, so he retreated to keep from being captured.

We heard he crossed the river and went to catch up with Johnston at Smithfield."

"And the citizens of Goldsboro just welcomed the Yankees with open arms?" Kitty blinked. "I don't understand."

"You sure don't," Travis snapped. "You don't realize that the damned war is about over. The South is soundly beaten."

Sam told her that early that morning the mayor of the town had ridden his horse out to meet Union officers and ask for their peaceful entry into Goldsboro. In return for that peace, the citizens had offered to share their homes. "General Schofield and General Terry already rode in."

"Mayor James Privett!" Kitty spat. "The coward! They should have taken up their arms and—"

Travis turned to stare at the angry woman waving her arms in the air. "Are you crazy, Kitty? Have you taken leave of your senses? We would have charged into that town and killed everybody in it and then burned it to the ground. A smart man knows when he's licked. And you'd be a smart woman if you'd realize that you are licked. Not only by the Yankees but by me, as well."

Sam laughed, and Travis joined him, and that just made Kitty all the madder. He was not going to treat her like a trophy of war. Damn him! "I'm not camping here," she cried, sliding off the back of the horse unceremoniously and almost losing her balance. "I refuse to march into town with the damn Yankees. I'm going on ahead. They will be needing me at the hospital."

Travis had dismounted and grabbed her before she took two steps. Swinging her back against him, he growled, "You are not going into town without me, Kitty Wright, now get that through your pretty little head. We're going to camp right here in these woods, tonight. We're going to dump you in the river to wash off the blood and mud, and when we march into town tomorrow morning, you're going to look like the beautiful woman you are. If I let you go traipsing in there alone, the way you look now, there's no telling what might happen to you. I don't know the situation there, and neither does Sam. He's only going by hearsay."

"I am not your prisoner." She tried to jerk away, but he held her tightly.

"You are now, damn it. If you act like a fool, Kitty, I'll treat you like one. I sometimes find your temper and spunk charming, but at other times, like right now, I find you quite annoying. If you continue, I'm going to turn you over my knee and give you the sound spanking you deserve.

"I love you, Kitty, with all my heart." He spoke more quietly now. "But I don't intend to let you ride over me. Now, when I say something, I mean it. You're high-spirited, and that's fine—in bed. But in ordinary circumstances, I expect you to do what I tell you to do."

"Then you will be expecting for a damn long time, sir!" She sputtered.

"And stop cursing. You sound like a trollop."

Sam laughed.

"I'll curse when I want. Damn you, you bastard! Just who do you think you are? One minute you're tender and loving, and the next you're hateful. I'll never marry you. I'll never subject myself to being your slave. I'll never marry any man. You're all alike. And I am going into Goldsboro, if I have to walk every step."

She whirled around and grabbed his sword from the saddle. Her fury only increased as Sam and Travis stood there with hands on their hips laughing until they were almost breathless. Kitty felt so foolish, standing there with the heavy sword held over her head. She didn't want to think about what she might do if either of them took a step towards her.

"Sam, I think the river is close by," Travis said. "Will you see if you can find me a nice, quiet spot?" Sam nodded, still laughing, and went crashing through the bushes. "Kitty, you know you're acting like a child. Now, put down that sword and come here and apologize. Then I might go easy on you."

"You bastard! You just step over there to the side of the road and stay out of my way while I get on your horse. I'm riding into town. I'm going to the hospital to see how things are. They probably need help badly, with wounded from both sides."

"I'm sure they do, and I will see that you get there tomorrow. But you aren't going in until I do, so I can see that you are protected."

"How noble," she said tartly. "You care for me as you do your horse, making sure I have plenty of oats and a roof over my head. You don't own me, Travis Coltrane, and with your attitude, I never will marry you!"

"Well, now, I'm not so sure I want to marry you now, anyway." His grin was infuriating. "I think I'll just make you my mistress. Then, when I get tired of your temper—as I'm sure I will—I can just boot you out."

"Oh, damn you, Travis Coltrane. I hate you!"

Just then Sam stepped out of the brush, his eyes shining. "I found a perfect spot, nice and private, right by the river's edge. We can bathe and rest up till tomorrow. Right now I'm going to hightail it after a rabbit I just spotted, 'cause I aim to see him on a spit for our supper."

Travis stepped towards Kitty and snatched the sword from her upraised hands so quickly that she had no time to hold on. He led his horse by the reins with one hand, gripped Kitty's elbow tightly with the other, and began to make their way down an incline and through the brush.

The river was not very wide, and it rolled along sleepily, undisturbed by the thousands of Union soldiers gathered along a bridge further down. Birds trilled in the trees overhead, and a large turtle plunged from his resting place on a fallen trunk as the intruders crashed through the brush near him.

"Take off your clothes." Travis gave her a rough shove as he tied the reins of his horse to a nearby tree. Kitty stood frozen, blinking at him in disbelief. His eyes flashed. "I said take off your clothes, woman. They're all you have at the moment, but if you want them torn from you so you can ride into town naked tomorrow, so be it."

He took a step forward, and she threw up her hands to ward him off.

Muttering an oath, Kitty began to remove the filthy uniform. Then she went to the river and bent down, trying to scrub some of the grime from the thin material. She was quite aware that Travis was watching her, his eyes raking over her naked buttocks and large, firm breasts.

When she had twisted, wrung, and beaten the clothes on rocks, sure that they were as clean as she was going to be able to get them, Kitty hung the garments on a bush to dry, then stepped behind the bush and crouched down. "I am not coming out of here until my clothes are dry. I am not going to parade around in front of you naked, like some trollop."

"Oh, you've been naked with me before and haven't minded. True, there were times when you pretended to object, for the sake of your silly female pride, but I remember nights when we slept in each other's arms, bare flesh touching, and you loved it. I remember that we even swam naked together on occasion, and you seemed to like that."

"Will you just shut up?" She covered her ears with her hands, furious. "And leave me alone? Why do you take such pleasure in tormenting me? You say you love me, yet you try to humiliate me at every turn. . . ."

When he spoke, he was right behind her, and she jumped in surprise. "I do love you, Kitty, and you force me to humiliate you to keep you in line."

"Does giving orders make you feel like a man? What will you do when the war is over and you can no longer order your men about?"

"I'm not worried about my men—just my woman," he murmured, pulling her into his arms roughly. "Now come here and be my woman. Show me how much you love me and want me. Seeing you like that tears me up and you know it. You've got the most exquisite breasts I've ever touched. . . ."

He reached to cup her breasts in his hands, and she shoved him away. "Don't you dare touch me after the way you have talked to me."

He chuckled. "You know, I'd almost forgotten that I promised you a sound spanking." And before she could turn to flee, he grabbed her by her wrists, sat down on a stump, and pulled her over his knees. Maneuvering to hold both her wrists with one hand over her head, he used his right hand to begin soundly smacking her bare bottom.

"Stop that!" she screamed, kicking her legs wildly. "How dare you, Travis? Stop that this minute, you bastard."

"Is that any way for a lady to talk?" he laughed, bringing his hand down harder, watching the white flesh turn a fiery red. "Aren't you ashamed? You, a genteel Southern woman, using saloon talk? I'd say you deserve a very hard spanking, my sweet, if you're to learn your lesson."

Kitty continued to struggle helplessly. But as Travis' hand kept slapping her bottom, his blows became slower, his fingers pausing to caress the tender flesh. And then he stopped spanking her altogether, fingers smoothly stroking her buttocks as he murmured, "Are you ready to apologize, my sweet? Wouldn't you rather have me love you than chastise you?"

And without waiting for an answer, he rolled her over on his lap, hands milking her breasts. He bent to touch his lips adoringly to each rosy nipple, working them to hard, tight points. Kitty closed her eyes, melting beneath his touch. He knew how to make her helpless with desire. The fight was gone from her body, replaced by the surge of passion only he could arouse so fiercely. Winding her arms about his neck, she pulled him towards her till their lips met. They tumbled gently to the ground, and he spread her thighs and positioned himself between them.

"My little spitfire," he chuckled, fumbling with his clothing. "You make conquest so sweet, my love, because your spirit is so stubborn and hot. But I have learned you well in the time we've had together. I know how to make you writhe and moan."

"Never leave me, Travis," she murmured. "When you hold me like this, I feel as though nothing can ever hurt me again."

"And if I can help it, nothing will. Trust me, Kitty. As I've told you, I never thought I could bring myself to believe in another woman, but I am taking that chance with you. Don't fail me. Do as I ask. Ride with the Union ambulance wagons till the war comes to an end. It won't be much longer. Then we can start our life together, and forget all the pain of the past."

He had moved from her body, and she struggled to her feet, suddenly embarrassed and self-conscious over her nakedness. Running to the river's edge, she threw herself into the water. Travis followed her. When they were side by side, submerged to their necks, Kitty turned to him. All her pain was in her gaze.

"I do love you. You must believe that, Travis. I know I am everything you say I am—stubborn, willful, and I know that sometimes I am anything but ladylike. When other girls were learning to tat and embroider and weave, I was slipping away to hunt and fish with my father. My real love was medicine. I had dreams of being a doctor one day."

"Kitty, I know all those things about you. Your father spent many hours talking of the daughter he loved with all his heart. But I don't see what that has to do with our future. I love you the way you are." He winked at her mischievously. "I know how to control that stubborn streak of yours, my love."

She tried to return his smile but the effort was futile. "Travis, you say you understand me. Then why don't you realize that I have to fulfill my father's dream? I must keep my promise to him about the Wright land. I can't leave here."

He smacked the water with the palm of his hand, sending an angry shower into the air. "Damn it, woman, why can't you see the obstacles you will face if you try to stay here? These people hate you as they hated your father. They burned the farm."

"But why should they hate me? I nursed their wounded. I've stood on my feet till every muscle in my body cried out for rest, trying to save the lives of the Confederate soldiers. I've gone without food myself to give my portion to a wounded man. People here know I did not share my father's feeling for the North. It was by accident that I fell into your hands and was forced to travel with you."

"They won't see it that way," he argued. "Kitty, the word will get out about Nathan Collins' death, and the version that spreads will be distorted. You will be blamed. He will be a hero and martyr for killing your father—a man your neighbors considered a traitor. They won't want you in Wayne County. Can't you get that through your head? And you are even so foolish as to think *I* could stay here with you. A Union soldier! Now, how do you think they would react to that?"

"But the North is going to win the war," she protested. "You said so yourself. The South is beaten. Who would dare make trouble with a Union soldier?"

He threw back his head and laughed, the sound echoing around them in the stillness of the forest. "Oh, my sweet, you are so naïve. You think the hatred between the two sides will end when the South surrenders? Sometimes I think it will be worse then. No, you and I would be wise to leave this part of the country and settle elsewhere."

"I won't leave my home."

"I think we had better talk about this later, Kitty. When we ride into Goldsboro, and you have a chance to see what kind of reception you receive, you will realize that our only chance for happiness is to put down roots elsewhere."

He began sloshing water over his body. Kitty began scrubbing herself, but her thoughts were on the farm, and her promise to her father. She loved Travis, but she had to make him see that part of her heart was here.

It had to work out, she thought fiercely, scrubbing at her skin. She had been through too much, suffered enough, without more heartache lying ahead. With Travis beside her, she could face anything. Together, there was no obstacle they could not conquer.

Chapter Three

TRAVIS reined his horse in line with General Sherman's troops as they prepared to ride into Goldsboro. Kitty, sitting behind him, arms about his waist, was self-conscious and uneasy. The other soldiers were staring openly at her. One of them, a burly man in a bloodstained uniform, grinned with rotten teeth and called, "Hey, Cap'n Coltrane, you already enjoying the spoils of war? That filly don't look spoiled to me."

The others guffawed.

Kitty felt Travis tense. Then he wilted the grinning soldier with a look. "Watch your tongue, mister, or you may lose it."

"It's going to be this way. I know it is, Travis," Kitty said nervously, clinging to him even tighter. "I can't ride into town with you. Just let me go. I'll find my way in alone. I know every inch of these woods. I can meet you later in town. Everyone is going to wonder why you have a woman riding with you."

"I can't let you go, Kitty. You see how these men are reacting, even when you ride under the protection of an officer. They're marching into a town they've taken without a fight, and they're out to celebrate. You wouldn't last five minutes before they'd have you stripped and raped." She shuddered. He felt the movement and reached to pat her thigh. "I'm sorry, Kitty. I have to ride in with my men. It's the general's orders.

Once we arrive, I'll find a room for you at the hotel and keep you out of sight."

"I want to go to the hospital."

"I thought you said you were sick of war, that you didn't want to be around dying and suffering any longer. The hospital will be full of soldiers from both sides."

"I know that," she said quietly, pushing back a strand of her strawberry hair. "I feel I have to go there. I'm not the only one who's tired of war. Everyone has had their fill. But Dr. Holt was understaffed when I left, and he'll have his hands full with both sides bringing in wounded."

"Johnston took his with him."

"I know. I was going, too, when Nathan forced me to go with him. Oh, God, if only he hadn't."

A bugle sounded and she felt Travis straighten in the saddle. All about them, men came to attention. They were bedraggled, weary, filthy—but at the sound of the brass, they came alive.

As the bugle's call faded, the men moved their horses forward in columns of four abreast. As though a silent command had been given, they broke into song. "Mine eyes have seen the glory of the coming of the Lord . . ."

Kitty frowned. The Battle Hymn of the Republic. They could sing of God in a battle song, as though using His name gave them the right to plunder and kill. She bristled. The song was a sacrilege.

They finished their patriotic tune, and before they could join together in another Yankee song, Kitty straightened and lifted her face to the wind, her voice ringing out clearly. "Oh, I wish I was in the land of cotton, old times there are not forgotten, look away . . . look away . . . look away . . . Dixie Land . . ."

She kept on singing, every line, every chorus, and her voice grew louder and carried farther, as the soldiers grew quiet, frowning, as they turned to stare at her.

Travis wanted to strangle her. Here he was, a respected cavalry officer in General Sherman's army riding with a woman behind him singing the anthem of the Confederacy! But he knew better than to try to make her stop. It was much better to just let her go on and finish, despite the scowls that were being cast in his direction.

Just as her voice rose to sing out the last few words, he heard thundering hooves and looked up to see the great general himself riding towards him, his greatcoat flapping in the wind. His approach did not silence Kitty. She kept right on till she finished her song, even adding an extra chorus after Travis reined to a halt to salute the glowering General Sherman.

"What is the meaning of this, Captain?" the general's voice boomed. "What are you doing with a woman riding behind you—a woman who dares to sing the infernal song of the Rebels?"

"*Our* song is not sacrilegious," Kitty snapped, as Travis fought the impulse to cringe. "*We* do not march into battle singing of God while we murder and rape and plunder. Everyone knows how you have let your men run amuck through the Southland, burning, robbing, killing. And *you* sing of God?"

For an instant, Travis feared she would spit in contempt, but she didn't.

"If I am so terrible, why don't I have you killed this very moment?" General Sherman was asking. His lips were curved in a sardonic smile, but his eyes looked menacing.

"Why don't you?" Kitty cried. "You allow other evils."

"Kitty, for God's sake." Travis twisted in the saddle, glaring at her, trying to decide whether to slap her to silence.

"Well?" Kitty's nostrils flared, her violet eyes sparkling with purple and red fires. "Aren't you the famous general who declared that a crow would starve to death flying over your trail? That war is hell? That you meant to punish the South? Go ahead and punish me. If it will make you feel like more of a man, go ahead and kill me! You will have to kill me to silence me, because I'll go to my grave singing 'Dixie.'"

General Sherman looked at Travis, his voice a harsh whisper as he asked, his body trembling with rage, "Captain Coltrane, who is this woman? I believe I have seen you with her before. Who is she, and how is it that she happens to be in your company?"

"Sir"; Travis took a deep breath and wiped a hand across his brow; "this is Miss Katherine Wright, the daughter of John Wright..."

General Sherman's expression changed immediately. "I see." He cleared his throat, then asked, "What is she doing with you?"

"Well, sir, John Wright was killed at Bentonville."

The general blinked, shocked, his grief evident. "Oh, no." The words came out in a whisper. "I didn't know. I had not heard." Then, his bitterness put aside, General Sherman looked at Kitty. "I am sorry, Miss Wright. I had the utmost respect and admiration for your father. He was a man of deep moral and religious convictions, a brave and courageous soldier . . ."

"A pity you aren't more like him," Kitty snapped, and Travis cringed.

General Sherman jerked his head back as if she had slapped him. "I could say the same for you, young lady. I know that John Wright was from the South, but his convictions were with the North. A pity you did not share those convictions. But I am not at all surprised that John Wright would have such a high-spirited daughter."

He turned his gaze upon Travis once more. "You

still have not explained to me why this woman rides with you, Captain Coltrane."

As briefly as possible, Travis told General Sherman about Kitty's work with General Johnston's field hospital at Bentonville, and her kidnap by a deserting Confederate officer. Then he told of the officer killing John Wright and of his own intervention and subsequent killing of Nathan Collins. "Collins is from around here," Travis went on. "So is Miss Wright. Their neighbors felt very bitter towards John Wright. They burned his farm. Kitty had been working in the Goldsboro Way Hospital, and I thought it best that I escort her back there. I feel sure there were Rebel soldiers about, deserters, who saw what happened and will spread the story, and when it gets out that Kitty Wright had anything at all to do with the death of Nathan Collins, the townspeople are going to turn on her. She is safer with me."

"Safer with you?" General Sherman raised an eyebrow. "And just what do you propose to do with her, Captain? Do you think they will feel any kinder when they see her in the company of a Union officer? And how do you think they will react when we march on, as we shall do quite soon?"

"I plan to take her with me." Travis met the steady gaze of his general, his voice firm. "I plan to marry her."

There was a murmur of angry voices about them, which Travis silenced with a flashing glare. He looked back at General Sherman, waiting for his reaction. But just then Kitty cried out indignantly.

"You all just wait a minute! You talk of me as if I were not even present. I've told you, Travis Coltrane, I'm staying here and tending my father's land. What business is it of yours, General Sherman, what I do? Now you either go ahead and kill me, since that is your way with women and children, or ride on and leave me be. I have no intention of traveling with your captain any longer than necessary. And it was *his* idea to escort me into town, not mine. I can assure you I fear the townspeople no more than I fear your soldiers."

Travis waited for the worst. But General Sherman did something that was seldom witnessed by his men. He laughed. He actually threw his head back and laughed at the fiery young woman. "By damn, I think you mean that, Miss Wright. Only John Wright could have sired such a daughter. Ride on with my captain, and do what you will when you reach Goldsboro. I pity Coltrane if he is so foolish as to wed you."

They crossed a covered bridge over the Neuse River, heading into Goldsboro by way of Waynesboro. The men jerked upright in their saddles at the sound of artillery fire, but the word quickly spread through the lines that there was no cause for alarm. General Schofield had ordered a battery of artillery placed on the brow of a hill and was firing salutes to General Sherman as he marched in.

The townspeople, hearing the gunfire, were gathering to watch the soldiers come in. They stood silently, blank expressions on their faces, which Kitty took to mean defeat and absence of spirit.

"Where are we going now?" Kitty asked of Travis, not liking her present situation. She knew she was the object of stares and exclamations. They probably took her to be a trollop picked up along the way, a woman of pleasure for all the men.

Travis asked her where she wished to go.

"I told you, Travis. I want to return to the hospital for now. Dr. Holt will need all the help he can get."

He was silent for a moment, then said in a sardonic tone, "You realize, my sweet, that there will be plenty of Union soldiers there now, wounded and needing treatment."

"Oh, Travis, be fair with me, please," she cried indignantly. "Did I ever show any partiality to the Union soldiers when I worked in your field hospitals? You, of all people, should know I did everything I could to help the wounded, and it never mattered to me on which side a man fought."

"All right, all right. I'm sorry," he acquiesced. "I know that you performed great services to my side."

"Take me to the hospital, Travis, please. I know I am needed there."

"As you wish," he sighed, weary of arguing.

Reining his horse out of the parade line, Travis moved in the direction of the Goldsboro Way Hospital. Suddenly a shrill cry pierced the air. "It's her! It's Kitty Wright, the traitorous slut. See her? There, riding with a damned Yankee. He's probably the one that killed poor Nathan!"

Kitty's eyes darted to her left to the hysterical face of Nancy Warren, and she gasped at the sight. Nancy was the young woman who had vied with Kitty for Nathan's affections, making no secret of her desire to marry him. Only bitterness existed between the two women.

"Who in the hell is that woman?" Travis hissed, spurring his horse on as the crowd began to surge forward.

"Nathan's old sweetheart, or so she thought," Kitty answered quickly. "Do move on, Travis. Those people are getting angry."

Nancy was hitching up her long skirt to run alongside them, screaming, "Is that your Yankee lover, Kitty? We've heard how poor Nathan died. You slut! How dare you come riding in here this way?" She reached out to grab at Kitty's leg, but Travis twisted in his saddle to shove her away. The gesture caught her off balance, sending her sprawling into the dirt road.

"That goddamned Yankee shoved her down," a man yelled. "They ain't riding in here treating our women like that. Are we going to let him get by with it?"

"Hell, no," another screamed.

Kitty felt something hit her cheek—a dirt clod—and before she could cry out, another flew threw the air, hitting Travis just above his ear, knocking off his hat. Swearing, he spurred his horse, trying to move through the tightening crowd quickly surrounding them. Hands reached out to pull them from the saddle. Kitty was terrified, knowing they would be torn to bits by the mob. Then she saw that Travis had yanked his rifle from his holding strap. He fired straight up into the air. The crowd backed off momentarily, then surged forward again. She saw him lowering the rifle in the direction of a man who was beating upon his leg with a stick.

Loud cracks of gunfire split the air, and the mob began backing away, terrified, as soldiers rode straight into them, knocking both men and women to the ground, charging to where Travis and Kitty had been trapped. "What the hell is going on here?" the officer in charge yelled, then looked straight at Travis and said, "Point out the ones who attacked you. General Schofield will not stand for an attack upon our men."

Kitty's arms were wrapped tightly around Travis' waist, her face pressed against his back. Her eyes were locked with those of Nancy Warren, and she shuddered beneath a gaze that was plainly murderous. Then someone was leading Nancy away, but not before she cried, "You'll pay, Kitty Wright. You'll pay for what you caused to happen to a courageous soldier like Nathan Collins."

Kitty could be quiet no longer. Straightening, she yelled, "Nathan killed my father. He shot him in the back."

"Your father was a goddamned traitor to the South,"

a man standing next to her shrieked. "I could have killed him with my bare hands and never felt a moment's guilt. The vigilantes should of gone on and hung his worthless neck when they had the chance."

"No . . ." Kitty's eyes filled with tears. Didn't they understand? Didn't any of these people understand? Her father had loved them, but he had to follow the convictions of his heart. Was there no way she could make them see that? She had to try. "Poppa loved the South, he . . ."

"Kitty, it's no use," Travis yelled. She lapsed into immediate silence as he twisted to look into her eyes, lowering his voice. "Kitty, I told you it was going to be like this. These people hate your father, they hate the Union, and it doesn't matter that they are defeated. They are going to go on hating until time heals, which may take forever."

"Captain, what's all this about?" The officer standing beside them asked. "What caused this riot?"

"Miss Wright is from Goldsboro," Travis said in a weary tone. "Her father was John Wright . . ."

"John Wright?" The officer's eyes widened, his voice echoing his respect. "I've heard of the man. He was quite a soldier. I knew he was from the South."

"From here," Travis said. "He was murdered, on the last day of battle at Bentonville, shot in the back by a local hero. Miss Wright was that man's betrothed. *I* killed him. The story has spread, and that's why the good citizens were wanting to drag both of us to the ground and kill us."

"Whew!" He let out his breath. "Well, the best thing for both of you is to get off the streets for a while and let things cool down."

Travis told him where he was taking Kitty, and the officer nodded and said they should proceed immediately. As they rode away, Kitty said, "Go ahead and say that you told me so."

"I don't have to. But maybe now you can understand why I say you have to leave here, Kitty. These people hate you, and right now, with feelings running so high, I don't think they would blink an eye at hanging you if they got the chance."

She chewed her lower lip thoughtfully. It would not be that way later, she told herself, not after everything calmed down. People were just upset at the moment. After all, the Yankees were riding into their town, and it had to be a very emotional time. After four long, bloody years, the war was coming to a close, and the South was beaten.

No, the time was not right but wounds would heal later. They had to. This was home.

They reached the hospital. Travis dismounted, then gently reached for Kitty, setting her upon the ground. She looked about her, Travis' arms still holding her. How long since she had left to go to Bentonville? Five days. It seemed like forever. Yet nothing had changed. The dogwood trees that lined the street were struggling to burst into bloom. There was silence. A few people walked along, heads bowed in desolation, footsteps plodded doggedly on.

A scream pierced the air, and both Kitty and Travis turned their gaze to the hospital. "I must go in now," she whispered against his chest as he pulled her closer. "They need all the help they can get."

He cupped her chin in his hand, raising her face upwards. "Kitty, I'll be close by should you need me, and I will try to get by and see you. I want you to promise me that you will consider going with me when I leave. You saw how these people feel about you. There is no life, no future, for you here. Come with me, and we'll make a future together. You know you have my whole heart."

"And you have mine," her voice cracked. She fought to hold back the tears. She had to find words. "Please understand me, Travis. I would marry you any time you wish, but I cannot leave my father's land."

"I ask only that you think about leaving with me."

"And I ask that you think about staying with me."

They embraced once more, then Kitty tore herself from his arms and ran up the path to the hospital. She did not look back.

Chapter Four

DR. W. A. Holt, medical officer for the way hospital in Goldsboro, had just finished amputating the right leg of a Union soldier when someone stopped to tell him that Kitty Wright had returned to the hospital. Wiping bloodied hands on his already stained apron, he moved out to the crowded hallway, maneuvering about the stretchers.

Kitty was already kneeling beside a soldier, trying to comfort him. "Thank God you are back," Dr. Holt greeted her, and she glanced up, then rose. He took hold of her arm and steered her on down the hallway to a corner where there were no stretchers. Compassion in his eyes, he said in a soft voice, "Kitty, I heard about your father. I know he was fighting for the North, but I also know how much he meant to you. I'm very sorry."

"What else did you hear, Dr. Holt?"

He looked away momentarily, then quickly said, "I *am* glad you're back, Kitty. We really have our hands full now, what with wounded coming in from both sides, and—"

"Dr. Holt," Kitty interrupted him without apology. "I have to know what you heard about my father's death. Do you see this mud upon my cheek? There was a near riot when I rode into town, thanks to Nancy

Warren's inciting a mob, screaming about Nathan being killed by my 'Yankee lover.' "

He sighed. "I suppose you do have the right to know what has already spread like wildfire. I don't have to tell you that Major Collins was revered by the people around here. The word came back from two Confederate soldiers who slipped into town rather than retreat with Johnston, and who had witnessed the whole incident from behind scrub brush. They said that Major Collins killed your father in self-defense in an argument over you, and then a Yankee came along and murdered Collins in cold blood. They gathered that you condoned the killing, that you knew the Yankee soldier well, that the two of you were apparently—"

"Lovers," she finished. "The truth is, Dr. Holt, that Nathan Collins was deserting. My father happened along, and to divert an argument between him and Nathan, I lied to my father and said I wanted to go with Nathan. I could tell by the anguish in that one eye those bastards had left him that he believed me when I said I wanted to go with Nathan. He turned his back to walk away, and that's when Nathan shot him . . . in the back. Travis Coltrane came along, and his temper got the best of him. He stomped Nathan to death. *That* is how it happened."

She brushed at tears with the back of her hand, and Dr. Holt patted her gently. "I believe you, Kitty, but you must understand that the townspeople will believe the other story, because it is what they *want* to believe. I am afraid you have much grief ahead, for they won't forget soon."

She jutted her chin up, angry and defiant. "You said you needed help, and that's why I'm here. I don't intend to let lies make me turn tail and run."

"Good girl," he said with a smile, clapping her on the back like a comrade. "Now, here is the situation. General Schofield just marched right into town with no opposition at all. Every available soldier in eastern Carolina was ordered to Bentonville. In no time at all, the Yankees covered the entire town with a circle of breastworks, and they camped inside, because Schofield knew General Johnston was close by. Well, things calmed down a bit. Schofield moved into the Borden house and made it his headquarters. Then we heard about Bentonville and Johnston retreating, and how Sherman was heading this way. Folks panicked."

"Justifiably so," Kitty said bitterly. "General Sherman allows his men to do as they please, burning and stealing."

"There is quite a contrast between the two armies. General Schofield has his men under complete military control and allows no disobedience. He knew folks would get upset when they heard Sherman was marching into town with his army of cutthroats, so he issued an order that anyone who wanted a guard to protect their homes could have one by applying to the provost marshal's office which they set up in Dr. John Davis' home. Provost marshal's name is Glavis, I think. He came by here yesterday to see if we needed anything. I tell you, girl, we can thank our heavenly Father that Schofield got here first. That saved our town from being plundered and burned by Sherman."

"And what about the hospital? I suppose the Yankees have taken over."

"Oh, yes, of course. General Schofield's medical officer has taken over the command, and the first thing he did was to order that Union soldiers be given preference over Confederates. 'Treat our men first,' he said. And you know what I told him? That he might as well go ahead and shoot me because I was treating a man according to the seriousness of his wounds, that it didn't matter a tinker's damn to me what color uniform he wore. The other doctors told him the same thing, so he didn't have much choice. There aren't that many doctors, you know. What galls the hell out of me, though, is those Yankee doctors. They'll step right over a dying Confederate to treat a whining Yankee with a minor wound. The damn bastards."

"Dr. Holt!" They whirled about to see a bearded, heavyset man in a bloodstained coat glowering angrily. "Men are dying and you find time to chitchat with women. No wonder the South is losing the war."

"You wait a minute, doctor. This is Miss Kitty Wright, and she probably knows as much if not more about medicine and doctoring than some of your pumpkin-head Yankee doctors. And as for me 'chit-chatting,' as you call it, I haven't stopped working in twelve hours, not even to eat."

The Union medical officer raised a bushy eyebrow. "They are calling for you in surgery. As for you, Miss Wright"—he turned those cold eyes upon Kitty—"you are hereby impounded to work at this hospital, since you have some knowledge of medicine. If you will see one of the nurses and properly attire yourself—"

"What I am wearing is fine," Kitty snapped. "And you do not have to 'impound' me, sir. I came here to work, and it is my intention to do so—not to stand around listening to some damn pompous Yankee try to browbeat me."

She whipped around and stomped down the crowded hallway, and Dr. Holt chuckled, ignoring the glare of the other doctor. Kitty Wright had been through hell and back and had not lost one bit of her spirit.

Kitty moved among the wounded men, not caring whether she ministered to Yankees or Rebels. Her heart went out to all of them. There was more she would have liked to do for them, but the Union medical officer did not trust a female Southern nurse, and he limited her responsibilities to giving drinks of water, changing bandages, and cleaning up. She lost all track of time, pausing only when ordered to eat. Once in a while she would curl up in a corner for a few hours of sleep.

Since reporting to the hospital, Kitty had lost all sense of time. She was dimly aware, however, that occasionally townspeople came to visit their relatives or to claim the body of a loved one. One day, as she bent over the form of a wounded Union soldier, she heard a familiar voice.

"How can you minister to these Yankees?" It was Mrs. Harriett Dewey. The old woman twisted a lacy handkerchief in her hands as she surveyed the sea of bodies lining the hallway. "I know of several ladies in my church who came here to offer their help to the Confederate wounded, and that nasty Yankee who took over said that if they were not willing to help with his men, then they could not help at all. Isn't that terrible?"

"No," Kitty said bluntly, not deterred by the cold flash that instantly appeared in Mrs. Dewey's eyes. "If those good women were Christians, they would care for all. The ladies of your church could take a few lessons from our own soldiers. They feel no hatred, only a deep fierce yearning to recover and go home again, to see all the suffering and anguish ended. I have seen Confederates on the mend go to the bedsides of Yankees when the staff was busy elsewhere. The time for bitterness and hatred is over, Mrs. Dewey. We would all do well to realize that and think about rebuilding our country."

"That's easy for *you* to say, Katherine Wright!" A plump woman who had been kneeling beside her wounded husband spoke. Her face was twisted with rage. "You would like mighty well for folks to forget the past, wouldn't you? You'd like for them to forget that it was by the hand of your Yankee lover that one of Wayne County's finest officers was brutally slain."

"After that same, so-called fine officer shot my father in the back," Kitty flared instantly.

"You're a fine one to talk, you little snit. You should be stoned right out of town. Everyone knows your father was a turn-coat traitor. He deserved what Nathan Collins gave him," the woman went on, unmindful of the scene she was creating.

Kitty felt as though the blood was boiling in her veins. Her arm that still held a water bucket shot up involuntarily. Just as she was about to send it flying straight into the shrieking woman's face, she felt a hand clamp down on her wrist while another encircled her waist tightly.

"Just calm down, Kitty. You might get some of your patients wet." Her heart skipped a beat at the sound of Travis' voice in her ear. She all but collapsed against him. "Forget her," Travis continued, as he lead Kitty down the hall, stepping around the wounded, moving out the front door into the cool air of the spring evening.

For a moment they just stood embracing in the shadows at the porch's edge. Travis tilted her face up to meet his tender gaze. "Have you had enough, Kitty? Have you realized that this can never be your home again?"

"Travis . . ." she shook her head slowly, tears filling her eyes. God, how she loved this man, but how could she make him understand how she felt?

"Miss Wright, are you out here?" Dr. Preston, the Union medical officer, stepped out onto the porch. Travis immediately clicked to attention and saluted. The doctor recognized him and smiled. "Oh, Captain Coltrane. I had heard Miss Wright was fortunate enough to have a Union officer courting her, but I did not know it was you."

"Sir, I request permission to take Miss Wright for a ride."

"Unchaperoned?" the doctor laughed, a nasty sound in Kitty's ears. "Of course. Try to be back by morning."

"Damn Yankee bastard," Kitty spat out as Travis steered her down the steps.

"You're talking like a trollop again, Kitty," he said, sounding amused. "What would the dear ladies of Goldsboro say if they could hear you now?"

She snapped, "Must we spend what little time we have together discussing my shortcomings?"

He mounted his stallion, then swung her up to position her in front of him, his arms about her as he held the reins. "You are turning into skin and bones," he said critically. "I could lift you with one hand. I know food is scarce, but I thought they would at least feed the hospital staff."

"I seldom have time to eat, and when I do, I have no appetite. Who wants to eat, surrounded by death and its smell all day and all night?"

He reminded her that it had been her decision to work at the hospital. "I offered to get a room for you at the hotel. We could have been together these past nights. My bed has been cold and lonely."

"That is easy for you to say. I have no way of knowing whether or not you found a woman to take my place."

"I told you that you are the only woman for me, Kitty. Until you betray me." He spoke between gritted teeth. "So don't hint that I have been unfaithful. I have never liked being called a liar."

"Oh, Travis, I'm sorry," she whispered, burrowing her face in his shoulder. They rode through the night. She didn't care where they were going, as long as they were together. He bent to plant a light kiss on her forehead. He was no longer angry, and their world was right again. She prayed this night would never end.

As she felt his heart beating rapidly, Kitty knew what would take place between them before the black skies turned to gold.

And she felt the beating of her own heart quicken in passionate anticipation.

Chapter Five

TRAVIS found a place on the banks of the Neuse River where they could isolate themselves. Honeysuckle vines had already begun to entwine their foliage skywards, bursting into early sweet fragrance. A tall weeping willow tree bowed forward gracefully to enshroud them in its protective arms.

Travis took a blanket roll from the back of his saddle, and lay down on it, rolling on his side to prop his head upon his hand, smiling at her through the thick, dusty lashes she adored. "Take your clothes off, Kitty. I want to see you naked."

She complied unabashedly, aware that his eyes took in every inch of her body. As her breasts spilled forward, he whispered, "I will never forget the first time I saw your breasts, Kitty. I thought they were the most beautiful objects I had ever seen—ripe, succulent, and just waiting to be devoured."

"You have seen many?" she teased, throwing back her long red-gold hair, feeling wanton and wicked and loving it. "You are a connoisseur of breasts? I am not sure I want hands fondling mine that have sampled so many others."

"You love for me to touch you all over, and you know it," he said lazily. "You always did. You were just too much of a lady to let it show."

"And you tell me I have the speech of a saloon

trollop?" Laughing, she raised an eyebrow in mock surprise.

"When that temper of yours is riled, you have quite a foul mouth, m'lady, and we're going to have to do something about that when we get married. It wouldn't be fitting for me to have a wife who could outcurse me."

"And you a brave Yankee cavalry officer." She shook her head. Standing before him, completely naked, she placed her hands on her hips, legs spread apart slightly, and asked softly, "Why do I not feel like a trollop at this moment, Travis? We are not married, and we have no right to this, but I feel no shame. Your eyes devour me, and I glory in their gaze. Yet I know it isn't just lust. There is something else, something warm, burning deep within our hearts. . . ." Soon he was naked before her. Her eyes devoured every line, resting at last on that throbbing pinnacle of manhood that rose for her alone. He knelt beside her, warm flesh melding against her own. Gentle, teasing fingertips touched her nipples, which were already taut and prominent. "Lovely," he whispered as his lips covered hers, tongue seeking. "So damn lovely, you are. . . ."

His strong hands explored the wonders of her body. His tongue touched one sweet nipple. He could feel her back arching as she strained to bring herself even closer, wanting to fill his mouth with the glory of her womanhood. He suckled until she was gasping, and then he began to move lower, his tongue trailing a path of fire as it moved across her trembling belly.

"Travis, no," she whispered in impassioned torment. "I . . . I don't think I can stand it . . ."

"Oh, yes, you can, my love."

Firm hands gripped her quivering thighs, forcing them apart as he pressed his seeking mouth into the softness of that delectable hub of pleasure. Her buttocks arched as a soft scream escaped from her lips. He knew his probing tongue and nibbling lips were bringing her to explosive release, and he pressed even harder, sharing her joy as she peaked, moaning and writhing beneath him. Then he lifted his body to cover hers, plunging his swollen member inside her, filling her with the fruits of his loins.

Kitty wanted him to remain inside her forever, and she raised her legs to wrap them around his undulating buttocks, squeezing against him to hold him even tighter. Nothing else mattered, not the war, not imminent separation, not even their dissent. They were one inviolate being. And for a moment, the world stood still.

Kitty felt the tears of reality stinging her eyes. She blinked furiously, but they spilled over, trailing down her cheeks and chin, and Travis felt a drop on his hand and instantly raised his head to stare at her in wonder. "You're crying, Kitty. Did I hurt you? I didn't think I was rough."

"No, darling, no," she shook her head from side to side as the tears ran freely. "Just never leave me. *Please.* You have to find a way to stay with me forever and always. I . . . I've had this horrible feeling for days now, that if you leave me, I will never see you again."

He sat up, staring out at the creeping river. "You can always go with me," he said quietly. "I can arrange it with General Sherman. He knows what a spunky woman you are, and he would allow you to travel with his ambulance wagons. The war will be over soon, Kitty. We could go home, then."

"I *am* home!"

"How can you call this damned place home?" He got to his feet and began dressing with quick, jerky movements. "You've seen how these people regard you. They don't want you here. Haven't you had enough of hatred and fighting? We can go back to the peace of the bayous of Louisiana and make a whole new life. We would never have to be separated again."

"You could stay here *now*, Travis." She got up and moved to stand behind him, wrapping her arms about his waist and pressing her face against his back. "Who would dare lift a hand against the wife of a Union officer? We could work the land together. Poppa always said the future crop was tobacco. One day, we could be rich. . . ."

He whirled around so abruptly that she was caught off balance and stumbled. He caught her, holding her tightly as steel eyes met violet, each gaze filled with despair. "Kitty, you don't understand. I'm leaving tomorrow morning, early. General Sherman is marching on to Virginia for a conference with General Grant to determine their next move. The word we receive is that Richmond is falling, and when that happens, it should be only a matter of days until Lee surrenders. But we are not certain of anything, so we leave for Virginia with the rising sun. Come with me, please."

"Travis, I can't. . . ." The words were wrenched from the very depths of her soul. "Please forgive me, but I cannot leave with you. If you love me, you will stay."

"If *I* love *you*," he asked incredulously. Then, giving her a shake that sent her head bobbing, he shouted, "If *you* loved *me*, woman, you would do as *I* ask. If you weren't so goddamned stubborn, you would see the folly of what you want. We can never be happy *here*. Why must you be so stubborn? Why must you always have your own way?"

Their eyes locked, blazing now. Suddenly Kitty remembered she was naked, and now she found no glory in that realization and began to scurry about, picking up her clothes and quickly putting them on.

"Kitty, be reasonable," Travis yelled at her.

"I will not be led around by the nose by any man."

She faced him once she was fully clothed, her chin jutting upwards in the familiar stance. "I have given you my heart, but I will not give you my mind. I will not be dictated to and told how I should direct the course of my life merely because I am woman and you are man. You have known me long enough to know that I am not a servile woman. I have a will of my own, and good reasons for remaining here on my father's land."

He inhaled deeply, chest swelling, nostrils flaring in his anger, but Kitty stood her ground. "I should have known better than to think you could love me or anyone, you selfish little vixen. You want me only as long as I bend to your will. Well, I must profess to love you, my dear, but the only way you will make use of my testicles is to have them plant you with the seed of a child, not to adorn your neck like a prize won in battle."

"If you love me, you won't go."

"I'm still a soldier." His voice softened, but his eyes remained hard. "I have to follow my general's orders. I couldn't stay now if I wanted to. Now, for the last time . . . I am asking you to come with me, Kitty. If you love me, you will follow me."

"Like an Indian squaw," she snapped. "Oh, Travis, don't you see? If it weren't for Poppa's land, I would go with you gladly, to the ends of the earth, into another four years of battle if need be. I'd fight right by your side to the death, because I *do* love you. You must believe that. But I loved my father, too, and I made him a promise to keep the land that meant so much to him. Travis, I am to blame for Poppa's death! I was blind to the kind of person Nathan really was. If only I had realized sooner! Oh, what difference does it make to you? You won't even try to see things my way."

Sighing, he walked over to where she stood and

placed firm hands on her shoulders. "Come. We have to go now. It's almost dark. I don't want some stray Reb to take a shot at us out here in the country. It isn't safe."

She let him lead her to his horse. Before he helped her up, he said, "Kitty, don't blame yourself for your father's death. You had no way of knowing just what a scoundrel Nathan really was. According to your father, Nathan disguised himself pretty well. And you did try to avoid trouble. You said you lied to your father so he wouldn't try to come to your aid. How were you to know Nathan would shoot him in the back when he turned away?"

"Thank you," she whispered. "Thank you for everything you have meant to me, Travis. If we had met another time, in another place, perhaps our love would not have been shadowed."

Then, overcome, Kitty threw herself into his arms and sobbed, "Please, Travis, say you'll come back to me when the war is over. I'll wait for you. I swear to God, I'll be waiting for you no matter *how* long it takes."

He cupped her chin in his hands, warm eyes gazing down at her moon-bathed face. Never before had he feasted upon such beauty or seen so much love written in a woman's face. "Do you mean that, Kitty? Would you wait for me however long it might be?"

"Yes, oh, yes, I swear on my father's grave, Travis. I could never love another man, never let another man touch me, now. If you believe me, you will return. I know you will."

"Kitty, understand me well. I do not promise to return. I am hurt, and I am angry that you won't go with me now. Later, I may feel differently. It's possible that I will return, but I make no vow. I'm proud, too, you see. I'm a man, and while you make me realize that fact more than any other woman in my life has ever been able to do, I can't let you damage my pride."

"Must I lose the only man I can ever truly love, merely because I want to keep a promise to the father I adored?"

He sighed. "Kitty, I will admit that you have a point. And I will give serious thought to what you ask of me. I do love you. More than that I cannot give you at this time. If you will leave here with me tomorrow, we will be married right away—"

"I can't go with you." She squeezed her eyes shut, wanting to close out the picture of his departure. "I love you, my darling, but I cannot leave my homeland."

"Then so be it," he said tightly, mounting his horse and drawing her up to sit behind him. She wrapped her arms about his waist and pressed her cheek against his back. He could feel the moisture of her tears through his clothes.

And so, they moved up to the road for what might be their last ride together. The night enshrouded them in a cloak of black velvet.

Chapter Six

"I don't believe it!"

Kitty had been spooning water through the parched lips of a wounded soldier. Straightening quickly, she looked up into the anguished eyes of Dr. Holt. "Tell me it isn't so. General Lee didn't really surrender."

But the graying medical officer could only nod, his face lined with the anguish of defeat. "He surrendered to General Grant at Appomattox. The word just came."

With trembling hands, she set down the water bucket, stumbled over the bodies in the corridor, and ran to the front porch of the hospital. For four long years Lee's army had been unconquerable. Twice his army had moved the war north of the Potomac. Time and again it was able to beat back the strongest forces that the North could send against it. Now it had come to the end of the road.

So it was time to quit, she thought. The war was over. It was time to think about the future, and rebuilding. Travis might be coming back soon. They would be married and start a new life. It was only two weeks since he last held her, and already she missed him so much that tears sprang to her eyes thinking of him.

"Miss Kitty? Miss Kitty? Is that really you? Lordy, I don't believe my eyes!"

She whipped her head around and, for a moment, could only blink in surprise as she recognized old Jacob, who had been her father's faithful servant for so many years. "Jacob, Jacob!" She ran down the steps with arms outstretched. "Oh, I was afraid you were long dead. Dear, dear Jacob."

They embraced, and then the dark-skinned man stood back, twisting his worn straw hat in his gnarled old hands. "Not me, Miss Kitty. Can't kill an old coot like me. Come close to it, though, with one thing and another. But I been doing fine. You know my Fanny, she took sick with the fever and died. But I got my young'uns, and we've made out."

Her hands pressed down on his shoulders, and she whispered, "I'm sorry about Fanny. I'd heard of her passing. But I am glad you survived, Jacob. You heard about Poppa?"

Tears sprang to his eyes at the mention of the man he had loved so dearly. "Yes'm, I heard," his voice broke. "I heard all the stories, but I didn't believe nothing 'cept that John Wright died in glory—just like he lived."

Kitty blinked back her own tears as she told him exactly how it happened, and then she told him of her father's admission that Nathan had been among the vigilantes the night he was beaten. The old Negro's milky, veined eyes bulged in anger. "If I'd a'knowed that, I'd have kilt Nathan myself." Then he stopped to stare at her in wonder. "But how come he never told you, Miss Kitty? How come he kept silent, knowing you planned to marry Mr. Collins?"

She bit her lip in painful remembrance of those final moments as she held her dying father in her arms. "He wanted me to find out for myself what a scoundrel Nathan was. But it took a tragedy for me to really see it."

"Don't blame yo'self," Jacob said gruffly, wiping at

his eyes with the back of his bony hand. "You'll find happiness again someday, Miss Kitty. I knows you will. General Lee, he done surrendered, and now we'll have peace. You know what I heard? Every black man is gonna have a mule and some land, *give* to him by the government. I'll have my own farm, me and my boys!"

"I'm happy for you, Jacob. I only wish Fanny were alive to share your new life. We were always so poor that we couldn't give you much, just a roof over your heads. My mother didn't make life any easier for you, either."

He bowed his head respectfully. "I heard she's passed on, too, Miss Kitty. I'm sorry."

"I'm sure you heard how my mother died. A drunk. A prostitute. The talk of the town. Maybe I could have saved her if Luke Tate hadn't kidnapped me *again* when I was going after medicine for her, but I doubt it. She destroyed herself. She was never happy. I hope she's found peace now."

"I hope *you* find peace, Miss Kitty," the old Negro said in a reverent whisper. "You's a fine woman. You deserves fine things. If you ever need me, I'll be around. Just spread the word among my people that you need old Jacob, and there I'll be, long as there's a breath left in my body. You believe in that.

"Maybe it's a lie, that talk about a mule and some land. Maybe I won't have nothing. You think you could use me and my boys on your Poppa's farm? 'Course, it's your farm now, ain't it? You going to keep it? Make it be what he wanted it to be? If anybody can, you can, Miss Kitty. I knows that with all my heart."

She forced a smile. "I'm going to try to do what Poppa wanted me to do, Jacob. And if your own dream doesn't come true, then come to me. You'll always have a home."

Just then Dr. Holt walked out on the front porch.

"Miss Kitty, we need you. An amputation. Will you come with me, please?"

"Sometimes I think the suffering will never end," she said to Jacob in parting. "We'll meet again. You take care, and I pray both our dreams come true. I want to tell you about my cavalryman, Jacob, the man I'm going to marry. He's wonderful, and he's going to help me make the farm prosperous, the way Poppa always said it would be."

Jacob stared after her, his heart warmed by her smile, by her nearness. She probably never left the hospital, he thought sadly, a place where screams could be heard at all hours of the day or night. So she probably hadn't heard the rumors yet, either, about how if the Yankees won the war, they were going to take the land away from the Rebels and give it to the slaves. He prayed they didn't take her land. Lord, her daddy had loved that land almost as much as he loved that girl. Miss Kitty would die if she lost that land, he mused, walking on down the street shaking his white head. Yes, Lord, she would lay down and die.

The soldier facing the amputation of his right leg was young, perhaps sixteen or seventeen. He screamed as soldiers tied him to the blood-soaked table. Kitty stepped forward and placed her hand on his brow. "God, don't let them do this to me, lady," he shrieked, seeing her through fevered eyes. "I've got to have my leg. God almighty, what good is a man with just one leg?"

She had heard the same plea so many times in the past four years that she knew by heart every word that would come from his trembling lips. Her eyes went to the exposed flesh of his gangrene-infested leg. It was amputate or die. There was no other way. "We want to save your life, soldier," she said, and pushed his damp hair back from his forehead. "Why, they make wooden legs nowadays that are just as good as real legs. You'll be dancing to a banjo in no time at all. God wants you to live, or He would have let you be blown to heaven, instead of just wounding your leg."

"I'd rather die than lose my leg." He arched his back, the veins in his neck nearly bursting as he screamed, "Don't . . . don't let them do it . . ."

Someone handed her the chloroform. At least the Yankees still had some of the precious drug. So many times she had been forced to amputate with no anesthesia at all, just other soldiers to hold a man down until he mercifully passed out from the excruciating pain.

She administered the drug placing a folded cloth over his screaming lips, letting it drip down, a bit at a time. It didn't take long. Soon he was out of his misery. She turned her head away as the sound began, steel cutting into flesh, blood dripping to the floor, the whining of bone being severed. "We'll leave him a good stump," Dr. Holt was saying. "He'll have enough for a nice wooden leg. So many times, there's just not enough left."

The smell of hot tar being slapped against the wound to close it. Then he was lifted from the table and carried to lie on the floor with the others. Soon, he would awaken to scream in agony throughout the long night, the sound echoing with hundreds of others who had been through hell along with him.

Dr. Holt wiped his bloodied hands on his apron and reached for the cup of water someone handed him. "I heard that General Grant was as anxious to end this damned war as Lee," he said to Kitty, who was trying to rinse the blood from the table in anticipation of the next poor soul. "I heard it said once that Grant believed the whole point of the blasted war had been an effort to try and prove that the North and South were, and always would be, neighbors. And he thinks as soon as the fighting is officially over, they should start acting that way—like neighbors. God knows, that's not going to happen. Not in my lifetime, anyway. I'll never live to see the day that Yankees and Rebs don't hate each other. And as for acting like neighbors, what meaning does that have? Look at the way your neighbors treat you!"

Dr. Holt sighed. "The story I get is that Grant told Lee to just have his men lay down their arms and go on home, and it's even in the terms of surrender that if they'll do just that, they won't be bothered by the Federal authorities. Thank God, the man did that. Think of the Northerners who want to see General Lee hanged. Now they can't do it, not by the terms of the surrender. And if they can't hang General Lee, by God, they damn well can't hang a lesser Confederate. That's some comfort."

"Then, if they don't intend to force their authority upon us, how do they plan to give the freed slaves mules and land?"

"That's just talk, girl. But let's face it. We can't be sure of just what is going to happen. Look around you. Right here in Goldsboro, people are starving. Have you seen the horses that wander around and die and rot in the streets from starvation? What's going to happen to all of us? The Confederate dollar isn't worth the blood that drips off my operating table. Time will tell what God and the Yankees have in store for us."

But not a great deal of time passed before the whole nation learned what was in store. Just six days later, Kitty was making her morning rounds when she heard the screaming. Louder and louder the sound came—some shouts of joy, others of anguish. Guns fired. Kitty ran to the window and looked out to see people running around in hysterical panic. Then a man ran up the steps yelling, "President Lincoln is dead! President Lincoln is dead!"

Kitty's hand flew to her throat as she stood watching the man talk with the officer. Then the officer turned and made his announcement to the deathly quiet room. "President Lincoln died this morning," he said, voice cracking. "He was shot last night. Assassinated."

He turned away, overcome. A few of the bolder Confederate soldiers lying about began to cheer. The Yankees who were strong enough cursed back at them. Soldiers restored order, but for a few moments there was almost as much pandemonium in the hospital as there was in the streets.

A gentle hand fell on Kitty's shoulder as she stood watching the jubilation. "They don't know what they are doing, the fools," Dr. Holt said harshly. "President Lincoln was their only hope . . . *our* only hope."

Kitty turned her head, surprised when she saw tears streaming down his cheeks. "I don't understand."

"President Lincoln wanted peace. He did not want to see the South punished. Vice-President Andrew Johnson feels just the opposite. And now he is our President, Kitty. God save the South. The government is in the control of radicals now."

A few days later word came that General Johnston had met with Sherman at Durham's Station, near Raleigh. Kitty's heart leaped. Sherman was in Raleigh! Was Travis there, too? If so, he would be back soon. He had to be. Her lips ached for his, and her body trembled each time she thought of his warm strength. He *had* to return.

"Kitty?" She jumped as Dr. Holt shoved a plate of beans across the table. "This isn't much, but you haven't eaten all day. Neither have I. Maybe they'll keep us from dying of starvation before morning. It's all I could salvage from the kitchen."

"I can't," she said, pushing her fist against her lips. "Thank you, but I can't. Those worms . . ."

"Worms?" he guffawed. "Kitty, girl, you've been through the war, and I imagine you've seen your share of worms and maggots in your food and learned to pick them out. What's wrong now?"

Shaking her head miserably, she whispered, "I don't know. I just haven't been feeling well at all lately. I'm tired. Tired of the war. Tired of the rumors. Most of all, I'm tired of missing Travis, wondering if he'll come back. If Sherman is in Raleigh, though, maybe Travis is, too."

"There's no telling where he is, girl. Haven't you heard there's a massive Federal cavalry force sweeping through Alabama and taking over the last war-production center in Selma? They're moving towards Montgomery, too, where the Confederate capital was once located. Mobile has surrendered, down on the Gulf Coast. And even though there's an army west of the Mississippi, it's rumored it will lay down arms any day now. No, honey, there's no telling where your cavalryman is. And, I don't mean to alarm you, but there's been a few skirmishes. He may not make it back to you."

Kitty stared in horror. She wouldn't let herself think of that. Travis couldn't be dead. He was too cunning, too strong. Shaking her head, she blinked back tears. "He'll be back. I know he will."

"Mind if I eat your beans?" he asked casually.

"No, no, go ahead." Her stomach was heaving again.

"I hear the paper Johnston signed covers not only his army but the rest of the Confederacy," the doctor said between mouthfuls. "He didn't have that authority, but General Breckinridge did, and he is . . . was . . . the Secretary of War for the Confederacy."

"Does that mean it's over? All of it?"

"Kitty, girl, there's so much turmoil going on that I can't tell what's going on. Every soldier that's brought in here has a new tale, a new rumor. But I do have it on good authority that the agreement Johnston signed went far beyond the terms Grant gave to Lee. Our boys are to march to the capital in the state they came from and deposit their weapons there; sign a paper saying they'll never take up arms again, and then disband. And each state government will be recognized as lawful once its officers take oath to support the Constitution of the United States. No one is to be punished for his part in the war. Political rights are supposed to be guaranteed. Everything is supposed to settle down and be peaceful." He snorted.

"You don't believe the Yankees will keep their word?" Kitty's eyes widened. She wanted peace as much as anyone. If the South had lost, then so be it. Rebuild. Think of the future. That was the only answer now.

Dr. Holt lay down his spoon and looked her straight in the eye. "You want to know the truth, harsh as it may sound?"

She nodded, a chill moving through her.

"That was not just a simple surrender document Johnston signed," he bit out. "It was a treaty of peace, all that any Southerner could hope to ask for. But there's not a chance that the government in Washington is going to ratify it. Lincoln would've. From the moment it became apparent that we were going to surrender, Lincoln insisted that the field generals were not to concern themselves with political questions. They were to give liberal terms to the surrendering armies. They were to leave all the details—about readmission to the Union, and the restoration of civil and political rights, abolition of slavery—all of that, in his hands. But now Johnson is President, and you can bet Lincoln's dreams for peace and all his plans will go right in the ground with his coffin."

Kitty got up and left the room, walking down the corridor and out onto the front porch. There was a full moon. The dogwood petals were starting to drop from the tree branches, and the ground looked as though giant snowflakes had begun to cover its surface. A gentle breeze sent the white flowers swirling and dancing about in the street.

Lifting her face to the blue-black sky, Kitty gazed up at the moon, thinking that the same glow was shining down on Travis, somewhere.

A cloud drifted across the night sky, obliterating the moon. Life is like that now, Kitty thought. For all of us. A cloud covers us all.

She whispered out loud, tears streaming down her cheeks, her whole body quaking: "Travis, I need you. I need you now more than I've ever needed you before!"

The worry that had been locked inside now flowed from her. She whispered into the night, "Travis, I need you . . . and so does our baby!"

Chapter Seven

SPRING turned to summer, and heat made the hospital intolerable. Gradually the number of patients began to thin. The Federal medical officers were discharging the Confederate soldiers as quickly as possible. Kitty overheard Dr. Holt arguing fiercely over several patients, saying they were not well enough, nor strong enough, to be sent out into the streets. The Federals argued back that they were not coddling any man, least of all a "damned Reb."

Kitty knew that soon she, too, would be discharged from services. There had not been any pay, ever, but at least there was a roof over her head. Food was becoming more plentiful. Where would she go? Who, in all of Wayne County, would befriend her? She knew she had to keep her pregnancy a secret as long as possible. Travis would return soon, and they would be married. He had to come back. It was the only hope she had.

But where was he? The only news was from a wounded Yankee cavalryman. Kitty questioned him anxiously.

"I was a cavalryman, all right, lady," he grinned, enjoying the attention. "I rode with the best of 'em. I was hot on the tail of old Jeff Davis himself when a Johnny Reb that wouldn't believe the war was over took a pot shot at me."

"Were you in Goldsboro when General Sherman first marched in?" Kitty could hardly contain herself, and her body began to tremble nervously. "Were you with his cavalrymen at the battle of Bentonville?"

He laughed. Damn-a-bear if the filly wasn't shaking, she was so impressed. He felt himself swell to bursting and made no effort to hide the bulge in the sheet. Let her see it. Let her know. Maybe she had so much admiration for cavalrymen that she wouldn't mind doing something about his needs. No one was looking. It was a fact that the dashing horsemen always impressed the young ladies. "Yeah, I was there all right, honey." He reached out and caught her wrist, pulling her hand towards him, as he lowered his voice to a whisper. "I swear if you aren't the prettiest thing I've seen around here."

She twisted out of his grasp, stepping back quickly. "You don't understand, sir." She made her voice steady. "I want information about a captain who rides with General Sherman. Captain Travis Coltrane. Do you know him?"

The soldier's smile faded. "I might have known. I heard about Coltrane's woman." He sighed, thinking of all he had missed out on. What a fool Coltrane had been to leave her. "He was my captain. He's chasing Davis now, with the rest of the men. They might have caught him by now. I don't know."

"But is he well?" she persisted.

"Coltrane?" He snorted. "I don't think a grizzly bear could kill that son of a gun. I should have known you were the one they talked about, the rest of the men. Hair like early morning sunshine. Eyes that dance with fire. A shape that could drive a man to insanity."

Kitty felt herself blush. She took another step backwards. "I'm sorry," he said sincerely. "It's just that you are lovely, miss. As for Captain Coltrane, I wouldn't worry none if I were you. He's as fit as he's ever been. He's one of the best officers the Union has. Just because the war is supposed to be over, he won't be asking for a discharge to get out of all the dirty clean-up work."

"Thank you," she murmured, cheeks still warm. "And Sam Bucher? Is he well, too? He was such a good friend."

"You can believe that he rides beside Coltrane every step of the way. Yes, lovely lady, they are both well."

"And you will be rejoining them when you are well? Would you tell him you saw me, and that I'm anxious for his return?"

He shook his head, a chagrined expression moving across his face. "As soon as I get discharged from this place, I'm heading home to Pennsylvania. I've got a wife and five kids waiting for me. I've done my part in this damned war. I won't be seeing Coltrane again."

He called out to her as she stumbled away, but she did not turn back. There was no way to get a message to Travis. How could she write to him when he was on the move?

Wiping perspiration from her forehead, she moved along the rows of beds. Once, she had to step over wounded men lying on the floor, but the hospital was no longer crowded. Still, the smell of dying and the stench of decay permeated the air. Nearby, a soldier had vomited and then passed out to lie unconscious in his own filth. She moved towards his bed, knowing he needed to be bathed. Flies were buzzing about his face, and the scene was nauseating.

She got as far as his bedside when she felt herself swaying dizzily. The heat, the flies, the sour odor—it all hit her at once. Groping out blindly, she found nothing to anchor herself and crumpled to the floor.

"Kitty. Kitty. Wake up, girl."

She blinked. Someone was gently slapping both

sides of her face at once. Dr. Holt was bending over her. "Oh, I'm sorry," she cried feebly, trying to sit up, only to be pushed back gently on the cot where Dr. Holt had placed her. "I'm all right now, honest. It was the heat, and the smells, and . . ."

"And the fact that you are going to have a baby," he said softly.

Their eyes met and held. She could not lie to this man.

"When do you figure it will be born?"

"It had to have happened right after the battle of Bentonville." She turned her face to the wall. I suppose that means I can expect the birth sometime around Christmas." She gave an unladylike snort. "Isn't that something? An unwed mother expecting a baby at Christmas. But not a virgin birth."

The doctor patted her shoulder. "Kitty, your captain will return. How could a man not return to someone as lovely as you? You will be married and have your baby, and a smile will touch your lips again. You'll see. You can face anything, and as bad as I hate to leave you in your predicament, I know you will come through."

Her head snapped back "What do you mean you hate to leave me? Where are you going?"

He spread his hands in a helpless gesture. "I haven't told you before now, because I didn't want to upset you. I have suspected for several weeks now that you were carrying a baby. Doctors sense those things, my dear. I have been told by the Union officers in charge of the hospital that my services are no longer needed. I'm free to go back home, to Raleigh, where my family needs me. The hospital will close soon, anyway. A few months at the most. But I hate to think of leaving you behind this way, with no one to look after you, knowing how the townspeople feel about you. Why don't you come with me? You'd like my wife, and she would welcome you into our home as though you were our own daughter."

"No." It exploded from her. "I can't leave here. Where would Travis know to look for me when he returns? I promised to wait for him."

He sighed, exasperated. "So what are you going to do in the meantime?"

"I'll find a way." Her chin jutted upwards, and he knew that the conversation might as well come to an end.

In three days, Dr. Holt bid her goodbye and was off to Raleigh. For him, the blood and anguish of broken bodies was over. Kitty could not hold back her tears. "You will write?" he asked anxiously. "You will let me know if you change your mind and want to come stay with me and my family?"

She nodded, but they both knew they would probably never meet again. Kitty was going to wait for Travis. Now, more than ever, they had reason to rebuild their lives on the land that was now hers. How happy her father would have been to see his grandchild growing up on Wright land. The thought brought a smile to her lips, a glow to her eyes, and Dr. Holt whispered, "You're going to make it, girl. I know you will."

And then he was gone.

She continued with her duties at the hospital, working harder than ever. She wore larger dresses as she could find them, bigger aprons. Her condition had to be kept secret as long as possible. The Union medical officers tolerated her because, she supposed, it was a known fact that she belonged to a respected cavalry officer. The other local women who had volunteered for hospital work had long since been sent away, except for the good ladies of the church who came and went with baskets of cheer for the wounded Yankees.

"They hate us, yet they come," a soldier laughed

once after the woman had left. "I guess they feel it's a sure way to heaven, being nice to the enemy. But it's obvious they despise us."

"You are no longer the enemy," Kitty told him. "We are supposed to be one union now, remember? There are no more sides. We have to think like that if we are to have peace."

One morning the sound of women chattering made Kitty look up from changing the bandage on a soldier's arm. "The do-gooders," the soldier snorted. "In they come with their baskets of stuff what ain't fit to eat nohow. Don't let none of 'em come around me. I ain't in no mood for no hymn-singing this morning."

"Now, Linwood, don't be so cantankerous," Kitty scolded good-naturedly. She had grown fond of the old man who had lost one arm in battle and half of his other. He was from Rhode Island and dreamed of the day he could go home, and she had been working to help his recuperation along. She was the only person in the hospital who could get him out of bed to walk around and exercise every day. He was getting stronger, as evidenced by his dismay over seeing the clucking women bustling down the aisles.

"Can't stand 'em," he snapped. "You can tell they can't stand to touch us. Remember that fat one that ran out screaming all of a sudden last week, saying she might be giving treats to the very soldier what shot her husband? Lord, I can still hear the way that woman was hollering. How come the doctors in charge let those old biddies in here, anyway?"

"Some of the patients enjoy their visits," Kitty said patiently, putting the last touches to the dressing on the stump of his arm. "The woman who ran out screaming didn't have any business coming, that's true. I heard later that she was talked into coming, because her preacher felt it might help her get over some of her hate when she saw that the North had suffered, too. Obviously, it didn't work."

"Yeah. Maybe her husband was the one what put a ball in me and blew off one arm and near 'bout all the other one. *I* didn't run out screaming." He spat a wad of tobacco on the floor, ignoring Kitty's scolding glare. "Just keep them hens away from me. Let 'em sing their hymns and pass out that gawd-awful food to somebody else. I'll eat the slop they serve me here."

Suddenly a shriek pierced the air. "That's her! My God, that's her. And look! She's going to have a baby. *His* baby, no doubt. The Yankee bastard that killed my nephew. Oh, God, God . . ."

Kitty whirled around, gasping at the sight of Nathan's Aunt Sue. Memories spun through her—the mansion where Nathan insisted she stay with his aunt and mother and Nancy Warren Stoner, his cousin. That awful night in the orchard when the Yankee foragers came through, and Nancy literally threw Kitty at them to save herself, when Kitty had been forced to kill them. Then, despite a promise to Nathan, she had left the plantation and returned to the hospital, refusing to live with those women any longer. Nathan's mother had died shortly afterwards.

And now Aunt Sue stood there, white-faced and screaming. "How dare that heathen she-devil be allowed around Christian folk? Even though these Yankees are enemies, they are God's children. And some of them are sure to be born-again Christians."

Sounds of "Amen" rang through the air—some from the patients. The loudest chorus came from the scowling women. Aunt Sue was making her way to Kitty. "I'd heard you worked here, and I prayed to God to give me the strength to keep silent if we ever met. But when I see you here, flaunting your sins, swollen with the baby of the man who killed my nephew . . . oh, Jesus!"

Before Kitty realized what was happening, the stout woman's arm flew up, her hand cracking across her face. Kitty fell backwards across the bed, stunned. "Jezebel! Child of Satan!" The blows rained down upon her. The others in the room seemed to be in a state of shock. No one moved to help her until Kitty heard a feeble voice crying out.

"You crazy fool. Stop it, I say." Linwood stumbled across the floor to the shrieking, striking woman and, with strength Kitty never dreamed he had, kicked her to the floor. "How dare you strike this girl, you hypocritical old biddy! You ain't fit to walk in her tracks."

"What is going on here?" an authoritative voice boomed, and Kitty raised her stinging face to see Dr. Theodore Malpass striding towards them. Three soldiers walked with him, all with grim, set looks on their faces. Dr. Malpass motioned for one of his men to help Linwood back to his bed. He stooped to help Aunt Sue to her feet. "Will someone please tell me what is going on here?"

Kitty rubbed the back of her hand across her cheek as Nathan's aunt launched into another tirade. "And I presume some of you Yankees are born-again," she snapped. "Look at her. She's carrying the baby of the man who murdered my nephew. He was a fine Confederate officer, brutally murdered. And here stands his mistress, his *whore*."

Dr. Malpass reached out and took Kitty's elbow, moving her to the waiting arms of another of his men. "Take her to my office and wait for me. I'll get things under control here."

Numb, Kitty allowed herself to be led away, Sue's words still ringing in her ears. Lies, all of what she said were lies, but what difference did it make now? The whole town believed what Nancy Warren Stoner had told. Everyone hated her as much as they had hated her father. "Oh, Travis, Travis," she cried silently, "Where are you now that I need you so? Dear God, Travis, where are you?"

A tear slid down her cheek, and she hated herself for being weak. She had always hated women who cried.

"No more," she said aloud, and the soldier steering her down the corridor glanced down in surprise. "I'm not going to let them get to me again. I got through four years of blood and hell, and I'm not going to let this damn town rip me to shreds now."

"Are you all right, Miss Kitty?" he asked in a kind tone. "Could I get you some brandy or something?" He could feel her arm shaking.

"I'm just fine," she said through gritted teeth. "That little scene back there just let me know how fine I really am. I'm not going to let them get to me. I won't."

"Well, that's wonderful," he said awkwardly. "I don't think I understand what all the fuss is about, but I'm glad you feel better about it." He was grateful to reach Dr. Malpass' office, where he could ease her into a chair and step outside to close the door behind him. Let Dr. Malpass handle it. He wanted no part of brawling women.

Dr. Malpass was not long in coming. "How is she?" he asked the guard, anger flashing in his eyes.

"Oh, she says she's fine, that she's not going to let this damn town rip her to shreds . . . sir," he added awkwardly. "Would you mind telling me what's going on?"

"Yes, I would mind," came the doctor's curt reply. "It is none of your business."

He opened the door to his office and slammed it shut behind him. "Well, Miss Wright, the parson who came with the ladies was kind enough to take your attacker away. I regret the incident. I had heard the rumors about you and Captain Coltrane, and the circumstances surrounding the death of one of the local

Rebs. It is most unfortunate. I never thought the hostility towards you ran so high."

"That woman was Nathan Collins' aunt," Kitty said dully. "She never was very bright, and she was always given to hysteria. Maybe the fact that I am expecting Captain Coltrane's child has already leaked out in town. I thought I was still hiding it. It makes no difference now," she added.

"Uh, I think you kept it hidden," the doctor said, a bit embarrassed to be discussing such a delicate subject, particularly with an unmarried woman. "At least, no one has mentioned it to me. May I ask what you had planned to do about your, er, condition?"

Kitty blinked at him. "What do you think I planned to do, sir? Have a baby! That's what a woman usually does when she is carrying one in her body. She goes into labor at the time Nature sets, and she delivers a child. You *are* a doctor, are you not? Do you need *me* to tell you about how babies come into the world?"

He colored, stiffened. "I am well aware of *how* a baby comes into the world, Miss Wright. I have delivered quite a few. I am also aware of how a baby gets *inside* a woman's body. In most instances, her husband puts it there. Were you and Captain Coltrane ever married?" Without waiting for an answer, he rushed on, "I thought not. That is a pity. But you should have thought of that before you—"

"Spare me your lectures, doctor." Kitty got to her feet, shaking. "I am not ashamed to be carrying Captain Coltrane's child, and we will marry as soon as he returns from whatever mission your General Sherman has sent him on. Now if you will excuse me, I have work to do. There are patients out there."

"Yes, there are patients out there," he snapped, leaping to his feet as he yanked at his moustache angrily. "Patients who should not be exposed to a woman of questionable morals. I have to ask you to leave this hospital at once. Not only for the sake of my patients, but for the sake of the relationship between the Federal government and the people of this town. Now that your condition is known, there will be much said about you. General Schofield has issued strict orders that our occupying forces are to maintain as good a relationship with the people of Goldsboro and Wayne County as can possibly be accomplished. In view of your situation, your presence at this hospital must be terminated at once."

She had known that sooner or later the time would come that she would be forced to leave her only shelter, but she had prayed that Travis would return first.

"I will leave as soon as I gather my things," she said crisply, turning to the door with a swish of her muslin skirt. "That should not take long!"

She was through the door and several steps down the corridor before he hurried after her. "Miss Wright, wait."

Turning, Kitty appraised him, aware that the guard was listening with interest. Let the whole world know. What difference did it make now?

"On behalf of the Union army, let me say that your services have been appreciated. I am well aware of how you worked with wounded men with no thought as to which side they had fought for. You worked tirelessly, even on the battlefields."

She gave him a mocking smile. "Are you giving me a citation, sir? Me? A trollop who would dare to bed with a man before marriage? I suppose if I carried the seed of a Confederate, you would not bother with your flowery words, would you? Well, I'll see that Captain Coltrane is informed of how 'polite' and 'gentlemanly' you were to this poor, tainted woman."

She looked to the guard, then to the doctor, and gave an insolent curtsy. "Good day, gentlemen."

She disappeared around a corner, and the guard leaned forward and quickly whispered, "Forgive me, sir. I don't mean to be nosy, but are you really kicking her out of here? She's more of a doctor than a nurse. I've heard all about her work, and if she is carrying Captain Coltrane's baby, and if the town folks hate her the way I hear they do, she's going to be in for a rough time out there. At least here she had shelter. How is she going to live?"

Dr. Malpass looked the soldier up and down. "I would suggest that you keep your thoughts to yourself, soldier. We don't know that she is carrying Captain Coltrane's baby. We don't even know that *she* knows *whose* seed she carries. We have to concern ourselves only with carrying out General Schofield's orders."

"It's still a shame, a damned shame," the guard mumbled.

The doctor sighed. "Soldier, just keep your mouth shut about what you heard here today. Otherwise you will find yourself on report. Is that clear?"

Heels clicked to attention. "Yes sir," came the snapping reply.

Chapter Eight

KITTY stepped off the hospital porch and turned to gaze one last time at the squat building where she had spent so many months. She wondered if she would ever be able to forget the blood, the stench of decay and dying, and the anguished screams. Men had been in need, and her heart had burned with desire to help.

She walked down the rutted street towards the heart of the small town. Children played and laughed, despite the rags they wore, oblivious to the Yankee soldiers that wandered about. She neared the home of Mrs. Eleanor Parrott. Once, she had sat up with her all night when she was having a difficult labor with her last baby. Memories of placing the red-faced, screaming baby girl in her mother's arms brought a smile to Kitty's lips. Several times she had been afraid she would lose both mother and child. "Oh, Kitty, how can I ever repay you?" Mrs. Parrott had cried gratefully, tears of joy streaming down her face as she gazed at her newborn. "If it hadn't been for you, my precious darling wouldn't have made it."

"Just seeing you together is reward for me," had been Kitty's fervent answer, overcome by the holy sight of new life. How could anyone see such a miracle and deny the existence of God?

Mrs. Parrott had showered her tiny daughter's face

with kisses, then, as the infant began to suckle at her breast, she looked up at Kitty and whispered, "Katherine. I'll name her Katherine, after you, Kitty. And when she grows up, she will know she was named for the woman who brought her into the world and saved her life."

Suddenly the door to the house banged open, and a little girl came running down the steps. A purple and gold butterfly was flitting around the honeysuckle vines, and the child chased after it gleefully. Kitty stopped walking and stared after her. Was that her namesake, she wondered, heart pounding.

The door banged open once again, and Eleanor Parrott came storming down the steps. "Katherine, you come in here at once," she cried, her voice a mixture of anger and exasperation. "I don't want you chasing about with these soldiers everywhere."

She stopped short, catching sight of Kitty standing at the gate. "You!" Eleanor spat. "You keep moving. Don't you dare stand at my gate."

Surely, Kitty wasn't hearing right. Not Eleanor Parrott. She wouldn't turn against her. Why, she had told everyone in the county how Kitty had saved her life and her baby's, how she had named her child after Kitty so the deed would never be forgotten. And now she stood glaring, eyes burning with hatred, body trembling with rage.

Kitty cleared her throat, took a step forward, then stopped when she saw the woman's fists clench. "Why, Mrs. Parrott, don't you recognize me? It's Kitty . . . Kitty Wright. Remember?"

"I remember nothing except that you're not fit to walk the streets with decent folk. Now you move along. I don't want people thinking you been to see me, and I sure don't want you around my child. Now git! Before I get Jed's gun and shoot you myself."

"Mrs. Parrott!" Kitty's heart wrenched. "How can

you talk to me that way? I helped you bring Katherine into the world, remember? Whatever have I done to you, of all people, that you turn against me?"

Mrs. Parrott shook both her fists in the air. "You know what you've done, you traitor. Sleeping with a Yankee, going to have his baby, if'n you even know *whose* bastard you carry. And a fine, Christian man like Nathan Collins lies in the ground because of the likes of you. Get away from my home."

The little girl, terrified by her mother's raging, had run to cling to her skirts. Peering out at Kitty, feeling protected with her mother's arms about her, little Katherine stuck her tongue out. Turning away, Kitty quickened her steps, heart pounding.

As she walked along, it became obvious that everyone shared Eleanor Parrott's feelings. Some just turned their backs when she passed. A few openly glared or hissed as she passed by. One old man even spat at her. There were at least a thousand Yankees left in town, maybe more camped around. The townspeople ignored them, but they vented their wrath on Kitty.

Where in all of Wayne County could she go for shelter?

Night came, and she huddled among trash barrels in an alley. Drunken soldiers passed nearby, laughing and singing. She knew if any man attempted to rape her, no onc would come to her defense. She would have to hide until daylight, till it was safer. Maybe she would have to accept Dr. Holt's offer to make her home with him. But what if Travis returned and she was nowhere to be found? There was no way she could leave word for him, and no way she could send him a message. Dear God, what was she going to do? Her stomach was rumbling and twisting with hunger, and she had no money to buy food.

A door opened nearby, and she crouched down even lower in the dirt. Footsteps shuffled in her direction. She cringed fearfully, afraid to breathe lest the slightest sound give her away. Close, so close that his breeches brushed against her arm, the man reached down and lifted the lid of one of the barrels. There was the sound of something being dropped inside the wooden barrel. Then the lid was replaced. Footsteps shuffled away. Kitty let out her breath.

The smell of food touched her nostrils. Garbage! He had put food scraps in the garbage barrel, and, no matter what it was, she had to have something to still the gnawing in her belly. No longer could she turn away from worms. She had to eat, had to keep strong. The baby had to come first now, no matter what.

Rising out of the shadows, Kitty reached out and removed the lid from the barrel. The odor was awful, but she reasoned that whatever had just been placed on top would not be rancid. Grabbing the wad of paper-wrapped food bits, she replaced the lid and sank back to her hiding place in the darkness.

She had no idea what she lifted to her lips with trembling fingertips. It was slimy and cold, and it was in tiny pieces that held together with difficulty. But soon, she knew she was in luck. Rutabagas cooked in fat meat. Hungrily, she wolfed the morsels down. She opened another paper wad to find fish scraps. Her stomach gave a heave, but she fought against it.

Pushing the fish bits away, she clutched her stomach and weaved to and fro, fighting nausea. The greasy rutabagas had not set well on her empty stomach, and the rotten odor of the fish had made things worse. Bile was slipping into her throat, and she held her breath, hearing footsteps approaching once again.

"We can get in this way." The gruff male voice punctured the solitude of her hideaway. "Ain't no damn body gonna kick me out the front door of no saloon and tell me I can't come back in."

"Me either," Kitty heard another man answer. He, too, spoke in clipped tones of rage and fury. "That son of a bitch bartender ain't got no right to kick me out and tell me I've had too much to drink. Shit, I'll go in there and bust every bottle on his goddamn shelf over his pumpkin head."

They were right alongside her. Kitty held her breath until she was about to pass out. Suddenly, the belch leaped from her throat.

"Who's there?" a voice cracked. "Tom, I know damn well I heard some drunk belch. Maybe he's got a bottle. Maybe we won't have to bust in the back door."

"Yeah. Shouldn't be too hard to find in this alley. He's around here somewhere. Hey, where are you, buddy? All we want is a little drink. Share a drink, will you?"

"Come on, you old fool. If you ain't nice about it, we'll steal the whole damn bottle and might bust your head just for the fun of it. Now speak up."

Kitty began to tremble. Her only hope was to leap from her hiding place and run for the street. Here, she was trapped. Pushing herself upwards, she screamed. She had leaped right into the waiting arms of one of the men, and his whiskey-sour breath in her face was overwhelming. "Hey, it's a woman. I found me a woman, Tom. How about that? I ain't had me no good lovin' lately. Ain't this a find? Better'n a bottle any day of the week."

"What does she look like?" the other asked dubiously.

Kitty continued to scream. She felt a beefy hand slapped over her mouth as another groped across her breasts. "Feels okay to me. Let's lay her down and spread her out and see what we got. Don't matter about the face. Hell, we can throw a Yankee flag over it and fuck it for revenge."

His sidekick guffawed as both began tugging at her

muslin skirt. Kitty tried to fight them, fearing not only for herself but what their assault might do to her baby. But the heavy hand stayed pressed on her face so hard that she was finding it difficult to breathe.

Her hands were clawing at them, at the dirt around her, and then her fingers touched a bottle. She picked it up and brought it swinging down. Glass cracked against a skull. There was a yelp of pain, and the beefy palm fell from her face. She brought her knee up into the other man's groin, and heard a shriek of pain. She scrambled to her feet and fled from the alley, leaving the two stunned men groaning in the darkness.

For a moment she stood in the dim glow of the saloon's lanterns, wondering where she could run to, where it would be safe to hide. Perhaps she should try to make it back to the hospital, beg Dr. Malpass for a night's refuge. In the daylight hours, she could make plans. Now, there was only danger about.

"Hey, look what I see!" She turned, trembling, at the sound of a voice to her right. Three men had just swaggered out of the saloon and stood there appraising her. One was tall and slender and wore a tattered Confederate uniform. He grinned at her with yellowed teeth. Another wore overalls and no shirt and was barefooted. He had flared nostrils like a hog, and his fingers dug into his groin as he looked at her with excited eyes. The man who had spoken was heavyset, a scar ran down one side of his cheek, and she saw that only a stump remained where his right arm should have been.

"I remember you," the one-armed man spoke, his upper lip curling in a snarl. "You helped chop my arm off."

"I . . . I'm sorry," Kitty stammered, rubbing one hand across her forehead. "There were so many. I was a nurse. I worked in field hospitals, you see. . . ."

"Yeah, I see." He stepped off the plank porch fronting the saloon. "I begged them fool doctors to just let me die. But no, they kept telling me I had to live. For what? To come back to this stinking hole and starve to death? What good is a one-armed man? And all the time, you was there, a syrupy smile on that picture-pretty face of yours, telling me God had a plan for me and all that bullshit. And you helped 'em take off my arm. I was crazy with pain, but I remember you was right there."

"Bert, I thought you said it was a Yankee doctor what took your arm off, a'fore you was sent to that prison." The man wearing the tattered gray uniform spoke. "If this little filly was there, how come she's here?"

"Oh, where are my genteel Southern manners." Bert gave a mock bow, sweeping his straw hat off with his remaining hand. "I didn't introduce this young 'lady,'" he sneered.

"This here," he continued, insolently grinning, "is Miss Kitty Wright. She worked for the Yankees. Had her a Yankee lover, too. Hard-fightin' bastard cavalryman by the name of Coltrane."

"I've heard of him," the overalled man said, awed. "I remember soldiers saying Coltrane would ride into hell and go after Satan himself with his sword, if it would clear the path to draw the blood of a Reb. That son of a bitch was her lover?"

"Oh, yes, he was," Bert snickered. "And you know what else? He's the one what murdered Nathan Collins. I didn't know the man myself, and neither did you-all, being we ain't from these parts, but I hear tell he was a fine Southern officer, and he was murdered by this trollop's Yankee-boy 'cause Collins had the misfortune of being her betrothed."

The overalled man spat a wad of tobacco juice into

the street. "Well, ain't that a pile of horseshit. Then what's she doing back here?"

"Well, I reckon she's looking for a man to take the place of her Yank." Bert started towards Kitty at the same time she began to stumble backwards. "You boys reckon the three of us could take the place of one Yankee and satisfy the little lady?"

"No, please." Kitty turned and started running in the darkness, the three men right behind her. She knew what would happen if they caught her. She would be dragged into the nearest alley and raped. She would probably lose her baby. They might even kill her. And no matter how loudly she screamed, anyone who heard would turn a deaf ear as soon as they realized it was Kitty Wright who cried for help.

She ran past several buildings, windows dark. If the men had not been drunk and staggering, they could easily have caught her, but their stumbling gave her an advantage.

Then she saw the dim glow of a lantern straining to cast a shadow through the cracks in a boarded-up window. Perhaps someone was inside to hear the shouts of a woman in distress. If they would only open the door quickly, Kitty prayed, she would rush inside before they could recognize her and shut her out.

"Please! Help me!" She banged on the door with her fists, voice hysterical. "Help me. You must help me, please!"

"Gotcha!" She felt a hand grabbing at her skirt, yanking her backwards. She would have fallen from the wooden porch if her attackers had not been upon her, supporting her even as they pulled her away from the door. Already hands were pawing at her breasts, streaking beneath her skirt and inching up her legs.

"Oh, we're gonna have us a fine time with this one."

She smelled their whiskey breath. "I'm first, remember."

Just as they reached the street, Kitty's feet digging and kicking up a dust swirl about them, the door to the little building opened. A man stepped outside, holding a lantern above his head. Kitty did not see the gun he also held. "What's going on out here? What are you men doing to that woman? Leave her alone."

He spoke as though he were used to being obeyed, and the mauling stopped as Bert spoke up quickly. "You don't understand, Mr. McRae. This here is Kitty Wright. Everybody in town knows she's trash."

Kitty shuddered as the explosion spit the air. "I said leave her alone. Unhand her. What right do you have to manhandle a woman? Get away from her."

The hand fell away from her mouth. She was allowed to slump into the dirt. Footsteps thundered as the men disappeared into the night. A few people had gathered out of nowhere, it seemed, at the sound of gunfire. Trembling, her nerves frazzled by the two confrontations, Kitty meekly allowed her rescuer to lift her out of the street and to her feet. In the lantern's glow, she saw two fiery black eyes staring down at her beneath thick eyebrows. The man had hard, chiseled features, a deep cleft in his chin. His dark hair had flecks of gray, and his moustache, clipped neatly, gave him an aristocratic air. She decided at once that she was not at the mercy of ordinary riffraff.

Then, for some reason, despite her gratitude for being saved, Kitty's bosom began to quiver with an unexplainable fear. There was something terrifying about the man. He exuded power, authority, and brute male force, yet his arm was gentle as he steered her up the steps.

"Are you all right, miss?" he asked, ignoring all the staring eyes. "Shall I have one of my men go for a doctor?"

"No, no, they didn't hurt me. They just scared me to death." Kitty allowed him to lead her inside and close the door. She didn't like those angry, staring faces. She doubted there was one among them who would do for her what this man was doing. Then why did she fear him? She tried to tell him how she appreciated his helping her. "I have many enemies in this town, and I have just been discharged from my work at the hospital, and there's no place for me to go, and . . ."

She stopped, realizing how hysterical she must sound. "I'm sorry. I didn't mean to rattle on so. My problems are no concern of yours. You have helped me enough for one night. I'll go now."

He had poured brandy into two glasses. Handing one to her, he smiled and said, "Go where, my lady? You just finished telling me that you have nowhere to go. It was terrible of Dr. Malpass to dismiss you because of that unfortunate incident at the hospital today. I realize he was only following orders, but I should think his heart would have overruled his obligations as an officer."

Kitty could only blink at him, stunned. "How . . . how is it that you know so much about me, sir?" She took a big gulp of the brandy, not caring that it burned her throat, which was raw from so much screaming. "I haven't even told you my name."

He smiled down at his glass, swirling the amber liquid around and around. He wore fine clothes, Kitty noted. His silk shirt was open at the throat, revealing a muscular chest covered in dark, curly hair. His boots were of genuine leather, hand-polished. She also noticed a large diamond ring. He was obviously quite wealthy.

"Your name is Kitty Wright, and you were born and raised in Wayne County." He spoke in words that sounded memorized. "You helped both sides during the war in the hospital tents. You were engaged to a Confederate officer from Wayne County by the name of Nathan Collins. You were the mistress, lover, whatever you wish to call it, of a Federal cavalry officer named Travis Coltrane. At the Battle of Bentonville, Collins and Coltrane fought, and Collins was killed. I have heard many reports of what happened, the most popular of which is that Coltrane ruthlessly stomped your ex-fiancé to death. You rode into Goldsboro with Sherman's army, then went to the Way hospital to work there. Coltrane left town a few days later with General Sherman and has not returned. You now carry his child. The people of Goldsboro and Wayne County despise you, and it is not safe for you to live among them as long as the scars of war still fester."

Kitty coughed, almost choking on the brandy. "How could you possibly know so much, when I have never seen you before in my life? I don't even know your name."

"Corey McRae, formerly of New York, at your service." He bowed with a flourish. "And I know everything about everyone in this county. I make it my business to know as much as possible about people where I live. Then I know when to turn my back and when not to. In your case, I visited General Schofield one day when he was about to make a tour of the hospital, and he mentioned to me the problems that your presence was causing. He also mentioned that you have a rare and tender beauty and a spirit unmatched by any woman he had ever known before. I was curious. I wanted to see this beautiful creature who could stir the ire of so many. I went with him and saw you that day, but you did not see me. You were far too busy ministering to the sick and wounded. I should like to compliment you on your work, by the way. You were wonderful with the men."

He downed the rest of his brandy, then refilled his glass. "I asked the general to keep me informed as to your activities, and he sent a messenger just this evening to tell me of your unfortunate discharge. I also learned that you are expecting a child. Is this child sired by Travis Coltrane?"

"Yes," she nodded, awestruck. Shaking her head from side to side, she murmured, "But I don't understand why you bothered yourself about my activities. Why should I be of concern to you?"

He interrupted by snapping, "Had I not been so busy with other matters, I would have seen to it before now that you were not bothered. The incidents tonight should not have happened." His nostrils flared with anger, black eyes sparkled.

Kitty had never before felt such a reaction to a man. Travis could be riled to extreme violence, true, but even so there had been an underlying feeling of tenderness.

With Luke Tate, there had been instant distaste. He was a useless human being who had never possessed an ounce of kindness.

But in Corey McRae, Kitty found a new phenomenon, one she could not explain. She sensed that while he was not as ruthless as Luke Tate, he was incapable of genuine feeling for anyone.

Yet he had saved her when no one else would. Why?

There was a sudden pounding on the door, and Kitty jumped, startled. Corey crossed the room. Would it be the townspeople, she thought apprehensively, demanding that she be turned over to them?

She watched, trembling slightly, as a huge, burly man wearing a bloodstained shirt and buckskin breeches entered the room. Vaguely, Kitty remembered his having been outside, appearing out of nowhere when Corey fired his gun. Corey had spoken to him as they entered the little building, but she had not heard what was said. Now he was removing his hat and speaking in a respectful tone. "Sir, we got those three. Me and the boys worked 'em over good. They'll know better than to bother the lady here again. They'll also spread the word that any man or woman what lays a hand on her will answer to you."

"Very good, Carl." Corey dismissed him with a wave of his hand. Backing out the door, Carl closed it quietly after him. Corey turned to Kitty and smiled. "That is what I mean, my dear. I could have kept unpleasantness from you. I have a large group of men working for me, all experienced gunfighters and barroom brawlers. Your good neighbors know this, and they fear them. You may now go anywhere you wish without fear of harm. Had I not been so tied up with business matters, all of this could have been avoided. An unpardonable sin, my sweet, to let business matters come before one so lovely as you." He lifted his glass in salute.

He walked over to where she sat and stood gazing down at her. Kitty was glancing around the room, taking in the disarray and clutter, the stacks and stacks of papers and maps. "What kind of business are you in?" she asked him bluntly, lifting her eyes to meet his.

For a moment he did not answer but stood there looking at her in a way that made her extremely uncomfortable. Then, with a slight chuckle, he said, "Real estate, my dear Miss Wright. I deal in real estate."

She shook her head in wonder. "Why would anyone come all the way from New York to deal in real estate in the South? Haven't you seen the devastation your General Sherman left in his wake? What do you plan to do? Start one big cemetery and have all the bodies from both sides buried in it, then charge admission?"

He laughed uproariously. "I had heard you had spunk, and now I believe it. You are precious, Kitty

Wright, simply precious." He waved his arm in the air. "Allow me to apologize for these miserable surroundings. I had to set up an office, and this building was left vacant by someone who was obviously fleeing our army. General Schofield was kind enough to allow me to use it. I plan to build my own office in the near future, as well as an estate in the country. But enough talk about me. You look pale. When did you last eat? I understand that rations are scarce at the hospital and unpalatable at that."

Pride would not let Kitty admit that her last meal had come from a garbage barrel behind a saloon. "I'm not really hungry," she lied, staring down at her worn boots. She had taken them from the feet of a dead soldier. Getting to her feet, Kitty thanked him once again for his kindness. "Now I'll be leaving. I have taken enough of your time."

"Leave?" He raised an eyebrow. "To go where, lovely lady? You have no place to go. I have some stew simmering in the back. I will get you a bowl, and then we can talk about what to do with you."

"You should not concern yourself with me . . ." she protested, but he left the room. Kitty looked about, perplexed. There was something about Corey McRae that she did not like, and she wanted to leave. She could take refuge in a livery stable until morning. Then she would decide what to do. Perhaps there was some way she could find shelter on her land, find a way to purchase seeds and grow a late garden.

Tiptoeing quietly, she walked towards the front door. Her hand reached for the knob just as a voice cried, "Why, my dear Miss Wright! You would not be so rude as to leave without saying goodbye, would you?"

She whirled about, frightened for some unexplainable reason. "Please. Just let me go. I can't stay here any longer."

"Of course you can." He set a bowl of good-smelling stew on a desk. "Besides, my men are stationed about. They would not let you leave unless I told them you could go. The thing for you to do is accept my generous hospitality and eat this food. And stop pretending, Kitty. You know you are famished."

The stew did look appetizing, and she was starved. Kitty sat down behind the desk and began to spoon the food into her mouth. "It's delicious," she murmured. "Thank you."

"When is your baby due?" he asked bluntly, sitting opposite her as he shuffled through some papers.

She almost choked. "Why . . . why are you so curious about me?" she demanded, that strange feeling moving over her once again.

He smiled. It was a sinister smile. Kitty did not like this man at all. "I like to know everything about my potential customers."

"Customers? I don't understand."

"You will. Tell me, do you recognize anything on this map?" He shoved a large drawing across the desk. Instantly she could see her father's land, now *her* land, diagrammed on the map. But, circled in red, she saw the diagram of Aaron Collins' plantation, and it was massive.

"Yes, that land is familiar to me. I knew Aaron Collins owned much acreage, but the sight of it drawn off on a map is overwhelming. It looks like half of the county."

"Hardly. It is quite large, though. Several hundred acres. I plan to rebuild the mansion. Foragers set fire to the original building and did extensive damage."

Kitty shook her head, remembering the lovely old house with is verandas and tall, white columns. There were large pecan and oak trees spread to the heavens as they stood guard, bordering the long, circular drive. She could close her eyes and smell the sweetness of the magnolias and the carefully tended roses. The lawn had looked like a giant carpet of green velvet. And in the spring, it was always a contest between the crepe myrtles and the dogwoods to see which would be the loveliest. Oh, how could anyone set a torch to so lovely a place?

Suddenly she looked at Corey. "You say *you* plan to rebuild the mansion? Did you buy the estate?"

"I told you, I'm in the real estate business." He tapped a finger against his moustache thoughtfully. "Aaron Collins, his wife, and son are dead. . . ."

"But there was a daughter. She would have wanted to rebuild the mansion herself. Everyone knew how the Collins family loved that place. She would never sell it."

Snatching the map from her hands, he began to roll it with quick, jerking motions. "Women should not concern themselves with business matters," he snapped, a nerve in his jaw twitching.

She spooned the last of the stew from the bowl, pushed it away, and said, "I would never sell my land. The house is gone and so is the barn, but I'll keep it, like I promised my father I would. It's the only thing I can do to preserve his memory, and I'll find a way to make that farm one of the most prosperous in all of Wayne County."

"And how do you propose to do that?" He sounded amused, and that infuriated her. "You have no money. You're expecting a child, and you aren't even married. Your Yankee lover has obviously deserted you. You would be better off to sell the land for whatever you can get, then use the money to take care of your child and yourself until you marry."

"I'll never sell my land! I would starve first. I may be a woman, but I know about raising cattle and horses and growing vegetables. Travis will return one day. I feel it in my heart. A woman knows such things.

I will be waiting when he does return. Now, if you will permit me, sir, I would like to leave your company. It would not be proper for me to remain here any longer unchaperoned."

Again he laughed, this time in contempt. "You speak of propriety as you sit there pregnant and unmarried. My dear, are you a hypocrite or just plain daft?"

She had had enough. She got to her feet with determination. "I will be leaving now, Mr. McRae. Thank you for your hospitality, but I do not care for your interference in my private life. I managed to survive all the atrocities of war, some inflicted directly upon me, all with no help from you. I feel quite confident that I can now face whatever the future holds, also with no help from you. Now"—she took a deep breath—"will you let me leave or shall I have you to struggle with instead of the street riffraff?"

His eyes glittered. She saw his fists clenching. Had she gone too far? It was too late now, and she prepared herself for the worst. "No," he said evenly, "you may not leave, and you will be wasting your breath and endangering your delicate state to attempt to struggle with me or my men. There is a cot in the back room where you will spend the night. In the morning, we will talk about what to do with you."

They faced each other. Corey's eyes were now mocking, daring her to rebuke him. "And will you force yourself upon me, sir?" she asked contemptuously. "Is a woman swollen with child the best you can get into your bed?"

His hand moved out slowly, and she did not flinch as his fingertips moved slowly up and down the smooth lines of her face. "So lovely, yet so angry." His smile made Kitty think of the way a cat looks just before he pounces on a mouse he has trapped in a barn corner. "Yes, my sweet, one day I shall have you, but not just for a few hours of lustful pleasure. Beauty such as yours is rare indeed, and just thinking of holding your body next to mine, possessing you completely, brings fire to my loins. However, you are fortunate that I do have some honor, however ruthless I may be in other matters. I would never force myself upon a woman in your condition. But when your child is delivered, rest assured that you will feel the heat of my manhood pulsating inside your belly."

"I doubt that, sir." Her chin jutted upwards. "Captain Coltrane will return before our child is born, and we will be married. Because you saved me from what could have been a tragic incident tonight, I won't tell him about your dishonorable intentions. He would kill you, just as he would kill any man who dared touch me."

"Then why isn't he here?" he laughed, making her face burn with humiliation. "Why hasn't he returned? If he is alive, he would have come to you *if* he loved you. No, Kitty, my lovely, I think you will soon have to come to terms with this. Travis is not going to return, and you are in a desperate situation.

"And as for what you term my 'dishonorable' intentions, have I said anything about forcing myself upon you? Have I even hinted that I intend to rape you, my dear? Oh, no, I certainly possess more integrity than to ravish you as though you were no more than a street whore."

He stood back, smirking at the glitter in her lovely eyes. He could almost see flames sparkling as she glared at him. Folding his arms across his massive chest, legs spread wide, he whispered, "I was speaking of possessing you as my *wife*, Kitty. My *legal wife*, with all the husbandly rights to which I would be entitled."

Kitty stepped from behind the desk to face him. "Have you taken leave of your senses? I happen to be in love with another man, and I carry his child and do so proudly and without shame. And I would not marry you even if I weren't. You have no appeal to me."

"You find me unattractive?" He raised a mocking eyebrow. "Strange. Most women find me quite handsome. Perhaps it's my fortune. I am quite wealthy, you know. Since you seem to find me so repulsive, I will have to give some thought to the matter. I do hate to think of those writhing, naked women in my arms merely pretending that they like me, when actually they are after my Yankee gold. Hmmm . . ."

"I didn't say you are unattractive, Mr. McRae. I merely said that you have no appeal for me. Now, if you will be so kind as to allow me to leave, I find our conversation distasteful."

She started to move by him, but he grabbed her arm and whirled her back, pinning her against his chest. He cupped her face in his hand, and his lips came thundering down on hers. She was caught in a vise and could not move. He practically lifted her from the floor. His tongue forced its way past her lips. Then, while continuing to grasp her with one hand, his other plunged down the bodice of her dress, squeezing her breast. She beat on his back with her fists, tried to claw his face, but he was undaunted, continuing to kiss her at the same time his fingers milked one nipple.

Suddenly he released her. She took a few steps backwards, almost falling. "Now," he said in a fierce tone. "Go into the back room and go to bed on that cot. I am going to the hotel where I sleep, and I will find a woman to take care of the need you have aroused in me. Do not try to escape, because I have guards posted outside. In the morning I will return, and we will talk once again about what to do with you."

"I . . . I hate you," Kitty spat at him. She whirled

about, looking for something to throw. Spying an ink well, she sent it sailing through the air. He ducked. "I think you're disgusting, and when Travis returns, I will tell him how you treated me."

"You are even more beautiful when you are angry," he said quietly, gazing at her with an expression of awe. "I don't think I have ever seen a woman quite as desirable as you, Kitty Wright. Yes, I think it would be best that we do marry. I will accept your bastard child. I will see that you have the best of everything."

He reached down and squeezed his swollen organ. "And night after night, I shall plunge this into your body, emptying myself in ecstasy. You will be worth waiting for, my dear, for I have much to give you, and I will take what I want from you once I own you."

"You'll never own me, you damn Yankee bastard," she screamed as he stepped out the door. He closed it quietly behind him. She ran across the room, tugged at the handle, but it was locked. "Never!"

She flung herself about, leaning against the door and covering her face with her hands in despair. Now she was really in trouble. The man was obviously rich and powerful and used to overcoming any obstacle to get what he wanted. And he wanted her. Oh, when Travis returned, Corey McRae would rue the day he decided he wanted her! There would be the devil to pay. Corey and all his hired gunmen would not be able to stand in Travis' way.

Suddenly her ears pricked to attention. Pressing the side of her face to the door, she heard voices. "Well, he's got him a fine one." She recognized Carl's voice. "Did you see the look on his face? Did you hear the tone he used when he said we better make damn sure she don't get away? I've seen him lust for plenty of women, but never like this one, and I've never seen one he couldn't have by snapping his fingers. This one's something new."

"And her all swollen with a baby," a male voice snickered. "What's he gonna do about that?"

"I heard 'em yelling in there. He says he's gonna wait till she has the kid, and then he's gonna marry her. What do you think of that?"

"I never try to figure out Mr. McRae. But I'll bet a week's wages that he gets her. And if she's smart, she'll jump at the chance to be his wife. What woman wouldn't, with the money he's got?"

"Oh, you know these stupid Southerners. They don't know their ass from a hole in the ground. But damned if she ain't a pretty thing. Did you see them eyes? God a-mighty, they glow like fire. And that hair. Yep, she's pretty, and even carrying a baby, there's something about her that makes you want to get it in her, you know what I mean?"

There was the sound of tobacco juice splattering on the plank porch. "Hell, yeah. I'd like to have me some of that myself. She's purtier than a speckled pup. What do you reckon he's going to do with her in the meantime?"

"I don't think he'll wait till she has the baby," Carl said. "I figure he'll marry her quick, before her Yankee lover does come back. Meanwhile, we got to keep a close eye on her. She's a spirited filly."

They both laughed, and Carl added, "But you know, I ain't never seen a filly yet, two legs or four, that Corey McRae couldn't break."

"Well," Kitty sighed, looking about at her surroundings. "Might as well get a good night's sleep." She headed for the back room and the cot. Corey McRae could be reckoned with later. Filly indeed! After all, she thought with a satisfied smile, he was only a man.

Chapter Nine

THE morning sun spilled through a wide crack in the boarded windows. Kitty stretched and yawned, wishing she could take a hot bath and put on clean clothes. During the war there had been nights when she was forced to sleep on the cold, hard ground, without even a blanket. There had been beds of pine needles, straw, mossy river banks. Her body had grown used to discomfort.

Suddenly she sat upright, gathering the blanket about her even though she was fully dressed. "What are you doing here?" she demanded, watching as Corey McRae puttered around the wood stove. It all came flooding back, and now anger was boiling through her veins as rapidly as the coffee brewing on the stove.

"I thought you might want something to eat this morning," her captor host said with a smile as he walked across the plank floor to hand her a tin cup of steaming brew. Gratefully, she took it and sipped cautiously lest she burn her lips.

"This is real coffee," she cried, astonished. "I haven't tasted real coffee since the war began. How did you come by it?"

"I have ways." He poured a cup for himself, then sat down in a rickety chair near her cot. "I like the luxuries of life, Kitty, and I make sure that I acquire as many as I desire. Right now, I have a fierce desire for you. Shall we talk about what to do with you, or do you want to finish your coffee and have a chance to fully awaken? Marriage is not a subject to be discussed lightly, my dear."

She jerked herself to a sitting position on the side of the cot and faced him with blazing eyes. "Marriage is not a subject I care to discuss with you at all, sir. I don't care how much money you've got or how much power. I happen to be in love with someone else, and I plan to marry him the minute he returns. I'm afraid I just don't understand you. Why would you ever contemplate taking a wife who carries the child of another man?"

"Many reasons." He took a long sip of coffee, set it aside as he pulled out an expensive-looking cigar and lit it. "I told you last night, Kitty, that I know all about you. I know everything about everyone in this wretched county."

She blinked, confused. "But why? You are from another state, and you say you deal in real estate. Why does Wayne County concern you so? Why are you so interested in me? True, I appreciate your coming to my rescue last night, and I am grateful for your hospitality, but that is as far as it goes. I plan to take my leave this morning."

His lips smiled but his eyes glowered with anger. "You are not going anywhere, Kitty. I not only deal in real estate, I deal in people, when it behooves me to do so. I possess them as easily as I possess the land I purchase. As for my interest in Wayne County, I feel I should know everything about everyone here, since I plan to own the whole countryside."

"Own it?"

"Yes. Haven't you heard? The South is destitute. Your Confederate money is worthless. How do you plan to pay the taxes on the property you inherit from your father? How do any of your neighbors plan to pay their taxes? They won't be able to, but I can buy their land, and yours, for the taxes owed."

Kitty leaped to her feet, coffee cup clattering to the floor. "You can't do that. It's . . . it's horrible to even think about. These people will find a way to come back and make a living from their lands. For you to even think of doing such a thing is horrible. You're a vulture, Mr. McRae, hovering over a dying land, hoping nothing will survive so you can swoop down and pick the meat from the bones."

She began to pace up and down the room, wringing her hands nervously. She hadn't thought about the taxes on the Wright land. The thought had not occurred to her. She had been too preoccupied with work at the hospital, worrying about Travis, the baby she was carrying. She had never thought about property taxes!

"Marry me, Kitty," he said quietly, almost in a whisper, "and I will pay your taxes for you and see that you retain title to your land. I will not take it away from you."

Whirling about, she glared at him in astonishment. "Why do you want to marry me? You know I don't love you. We've been all through this. You just won't listen, will you?"

"With proper dress and care, you can once again be the fairest woman in the county. Corey McRae must have a wife who is the most beautiful to be found. Corey McRae must be the envy of every man about."

"Corey McRae rambles on like a soldier with a fever," she snapped. "I think I am in the hands of a madman."

He laughed. "God, I love your spirit. That, in addition to your beauty, is why I must have you for my wife, Kitty. I will be the most hated man in this county when I acquire vast holdings of land. But I will also be the most respected. I want to give balls, parties, have a gala social life. I don't want to live the ostracized life of a despised land baron. With you as my wife, my dreams can all come true."

"You *are* mad. These people already hate me. You know that. If you want a wife others will respect, go marry that snotty little Nancy Warren Stoner. Everyone is fooled by her and thinks she is sweet and gentle. I know what a little liar and conniver she is. I'd say the two of you would be a perfect match."

"Nancy Warren Stoner has already let me know she is available. And it does not bother me how the people feel about you, Kitty, because they won't dare say a word against you once you are my wife. They will bow and scrape. You will be the most powerful social leader in the state."

She shook her head, "It's absurd. I won't marry you. If Nancy has made it obvious she would like to be your wife, I suggest you propose to her."

He threw back his head and laughed. "I have already had her in my bed, Kitty. She's cold and tasteless. She cannot hope to match your beauty or your spirit. No, my dear, it is you I must have, and you I will have. What other choice do you have? Your Captain Coltrane is not coming back, or he would have returned by now. The war is over. He could have written to you, at least. You have no money, not even a fit pair of shoes. And you carry a child. Where will you go?"

Pressing her fingertips against throbbing temples, she whispered, "I don't know. God, I don't know. I just wish you would leave me alone so I can think."

He stood up, walked to where she was pacing, and pulled her unyielding body into his arms. Kissing her cheeks tenderly, he said, "I'm going to buy you some clothes. Then I will have you brought to the hotel, where I will reserve a room for you. You can soak in a hot tub of scented water. Dine on the delicious food I will have sent to your room. Take an afternoon nap, then dress in one of the exquisite gowns I will buy for you. Then, tonight, I will take you to the hotel ballroom for dinner and let everyone know that Corey McRae has chosen his queen."

He left her standing there, dazed. Was the man insane? She didn't know. She just knew that she wanted to get away from him as quickly as possible. But how? Tiptoeing to the door, she turned the handle. It opened easily and she stepped into the front room. The boards squeaked as she walked across them to the front door. Peering out through a crack, she cursed silently at the sight of the guard leaning against the porch post.

She returned to the back room. There was a window, boarded over. She peered through a crack, and her fingertips happened to touch a loose board. It swung outwards with a slight squeaking sound, and she tensed, expecting a guard to come running. She waited a moment longer, then pushed the board outwards. Then she shoved at the next one, and the rotten wood popped and fell to the ground. Again she froze, waiting fearfully. She could see that there was an alley, with no one about. The drop to the ground was not a great distance. If she could push out the rest of the boards, she could hoist herself to the sill, drop down, and escape. Where she would go was something she could not think about at the moment. The immediate need was to escape Corey McRae.

The other boards were not rotten and they held tight as she pushed against them desperately. The two that were out did not leave an opening large enough through which she could escape. It was no use.

A clattering sound made her jump and peer out the window. Had a guard seen her futile attempt? No, it was an old Negro, moving down the alley, picking food scraps from the trash barrels just as she had done the night before. He was bent and stooped with age, a straw hat shielding his head from the sun that was already scorching the ground. He wore patched overalls, no shirt, and his feet were bare. She wondered how Jacob was faring. Was he starving and picking food from trash barrels, too?

Jacob! That was it! She strained to poke her head through the opening and made a hissing sound. The old Negro glanced up, frightened. He turned and started to run away, figuring he was about to be chastised for stealing from the barrels, but Kitty called out as loudly as she dared, "Please! Don't go. I'm a friend of old Jacob's, and I need help."

Warily, he slowed and turned to stare at her suspiciously. "What you say? You say you is a friend of Jacob's?"

"Yes, yes, my name is Kitty Wright," she said anxiously. "Jacob used to live on my father's farm. My father was John Wright."

At the mention of the name, the Negro's eyes widened in recognition. "Yes'm. Yes'm." Tipping his straw hat to her, he smiled. "I knows who you is now. What you want?"

He moved closer, and she whispered, unable to keep the desperation from her voice. "Tell him that a man named McRae is holding me a prisoner in the old feed store, and he has to help me get out through this window. As quickly as possible. Tell him he must be careful, because there are guards posted about. We can't wait till night. He must come right now. Hurry, please."

The old Negro took off running down the alley as fast as his old bones would carry him. Sinking back down on the cot, Kitty prayed he would find Jacob in time. Jacob and his people would hide her. They were the only ones in the county she could trust. If only he got back in time . . .

She poured another cup of coffee, gulped it down, and then she began to pace the floor. An hour passed. How long would it take the old Negro to find Jacob? What if he were way out in the county some place? Oh, God, Corey could return at any moment to take her to the hotel.

She jumped at a sound. "Miss Kitty? Miss Kitty? You in there?" Joyfully, she recognized Jacob's whispered call.

Running to the window, she poked her head out and said, "There's no time to explain everything now, Jacob. Just get me out of here quickly, please. And do be careful. Corey McRae has guards stationed about."

"I know. I seen 'em." He was already prying at the other boards with an iron bar. "I'll have you out of here fast, Miss Kitty. I know all about that Mr. McRae. Everybody knows 'bout him. Just don't you fret. I'll have you out of here and take you to my people. We got us a hideout."

The board popped out, then another. Kitty was slithering through the narrow opening into Jacob's waiting arms. When her bare feet touched the ground, she felt the heat from the parched soil and wished she had taken time to slip on the boots, uncomfortable though they were. It was too late for that, though, and, with Jacob holding her hand, they ran together down the alley.

There was a rickety old wagon waiting at the end. She recognized Jacob's two sons as they glanced about nervously. One sat in the wagon, holding the reins of a tired-looking mule. The other stood behind, ready to hoist her up and help her cover herself with straw.

"Just you lay still," Jacob ordered. "We'll have you out of here quick-like."

Despite the straw tickling her nostrils and poking into her exposed flesh, Kitty sighed with relief. She had escaped Corey McRae, and the thought of his anger when he discovered she was gone made her want to giggle. Used to getting his own way, was he? Well, he had not reckoned with her.

It seemed like hours before the wagon finally jolted to a stop. Instantly, Jacob and his two sons were knocking hay from on top of her, helping her up and onto her feet. "You okay, Miss Kitty?" the old Negro asked anxiously. "The ride didn't hurt you none?"

"I'm fine, now that I'm out of the clutches of that man. Just who is he, anyway, Jacob? Have you heard anything about him at all?" She dusted bits of straw from her dress and glanced at her surroundings. They were in the swamps, and she could see little makeshift huts here and there. A dozen or so Negroes moved about, staring curiously at their white visitor.

"I heered about him all right," Jacob snapped bitterly. "He's goin' around buyin' up land dirt cheap, for the taxes. Southern money ain't no good no more, you know, and this Mistah McRae, he got plenty of Yankee money. He even bought Mistah Aaron Collins' place. All of it."

"Yeah." Kitty turned to see a boy of fourteen or fifteen. "And Miss Nancy Warren is a chasin' after Mistah McRae, too. I reckon she figured if she couldn't get in that fine house by a'marrying Mistah Nathan, she'd get in there by marryin' up with the new owner."

"Luther, you watch that sassy mouth of yours," Jacob thundered. "You got no call to go talkin' about no white woman that way."

Kitty blinked, surprised. "This is Luther? Oh,

Luther, you were just a tiny thing when I saw you last. Now you're almost grown."

She gave him a hug and he twisted away, embarrassed. "That was a long time ago, Miss Kitty. I is grown up now."

"You ain't too big to be taken down a notch or two, boy," his father scolded him. "Now go get Miss Kitty some cool spring water, and tell Nolie to fix her a place where she can lie down in the shade. That ride didn't do her no good."

He lowered his eyes, realizing that he had made reference to Kitty's condition, and she smiled and told him not to worry. "Everyone in the whole town knows by now, I guess. I am carrying a baby, Jacob. Travis Coltrane's baby. I was asked to leave the hospital yesterday, and I have no place to go."

"You got a home now, Miss Kitty. Long as you want one. We ain't got much here. Just a bunch of us nigras joinin' together to try and find some peace. We don't want no part of the Yankees, and the Southern folks hate most of my people 'cause they is free now. They want to see us starve. But we gonna show 'em. We waitin' to get our mules and our land, and then we gonna farm and make a good livin' off our land. We'll show 'em we don't need to work for white folks to keep from starvin'. We'll make it, workin' for ourselves."

He had led her to a cool, mossy bank beneath a spreading pecan tree. She sat down, weary in mind and body. "I was almost attacked twice last night," she said drily. "The second time, Corey McRae saved me. But once he got me inside that old feed store, he wouldn't let me leave. Says he wants to marry me, of all things. Oh, Jacob, Jacob, whatever am I going to do? I can go to Dr. Holt in Raleigh, and stay with his family till the baby is born, but what if Travis comes back? Oh, I've said it again." She shook her head.

"Said what again, Miss Kitty?"

"I said 'if' instead of 'when.' I've got to stop letting myself think of the possibility that Travis won't come back. He must be hurt, Jacob. I know he would come to me if he could. He loves me."

"Yes'm." He lowered his eyes. It wasn't his place to voice an opinion. It was no concern of his. All he wanted was to help the daughter of the man he had loved and respected. "You know you're welcome to stay here, Miss Kitty. Mr. McRae won't find you here. Nobody knows these swamps like we do. He won't even suspect you of comin' to live with us nigras."

She took his hand and squeezed it. "Then I will stay here, Jacob, and I'll be mighty obliged to you for letting me. Your sons and your people can keep their ears open when they go into town, and when Travis comes looking for me, they'll hear about it and let me know. The baby is due around Christmas as best I can figure. Surely we'll hear something before then. Travis won't desert me."

"Yes'm." Again he lowered his eyes. He doubted that the Yankee soldier would ever return, but he sure wasn't going to tell her that. She had to have hope to see her through the long months of struggle that lay ahead.

A plump black woman appeared. She wore a faded but clean gingham dress, a white apron tied about her waist. A bright bandanna covered her head, and she smiled to show sparkling white teeth. She handed Kitty a tin of cool water. "I'm Nolie," she introduced herself. "You don't remember me. I used to be a cook for Mr. Aaron. I was at the barbecue the day you poured that pitcher of water on Miss Nancy's head." She laughed, her large belly jiggling.

"I was also there when you took that whip away from Luke Tate. I didn't actually see it, mind you, but I heard the commotion and went a'running from the house like all the other help. I seen him yank that whip out of your hand and take you into that house. Then I seen Mr. Nathan come a'runnin' . . ."

Kitty had closed her eyes, body swaying to and fro in painful remembrance. It all flashed before her as though it was happening again. She had become angry at the party, incensed over Nancy Warren's constant needling. Finally she lost the temper she found so hard to control and dumped a pitcher of water on the girl's head. Then she had started for home, preparing to walk. Hearing the sound of leather slashing into flesh, and a woman's anguished screams, Kitty stumbled through the brush to the slave quarters to find the Collins' overseer, Luke Tate, beating a pregnant slave girl.

Kitty ran forward, yanked the whip out of the astonished man's hand, and let him have a taste of his own torture, but she was no match for his strength. When he recovered the whip, he had picked her up and dragged her into one of the slave houses, ripping her dress, exposing her breasts. Nathan charged in and took the whip from Luke and gave him a sound beating before ordering him off the property.

Then Nathan had turned on Kitty, admonishing her for interfering. It hadn't mattered that the slave girl was pregnant. Nathan was a strong believer in social "appearances," and he was embarrassed that Kitty had intervened on behalf of a lowly slave.

All of that had led up to her father's brutal beating by the vigilantes. She shook her head from side to side, trying to blot out the memories.

"You got a big mouth, Nolie," Jacob was scolding the woman. "See? You done got her all upset, making her remember them bad times. They's over and done with now. We can't help what's happened in the past. We got to look to the future, so you hush up making Miss Kitty think about them bad times."

"Oh, Miss Kitty, I am sorry." Nolie's big hand flew to her mouth, her eyes growing big. "I does go on too much."

"Nolie, it's all right, really. But Jacob is wise to say we shouldn't look back. We have to think about the future. Just think, Nolie, you're free now." Kitty looked at all the black faces now surrounding her. "You're all free."

"What good does it do if we gonna starve to death?" Jacob asked grimly.

"We had to run when we heard the Yankees was comin'," Nolie spoke up. "Miss Nancy and Miss Sue, they took off for town, but they left us to look after ourselves. We's scared of Yankees. We heered how they took slaves and made 'em march with 'em and fight. We didn't want to fight, so we ran away."

"Now the white folks hate us 'cause we're free," Luther said, teeth clenched in bitterness. "They call us 'uppity niggers' and say now that we free, we can look after ourselves. And how we gonna do that when nobody gonna give us a job? What we gonna do? Live here in the swamp and eat roots and drink muddy water for the rest of our lives?"

The angry desperation in the young man's eyes frightened Kitty. She knew that many of the Negroes who surrounded her probably felt the same way. The older ones had been conditioned to bending to the white man's will. The younger ones, like Luther, had not had the rebellion beaten out of them.

She motioned to Luther to sit down. Eyes wary, he did so, crossing his legs. His pants were ragged and hung just below his knees. He was barefoot and wore no shirt. They were probably the only clothes he had. What would happen when winter came? "I'll do what

I can to help you," Kitty said, taking all of them in with a sweep of her eyes. "You know I now own Poppa's land. I don't know about the taxes. I'm going to have to look into that. Somehow, I'm going to find a way to work that land and make it prosper. I know it's good land and I can make a living there. Those of you who want to help me, I'll see that you are rewarded. But I can't pay you anything now."

"You saying you wants us to go to work for you for nothin'?" Luther asked incredulously. "We ain't got nothin' now, and we ain't workin'. So how we gonna be any better off breaking our backs for you?"

A few of the younger Negroes snickered, and Jacob stepped forward and shouted, "Shut up. All of you. You show some respect for Miss Kitty and hear her out. She's a fine lady. Her poppa was a fine man. We'd do well to help her out if there's a chance we might get paid somethin' later on. It's better than no chance at all. And it's sho better than you sneakin' around town, Luther, stealin' things."

"Other white people will have to hire you later on," Kitty continued. "Those that keep their land are going to have to have field hands to work. You aren't slaves any longer, so they're going to have to pay you. Those of you that can get jobs, do so. I can't pay you anything. I haven't a cent to my name. It's going to be a very hard winter for me unless Captain Coltrane returns."

"Miss Kitty gonna have a baby," Jacob interrupted, a happy ring to his voice. "She gonna have Captain Coltrane's baby."

"I don't know no Captain Coltrane," Nolie mused. "He from around here?"

"He's a Yankee," Luther spoke up, a proud gleam in his eye because he knew something the others didn't. "I heard about him from time to time just listenin' to the white soldiers in town. He's one of the bravest men in the Yankee army. You gonna marry him, Miss Kitty?"

She nodded, smiling. "Yes, I am. I love him very much, Luther. And every time you go into town, I want you to listen for any word of him. He'll be coming back soon, and he's going to be looking for me. Until then, I'm going to have to stay with you till I can build a little place on Poppa's land."

"First of all, you better find out if that Mistah McRae done bought yo' land," Jacob pointed out. "And how you gonna do that? He gonna be looking for you."

"Yes, I've been thinking about that," she said, more to herself than to those around her. "He had me at a disadvantage, but not anymore. Captain Coltrane and Sam Bucher buried Poppa's pistol in a gunnysack near his grave. I'm going to go there and dig it up. They thought I might want it for a keepsake one day, but I need it now for protection. I believe his rifle is there, too. I'm not going to hide from Corey McRae. I'm not going to hide from any man."

"You sure that's wise, girl? In your condition?" Jacob cried, leaping up from his crouched position. "He's got lots of men—"

"He can't go around kidnapping women and forcing them to marry him," Kitty snapped, angry with herself for having been frightened of the man in the first place. "Poppa may even have some pay coming to him from the Federal army. I'll go into town and see General Schofield and find out. Even if it isn't much, it might be enough for me to buy some seeds and get some food growing."

The Negroes whispered among themselves. Most of them knew Kitty Wright, or knew her reputation for spirit, but to hear her talk about facing up to a powerful man like Corey McRae was astonishing.

Kitty leaned back against the rough bark of the

tree and closed her eyes. It was not going to be easy. For the past four years everything had been difficult. But she would find a way. After all, she was John Wright's daughter.

Chapter Ten

THE next day, Jacob took Kitty into town, and she went directly to General Schofield's headquarters, ignoring the curious stares of the soldiers and townspeople. The guard stationed outside stepped forward, rifle in hand, but she pushed him aside, leaving him with an astonished look on his young face.

Several other soldiers milled about in the outer room, their attention turned to the young woman in the tattered, dirty muslin dress, obviously in the family way, who glared back at them with defiance. "Hey, lady, you can't go in there," one of the men said, stomping towards her as she headed for the closed door at the rear. "The general is busy—"

"My name is Kitty Wright," she snapped, her chin jutting upwards, violet eyes flashing fire. "You tell General Schofield I have to see him. He knows who I am."

The soldier swallowed, Adam's apple bobbing. "He does?"

"Just tell him the trollop he had dismissed from the hospital is here."

He glanced at his fellow soldiers. One of them shrugged, the other shook his head as though he didn't know what to advise. Finally, he knocked on the general's door, and instantly a voice boomed, "Yes, what is it?"

The soldier looked extremely uncomfortable. Looking warily at Kitty, he called out, "Sir, there's a . . ." and then he hesitated.

"I asked what you wanted!" the voice thundered.

Clearing his throat, the soldier called out, "Sir, there's a . . . *lady* here to see you. Says you know who she is. She's very persistent."

"I have no time for visitors at the moment. Take her name and have her come back later."

Elbowing the astonished soldier aside, Kitty opened the door and stepped into the room, muslin skirt swishing around her ankles. Major General McAllister Schofield leaped up from his chair and glared at her indignantly. "Just what in thunderation is the meaning of this, young woman? How dare you barge into my office this way?"

Kitty pursed her lips, folding her arms across her chest as she narrowed her eyes. Short, heavyset—it was obvious he hadn't lacked for food during the war, while others starved. His eyes were dark and piercing, and his nose was huge. He was almost completely bald, but thick, bushy white hair grew down the sides to form a long beard on each side of his clean-shaven chin. A thin moustache edged the top of feminine lips. Here was a man quite used to having people wilt before his command, but she was not the wilting kind.

"My name is Kitty Wright, General, and you know who I am." She walked over and sat down in a chair opposite his desk.

He continued to stand, leaning forward, knuckles turning white as they pressed into the wood. "I can't say as I recall your name, Miss Wright." He took a deep breath as though trying desperately to hold his temper in check. "Now, my good woman, everyone knows that I do everything in my power to maintain a good relationship between my soldiers and the citizens of this town and county. However, I do demand respect. Will you leave my office peacefully, or shall I summon my soldiers to throw you out?" There was the play of a smile on his lips, but it quickly faded with Kitty's next words.

"Oh, I know all about how you strive to maintain good relations with the civilians," she laughed bitterly. "I'm the 'trollop' you wanted dismissed from working at the hospital, remember? You wanted to appease the good Christian ladies of this town. They blame me for the death of their local hero, Nathan Collins, who was actually a black-hearted snake and a coward. He deserted General Johnston's command and shot my father in the back."

She paused to take a breath, then rushed on. "But I did not come here to talk about that. I came here to demand that you pay me, as my father's only heir, whatever back pay the Union army owes him for his service. Thanks to you and your 'good relations' policy, I no longer have a roof over my head. I was never paid for my services at the hospital, but I did have a place to sleep and a little food.

"And"—she forced a bright smile—"I also happen to be carrying the child of one of your cavalry officers. But of coarse you must have heard by now that the town trollop is pregnant."

His huge nose turned redder than his cheeks. "Miss Wright, I do not wish to hear about your personal problems."

She went on as though he had not spoken. "The father of my baby is Captain Travis Coltrane. He happens to be one of the bravest soldiers you Yankees had, with the exception of my father. There was never a man better than he. Now, back to my situation. Now that I no longer have a home, thanks to you, I must demand that you turn my father's back pay over to me at once."

Very slowly, General Schofield lowered himself into

his chair. "Now I realize who you are," he said quietly, evenly. "And I am sorry for any distress you feel I may have caused you, Miss Wright. Your expecting a baby is your fault, you know. That was something you should have considered when you and Captain Coltrane . . ." He trailed off, embarrassed.

"I did not come here to discuss my relationship with Captain Coltrane. That is my concern and no one else's," Kitty snapped. "I came here to discuss the pay owed to my father. I am quite sure something was owed to him at the time of his death, and he did not have any money on him. I feel the money is rightfully mine now, and I also expect you to expedite matters and see that it is paid to me at once, due to your being indirectly responsible for my being thrown out on the streets."

The general raked stubby fingers through one of his side beards, a sarcastic smile twisting his lips. "And who was your father?"

"John Wright."

His eyebrows raised, and his eyes widened. He coughed and cleared his throat uncomfortably. "Well, of course I knew of your father. He was a fine soldier, a very fine soldier, indeed. One of our bravest."

"Nathan Collins shot him in the back," she spat out. "Captain Coltrane merely revenged his death by giving Nathan what he deserved. What the people of this county believe is of no concern to me. What *does* concern me, sir, is keeping the land that belonged to my father. It meant everything to him, and he meant for me to have it. Now, I don't have to tell you about the Yankee vultures hovering about waiting to buy up Southern land for delinquent taxes, now that Confederate money is worthless."

"Such are the consequences of war," he said with a shrug. "I can do nothing to stop such investments, Miss Wright. If I were not a military officer, perhaps I might become interested in such business ventures myself."

"Are you sure you aren't already involved? Don't pretend that you don't know the lecherous Mr. Corey McRae. He told me himself that you were the one who informed him of my unwanted presence at the hospital. I also know that you gave him permission to use that old feed store for his office while he pursues his real estate business."

He sputtered indignantly, "I am only befriending the man. The store was standing there useless. Miss Wright, I must say that I resent your implications."

She ignored his outburst and continued calmly. "I plan to live here and work my land. I do not intend to have Mr. McRae or any of the other vultures take it away from me. If Captain Coltrane is not dead, he will return and marry me, though God only knows when that will be. Until that time, I need money desperately, and all I am asking of you is that you check the military pay records and determine just how much money my father had coming to him at the time of his death. I want this done as soon as possible."

He started to tell her that it didn't make a damn bit of difference what she wanted, but he knew the persistent woman would not take no for an answer. "Yes, I understand, Miss Wright," he sighed. "But you must understand that this is going to take some time. The final terms of surrender are still up in the air, due to President Lincoln's tragic death. Washington is in turmoil. There is much paperwork going on. In addition, there are soldiers begging to be discharged so they can return to their homes. Relatives must be notified as to where their loved ones are buried, so they may move the remains elsewhere if they so desire. As for pay records of the dead, that is not of primary concern. I would say it is on the bottom of the list."

"It is of primary concern to *me*, General, and it is

on the top of *my* list!" She slammed her hands on his desk to emphasize her desperation. "I am starving, do you understand? For my supper last night I ate swamp bottom roots with the only friends I have . . . freed slaves . . . Negroes . . . good people who were glad to take me in. I drank hot water for my breakfast this morning and chewed more swamp roots. How long do you think I can survive this way? How long do you think those Negroes can survive? My God, General, they were better off before you damn Yankees set them free. At least they had food in their bellies and a roof over their heads. I need money to pay the taxes owed on my father's land and get a late crop of food growing so there will be food for this winter. I need to buy cows for milk, calves for meat. I want to befriend the Negroes the way they have befriended me. Corey McRae will never get that land. I'll die first. Which is probably what I will do, and my baby too, if you don't get up off your pompous butt and find my father's pay records and get me some money."

She took a deep breath, then said loudly, "Do I make myself clear, General? I hope so, because if I haven't, you are going to get very, very tired of seeing me march into your office every single day. You may be assured that I will return daily until I get that money.

"Maybe other Southerners are content to grovel about with their heads down in shame because we lost the war," Kitty said, pounding the desk again. "But I, sir, do not intend to grovel. I have no shame. I never turned from a wounded man on the battlefield because of the colors he fought under. I doctored hundreds—maybe thousands. Now I figure the Yankee army owes my father something, and I intend to receive it."

With that, she got up and stormed out of the office. As soon as the door slammed behind her, General Schofield banged his fists on his desk, yelling for the three soldiers stationed outside. They came rushing in, all three talking at once. "Shut up!" General Schofield ordered angrily. "I don't want to listen to your sniveling about how you are unable to control a helpless female."

"Helpless? Her?" one of the soldiers screeched. "Sir, you just don't know—"

"Yes, I *do* know!" The general withered him with a look. "And that is why you are immediately going to prepare pay records for a dead soldier named John Wright. When she comes back in here, you will have some money to give her and a paper showing that it represents the amount owed to her father. I have no intention of going through another scene with that woman."

The soldier stared open-mouthed, then gestured helplessly as he said, "How am I going to come up with pay records for a soldier when I don't know anything about him? Who's John Wright? What regiment did he fight with? What was the date of his death? Who was his commanding officer? I have to have more information sir, before I can even send out an inquiry."

"You idiot, you aren't going to send out an inquiry. We aren't going to go through channels on this. I said I wanted no more dealings with that woman. You prepare an official-*looking* document and state that we have found the United States Government owes John Wright the sum of, let's say, three hundred dollars. I will take the money from my own funds and give it to the girl to be rid of her. I certainly cannot have her storming in here every day. And perhaps I do have to assume some of the responsibility for her plight. Blast Coltrane!" He slammed a fist into the palm of his hand. "Send an inquiry as to his whereabouts. Request that General Sherman order him to return to Goldsboro as soon as possible."

He was pacing up and down the worn wooden floor, boots thudding with each step, hands folded behind his back. The soldiers exchanged uneasy glances. After a few moments he stopped pacing and stood in front of the Union flag, staring at it for long, brooding moments. Finally, sighing deeply, he shook his head and said, "No. Forget what I said about preparing a false document. I have never falsified government papers, and I do not intend to start now. I will just have to offer Miss Wright a loan until we can go through the right channels to ascertain how much, if any, money is owed her dead father. I cannot be a party to deceit."

The soldier who had been doing all the talking, Jesse Brandon, quickly said, "I agree with you, sir. It sure wouldn't be right. I guess we could all get in a heap of trouble. But you know it may take months—"

"Just do it," the general snapped wearily. "Get started right away. When she returns, show her into my office. I will offer her a loan. That is the best I can do."

Once outside the general's office, Kitty headed in the direction of the tax office. As she passed two pinch-faced women dressed in black, one of them said, loud enough for her to hear, "I don't see how some women have the nerve to show their faces in public."

Kitty whipped her head around and snapped, "I agree, madam. I know you can't help being ugly, but you could stay home where people wouldn't have to look at you." She could hear them gasping as she marched on, and Kitty laughed. No longer was she going to take abuse. She owed no one an apology for anything, and she had as much right to live here as anyone.

"Well, if it isn't the lovely butterfly who escaped the evil spider's web."

Kitty stopped short, turning to the doorway on her right. Corey McRae, resplendent in a white linen suit and fancy white boots, stood smiling down at her. The black silk shirt he wore made his dark eyes glow like shining coal. He touched a finger to his moustache, the huge diamond she had admired the night before gleaming in the mid-morning sunlight. In a mocking tone he said, "I thought you were a gracious lady, Miss Wright. Yet you rudely left without a word of appreciation for my hospitality."

"You scoundrel!" Her violet eyes glittered with red sparks of anger, and she faced him, hands on her hips. "How dare you speak of hospitality. You were holding me your prisoner, and you know it. You were planning on setting me up in the hotel as your mistress."

He laughed so loudly that several passersby paused to stare, then moved on when Corey glared at them. To Kitty, he said, "Come now, my dear. I offered you the respectability of matrimony. I asked you to be my wife. As I explained to you during our brief time together, I find you most beautiful, even though you carry another man's child. I plan to control this county once I buy up all the land that I possibly can, and I need a lovely, high-spirited woman at my side."

"You damn vulture. These people around here are going to be forced to lose their land to you because their money is worthless. You prey on them like a hungry wolf stalking a trapped rabbit. I find you despicable."

"And I find you enchanting . . ." He reached to touch her cheek, but she slapped his hand away.

"Don't you ever touch me again," she hissed, her body trembling in rage. "Don't you ever come near me. I am cowering no more, not for you or anyone else."

"Oh, come now, Kitty. You are being dramatic. You must learn to face reality. Do you want to give birth to a bastard? Do you want to continue to grovel in trash barrels for your food? I am offering you respectability, a home, a name for your child. You should be eager to accept."

Kitty shook her head slowly. "You are mad, Corey McRae. I thought perhaps you had been nipping brandy before I happened along last night. Now I can see that in the daylight, completely sober, you are actually insane."

He chewed his lower lip thoughtfully, eyes glittering with smoldering anger. Kitty did not wilt before his gaze. Instead, she gave her long strawberry-gold hair a flippant toss and turned to continue on her way. Corey's hand shot out and gripped her arm so painfully that she cried out sharply, and, with her free arm, she brought her hand up in a stinging blow across his stunned face. "Now let me go," she shrieked. "I want no part of you."

He snapped his fingers, and two surly-looking characters came running across the street. Kitty reached inside the deep folds of her skirt, down into a pocket, and pulled out her father's gun. Only that morning it had been dug out of its hiding place near his grave.

Backing against the wall of the hotel, she pointed the pistol at the men, but it was to Corey that she addressed her warning. "Be aware, sir, that I do not intend to be intimidated by you any further. I will not go along with your insane proposal, nor will you ever own my father's land. I have been to General Schofield and demanded the back pay owed my father. Go and swoop down on the carcass of some other crippled Southerner. This one stands tall and unafraid.

"And you scoundrels would be wise to believe me when I assure you I know how to use this gun. Ask any of the townspeople, and they will tell you I am as skilled with a pistol or a rifle as any man about."

She replaced the pistol in the deep pocket of her skirt, turned on her heel, and continued on her way, head high.

"Damn almighty," Jethro Quarry said to his boss.

"What for in the world you want to go getting messed up with a feisty filly like that?"

"Because she is feisty," Corey chuckled, watching Kitty strutting down the street. "And one day she will be mine. For the present, we will let her flounder on her own. She will come crawling to me sooner or later."

He took his time removing a long, expensive cigar from a gold case and lit it. "Jethro, what do you know of Captain Coltrane?"

The rough-looking gunman spat a wad of tobacco into the street, then wiped his mouth with the back of his hand. "I told you all I could find out. They say he's one of the best cavalrymen in the whole Union army. If General Sherman had a job that needed doing, one that was practically impossible, he always ordered Coltrane to do it. And Coltrane never let him down. He and his men were the toughest there was."

"Find him!"

Jethro blinked. "How the hell am I supposed to do that?"

Corey withdrew the cigar from his lips and gave him a withering glare. His lips trembled with anger as he barked, "I don't give a damn how you do it. Just do it. Get Carl to go with you. He's one of my best guns. Hire some new men to go with you, because I will be needing the ones I have working for me here. Find Coltrane and make sure he does not return to Wayne County."

"You mean kill him?" Jethro's slow grin displayed chipped, yellowed teeth.

Corey shrugged. "Just make sure he does not return. Those are your orders. I expect them to be carried out. I pay you top wages and I expect results. If Coltrane is permanently removed, Kitty Wright will be quite vulnerable. Sooner or later she will have to face the fact that he will not return. Now go."

Corey walked briskly down the street and entered General Schofield's office. Jesse Brandon glanced up from where he was sitting with feet propped on his desk. "Mr. McRae," he cried with recognition. Jumping to his feet, he grinned and asked solicitously, "What can I do for you, sir? The general isn't in right now. I'm sorry."

"Then I'll talk to you."

Corey sat down in a wooden chair near the soldier's desk. He folded his hands on top of his knees and was about to speak when he looked sharply at the other two soldiers, both watching and listening intently. "Why don't you men go for a walk?" he snapped.

They looked at Jesse, who nodded his approval, and they hurried out of the room, delighted to get a break.

"Miss Wright was here today. What about?"

Jesse twisted uncomfortably in his chair. "Mr. McRae, if the general ever finds out I tell you things I overhear, he's gonna have my scalp for sure."

With an exaggerated sigh Corey reached inside his white coat and took out a leather wallet. Laying several bills on the sergeant's desk, he said drily, "This will help you buy many hats to cover your baldness, Brandon. Tell me about Miss Wright's visit. I do not have all day."

Jesse quickly stuffed the money into his desk drawer. "I shouldn't do this, Mr. McRae. I don't feel right about it."

"Oh, your conscience never bothered you in the past when you answered questions for me. Now get on with it, man."

The sergeant took a deep breath and told him. When he had finished, MacRae spoke. "First, forget about finding Coltrane. Second, you will proceed at once to falsify documents showing back pay due to John Wright for the full time he served the Union army."

Jesse shook his head, bewildered and confused. "Mr. McRae, you're asking a whole hell of a lot of me."

"Oh, don't worry." Corey waved his hand. "If you do as I say and use your head, no one will find out about it. Now what was the rate of pay for a Union private?"

"They got thirteen dollars a month to start with. Then there was a raise in June of '64, and they started getting sixteen."

"There were also military bounties, right? To stimulate Northern enlistments? I remember that in the militia draft of 1862 the Federal government gave twenty-five dollars to men who volunteered for nine months, and fifty dollars to those who signed up for a year."

Jesse nodded. "That's right, and back in March of '63 they were paying as much as four hundred dollars to anybody who would sign up for as long as five years."

"Miss Wright won't know the exact dates or amounts her father would have received for reenlistment." Corey's face was bright with excitement. "Prepare the papers, Jesse. Show that Private John Wright refused to accept any money at all from the Union army, that he had requested that it all be kept in trust for his daughter. Figure in enough bounties so that she will receive at least a thousand dollars."

"A thousand dollars?" Jesse's eyes bugged out. "Who's going to put up that thousand dollars? General Schofield didn't say nothing about a loan that big. He mentioned something like three hundred."

"You fool!" Corey's fist slammed onto the desk so hard that it bounced off the floor. "I don't intend for the general to know a damn thing about *any* of this. You prepare the papers. Make them look authentic. I will give you the money with which to pay her. If she comes in when the general is here, keep stalling. Wait until he is out, and then send your other men out. Make sure you are alone when you give her the papers and the money. But do not let her keep the papers. Have her sign a receipt, then destroy all the documents you prepared. Tell no one about this."

"And what about when the general wants to know how the search for the real pay records is coming along? And what about when he asks have we received a reply to the request to General Sherman to find Coltrane?"

Corey smiled confidently. "Once Miss Wright stops coming around to pester him, the general will forget all about her. He has too many other matters to occupy his mind. He won't even think about his wire to General Sherman. Now, is there anything else you can remember that I should know about? Did she say where she is living?"

The sergeant snapped his fingers excitedly. "Yeah, that was the part that really got me. She's living in the swamps with a bunch of niggers—freed slaves. Says she had swamp bottom roots for supper last night and breakfast this morning. Says she's going to work her daddy's land and give them a job, 'cause they're the only friends she's got."

Corey shook his head in disgust. The woman was astoundingly independent. It was going to take some doing to bend her to his will. But he would succeed. He always did.

He got to his feet and Jesse rose also. They shook hands as Corey smiled. "You know what to do, Sergeant. Do your job well, keep your mouth shut, and I will see that you are handsomely rewarded. If you have any questions or problems, find me at once. But always be discreet. It would be best if we were not seen talking again, at least not as though we were acquainted."

"Yes sir." Jesse nodded vigorously. "I want to keep

this a secret as much as you do. Lord knows I can use the money. But I sure as hell don't want to get found out and wind up in big trouble."

"You do as I say and no one will find out," Corey assured him. Then he reached into his coat once again, removing his wallet. Counting out a little over a thousand dollars, he handed the money to the sergeant. "I'll stop by in a few days to see how things went."

Jesse looked at the money incredulously, then murmured, "Won't the general be suspicious at how fast this came about?"

"Tell him General Sherman was most concerned when he received your inquiry about pay records. Because of his deep respect for Kitty Wright's father, Sherman ordered the paperwork rushed through. General Schofield will be so delighted to have the matter settled that he won't question a thing."

Jesse nodded, and Corey walked quickly out of the office, nodding pleasantly to those he passed. The whole venture of making Kitty Wright his wife was going to be delightful. Yes, he decided, it was better this way. Had she jumped at the chance to become his wife and be financially secure, he would probably have tired of her as he had the others, finally having to do away with them. Kitty was a challenge. He would enjoy her much more.

Chapter Eleven

JACOB reached down and helped Kitty hoist herself up to the rickety old buckboard wagon, both aware of the looks of anger and disgust directed at them by the white townspeople. The mules began to pull the wagon forward. "Lordy, Lordy," Jacob shook his head. "You reckon it's ever gonna stop, Miss Kitty? All the hatin' looks? Folks had it in for you bad enough before. When they hear you is a'livin' with me and my people, they is really gonna be mad."

"Oh, Jacob, what business is it of theirs what I do?" Kitty was disgusted.

They rode along in silence until they were out of town and across the narrow river bridge. Then Jacob glanced at her. He could tell how upset she really was. "Things go bad with the tax man? Did you get bad news from the general feller about your daddy's back pay?"

She sighed. "The general was not very cooperative, and I'm afraid I am going to have to make many scenes in his office before he realizes I mean to collect that money. As for the taxes, well, it seems Poppa really didn't know just how much land he did own. He had sold off some of it a while back, you know, but I certainly had no idea he still owned so much. The taxes have not been paid since 1860. I suppose he had meant to find a way to pay them, but then you know how he became after that terrible beating. He probably didn't even think of taxes. Anyway, there is quite a large sum of money due, and the tax collector says that the land can be sold for taxes. In fact, he says it will come up on the delinquent tax list within the next thirty days and be offered at auction. I am sure Corey McRae already knows all this, and is just waiting for his chance. Oh, Jacob, I can't lose that land. Poppa would just turn over in his grave if I did. It meant everything to him."

Jacob nodded. "It sho did. Yes'm, that's a fact. I heered him say over and over that a man's land is ever'thing. Take that from him, and he ain't got nothin'." He paused a moment, then said, "I ain't worried about you keepin' that land. Yo' pappy is in heaven, sho as we is a'sittin' here, and he's probably talkin' to God, Himself, right this minute, sayin', 'Look down there at my girl, Lord. She's worrin' herself to death over the land, and that ain't good for her in her family way. You jus' got to help her out.' And the Lord, He gonna think about it awhile, and then He's gonna say, 'John Wright, you is a good man, and you served me well while you was on earth, and that daughter of yours, she is a fine woman, too. I gonna help her out.' You wait and see, Miss Kitty. Ever'thing gonna work out just fine. I ain't gonna worry a'tall about it."

Kitty's heart was warmed by the old man's faith, and she chided herself for not having more herself. There was going to be a way for her to pay those taxes, just as surely as Travis would one day return.

When they bumped along the rutted path to the swampy campground, they could see a crowd gathered in the center around the spot where the cooking fires were made. "Wonder what's going on?" Jacob gave the mules an extra slap on the reins, his eyes wide. "Looks like some excitement."

"Maybe someone shot a deer," Kitty mused. "I heard some of the men say they were going hunting today. Luther said they had seen some wild turkey tracks this morning. Fresh meat would sure taste better than those horrid swamp roots." She made a face, remembering the putrid smell and moldy taste.

"I don't believe it," Jacob cried happily. "See that man in the blue uniform? Praise God, I think it's Gideon. Gideon done come home from the war. Oh Lordy."

The old man burst into tears of joy, and Kitty blinked in bewilderment. "Gideon? Who is Gideon, Jacob?"

"You don't remember Gideon, missy? He be my sister Nolie's boy. He ran away and joined up with the Yankees when the war first broke out. Never did come home for a visit, 'cause he knowed he'd be shot on sight if he did. Made the white folks around here plenty mad that he run off, 'specially to join up with the Yankees. That there's got to be Gideon. I don't know of no other colored boy that'd be wearin' a suit of blue. Not from these parts."

The wagon bumped nearer, dust thickening in clouds about them. Kitty was about to ask Jacob to please slow down before she was bounced clean out of the wagon, when he let out a shriek. "Lord, God, it is you! Gideon! Oh, Gideon, I was a'fearin' you'd died." He yanked the mules to a stop so fast Kitty was almost flung across their backs. As she righted herself upon the bench seat, Jacob scrambled down to meet the running boy. She watched as they embraced, dancing around and around, both crying.

"You know no damn Reb can kill me," Gideon was shouting. "I told you-all I'd be back soon as it was safe. I got my discharge. I'm a civilian now!" he said proudly.

The other Negroes had gathered around them, forgetting about Kitty as she sat in the wagon watching. Then she felt piercing eyes. "Who's that?" Gideon demanded, pointing a finger in Kitty's direction.

"You remember Miss Kitty Wright, Gideon," Jacob said. "I lived on her and her poppa's land. You and yo' mammy used to come visit me there. John Wright fought with the Yankees, too. Miss Kitty, she a'livin' with us now, 'cause she ain't got no place else to go."

"What do you mean, she has no place else to go?" Gideon glared at her with distrust. "She's white, ain't she? What's she doing here with our people?"

"I tol' you, boy, she ain't got no place to go." While Kitty helped herself down from the wagon, Jacob proceeded to tell Gideon her story. She found herself becoming annoyed at the way the other Negroes stood back, their eyes distrustful suddenly—just because Gideon had arrived.

Gideon snapped, "It don't look right, having a white woman here with us. I don't like it. We're going to have enough trouble with the white folks as it is without giving shelter to someone they already have a quarrel with."

Kitty stepped forward then, lips set in a determined line. "You may stop talking about me as though I were deaf and dumb, Gideon. You may address me directly. It's true that I have no place to go at the moment, but I expect to be able to get some money soon. I have offered your people shelter on my land, once I am able to move onto it myself and start a late crop. As for my staying here, why do you object so violently?"

The whites of his eyes were the color of milk, surrounding pinpoint dots of chocolate. "You are white, missy," he ground out. "You look down on us freed slaves. All you Southern whites do. You're planning on tricking my people into working for you for nothing. You won't never want to pay no nigger, and you know it."

"I would pay any man or woman who worked for me if I had the money! But I have told them all that this year I can only offer them a share of what food we can grow. If the land prospers, I will even deed some to them, so they can build a house, plant their own garden. Even my own father did not know exactly how much land he owned. I checked today, with the tax collector—"

"I am not interested in all that." He waved his hand in disgust. "Do you think I believe anything you say? You are using my people, just like all the white Southerners will want to use them. And thank the Lord I returned in time to put a stop to it."

Kitty stepped closer, bristling with anger. "Gideon, you may as well have called me a liar, and I do not appreciate it. Just who do you think you are to come riding in here like some great messiah? Ready to incense these people into distrusting every Southerner with white skin? It's peace we are after now, not revolt."

"You listen to me," he shouted, eyes rolling around wildly, his fists beating into the air about him. The others stepped back in fright, but not Kitty. She stood her ground, facing him in equal defiance. "I fought with the North. I learned a lot of things. I learned to read and write and talk proper. The soldiers took time with me. They felt sorry for me, because they knew I'd been treated like a mindless animal all my life. I read the Bible, read about the man my mammy named me for, how he delivered his people. The soldiers, they told me how the white folks down here is going to hate the niggers because they can't own them now like they was cattle. They can't take a whip and beat 'em when they feel like it. We are citizens, too, now. We is free. We gonna stay free. We gonna take what is rightfully ours, and the government is gonna help us."

Kitty looked at the tall, thin black boy. He was eighteen or nineteen years old. His eyes were narrowed with hatred, his thick lips set in an angry pout. Perspiration dotted his forehead, and he wiped at it with the back of his hand. He glared down at her.

"I don't think you talk so proper," Kitty said, smiling. "I think you're a big put-on, Gideon. I think you have made yourself believe you are some sort of savior for your people. If they listen to you, they will be making a tragic mistake."

"A mistake?" he echoed, his voice thundering. "It will be a mistake for them to listen to people like you—hypocrites and deceivers who will use them because they are uneducated and stupid."

"You call your own people stupid?" Kitty raised her eyebrows and smiled sarcastically. "Gideon, I think you have fallen victim to some witless Yankees who knew what they were doing when they aroused your hatred and anger. They knew you would come back here to cause trouble. Can't you be reasonable? Let life settle into peace. Where do you plan to lead 'your people'? Tell us about this great revelation of yours."

"We ain't gonna work for no white folks without gettin' paid—"

"You are not talking properly," Kitty interrupted. For a moment it looked as though the young Negro were actually going to strike her. Even a few onlookers gasped. He had raised his hand, then lowered it, his eyes bulging.

"We *aren't* going to walk around with our heads down, like we are ashamed of our color." He bit off each word, making his diction crisp and clear. "We are free souls, and we are going to live like free souls. If anyone tries to push us around, then we will take up arms if need be. The first thing we are going to do is return to the slave shacks that are still standing and take what is rightfully ours—beds, blankets, clothing. We will strip the wood from the shacks to build our own elsewhere. These people ran because their white owners told them they were going to have to take up arms and fight the North. And they wouldn't do it. They chose to run to the swamps instead. When we ride out of here, we ride with heads high, afraid of no man."

"You work fast," Kitty said quietly, looking about her at the excited faces of the young black boys. They were almost trembling in their eagerness to follow Gideon. Her eyes went back to the young Negro who stood smiling down at her triumphantly. "You have only been here for a few hours, but you already have a small army ready to charge off to battle. Surely they are not all mad."

"We ready to go now, Gideon," Luther screamed, stepping forward and waving his arms over his head. Others did the same, till the air was filled with excited cries.

Jacob was shaking his son, yelling that he was going nowhere. "You ain't going to go stealin' beds and stuff from slave shacks, Luther. You goin' to stay right here and act like you got some sense. Now we in for some hard times, sho, but things won't get no better by startin' another war."

"Who rides with me?" Gideon yelled, moving towards his horse. "We go now, and we return when we have wagons filled with food and supplies."

Kitty watched helplessly as all the young Negroes ran to gather around Gideon. Except for Luther. He struggled and screamed like an infant in the throes of a tantrum as his father gripped him tightly. It was quite a struggle for the old man, and another stepped up to help him hold on to the youngster.

"Gideon!" Kitty called out, furious now. "Tell us about this man for whom you were named. Tell us if he would have incited young people to steal."

"The story of Gideon appears in the Book of Judges," he said quietly, reverently. "The Book of Judges is a collection of stories and national traditions of the Jewish people dating all the way back to a thousand years before Christ was born. One such story tells that the people abandoned God to worship the local deities of their neighbors in a place called Palestine. They suffered defeat from their enemies. And the Lord, in His mercy, every once in a while would raise up strong leaders who, under His guidance, led the Israelites to victory against their enemies. This way, God was showing the little people that, despite their smallness, He was a good God, who would come around to help them in time of need."

He paused to take a breath dramatically, smiling down at the awe-filled eyes that stared upon him. Then he cried out exuberantly, "Gideon was one of those leaders. He was called a Judge. The Lord chose Gideon to lead the Israelites when the Midianites swept in from the desert to steal their crops. The Lord came to young Gideon while he was threshing wheat in a wine press to hide it from the Midianites. The angel of the Lord came to Gideon and said God had chosen him to liberate his people. Just as I am going to deliver mine!" He slammed his fist against his chest. The Negroes sighed, overwhelmed by his vast knowledge. It was obvious that Gideon was a heaven-sent leader.

"I know of this story." Kitty spoke reverently, and all eyes were upon her. "Gideon was not even the head of a family. His father worshipped the Baal of the Canaanites and fertility symbols. Gideon was hardly a likely choice. Yet, despite his background, he was capable of faith. When he was convinced that the call from God was real, he did something drastic, something that could easily have caused his death."

Everyone waited, hushed, expectant. Gideon's eyes were blazing. It was obvious he did not like Kitty expounding on her knowledge of the Bible. The Northern preacher who had told him the story had instructed him well. So had the Yankee soldiers, who said he didn't have to go back home and be afraid of the white-trash Rebels who would still try to treat him like a slave. He was going to be a leader!

"Gideon went in the middle of the night and destroyed his father's altar to Baal," Kitty continued. A few cries of astonishment went up from her rapt audience. "But his father, Joash, defended his son from the angry devotees of Baal, saying that if Baal could not protect his altar against Gideon, then he was weaker than Gideon. Since Gideon had proved the strength of both himself and God, the Jews returned their loyalty and God led them to victory.

"So Gideon went out and raised an army of thirty thousand, and the Lord said it was too large an army. A victory would cause credit to go to the Israelites and not the Lord. Gideon weeded out the army. Do you know how he did this, Gideon?" She challenged him.

Gideon frowned. "That ain't important. You done said Gideon was the chosen leader by God Himself," he snapped defiantly.

"You aren't talking properly again," Kitty said sweetly, making his eyes dance with fire. "And it is important if you consider yourself the reincarnation of a great Biblical leader, and chosen by God Himself."

There was silence. All eyes were on Gideon. Finally, he mumbled, "I said it isn't important."

"Ah, but it is important," Kitty went on. "The final test was the manner in which the men drank water out of a stream. If they got down on their bellies and drank directly, causing them to ignore for the moment any enemy who might be lurking about, they failed the test. But if they cupped the water in their hands and drank standing upright, alert for the enemy, they passed. Three hundred men passed the test, and Gideon was able to launch an offensive against the Midianite camp. Do you know the details of the battle?"

"I know he won," Gideon cried. "That's all that is important. We waste time listening to the arguing of a white woman who just wants to use us."

She ignored the accusation. "Gideon equipped each man with a trumpet and a lighted torch set inside a jar. Secretly, the Jews surrounded the Midianite camp at night. Then, when Gideon gave the order, they smashed the jars, took out the torches, and blew their trumpets. The Midianites thought they were being attacked by a much larger force, and they panicked and fled."

"So? Gideon led his people to victory, just as I will lead mine. We're wasting time. We have to go now and take what is ours, unless you want your bellies to swell with the rot of swamp roots till you die."

"Wait!" Kitty called out, raising her hand. "Don't you see, Gideon? The true Gideon, the one chosen by God, led his people to victory by using intelligence and wit, not by shedding blood and taking up arms. God told Gideon to do this. What you plan to do is entirely different. You want to ride rampant upon the countryside and take what you want by force, shedding blood if necessary. That was not the way the true Gideon of the Bible led *his* people. You have much to learn. Violence is not going to accomplish anything except to breed more violence. Haven't you seen enough of that in the past four years? Aren't you ready for peace?"

"I'm ready to lead my people to take what's ours," he roared, leaping on his horse, yanking the reins to make the animal rear. "I bow to no man, ever again. Those of you who wish to go with me, come now. The rest of you can stay here and eat swamp roots."

"Gideon, you get yourself down off that horse!" All eyes went to the plump colored woman who stepped out of the crowd. She wore a tattered dress, and her feet were bare. Her face was lined with age and hard work. "You gone plumb crazy, boy? Your pappy and me didn't raise you to be no troublemaker. Things is a'gonna work out for all of us. So what if we eats swamp roots for a time? They ain't gonna kill us. Stealin' will. Now you get down off that horse and shut your mouth and quit talking about being some kind of religious leader sent by God. The only reason I give you that name was because my mistress tol' me to call you that. She studied the Bible like Miss Kitty here, and she told me to give you that name. I never knowed what it meant. It didn't matter then, and it sho don't matter now. So you hush up that big mouth of yours."

"Momma, I been called," Gideon cried. "You can't stop me. Nobody can. We're leaving."

He nudged his horse into a slow walk, so that the twenty or so followers could keep up on foot. Nolie began to cry, and another woman gathered her in her arms as she sobbed, "That boy always was a'tryin' to cause trouble. Never did know his place. He done fought in the war fo' years, and now he come home to die, 'cause these white folks ain't gonna put up with no niggers roamin' around stealin'."

Kitty lifted her worn muslin skirts and ran a few steps after them, calling out, "Those of you who stay will have a home on my land, I promise you. But those of you who ride out with Gideon need never come to me. I cannot tolerate those who do not want peace."

No one turned back except Gideon, who twisted in his saddle to give her a triumphant smile. Then he began singing the "Battle Hymn of the Republic" as he led his little group away. The others didn't know the words, but they caught onto the melody quickly enough. It wasn't long before they were all humming as Gideon sang, like one big choir marching across the dusty field.

"I'll join you when I can," Luther screamed hysterically, still being held back. "Gideon, I promise you I'll escape and come with you. I wants to be free, too."

"Oh, Luther, Luther, you are free." Kitty looked at him compassionately. He glowered at her. "You must understand. Gideon is only asking for trouble."

"Others are going to follow him. He'll have an army of hundreds of niggers, and they'll all fight right with him to take what's ours."

"And what is yours?" Jacob gave him a shove that sent him groveling into the dirt. "Right now, we ain't got nothin', any of us, but we gonna work and have somethin'. It may not be easy. But we'll do it with our own hands and the help of the Lord. We ain't gonna do it with no guns."

"You wait." Luther scrambled to his feet, backing away towards the swamps. "You wait and see. Gideon and all those who go with him are gonna be rich. They gonna live in fine houses one day, and white folks are gonna be a'workin' for them this time. But people like you, pappy, you gonna die here in the swamps with your belly full of ol' swamp roots, just like Gideon say." He turned and ran, disappearing into the great, silent wall of cypress and weeds.

Jacob's veined eyes filled with tears, and Kitty's heart went out to him. "He'll change," she said and touched his shoulder. "He's young, and he's bitter, but he'll see the wisdom of your words, Jacob, I know he will."

"Gideon!" Nolie spat out the name, hating it. "He's gonna cause the death of some good folks 'cause he listened to some Yankee soldiers who knew he was crazy enough to come back down here and get somethin' started. He ain't got sense enough to know there's white folks jus' waitin' for a chance to start shootin' freed slaves. Lord, Lord, what's gonna happen to us? I thought when the war ended we'd all have a new life. Now I wishes I was back on the plantation, even if it means being a slave. At least I wasn't starvin'. I look back now and see how it wasn't so bad, not for any of us, long as we kept our mouths shut."

"No, Nolie, don't think like that," Kitty whispered as the old woman began to cry. "You're free now, the way God meant you to be. There's going to be some bad times, but there will be good times, too. And try not to think harshly of Gideon. He really doesn't know what he's doing. He just listened to the wrong people.

"Hey," she cried, making her voice sound happy. "I thought someone said they saw turkey tracks. I'll bet a drumstick I can bag the first one. If we get busy, we won't have to eat swamp roots for our supper."

Gleeful cries went up from those anxious to forget the tense moments. They scrambled for their guns, though there were not many to be shared. They wouldn't have had even those had they not been stolen from the bodies of fallen soldiers. Kitty followed them into the swamps, eager for fresh meat, wanting to think of anything but that disappearing group that had followed Gideon so proudly.

"Look ahead," Kitty murmured to herself as she followed the others. "We have to keep looking ahead, because if we look back, God help us. If *I* look back, I don't think I can keep going forward."

Chapter Twelve

KITTY stared incredulously at the large stack of bills Sgt. Jesse Brandon had pushed across his desk. "That's . . . that's Yankee money," she stammered, ". . . and a lot of it. Are your sure the Union government owed my poppa that much?"

"You think we'd be paying it to you if it wasn't owed to him?" Jesse snarled, keeping his head down. He knew he had to make this transaction fast. No telling when General Schofield would come back, and the two soldiers working under him had looked suspicious when he sent them out as soon as Kitty entered. They probably figured he was going to make a pass at her.

"Here. Sign these papers. We have to have a receipt that you collected the money." He shoved the false documents across the desk. "And don't take all day, please. I've got other things to tend to."

Kitty reached for the quill, fingers trembling. Scrawling her name on the line he pointed to, she took a deep breath and stood back, still awed. "I just can't believe it. Why, I expected a hundred dollars or so, but there must be much more than that . . ."

"Just over a thousand," he snapped. "Like I told you, we found out your father never drew a cent of his pay. Left instructions that it be kept in trust for his daughter. You're his daughter, so it's your money."

With that, she snatched the large stack of Union

notes to her bosom, laughing a bit hysterically as a few fluttered to the floor and she stooped to pick them up.

"I asked you to hurry up," Jesse said nervously, wiping at the perspiration that beaded his forehead. Damn that Corey McRae for getting him involved in this mess. If the general found out, he'd probably face a firing squad.

"I want to wait to thank the general," Kitty said, pushing the money into the little bag the sergeant handed to her. "He was so nice to rush this through."

"Hey, don't do that," Jesse said quickly—too quickly, for she gave him a puzzled look. Forcing a smile, he said, "I sort of went around regular channels, you know? Some friends owed me favors, and I put the squeeze on them to rush things up. The general might not like it. I mean, he's real strict when it comes to following standards and procedures, you understand, Miss Kitty? I'll tell him in a week or so that things are straightened out, but if he found out right now that I'd gotten it all taken care of so quick, he'd ask a lot of questions. Me and my friends could wind up in trouble. You wouldn't want that, would you?"

"Oh, no, no, dear me, no." She shook her head from side to side. "I'll take this right over to the bank, and I won't say a word to anyone. I will pay my taxes, though. Oh, thank you, Sergeant. Thank you so much." He blushed guiltily as she ran around the desk to kiss his cheek. Then, her bag of money held tightly against her bosom, she hurried out of the office.

Jacob was outside, standing beside the old wagon. She threw her arms around his neck and hugged him happily. "Jacob, do you see this bag?" She swung it under his nose. "There's over a thousand dollars in here. A thousand *Yankee* dollars. I'm going to go pay my taxes, and then you and I are going to go buy some lumber, and we're going to start at once to build on Poppa's land. We'll buy seeds, plant a crop, build shelter for you and your people. Oh, Jacob, Jacob, I knew our prayers would be answered. We're going to make it. I know we are."

She swirled around and around beside him, face lifted to the hot July sun. She danced until she was dizzy, laughing as the old Negro righted her on her feet. "Oh, let's hurry and get started, Jacob. I'm going to sleep on my own land tonight, on the ground. *My* ground. And we're going to have food, real food. Tomorrow we plant corn and potatoes, and we'll even buy some chickens and a cow. Jacob, Jacob, God is good! Life is good!"

Grinning, Jacob followed her to the tax collector's office, where she paid the delinquent taxes and then waved her receipt in the air happily. The collector frowned. He was a Yankee, brought in to take over the job, and Kitty could tell he hated to see a Southerner able to keep his land. She even waved the receipt under his nose, just as she had the precious Yankee money. Then, with Jacob still beside her, she danced out of the office and onto the street.

They went to a feed store and bought items to get their garden planted. Then Kitty went to buy staples—flour, sugar, coffee. She even bought material to make a few new dresses to replace the muslin one she wore in tatters. Once this was done, they went together to buy lumber, demanding it be delivered out to the Wright land that very afternoon.

As they were walking back towards the wagon, Kitty stopped suddenly and said, "Jacob, you wait for me. I want to get some more cloth. I want to start making baby things."

"Miss Kitty, where you gonna put all this stuff?" Jacob asked worriedly, looking ahead to the loaded wagon. "You said you wants to sleep on yo' land tonight, and what if it rains? This stuff gonna get ruint. Why don't you wait befo' you buys anythin' else?"

"I want to have something for my baby," she said stubbornly. "Now you just go ahead and wait in the wagon for me. I won't be long."

Kitty turned and started back to the store. She had not gone far when Corey McRae stepped out to block her path. He seemed to come from nowhere. Yet she had the feeling that he had been nearby, watching her every move. Her eyes raked over him coolly. He was dandily dressed, as usual, this time in a suit of blue, and he stood smiling down at her, tipping his flat straw hat. "Morning to you, Miss Wright. It seems you are busy today. I watched your nigra loading your wagon. Suddenly you are a lady of means."

"It is none of your concern," she said angrily, sidestepping to move around him, but he quickly moved to position himself directly in front of her. She sighed. "Will you please let me pass? We have nothing to say to each other."

"Oh, yes, we do, Miss Wright. I want to apologize to you for any inconvenience or stress I may have caused you in the past. I was totally in error, and I would like to have your hand in friendship."

She cocked her head sideways, eyeing him suspiciously. "Just what are you up to, Corey McRae? I have made it quite clear that I want nothing to do with you."

"As I said"—he bowed graciously, sweeping his hat from his head and smiling—"I want to apologize. I understand you have paid your delinquent taxes and plan to rebuild on your land. Since we are to be neighbors, I think it would be nice if we were at least civil to each other. You are going to need help in getting a new start, and I have men, and supplies—"

"And so do I," she snapped, cutting him off. "I do

not need your help. As for being neighbors, you will live far enough from me that I doubt we will be running into each other. Now, I do have errands to tend to."

"Ahh, Kitty, Kitty." He rolled his eyes upwards, sighing with mock exasperation. "What am I to do with you? Never have I met such an obstinate woman. I offered you marriage and respectability, which you indignantly refused. Now I offer you neighborly help and friendship, and this you refuse also. What do you want of me?"

Her eyes widened incredulously. "Are you deaf, sir? I ask merely that you leave me alone. I want nothing to do with you."

He laughed. "Do you think I can leave such a beautiful woman alone? No, I have realized that I went about my pursuit of you in the wrong way, my lovely. I tried to force my attentions upon you, but you are obviously the sort who must be wooed and courted. This I plan to do. It causes me no distress to know that you are unwed and expecting a child. I find you extremely desirable, and I still intend to marry you one day."

"And I find you mad! Now, sir, if you do not let me pass . . ." She was reaching into the pocket of her skirt once again, feeling for the pistol she carried there.

He held his hands up in a helpless gesture. "Please! No guns today, milady. I give up. But only for the moment. I will still pursue you until you give me your hand."

Kitty pushed against his chest with both her hands, catching him off guard. He stumbled backwards and she was able to start by him. His hands moved quickly, however, and his fingers tightened about her wrists. Leaning very close to her upturned, angry face, he whispered harshly, "Kitty Wright, heed me well. The day will come when you will see the wisdom of the life I am offering you. I have made it my business to find out all about you, and I know that your Captain Coltrane left town very angry because you would not go with him. He does not want to live in Wayne County. He does not understand what your father's land means to you. I *do* understand. I understand much about you and the high spirit that makes you the desirable, passionate woman you are. And I shall have you. There has never been anything in this life that I could not have once I set my mind to it. And I shall have you. On this, I swear my life."

Kitty's lips parted, but just then a high-pitched voice cried, "Just what do you think you are doing, Kitty Wright? Do you dare to throw yourself at men in broad daylight on a public street? I should think your kind would know your place and roam the shadows of night to sell your wares."

Nancy Warren Stoner stood there, her face a mask of anger. She was wearing a bright yellow gingham gown. A matching parasol shaded her from the relentless sun. She tapped a foot as she looked at Corey petulantly. "You were going to take me to lunch at the hotel, remember? Must you embarrass me by conversing with this . . . this *slut* in public? I know how she throws herself at men, but—"

"Nancy, you are pushing me too far!" Kitty straightened as Corey's fingers fell from her wrists. "I will not stand for you calling me names. I have no quarrel with you. I want only peace."

"Peace!" Nancy spat out the word, eyes narrowed to evil slits. "You talk of peace? You, who are responsible for Nathan moldering in his grave. You are a traitor to the South, and you should be tarred and feathered and run out of town. You are just as sorry and no account as that no-good daddy of yours."

That did it. Kitty grabbed Nancy by the shoulders and sent her sprawling from the boardwalk into the horse watering trough, where she landed with a loud splash. As she floundered helplessly, hair and dress drenching in the sour water, screaming indignantly, Kitty leaned over and stared down at her, hands on her hips. "I told you, Nancy. You push me too far. Next time I will mash that hateful, arrogant face of yours right into the mud where it belongs. I have as much right to live in this town as anyone here. And I intend to do so, without being harrassed."

"Corey, Corey, don't just stand there," Nancy was screeching as people gathered to stare. They laughed, despite their feelings against Kitty. It was a sight!

"Corey, get me out of here."

Corey, trying to keep from bursting into laughter himself, was reaching for her as Kitty turned back towards the wagon. There would be no joy now in shopping for the baby. That would have to come another time. Oh, she hated it when she lost her temper that way.

Kitty's pace slowed as she saw the Negroes gathered around the wagon, saw Jacob's frightened eyes, his slack jaw and quivering lips. She hitched up her skirts and broke into a run, reaching the gathering to elbow her way into the group. "What is going on?" she demanded. "Jacob, why do you look so terrified?"

Finally a stoop-shouldered man in rags, his hair the color of snow, said in a faltering voice, "Missy, there's been a heap of trouble. A bunch of colored boys stole some horses last night . . . stole some other stuff, too . . . guns . . . food . . ."

Now others began to talk excitedly. "The townspeople are plenty mad. They went to General Schofield this mornin' and said they wanted them niggers hung."

"Somebody said old Jed Wesley got shot at."

"They say the vigilantes gonna ride."

"Somebody gonna kill them niggers, and it's gonna mean bad trouble for us all."

"Yeah. White folks, they might start shooting any colored man, just out of meanness."

Kitty bit her lip angrily. Gideon and his band had done what they set out to do. She saw the tears of fright welling in Jacob's eyes. "Let's go," she whispered, touching his arm. "There's nothing we can do now. It's out of our hands."

Just then two soldiers walked up, hands on their side arms, and one of them commanded, "All right, let's break this up. There's been enough gossip making the rounds this morning without darkies congregating."

The other snapped, "The white people are in a rage over last night's raids. It would be wise for you to stay off the streets." His eyes swept over Kitty. "And what are you doing in the middle of all this, miss?"

She didn't like the contempt in his voice, and she was exhausted from her shopping, her encounter with Corey, and her scrap with Nancy. She looked at the soldier wearily and said, "None of your damn business, soldier. Now get out of my way."

He stepped back, astounded, as Jacob helped her up to the wagon. He followed quickly, and, with a pop of the reins, the old mules began to take them out of town. "I know it was Gideon, and so do you," Jacob said as soon as they reached the outskirts and turned towards the river. "He gonna get hisself killed. I know he is. He ain't gonna stop with just stealin' food and blankets, like he said. He gonna run wild. You wait and see. And the rest of us, me and my people, we the ones what gonna pay for it."

"Not if you mind your own business and obey the law," Kitty said in her firmest voice. "Now, Jacob, don't you worry. You tried, Nolie tried. So did I. Gideon wouldn't listen, and neither would those who went with him. So now they are going to have to suffer the consequences. There is nothing more we can do for them. Except pray."

"Gideon always was rebellious. He hated bein' a slave. He never got over his sister being raped by whites. I wasn't s'prised a'tall when he run away to join the Yankees. And I ain't s'prised he's come back to make trouble now."

"The whole Southland is in a turmoil." Kitty tried to comfort him, though she could tell by the expression on his face that her words were of little solace. "I heard talk today when I was in the stores how the Negroes are causing trouble all over. Vigilantes are doing what the Federal troops won't do—and that's ride out and shoot them. It seems the Negroes are glad for the chance to punish the white man for all their years of slavery, and the whites are eager to fight back, angry because they can no longer hold the black people slaves. I don't think the winds of peace are ever going to blow across our land, Jacob, not in our lifetime anyway. But just try to remember that it isn't by your hand, or mine, that any of this is happening. We have to find some comfort in that."

"Yes'm," he nodded, a little more relaxed. "I knows I got lots to be thankful for. Your pappy freed me and mine a long time ago, and he still let us live on his land, paid us when he could. Saw to it we never went hungry. We always had wood to burn in the winter. If we got sick, you or Doc Musgrave took care of us. We always loved you and Mastah John fo' yo' goodness, and I'm proud to be able to try and pay you back now, by helpin' you when nobody else will."

"We won't tell them about the news," Kitty said to Jacob as they approached the swamps. "They'll hear soon enough. Let's let them rejoice in our good fortune, knowing that we do have a real home now."

"I think yo' right," Jacob nodded. "Like you say, they find out soon enuff. No need in me a'breakin' Nolie's heart. Look at her. Standin' to one side, away from the others, wringing her hands and a'cryin'. I know what she's a'doin. She's prayin' I don't have no bad news, and God forgive me, but I gonna lie and say I didn't hear one word."

They got down out of the wagon, but none of those gathered around made a move to come forward. "Hey, what's wrong with everyone?" Kitty called out merrily, moving to the back of the wagon. "Come and see what we have. Food. Supplies. Lumber is being delivered to my land this afternoon. Tonight we feast and celebrate, and tomorrow we start building and planting crops. I even bought a cow, and some chickens . . ."

Her voice trailed off as she realized that no one was paying her any mind. Nolie stepped forward, tears pouring from her veined, puffy eyes.

"Jacob." It was a moan, deep in her throat. Her hands covered her chest as she swayed. Someone steadied her.

"Nolie, what's wrong with you?" Jacob was hurrying towards her. "What you tryin' to tell me, sistah?"

Her eyes rolled back and she clasped her hands together in prayer. "Oh, Lordy, Jacob, it's happened. Gideon come back. He come back with horses and guns."

He grabbed her, shook her gently, crying himself. "Nolie, I heard about it in town, me and Miss Kitty. We weren't gonna tell you. We didn't want to worry you. We can't do nothin'. Gideon is in a heap of trouble, but it's his own doin'. We can't help him now. We got to think of ourselves, and the new life Miss Kitty is a'offerin' us. Get hold of yo'self now. God will look after Gideon, make him come to his senses. We pray for him. We get down on our knees now, and we'll pray."

He looked about at the others, gestured to them to get to their knees as he got to his. No one moved. He looked up into Nolie's face, and, with an anguished cry, she fell to her knees and clasped her big arms around him. "Oh, Lordy, Jacob. Gideon took Luther with him. He said he'd kill anybody who tried to stop him. And Luther wanted to go. He's gone, Jacob. They both gone. Yo' boy and mine."

And the two old Negroes wept, arms about each other. One by one, the others got on their knees, their bodies swaying. They prayed out loud for the deliverance of Gideon and Luther and all the others who rode with them.

Kitty bit her lip and turned away from the scene. She would not cry. Crying would not help. Crying made for weakness. Only the strong would survive these times.

She began to walk across the barren fields, head held high, the wind blowing her hair about her upturned face. And she kept on walking, till the weeping and wailing of the Negroes was only a distant echo.

Chapter Thirteen

JULY melted into August, and September crept across the lands to cool the air. The late crop had been abundant. The new barn held much corn and hay. Two cows gave milk. A calf was fattening. There would be meat for the winter.

The house Jacob and the Negroes had built for Kitty on the site of the old one was small but adequate. The furnishings were sparse. Frayed blankets covered the windows. The bed was roughhewn and had a worn, lumpy mattress filled with pine needles. She would not have had even that if she had not awakened one morning to find it in her front yard. Jacob said Gideon and his men had brought it. It was obviously from an old slave cabin. She wanted to leave the stolen item where it had been left, but her pride bent to the aches in her bones. The same was true of her kitchen stove, a nice, wood-burning model, hardly used. One morning she awoke to find it sitting in the back yard. Jacob and another man brought it inside. Kitty sighed reluctantly. She told herself it was really too cold to be cooking over a fire outside.

Other items appeared mysteriously—chickens, two pigs, a basket of apples, a thick quilt, some muslin. "I know Gideon is stealing these things," Kitty wailed to Jacob one morning as they stood together looking at a badly needed washtub. "I feel terrible taking them.

Maybe if I just left them sitting where he leaves them, he would stop it."

"He'd give 'em to somebody else," the old Negro said, shaking his head. "He got quite a gang now, missy. I heers all about it when I goes to town. The whites done formed a vigilante group, and they go out a'ridin' ever night, but they can't catch 'em. They done stole the fastest horses, so they can outrun anything the whites got. At first they just went to the empty places, houses where the folks had run off a'fore the Yankees came. Now they robbin' anybody they pleases. You heered about 'em even robbin' Mr. Calvin Potts?"

"Jacob, I don't hear anything unless you tell me," she pointed out. "I have not been to town since we settled in here over three months ago. People don't want to have anything to do with me, and I'm certainly not going to seek them out. I don't know what I would do if it weren't for you and your people."

"Well, my people is thinnin' out," he said apologetically. "The white folks is seein' they gots to have help, so they's started payin' a little. An' the shacks they offer is some better than what we wuz able to build on yo' land, Miss Kitty. So they been takin' off right regular. I tol' 'em how ungrateful they were, how it was a sin to walk out on you after what you done for us, but they's afraid you ain't gonna be able to make it, what with the baby comin', and the cap'n not comin' back."

She squeezed back the tears. "I understand, Jacob. They realize my money can't last forever, and that is certainly true. I'm trying my best to hang onto enough to plant my crop come spring, but that isn't going to be easy if I don't have hands to help me. Poppa always said the future of North Carolina lay in tobacco, and I wanted to plant a crop this year. And corn—lots of corn. And then there are the scuppernongs, and the beehives. But I am going to need help." Biting her lip, she asked fearfully, "Just how many of you are left, Jacob?"

"Tom and Hildy left yestahday to go to work for Mistah McRae."

"Mr. McRae?" Kitty screeched. "Jacob, Will and Addie went there last week. That makes four families I have lost to that man. What is happening? Is he paying them pure gold or something?"

"Just about." His frizzled gray head bobbed up and down. "He built that big fine mansion, you know, right where the old Collins place stood, but this one is even finer. It has real marble terraces and steps. He had furniture sent from England and France to furnish it. Dulcie, she one of the first 'uns to go, she say she never seen nothin' as pretty as that house. He got velvet drapes and silk drapes, and she say the floors is some kind of special wood."

"Mahogany," Kitty said quietly.

"That's what she called it. She heard Mistah McRae say most folks just made stair railing's and trim out of it, but he made his floors like that. She has to polish 'em by hand, but she say she likes it, 'cause they looks like mirrors when she through. That house got three floors, and Dulcie, she can't count but to ten, and she say she counted to ten two times, and they is some rooms lef' ovah. He payin' his help good, and he fixed fine cabins for 'em, with fireplaces. He give 'em all the food they can eat, too. So that's why they leavin', Miss Kitty. If they can go to work for Mistah McRae, they think they is in heaven. Treats 'em kind, he do. Nevah yells, says Dulcie. She thinks the whole world of that man. She don't like Miss Nancy, though."

"Nancy Warren?" Kitty raised an eyebrow. "Is she living there?"

"Not yet, but she comes around a lot. Dulcie says she Mistah McRae's mistress. She say she stay all night some times, and she hears 'em arguin' about how Miss Nancy wants to be Missus McRae, and Mistah McRae, he don't want to get married. Dulcie, she a'hopin' he don't, leastways not to Miss Nancy. She say that one mean woman."

"Dulcie should learn to keep her mouth shut about what goes on in her master's house, Jacob. It's wicked when servants gossip."

"Yes'm." He bowed his head guiltily, knowing that he was just as bad as Dulcie, having repeated her tales.

Kitty folded her hands across her swollen body. It was getting harder and harder to move about. "How many are left, Jacob?" she asked quietly. "How many families do we have now living on Wright land to help with the spring planting? I don't know because I seldom get out anymore. I'm so clumsy lately."

He looked everywhere but at her. He heard her patting her foot impatiently and finally mumbled, "Me and Nolie's bunch. That's it."

"You and Nolie's bunch?" Kitty grabbed the porch railing for support as she swayed. "Jacob, why haven't you told me this before? My God! You have two small grandchildren, hardly big enough to pick peas, and if their daddy ever comes back from the war, he'll, likely as not, take them off and try to make a home for them. You told me so yourself."

"I don't think he's a'comin' back." A tear rolled down his wrinkled cheek. "He took his daughter's dyin' mighty hard. I don't imagine he tried too hard to dodge any balls."

Kitty had no idea the situation had grown so desperate. "Why haven't you told me this before, Jacob?"

"I didn't want to worry you none, in yo' condition and all," he said humbly. "Nolie, she tell me not to say nothin'. She say the cap'n come back and then ever'thing be just fine. He'll know just what to do. And

Nolie, she said she'd never leave here. She got two girls, too, fine workers. Ever'thing gonna be all right, Miss Kitty. You just wait and see. You don't worry. The Lord look after all of us."

The sky overhead was gray and overcast. A damp, chilling wind blew across the lands. Kitty tightened her shawl about her shoulders as she began to pace around the washtub, deep in thought. Suddenly her head jerked up and she eyed Jacob suspiciously. "Why is Nolie so loyal? I never even knew the woman until I went to the swamp campground with you that day. Why does she refuse to leave here? With two healthy, strong daughters, and her experience as household help, she should have no trouble at all getting a very good job. I am sure Mr. McRae has tried to hire her away from me."

Jacob wouldn't look at her. He knelt down beside the washtub and ran his fingers around the edges. "I'll get this cleaned up today, missy, and bring it into the house fo' you. I know you gonna like havin' a washtub—"

"Jacob, answer me," she cried, whirling to stare down at him. "Why does Nolie stay here? She has no reason to be loyal to me. I want the truth. You have been keeping too much from me lately. I suppose next *you* will be leaving me, just like all the others?"

"Oh, no, missy, no." He straightened quickly, eyes wide. "Miss Kitty, I'd never walk out on you, not for any kind of money. Mistah McRae, he knows that, too. I told the man he sends over here to tell him old Jacob would never leave. No sir, I owes it to Mistah John to take care of his daughter."

"Mr. McRae sends a man over *here*?" She blinked incredulously. "He sends someone right onto my property to talk to my help and hire them away from me? How long has this been going on?"

"All along." Jacob shook his head from side to side

in misery. "It seems like he'd come up out of nowhere, and he'd just talk to one man about his family. Sometimes, others'd be willin' to go right then, but he'd say Mistah McRae didn't need nobody else right then. Then, a few days later, or maybe it'd be a few weeks, he'd come back. Nolie and me talked about it, and we knowed they wasn't nothin' you could do, Miss Kitty, so why make you fret, jus' like you a'frettin' now? T'ain't right, you in yo' shape and all. But don't you worry none. Me and Nolie, we'll do all we can. Maybe by spring some of the others will get dissatisfied and come back. Like Dulcie. She'd never stay over there if Miss Nancy was to be mistress of the house."

"Oh, she would find somewhere else to go. Once a Negro girl gets to do house work, you know she finds the fields degrading and those in the fields taunt her for her new, higher status in life. Dulcie is lost to us, just like all the others. Oh, I hate Corey McRae!" She clenched her fists at her sides. "Why did he take it upon himself from the moment we first met to make my life miserable? He even had the nerve to ride over here himself, right after we finished the house."

"Oh, I remember that." Jacob laughed. "He brung that big basket of fruit, and you yelled at him and tol' him never to come back or you'd meet him with a gun. Then you threw that fruit at him, a piece at a time. Hit him right in the back of the neck with a peach, you did. Those of us who was a'watching rolled on the ground laughin', the way it went a'dribblin' down the back of that fancy white suit."

"Don't make me sound like a madwoman, Jacob." Kitty had to suppress a smile as she remembered the sight, the way Corey had spurred his horse, trying to muster his usual dignity, peach juice dribbling down his neck. "He didn't just come to bring me a basket of fruit and wish me well in my new home. He came to tell me how clumsily it was put together, how it would probably fall apart the first time we had a bad storm. And he asked me when would I come to my senses and marry him, that I had to realize Travis was dead. That's when I went into a rage."

Then they both giggled, but the moment passed. Kitty demanded once again the reason for Nolie's sudden devotion. Jacob took a deep breath and then spoke the words that Kitty had feared. "Gideon. He slips in to see her here. She says he wouldn't try it nowhere else. If you was to see him, you wouldn't shoot him or sic the vigilantes on him. Ever'body else would. So she stays, 'cause she knows that's the only way she ever gonna be able to see her boy."

Kitty was quiet for long moments, then she murmured, "And Luther. Does Luther come, too, Jacob? Does he slip in with Gideon?"

He turned away, covering his face with his hands for a moment, then lifted his tormented face to the gray sky. "No, he don't come. He knows I can't hold to what he's a'doin', ridin' around and stealin'. One of these days, somebody gonna get killed. It might be Luther. If he ain't killed, he gonna get caught, and when he does, they gonna hang him, and Lord knows I can't see my boy hung." He lowered his eyes to the ground, his shoulders heaving. "I wants to see him, Miss Kitty, Jesus knows I do, but I can't hold to what he's a'doin', so I told Gideon to have him stay away till he can come to his senses and come home for good. Gideon promised me he tried to tell Luther he was too young, and I believe Gideon. But Luther was always stubborn. I hear he's one of the fiercest gunmen Gideon's got. Oh, Lordy, Lordy, his momma has probably turned over in her grave by now."

Kitty walked over and put her arm around the old man's shoulders. "You tell Nolie that she is welcome to stay here as long as she likes, and that Gideon will always be safe here, if I have anything to do with it.

The same goes for Luther. I don't approve of what they are doing either, Jacob, but the whole Southland is in a state of turmoil. It will be years before the agony starts to recede from these lands. If only Travis would come back and help us."

"Do you really think he's gonna come back?" Now Jacob sounded bitter. He turned to look into her sad eyes. "Miss Kitty, I hate to hurt you, Lord knows I do, but I think you better start thinkin' about the truth. And the truth is, if he was a'comin' back, he woulda done been back by now. You knows it, and I knows it."

"Jacob, I just won't listen to that kind of talk." Kitty stiffened, her cheeks reddening. She lifted her skirts and started back for the little house. "Would you mind seeing if Nolie's girls will look down in the swamp for some herbs today? I've been feeling poorly, and I'd like to brew some herb tea. And when you get a chance, bring that tub in. I might as well use it, and if I leave it sitting out here, there's always the chance someone will see it and think *I* stole it. Heaven forbid if anyone should think I'm a thief, in addition to the other sins they hold against me."

She was almost inside the cabin when the sound of thundering hoofbeats echoed about them. "Jacob, see who that is," Kitty said quickly. "If it's Corey McRae, by God, I will meet him with a gun."

She started inside, but Jacob called out for her to wait. "It ain't Mistah McRae. This man's ridin' a yeller horse, one of them palominos, and Mistah McRae don't nevah ride nothin' but his black stallion or his white stallion."

Kitty moved quickly back down the steps as fast as her condition would allow. She had just stepped onto the ground when the rider reined his mount to a halt a few yards away. His handsome face was unfamiliar, and her pounding heart skipped a beat as it settled back to a normal pace. It was not Travis, as she had fleetingly dared to hope. He was of average height and build, neatly dressed in buckskin pants with matching vest. Removing his tan suede hat, he bowed, his moustache twitching as he smiled. "Good morning, Miss Wright. My name is Jerome Danton."

"I don't believe I have heard the name," Kitty said suspiciously.

Jacob turned to her excitedly and said, "I knows him now, Missy. Mistah Danton, he owns a store in town, called Danton's Dry Goods."

She nodded, looking straight into Jerome Danton's hazel eyes. His hair was a dark auburn, streaked with gold, neatly trimmed a scant inch or so above his collar. "Why have you come here, Mr. Danton? I usually have no visitors."

"I know." He sounded almost pitying. "That is why I'm here. You see . . ."

Pausing, he looked pointedly at Jacob. Kitty turned to the old Negro and said, "Would you ask Nolie's girls about getting the herbs for me right away, Jacob? I suppose I should offer my guest tea." Reluctantly, Jacob turned away, casting wary glances over his shoulder.

Jerome laughed. Kitty liked the way his eyes sparkled. "Your servant is very devoted, obviously," he commented. "He certainly did not want to leave you alone with me. Do I look that ominous?"

"I suppose everyone is ominous as far as Jacob is concerned, considering the way the good citizens of this county have treated me. Jacob is very loyal, and I am extremely grateful." She started back up the steps and was about to invite him to follow when he moved swiftly to take her arm and help her up.

"Thank you," she murmured, and they moved through the door. There was a small wooden table and two chairs. She gestured for him to sit, then set about poking wood into the stove and lighting a fire beneath a kettle of water. She again asked why he had come.

"Oh, I suppose a combination of reasons. First of all, I was curious to see the infamous Kitty Wright."

She bristled slightly. "People never forget, do they? Forgive me if I sound rude, Mr. Danton, but I do not feel I owe you any narration about my past."

"As I said," he went on, "I was curious. I bought a dry goods store in Goldsboro and built onto it. It's now the largest one in town. You would know that if you ever came into town, but I've heard you never do. Well, I began hearing about you from different people in the store, about your Northern cavalry officer, who promised to return but hasn't, and about your dead fiancé, who died at the cavalryman's hand. I also know about your father, his reputation as a brave Union soldier, and also about how everyone in these parts seems to have despised him."

"Well, I do declare! You have a nerve, Mr. Danton, riding all the way out here to meddle in my private affairs. I think I shall have to ask you to leave without the courtesy of a cup of tea."

"Now, wait a minute, Miss Wright." He held up a conciliatory hand. "I did not come here to talk about your past. I just wanted you to know that I know who you are. I think you have been treated extremely unfairly and I don't believe a word of what I have heard. It is none of my business, nor am I concerned with gossip. Perhaps I had better start over and tell you exactly who *I* am, and then we can get into my reasons for being here."

She nodded, taking a seat opposite him, still wary.

"I'm what the Southerners are calling a 'carpetbagger,'" he said, obviously amused. Kitty looked puzzled. He noticed her confusion and said, "My, you have been out of touch, haven't you? The carpetbaggers are terrible people, my dear. We come down from the North and buy up Southern land dirt-cheap, making a fortune from the spoils of war, taking advantage of the whipped Confederates. In my case, however, it is inaccurate of the citizens about to label me a 'carpetbagger.' Actually, I am a Southerner, originally from Virginia. I fought for the Southern cause. When the war ended, however, it was to my advantage not to return to my home. I came here. For some reason, unknown even to myself, I decided to settle here. I bought the store, and now, as I have told you, it is the most prosperous in Goldsboro. But that is not enough for me, to be merely a shopkeeper. I believe in farming. I believe in the future of tobacco. Most of all, I believe in *land*. Which brings me to why I have come to see you."

Kitty's eyes narrowed once again, and she pressed her hands together in her lap. She sensed what was coming.

"You know the Griffin land that borders your land on the north side?"

She nodded slowly.

"And the Moseley land on your west side?"

Again she nodded.

"And the Temple property across the road, on the east?"

Exasperated, she cried, "Just what are you getting at, Mr. Danton? You are playing games with me, and I am in no mood—"

"I am getting to my point." Again he held up his hand for silence. "I own all that property."

"*You* own all that property? You bought out the Moseleys and the Temples and the Griffins? How was that possible? I don't believe it. They must have had over two thousand acres between them."

"Quite true." He curled one tip of his moustache as he smiled. "They also owed quite a bit in back taxes which they could not pay. Their Rebel currency was quite worthless. I bought the land for the delinquent taxes."

"You scalawag!" She leaped to her feet, despite her awkward bulkiness. "You're another vulture, preying on people's misfortunes. Well, I can tell you one thing, Mr. Jerome Danton, you have come to the wrong place if you think you can swoop down and pick my bones. If you had taken the time to check the tax records, you would have seen that my taxes are *not* delinquent. At least not through 1864. You people make me sick! And I am happy to say you have wasted your time in coming to my door, sir."

He ignored her outburst and continued in a calm tone. "I did check the tax records, Miss Wright, and I am well aware that your land is, at the moment, unencumbered. However, I did come here to offer you a handsome price for your land. By now, I think you should have come to your senses and realized that it is going to be impossible for you, an unmarried woman, soon to have a child to raise alone, to work this land. As I said, I hear many things in my store, and I have also heard how, little by little, Corey McRae has stolen your devoted Negro friends right out from under your nose. You are left with that old cottontop nigger and an old nigger woman who happens to be the mother of the outlaw every white man is itching to kill. He even robbed my store one night. But that is beside the point. I am prepared to offer you a generous amount for your land."

"You are wasting your time. I have no intention of selling my land."

Jerome Danton's amiable expression did not fade, though his voice was tight. "You will see the day come, Miss Wright, when you will beg someone to take this place off your hands. I might not be so generous then, however deeply your beauty touches my heart. I am a businessman, and I suggest you think this over carefully."

There was a quick knock on the door. Without waiting to be told to enter, Jacob moved quickly into the kitchen, a bag of herbs in his hand. His fearful eyes went from Kitty to the man staring at her so intently. "I brung the herbs," he said in a voice barely audible.

"Our guest will not be staying for tea, Jacob."

"Jacob!" Jerome moved his gaze from Kitty to the old Negro. "I would like you to take a message to the mother of that outlaw Gideon. Tell her that if he dares rob my store one more time, I will track him down and hang him myself."

Kitty saw Jacob's hands tremble. She was not about to see her faithful friend be intimidated by the likes of Danton. "You will say nothing to Nolie, Jacob," she spoke quietly. "She has enough worries without being frightened further." To her visitor she said, "I will thank you to leave now."

He got up slowly, moving towards the door, still watching her intently. "I mean what I say, Miss Wright, and I think you would do well to be warned also. That stove upon which you now cook was stolen from my store. I know, also, where that tub in the yard came from. It's obvious that you are the recipient of stolen goods, which makes you as guilty as the thieves. Gideon and his band are apparently taking refuge here—"

"That is not true," she screamed, slamming her palms on the wooden table. "I have not laid eyes on him or any of his men. I find these things in my yard, and I have kept them because I needed them. If you would like to send a wagon, I will be glad to return anything you claim is yours."

"No, I am glad for you to have them." He smiled, a nasty grimace. "As I have already told you, I am a man of means. A stove, a few things here and there, what are these to me? It angers me for someone to steal from me, true, but I certainly do not mind a needy woman having them. But you realize that I cannot let this continue."

"Take your damned stove." Kitty's eyes were stinging with tears of anger and humiliation. "I want nothing of yours. You came here like all the rest, wanting to see me fail, to grovel at your feet. That day will never come, sir. I will die first."

"And your baby? What of your baby? Your captain is not coming back. Really, I don't see how you can continue to be so obstinate, Miss Wright. You are living in a dream world, like so many other foolish Southerners."

Kitty pressed her fingertips against her throbbing temples. Would he never leave?

"I bid you good day," Jerome Danton was at the back door, pushing it open to step out into the late fall sunshine. "If you come to your senses, you know where to find me."

The door closed. She was alone with Jacob. The silence seemed to scream about them from the thin walls of the little house. Finally Jacob whispered, "It's gonna be all right, missy. You'll see. The Lord gonna look after you and your baby, even if Mr. Travis don't come back."

Any other time, she would have screamed. Lifting her face to Jacob, she forced a tight smile. "If Captain Coltrane does not return, Jacob, we will survive. Now, you go to Nolie and tell her that the next time Gideon comes here that I want her to warn him that it is no longer safe. This Danton fellow may have people watching. And please, have her tell Gideon not to bring me any more gifts. I do not want stolen goods, no matter how desperately I might need what he brings me. I have worries enough."

"Yes'm." He set the bag of herbs on the table and backed out the door.

Kitty finished making her tea, then lowered her heavy, swollen body into a crudely made chair. Things would get better, she promised herself and her unborn child.

Then she bowed her head into her folded arms, her body shaking. But she refused to let the tears flow.

Chapter Fourteen

AUTUMN yielded to winter. Kitty spent her days before the fireplace, which Jacob kept stoked. She whiled away the long, lonely hours making tiny garments for the baby, trying not to think what the future would be like if Travis did not return.

Corey McRae continued to send invitations to visit him at his mansion. Each message was thrown into the fire without the courtesy of a polite refusal.

It was late. A bitter wind howled outside, causing the thin plank boards of the little house to tremble. Kitty had fallen asleep in her rocking chair, her head nodding over the tiny gown she was stitching. Suddenly, her head jerked up as a chilling spasm shook her. It was freezing, she realized with a start, and she saw at once that the fire had burned down to ashes. Where was Jacob? How late was it? He never retired for the night without first making sure that her fire was stoked with enough logs to last till morning. Perhaps he was sick. If it were not so cold, and if she were not so big, she would take the lantern and walk to his cabin and see about him. But Nolie was there. If he were ill, Nolie would take care of him.

Suddenly she snapped to attention. Horses. Many horses. Hooves thundering and crunching upon the frozen ground. Riders were going by, fast. Pulling herself up, she began to grope in the darkness for the wooden shoes Jacob had so skillfully carved. Who would be coming here in the middle of the night? She had told Jacob that Gideon was not to come here again, that it was no longer safe.

Terror closed an icy fist about her heart as the sound of gunfire split the silence. Stumbling, she made her way to the back door. Flinging it open, she could see torches casting eerie, ghostly shadows among the woods. And what were those white things floating about? It looked as if ghosts were back there. But those were not ghosts screaming. That was Nolie shrieking. And those curses and yells were being made by men, many men.

Another shot rang out. She moved as quickly as her bulk would allow, and she was almost down the steps when she heard Jacob's pleading screams. Turning around, she reentered the house to find her father's gun. Then she once more made her way outside, her feet touching the frozen ground as she hurried among the ruts and ridges of the path, heading straight towards the scene.

"Hang the nigger," a man's voice rang out angrily, loud and clear in the blackness of the night. "Hang him high and leave him for the buzzards to pick. That oughta teach these damn, thievin' bastards a lesson."

"Not my boy. Oh, Lordy, God, not my boy. Please, no. Have mercy. He ain't never hurt nobody. You done shot him. Don't hang him, please, God, God . . ."

That was Nolie screaming. Kitty tried to quicken her pace, but the path was slippery. She could not risk falling and injuring the baby. Closer. She had to get closer so she could take careful aim before shooting. Trying to hold up her skirts with one hand so she would not trip, she held tightly to the gun with the other. She could make out the scene now. Six men, dressed in what looked like white robes, stood in a semicircle around someone lying on the ground. She could not see their faces, for they wore hoods, with slits cut for the eyes, noses, and mouths. Why would they dress like that, she wondered, like a child's image of a ghost?

But there was no time to wonder. She could see Nolie holding Gideon as she rocked back and forth, moaning and sobbing. Kitty was close enough. She stopped walking and stood there, taking in the scene. So Gideon had slipped in to see his mother. And he *was* an outlaw. But by God, this was *her* land, and there would be no more shooting here and no hanging. These ruffians were obviously not law officers, and they were not going to take the law into their own hands. Not on her land, by God.

She saw Jacob crouched near Nolie, his eyes wide with fear. Three of the men carried torches. The others all held guns. One of them roared. "Get away from him or we'll shoot the two of you."

Kitty fired over their heads, and they jerked around to stare at her through their slitted hoods. She yelled, "drop those guns!" And she fired quickly at one man who started to raise his rifle, knocking it from his hand. Incredulously, he shook his tingling hand and stared at the pregnant woman with a gun. The others made no move to raise their weapons against her.

"Jacob, take their guns," she ordered.

The old Negro looked at her uncertainly, dazed. Nolie continued to rock her badly bleeding son, weeping and wailing.

"Jacob, I said take their guns," Kitty repeated, her voice stern. "Do it now."

Very slowly the old Negro got to his feet. Moving cautiously and uncertainly, he went from man to man until he had collected all their guns. "Toss them over there." Kitty nodded towards a nearby huckleberry bush. With several loud plops, the guns were thrown into a pile.

"You're makin' a heap of trouble for yourself, Kitty Wright," the man closest to her snapped. "This nigger is an outlaw, and we aim to hang him. You knowed all along he's been slippin' in here to see his ma, ain't you?"

"I owe you no explanation for anything that goes on here. This is my land. If Gideon is an outlaw, then let the courts decide what to do with him." Her voice was crisp, steady, but she was terrified. "Jacob, take one of their horses and go for help. Go all the way to town if you have to. But find someone who is decent enough to help us with Gideon. We will then turn these men over to the sheriff."

"Nigger lover," another man said as Jacob scurried towards a horse, mounted, and galloped across the frozen earth. "Look at her! Belly all big and swollen with that Yankee soldier's young'un. We oughta kill her, too, havin' a damn half-breed bastard!"

Nolie stopped her rocking and moaning to raise tear-filled eyes to Kitty, her face glowing in the light from the torches. "Miss Kitty, I tol' my boy not to come here no more. But he was sick. He come here tonight for me to fix him somethin' fo' his fever. They musta been watchin' and waitin' fo' him to come. And now he's hurt bad." Tears streamed down her black cheeks.

"We'll take care of him, Nolie," Kitty said softly, her heart going out to the old woman.

Kitty's fingers were cold and stiffening, and she wondered how long she could stand there holding the gun. It felt like ice against her numbing skin. There was no way of knowing how long it would take Jacob to find help. If only someone else were around to tie up these animals, she thought anxiously, she could put the gun down and warm her hands and see what she could do to help Gideon. She could see that he was bleeding profusely from a wound in his chest. It looked bad, very bad.

"He is an outlaw," one of the men said. His voice was calm. There was something vaguely familiar about his Southern accent with the slight rise at the end of each syllable. "You know the law has been after him for months."

"Then let the *law* deal with him, not you. Who do you think you are? How dare you ride onto my property this way, in the middle of the night, dressed in robes and hoods? Why, you look like bandits yourselves."

"The law cannot be everywhere at once, but with enough followers who believe as we do, *we* can be everywhere, Miss Wright. So make it easy on yourself. Put down your gun and let us take this outlaw and hang him. Then we'll go and leave you in peace."

"You are in no position to bargain," Kitty snapped. "And I think the sheriff will be very interested to find out what has taken place here tonight. There are also laws to deal with scum like you, who dare to take the law into your own hands."

She saw his hood suck in as he drew a deep breath. "This is your last chance, Miss Wright. Either put down your gun and step out of our way or you give us no choice but to possibly harm you. We need the support of white people if we are to keep these uppity niggers in line, now that the Yankees have turned them loose. The white Southerners must stick together or perish."

One of the other men snorted. "Hell, you think she gives a shit about the South? We done tol' you, her daddy was a goddamn traitor, and everybody in the county knows her Yankee lover put one of our finest officers in his grave. You're wasting your breath trying to talk *her* into taking *our* side. She knowed all along Gideon was coming here. He never would of come if he hadn't figured he was safe."

"Miss Wright." The familiar voice spoke again, still

quite calm, as though he were confident he could make her see things his way. "I don't think you understand what you are doing. You never leave this land, so you don't realize how the niggers are running wild now. We whites have to join together to do what the courts are unable to do. And when word spreads about how you took up for an outlaw, you are going to suffer grave consequences."

"That accent . . ." Kitty said in wonder. "Virginia. Yes, a Virginia accent. I know who you are now, Jerome Danton."

Kitty was momentarily dazed by her discovery, and Jerome and the others saw and took advantage. The three men holding torches dashed them to the ground, and in the sudden confusion, Kitty was no match for the man who grabbed her arm and knocked the gun from her hand. She found herself being flung to the ground, her arms yanked painfully behind her back as she was pulled back up to her knees.

"Hold her there," Jerome ordered. "Try not to hurt her. We have control of things now, so there is no need to rough up a pregnant lady."

"Lady, my ass," the man holding her snorted. "You call this pregnant bitch a lady? I say let's show her what she's good for. She ain't one of us. She's a goddamn traitor like her no-good daddy. And I don't give a shit how good-lookin' she is, and how the menfolks talk about how they'd like to tap her honey hole. I say let's strip her naked and teach her a lesson."

Jerome moved so quickly that Kitty almost didn't see the fist strike out and smash into the other man's hooded face. Staggering but not falling, he dropped her arms. She fell forward, twisting to watch as blood seeped through his white hood. "I oughta kill you for this, Danton," he snarled, spitting out a broken tooth.

Jerome laughed shortly. "You have more sense than

to try, you fool. Next time, follow orders and keep your mouth shut. Now, let's get on with the business at hand. Your opinion of Miss Wright has nothing to do with why we are here. We do not stoop to torturing pregnant women, do you understand? She can do us no harm now."

Wiping at his bloodied mouth, the man glared at her through his slitted hood. "One of these days, I'll fix you up good, Kitty Wright. I'll show you what a real man feels like."

Jerome Danton knelt in front of Kitty, cupping her chin gently in his hand, forcing her to meet his gaze. Someone held a torch down closely, illuminating her face, and hatred blazed in her eyes. "I told you you were very foolish," Jerome whispered, genuinely apologetic. "You are such a lovely creature. It would be a pity to have to harm you."

"Hey, this nigger's dead," someone yelled. Jerome left her and rushed over to where Nolie still held her son against her bosom. He felt for a heartbeat, then nodded.

"Hell, we ain't gonna have the fun of seeing him swing and hearing his neck break," one of the men said.

"Yes, we will." Jerome stood up. "We'll take his body to the fork in the road by the river and hang it from a tree there. None of the niggers about will dare cut him down for fear that we are watching. When the buzzards have picked him to the bone, they can stare at him and think about how the same thing can happen to them if they dare get out of line."

"No, no, you can't have him," Nolie screamed as Gideon's body was yanked from her arms. One of the men hit her with his fist, and she slumped to the ground, unconscious. Kitty watched as the limp body of the Negro boy was slung over the back of a horse.

"Don't . . . don't do this thing." Kitty was struggling to get to her feet, knifelike pains slashing down her back. "Go now. Leave us alone. You've done enough."

"Oh, no, missy, we ain't through yet." The man who had first held her laughed in the night wind. "I'm going to throw my torch on the roof of the Wright house one more time and see you burned out. You're gonna learn, once and for all, that we don't want your kind around here."

He spurred his horse, charging into the night, and Kitty watched as he approached her little house, flinging his torch upon the roof. Two of the other laughing riders followed suit. The others, one of them carrying Gideon's body on the back of his horse, moved slowly up the path.

The house leaped into flames, a brilliant orange and red splash against the blackness of the night. Jerome Danton hung back, staring down at Kitty, who watched the house burning, a frozen look of horror on her face. "I know what you are thinking," he said quietly. "You are thinking how you will tell the sheriff that you can identify me as being a part of all this, but let me assure you I have an alibi ready for my defense. A charming young lady in Goldsboro will say that I have been with her all evening, so I will not be implicated in what has taken place here tonight. Don't waste your breath making any charges against me. And be thankful I did not turn my men loose on you, for it would not have mattered to them in the least that you are very much pregnant. They would have taken you like an animal, for they hold only contempt for you. So you have that to thank me for."

He paused. "And I can give you more for which to be grateful. Come to see me in a day or two, and I will offer you a fair price for your land, even though your house will be gone. You see, I am not altogether the unscrupulous scalawag you think I am."

Her cold, stiff hands opened and closed slowly. How she longed to rake her nails down his face. Had it not been covered with that ridiculous hood, she would probably have given in to the temptation, no matter what the consequences. She was about to tell him just how contemptible he was when the sound of gunfire once again split the night air. "What . . . what is that . . ." she whispered in fearful anguish. "Jacob . . . they shot Jacob . . ."

There was more gunfire, and Jerome laughed. "No, that old nigger is probably miles from here by now, running as hard as he can to get as far away as possible. That's your livestock my men are shooting, my dear, and your chickens, and anything else that breathes. They will destroy everything. We had planned to burn you out tonight before you attempted to intervene. It was all part of the plan, as punishment for harboring that outlaw."

"Oh, dear God," she murmured, her heart constricting with pain as she watched the house explode in a final shower of sparks and hungry, licking flames. Covering her face with her hands, she could watch no longer. Everything was gone now. There was nothing left. Here, in the dead of winter, her home was burned to the ground, the livestock dead. Nothing left. It was over.

"Danton. . . ." One of his men came charging back down the path, yelling at the top of his lungs. "Riders coming down the road fast. That nigger must've found help. We gotta get outa here, fast. We dropped the body. No time for that now. Gotta cut through the swamps. . . ."

The others were scattering. Jerome was swinging himself up behind the man, upon the horse's rump. They were one mount short due to the one Jacob had taken. In the illumination of the smoldering house, the flames still licking against the night sky, the two retreating forms were a perfect target. Kitty moved fast, despite the pain racking her body.

Her hands closed on the gun that had been knocked from her earlier. There was not much time to take aim, for they were moving towards the woods and the swamps beyond at a rapid pace. But she was an accurate shot, and she bore down and squeezed the trigger, and one more shot exploded in the night. A scream pierced the air. The horse kept moving. They disappeared into the forest . . . but one was injured. She hoped it was Jerome Danton. She prayed he was dead, his black soul on the way to burn forever in hell.

"Nolie . . ." Kitty gasped as another pain bore down upon her. The baby was coming. Dear Lord, the baby was about to be born. "Nolie, you've got to help me. Please. . . ." She groped her way along the frozen ground, moving slowly on her hands and knees. Reaching the old Negro woman, she looked down at the face illuminated by the glow of the raging fire beyond.

Nolie did not move, even when Kitty reached out to slap her face gently. What could she do, here, alone, with her baby about to be born? And it was cold. Oh, precious God, it was so cold. She and the baby would both freeze to death. Where was Jacob? And why couldn't she rouse Nolie? She prayed for strength to crawl into one of the shacks. There, at least, she would have shelter for the night, and she could only hope to endure the agony of labor and stay conscious to bring the baby into the world herself.

Suddenly voices pierced the air above the sound of horses' hooves crunching into the frozen earth. "The shot came from back here. Hey, over there. I see bodies."

Kitty wrapped her arms protectively around her swollen, contracting stomach, as she rolled over onto her back. The pain was swooping down like an eagle in pursuit of its prey. "Help me," she cried feebly. "My baby . . . help my baby . . ."

Someone was bending over her, smoothing her hair back from her brow. "It's going to be all right, Kitty. I'll take care of you. Trust me, please . . ."

Her eyes fluttered open. Everything was blurry, there in the strange red glow of night. Sweet oblivion begged to take her away from the nightmare, the pain.

She struggled to focus her eyes. The man's face glowed orange in the light from the burning house and barn. For one precious moment, she saw eyes the color of steel. Her heart raced. *Travis.* He had returned, just as she always knew he would. But then, painfully, the gray faded, and she saw two fiery black eyes staring down at her beneath thick brows. She saw the cleft in his chin, the neatly clipped moustache.

And she allowed oblivion to engulf her. For it was Corey McRae who scooped her gently into his arms and carried her to his horse.

Chapter Fifteen

COREY McRae stood before the marble fireplace, his hands folded behind his back as he gazed into the crackling flames. Above the mantel hung the portrait of himself that he had commissioned a Pennsylvania artist to paint. The expression in the oil-stroked face was much like the one Corey wore at the moment—pensive, cold. A look of power and confidence shone in the piercing black eyes.

The first rays of dawn streaked across the imported Persian rug, casting a bluish purple hue upon the vivid scarlets and golds and yellows. The room smelled of lemon oil. His servants knew that every piece of the fine mahogany furniture was to be hand-rubbed and polished to a glossy sheen, every day. He would tolerate no disarray in his house or in his life.

His gaze moved from the red flames to survey the beauty of this, his personal parlor. He loved the thick velvet drapes, a rich purple. He felt it gave him an air of royalty. Rich tapestries adorned the walls, and the white brocade sofas accented the splendor of the decor.

Beautiful, he thought, and smiled. This room, the whole mansion, the entire plantation, his hundreds and hundreds of acres of land, all splendid and beautiful. He had come a long way!

He was a happy man—except for two things.

He turned his gaze back to the fire, eyes glittering with anger and impatience. Jethro and Carl had not returned since he had sent them to kill Coltrane. That was months ago. There had been no word. He had sent out other men to find out what had happened, but they had returned dumbfounded, unable to learn anything. Coltrane had not returned either. That was a good sign. Perhaps there had been a gun battle with everyone killed. Fine. Then he did not risk being implicated in the killing.

He stared upwards. His other goal lay in a bed in one of the upstairs bedrooms. He wanted Kitty Wright for his wife. But he did have his pride. He was not going to beg her. He wanted her totally submissive. There were many things he wanted to do to that spirited flesh. When he took her to bed, he wanted her docile, ready to grant his every wish, no matter how strange it might be.

But he also wanted her to enjoy the pleasures of the flesh with him. He thought of the little trunk he kept hidden in the back of his bedroom closet, the devices that could bring pain and pleasure simultaneously. He would spread-eagle her upon his bed, tying her legs apart as far as possible, and then he would do the things to her body he had dreamed of doing. He would turn her on her knees, and lift her buttocks to him, and his organ would penetrate her from the rear, like an animal, and she would love it and beg him to do it again and again.

The throbbing between his legs was becoming unbearable. As much as he hated to satiate himself upon Nancy, he had to have relief. Stepping to a bell cord, he rang for a servant. Within seconds, the door to the parlor opened. Without turning around, he snapped, "Bring Mrs. Stoner to me at once."

"Uhhh, Miz Stoner, she say she gonna stay in her room till Miz Wright out of the house." The Negro servant spoke fearfully. "She say—"

"I don't give a damn what Mrs. Stoner said," Corey's voice cracked like a whip. "I want her brought to me immediately, even if you have to carry her. And you can tell her she will regret it if she does not comply at once."

"Yassuh." The door closed with a quiet click.

He began removing his clothes, tossing them carelessly upon one of the sofas. Nancy was a despicable bitch, and he was anxious for the day when he could turn her out of the mansion for good. She did, however, have a nicely shaped body, and she did give in to his every whim, wanting only to satisfy his lust. But she was quite blunt about her intentions. She was not content to be his mistress. She wanted to be Mrs. Corey McRae, and he had no intentions of marrying her.

The door opened, and he turned to see Nancy standing there, her face an angry mask, eyes glittering. She was fully clothed. Damn, he thought in exasperation, she should have known what he wanted. He summoned her only when he wanted sex. She should have put on her dressing gown. "Take your clothes off," he snarled impatiently, his eyes flicking over her. "And be quick about it."

Nancy's smile was mocking. "What's the matter, Corey? Have you become aroused over the mere thought of having that bitch upstairs? Do you actually think you are going to take out your passion on me? I have pride, you know, and I will not tolerate—"

He was across the room almost before Nancy realized he was moving. With one quick jerk of his powerful hands, her gown was ripped to her waist. He continued tearing until she stood before him naked, and then he threw her roughly to the floor.

"How dare you . . ." she cried indignantly, wrestling against his caresses as he squeezed her breasts painfully. "I won't have it, Corey. I won't let you take me this way."

He slapped her hard. Stunned, she could only lie there as he grasped her knees and yanked them apart, plunging into her roughly. He wanted only satisfaction, as quickly as possible. Kitty's breasts were the ones he wanted to kiss and suckle. Kitty's lips should be melding against his. Now he wanted only to empty himself of the gnawing desire.

Kitty . . . Kitty . . . Kitty . . . his brain screamed as he thrust his hips to and fro, pummeling his organ into the woman lying on the floor, helpless. It was not long in coming, the sudden rush from his loins that exploded to leave him spent. He opened his eyes to look down at Nancy's cold, angry face, and he wished with all his being that Kitty were lying beneath him, staring back with love.

He got up and began dressing hurriedly, mumbling to Nancy that she could go.

"Oh, I can, can I?" She leaped to her feet indignantly. "You call me in here like a . . . a servant, and then you rip my clothes off and throw me on the floor and rape me."

"Rape you?" he snorted contemptuously. "No man ever had to rape you, Nancy. You were merely angry and wanted to play games, that's all. Now go. I want to be alone."

"I will not leave until I have had my say. I want that woman out of this house. I may be just your mistress and not your wife, Corey, but I am due some respect. Everyone knows what she is. How dare you bring shame upon this house by allowing her to give birth to her bastard here? How could you do it?"

"I don't owe you any explanation for what I do, Nancy."

"I refuse to remain here as long as she is here."

They faced each other, both incensed to the point of trembling. "I want you out of my house," Corey said in a harsh whisper. "I want you out within an hour. Kitty has had a rough time of it, and she is very weak and will need much time to regain her strength. Having you about can only cause tension."

"Because I make no secret of the fact that I despise her?" Nancy gave her long hair a defiant toss. "I have my reasons."

"Yes, yes, I have heard your reasons," Corey said wearily. "Now will you just go?"

Her eyes narrowed to slits. "You are serious? You are actually telling me to leave this house after I have been your mistress all these months? How dare you, Corey McRae, to treat me so shabbily? I demand respect. . . ."

"Nancy, I never promised you anything. I did not even invite you to come here and live with me. It just happened. You kept staying and staying, and the next thing I knew, you'd had your things moved in and become a permanent fixture, or so you thought. I never had any intentions of having you stay here forever. The time has come for you to leave. It's that simple."

"Simple?" she screeched, her face contorting with rage. "You call it simple to just kick me out because that bitch lies upstairs, making herself at home? What will my friends think? How can I face people when they learn that I was tossed aside for Kitty Wright? She has caused me scorn for the last time. I won't stand for it, Corey. I swear to you I won't."

She began to pace up and down the room, unconcerned that she was still naked. "First she took Nathan from me, even though he loved me. He was only a man, young and anxious to sow his seed. Kitty gave him favors that no decent young lady would think of bestowing outside of matrimony. She drove him crazy, as only a trollop knows how to do to a man."

He walked over to a sideboard and poured himself a glass of brandy. Tossing it down unceremoniously, he whirled about to face the wide-eyed, staring woman who stood before him naked. "I'll tell you what I believe, Nancy. I believe that Nathan Collins never loved you, that it was Kitty he wanted, and with good reason. Not only is she beautiful, but she is a lady. High-spirited, I will be the first to admit, but she has a quality you wouldn't understand. I've heard other stories, too, from Rebel soldiers who were at Bentonville, and they say that Nathan was actually deserting his men, kidnapping Kitty to head for Virginia, where he thought he could escape the rest of the war. I have heard, also, that he shot Kitty's father in the back. Captain Coltrane just happened along at the right time, and he took revenge for a man he admired greatly. I believe Nathan was a coward, Nancy.

"And"—he paused to smile—"who are you to condemn Kitty for giving herself to a man outside of marriage, when you do the same thing yourself? I have also heard that your husband is not really dead, as you would have everyone believe. That makes you an adulteress, my dear, which is much worse than what you condemn Kitty for having done. She did not betray a husband."

Nancy paled. "David *is* dead," she spoke in a barely audible whisper. "I don't know who has been telling you lies, but he is dead."

"Did you ever receive official notice from the Confederate Army?"

"Many men are missing in action. No one knows what happened to them. David is dead. I know he is."

"Have you bothered to inquire? I think not. You see, my sweet, I heard that he returned home an amputee, and you were repulsed. The fool loved you, and he was heartbroken when you rejected him. So he returned to the war. It's said that he is living in the mountains with an old couple who lost their son in the war and adopted David."

"I don't know where David is," she said flatly. "Nor do I care. As far as I am concerned, he is dead."

He poured himself another glass of brandy, sipping it slowly as his eyes raked over her body. She was not unattractive, but she had a vicious, ugly way about her. He found her quite unbearable at times. "Would you please go?" he said quietly. "I wish to bathe and dress and go in to see Kitty. She will rest more comfortably when she learns that you are out of the house."

Suddenly Nancy's face contorted with pain, and tears sprang to her eyes. She threw herself on her knees before him, wrapping her arms about his legs, and cried, "Please, Corey, don't send me away. I love you. I love you more than my life. I want to marry you and be with you always. I'll do anything you want, anything you say, but please don't send me away. I can't live without you."

He felt no pity. She had known her position in his life, and he had never promised her anything. True, she tried in every way to satisfy his sexual desires, no matter how painful or vicious they might be at times. Never had she complained. It was her possessiveness that he found so difficult, that and her fanatical hatred of the woman he adored.

He set down his brandy glass, then pushed her aside and walked over to pull the ball cord. She was sobbing, beating her fists on the floor hysterically. "I won't leave you, Corey. I won't let her take advantage of you. I have to stay to protect you. You'll see I'm right. . . ."

"Yassuh?" The Negro servant, dressed neatly in the red coat and white pants that Corey required, looked at his master and not at the screaming, naked woman writhing on the floor. He deliberately kept his eyes averted.

"Get some of the women servants to pack Mrs. Stoner's belongings," Corey's voice boomed as he walked past the Negro and out of the parlor. "Have one of my carriages take her to the hotel in town and pay the bill for a week. After that, she is on her own."

"I'm not leaving!" Nancy screamed, reaching to grab the bottle of brandy from the sideboard and send it crashing into the fireplace. Glass exploded, and the servant looked to Corey helplessly.

"Drag her out of here if she keeps acting like a madwoman," he snarled. "Leave her in the main road, naked, if she continues this tirade. I want her out of this house in fifteen minutes. Is that clear?"

"Yassuh." The Negro shook his head, eyes wide with fear.

Corey hurried up the stairs, anxious to remove himself from Nancy. God, why had he allowed himself to become so involved with her? He should have seen what it was all leading up to. It would have been far better to bring in a prostitute from town.

Hugo, his personal manservant, was waiting with a tub of hot water and fresh clothing. "How is Miss Wright?" Corey demanded at once. "Has she awakened yet?"

"Sir, I spoke with Dulcie in the kitchen a short while ago." Hugo spoke with the distinct "white" pronunciation that Corey had ordered him to master, though the tone was still slurred with the Negro accent. "She said Miss Wright was stirring a bit, but still asleep from the laudanum the doctor gave her. She said she was going to fix her something to eat and take it into her and try to get her to wake up. She said the doctor said it was important that Miss Wright eat and get her strength back, 'specially with the baby to be nursed."

Corey had stripped off his clothes and was about to sink down into the deliciously warm water, but he stopped to glare at Hugo and snap, "She will not nurse that baby."

"But, sir—"

"Don't argue with me, man. You go to Dulcie at once and tell her that baby is not to be put to Miss Wright's breast. Find a wet nurse. I'm sure there are plenty of women about with nursing infants. I will tell the good doctor myself that I do not want Miss Wright nursing her baby. Now do as I say."

Hugo nodded and turned to leave, but Corey called out once again, "And the baby is not to be taken in to her until I have seen her. Tell Dulcie I will personally take the tray in myself. Do you understand?"

"Yes sir." Hugo nodded and hurried out, closing the door behind him, but not before Corey heard Nancy, still screaming.

Damn, he cursed, slipping into the water. He wished they would hurry up and get that woman out. When he went in to see Kitty, he did not want that infernal shrieking in the background. Giving birth was a joyful experience for a woman, he supposed, no matter what the circumstances, and she would naturally feel a fondness for the person who visited her first and told her about her newborn. He also reasoned that she was going to be extremely grateful to him for saving her life by bringing her here. It was a step towards his goal.

But there would be no nursing of the infant, he thought with disgust as he lathered his body with the fragrant soap. No, he would not see another man's child suckling upon the breast of the woman he intended to marry. Besides, the sucking might cause her breasts to sag. He wasn't too sure about such things, and he wasn't going to worry about it. He just wasn't going to allow it. The milk would dry up. A wet nurse would be found. Everything would turn out all right, and it would be his lips that devoured her nipples hungrily, not some illegitimate brat sired by a man who had known what he had yet to know. No, he just wouldn't have it.

Hugo returned in time to wrap his master in a thick towel and pat him dry. A devoted servant, he was paid well, and was eager to remain in favor. He said that he had given Dulcie the instructions, and she would leave the tray for him to take in to Miss Wright. She was sure a wet nurse could be found. Corey was also relieved to hear that Nancy Stoner had been removed from the mansion—still screaming, half-dressed, her belongings piled messily in the back of the carriage. Thank God, she was on her way to town and out of his life.

He dressed carefully, wanting to look casual, to create the right atmosphere for his meeting with Kitty. He wore dark trousers and decided on a pale blue muslin shirt, left open at the throat so that the hairs on his chest would show. Let her see that he had a good body. Let her see him as a real man. Splashing just a hint of cologne about his neck, he decided that he gave the appearance of a warm, friendly neighbor, seeking only to rescue a damsel in distress.

"You look real nice, sir," Hugo commented, not used to seeing his master dressed so informally, even about the house. He always wore silk shirts and frock coats, obviously enjoying his station in life.

"Yes, I think so," Corey agreed as he looked at himself. "We must not overwhelm Miss Wright, Hugo. Like all females, she loves the finer things of life. However, if they are flaunted before her, she lets her pride build a wall about her. We must be very subtle."

His servant looked confused. "I don't think I understand, sir. Miss Wright, she going to be here just a little while, till she gets well. So why you talking like you are?"

Corey whirled around angrily. "And why are you talking as you are, you fool? I spent a great deal of money bringing in tutors to teach you how to talk, so people would know that Corey McRae would not stand for an ignorant nigra to be his manservant. 'Miss Wright, she,'" he mimicked. "What kind of grammar is that? You know better, Hugo. Don't let me hear you make such a blunder again."

Hugo hung his head. "Yes sir. I'm sorry, sir." He spoke very clearly, trying not to drawl. He knew Mr. McRae hated the accent he had been unable to lose completely.

Corey turned back to the mirror, decided to unbutton his shirt one more buttonhole. "As for how long Miss Wright stays, I will let you in on a little secret, Hugo. I hope she remains forever. I would like to marry her. That is why I wanted Mrs. Stoner out of the house. The two do not get along, and Miss Wright would feel uncomfortable in her presence. We want to make her feel secure here. Since her home was burned down, she has nowhere to go. I want you to make sure that all of the servants give her every consideration and courtesy. Is that clear?"

"Oh, yes sir, yes sir," he said quickly, bowing in his anxiousness to please. "We'll all take very good care of her. You can be sure of that. As for Mrs. Stoner, if you will forgive me for saying so, sir, I'm happy she's gone. That was one woman that just couldn't be satisfied. She was always complaining about something or yelling at somebody. We are all glad to see her leave. But I think I should tell you, when the carriage was driving off, she turned around and screamed out to tell you that she would get even with you if it was the last thing she ever did. She said you'd pay for hu . . . hu . . ." He shook his head, embarrassed. He had studied so hard, wanting to please his master, but there were still words he couldn't always remember.

"Humiliate," Corey laughed scornfully. "That's the word, Hugo. Mrs. Stoner thinks I have humiliated her by forcing her to leave my home. I'm not worried about her threats. She should be thankful I allowed her to stay here and enjoy my hospitality as long as I did. She served her purpose well while she was about, but I was tiring of her. It's just as well that circumstances changed. Now I have the woman I really want."

"You really think she'll stay?"

Corey pursed his lips as he looked at himself in the mirror. He was attractive, rich, and powerful. Kitty Wright was beautiful, poor, and helpless. The only thing he had to overcome was that infernal stubbornness of hers. Perhaps the baby was the answer. She would have to realize that Travis Coltrane was not coming back, and she was left with a child to raise alone. She was extremely vulnerable. That was very much in his favor. "Yes, Hugo," he said with a little smile. "I think she will stay."

They left the bedroom together, stepping out into the wide hallway that ran down the center of the second floor. Corey slept on the third floor in a special room when he was with a woman, and it remained locked when not in use. The servants had explicit orders that they werc not to go into that room, ever, for any reason. He would keep it up himself, he had told them. And, of course, there were whispers and speculation about the "secret" room.

The polished mahogany floor smelled of lemon oil, and the crystal chandeliers along the way displayed the lavender-and-pink floral wallpaper attractively. There were marble statues along the sides, imported from Italy. Corey found that they impressed guests. He was relieved that no one asked him who the statue was supposed to be or who the sculptor was. Either they already knew or did not want to expose their ignorance by asking. He had no idea, himself.

"Which room is the baby in?" Corey whispered as they moved towards the end of the hall and the room where Kitty had been placed.

Hugo stopped before the door just opposite their guest's. "In here." He turned the knob, and walked in to find a Negro woman sitting in a maple rocker by the window. Her dress was open to the waist, and one large breast hung out, her fingertips holding the nipple to the sucking lips of the infant she held in her arms.

"I'll take the baby now," Corey said, turning his eyes away from the scene he found so disgusting. Women's breasts were so lovely, some of them, and he could find a much better use for them than feeding babies. He never liked such a spectacle and knew he could never have endured seeing Kitty's breasts bared for any lips other than his own.

"He ain't through suckin'," the wet nurse protested.

"You heard Mr. McRae," Hugo snapped, and she immediately pulled her nipple back and handed the infant to Hugo. All the servants on the estate knew that, next to Mr. McRae himself, Hugo was the highest authority. He had the power to fire a servant at will, or order one punished should he or she choose the lash rather than be discharged.

The baby smacked its lips a few times, pursing them as though ready to cry. Instead, the eyelids fluttered a few times, then closed in sleep. Hugo breathed a sigh of relief. He knew how much this moment meant to his master, carrying the baby in to Miss Wright for her to see it for the first time. It wouldn't do for the child to be crying with hunger. He turned to his master and held out the baby.

Corey looked down, eyes flashing with resentment. Another man had sired this child, a man who had tasted the sweetness he had yet to savor. He would forever have to be on guard to hide the revulsion he felt for the infant.

"Get the tray from Dulcie," he said to Hugo as he walked across the hall. Bring it up in about ten minutes. I'm going to take the baby in to her myself. Open the door for me."

Hugo twisted the knob, then turned on his heels and hurried away. Corey stepped inside the room, smiling at the lovely creature lying asleep on the huge, canopied bed. No one had ever used this room before. Perhaps he had subconsciously intended it for Kitty all along. The wallpaper was patterned in white and yellow roses, the furniture was of mellowed pecan, and a soft, pale blue carpet covered the floor. The spread and canopy were a deeper shade of blue, and the curtains that hung upon the doors to the front balcony were designed of the finest imported satin and velvet, the color matching the bedcoverings.

He leaned over to stare at the beautiful creature before whispering, "Kitty . . . wake up, my dear. Kitty . . ."

Her long lashes fluttered, her head moving slightly. He spoke her name again, and this time her eyes opened, frightened, bewildered. She could only stare at him silently as she tried to remember where she was, what had brought her to this place. Then her gaze went to the bundle Corey McRae held in his arms. "My baby," she cried, holding out her arms. "My baby . . . oh, dear God, is it all right?"

"Yes, yes, he's fine," Corey chuckled, amused at her delight. He handed the infant to her, and she moved to her side, opening the blanket to examine fingers and toes.

"It's a boy." He forced pride into his voice, proud of the way he was carrying the moment. "A fine, healthy boy. The doctor says he probably weighs seven pounds, at least. And all his fingers and toes are there. I counted them."

Kitty looked up, bewildered. "You did? You mean you were here when he was born?"

"Well, not in the room," he laughed. "But I brought

you here and summoned a doctor, and when the baby was born I was right outside the door, pacing the floor. As soon as he was cleaned up, they handed him to me, and I had to check him over and be sure, myself, that he was all right. He's perfect, Kitty, just perfect, and quite beautiful."

He was surprised he hadn't choked on his own lies. He had waited out the birth downstairs in his parlor, sipping brandy and hoping the baby died. He hadn't laid eyes on him till a few moments before. For all he knew, it had six toes on each foot. But Kitty was looking at him appreciatively.

"My son," she breathed in wonder, kissing the baby's forehead. "Oh, I can't believe it, Corey. I can't believe he's really here in my arms."

"Well, he is." He pulled up a chair and sat down to cross his legs and watch the happy new mother fondling her newborn son.

"Do you suppose he's hungry? He keeps smacking his lips. I suppose I should try to nurse him . . ."

"Oh, no." He spoke too quickly. Her head jerked up to look at him quizzically. He cleared his throat self-consciously. "The doctor says you are much too weak, Kitty. You had a hard time delivering. He does not think you should try to nurse the baby, that it wouldn't be good for you or him. I have already found a wet nurse."

She protested, "but I want to nurse him myself. I'm his mother."

"Don't you want to do what is best for him? And what about yourself? Don't you want to recuperate quickly so you can care for him?"

"I suppose you're right," she sighed. "But it is disappointing."

She closed her eyes, and the horror of the night before came flooding back. Gideon shot. Her home and barn burned, the livestock and chickens slaughtered. Why? A tear slipped down her cheek, and Corey saw and reached to brush it away.

"I know you're remembering what happened, Kitty," he whispered, "but you have to try and forget. It's over now. I only wish I could have gotten there sooner. Jacob came here. He knew it was closer than riding into town. I got there as fast as I could get my men together. I was afraid something like that would happen, because I heard that Gabriel was slipping in to see his mother."

"Nolie!" Kitty's eyes flashed open. "What about Nolie?" She looked at him beseechingly, saw the truth in his face, and then shook her head from side to side as the tears came.

"I'm sorry. She died there on the spot. I had her brought back here, and the doctor checked her and said she probably died of a heart attack. It was a terrible thing for her to witness seeing her son gunned down. Jacob took it pretty hard. I've housed him in one of the servant's cabins, and he's resting. I have instructed Dulcie to take care of the funeral. She's holding up quite well."

"Why?" Kitty whispered bitterly. "Why did any of it have to happen? And why did they burn me out? Now I have nothing . . . nothing at all. Oh, if only Travis would hurry and come back. I have to find him, somehow, if I have to go to General Sherman myself. Travis should know he has a son . . ."

Corey gritted his teeth, forcing himself to remain silent. He reached over and patted her shoulder and said, "Kitty, everything is going to be all right. I will look after you and the baby. Don't worry. Just concentrate on getting your strength back, because your son needs you. I won't let you suffer anymore."

Her violet eyes flashed. "Why should you feel an obligation to help me, Corey? I have always detested you and you know it. You took my workers away from me behind my back, sending your man over to lure them away until I had no one left but Jacob and Nolie. You were trying to break me. So why do you pretend to want to help me now?"

He leaned forward, hoping his expression looked sincere. "I regret that we started off our relationship the way we did, Kitty. I was wrong. I admit it. When I saw what those . . . those animals did, destroying what you had worked so hard to build, something just snapped. I wanted your land and was willing to do anything to get it, and now I wish I had just left you alone. If I hadn't hired away your help, maybe those men would have thought twice before riding in the way they did. You would have had some protection. I am truly sorry, and I hope you will forgive me. I hope you will let me make it up to you, Kitty, by helping you and your son."

He forced himself to reach out and touch the downy fuzz on the baby's head, a move he hoped looked tender and adoring. "I guess I feel as though the little tyke is partly mine now, since I helped bring him into the world. If we hadn't gone back there and found you, you would probably have both died. So, since I helped get him here, it is only fitting and proper that I help provide for him until his real father comes back." He lifted his eyes to meet hers. "That is, if you will let me, Kitty."

"Of . . . of course," she stammered. "I'm very grateful to you, Corey. We would have died out there in the cold. But as soon as I'm able, I will be on my way."

"On your way? Where will you go? You're burned out, my dear. You have no roof over your head. No, you must stay here for a while at least. There is no other way."

She was confused, her body sore and weak. There had to be another way. She could not live here in the house with Corey McRae. Travis would not like it.

It took all the strength she could muster to make her tone sound fierce and determined. "I appreciate your kind offer, Corey, but as soon as I'm able, I'll find a way to take care of my son by myself."

He suppressed a smile. He saw the way her chin stubbornly jutted upwards. The girl had spirit, and how he was going to enjoy it in his bed. "Whatever you wish, Kitty," he murmured. "But please remember this is your home for as long as you desire."

Hugo's soft rap upon the door could not have come at a better time. Corey told him to enter, which he did, carrying a tray of food, with Dulcie behind him. Reluctantly, Kitty handed over the baby. She told the Negro girl that she was sorry about her mother.

Dulcie blinked back the tears. "Yes'm, I knows you did a lot fo' her. She's at rest now. Gone to join the angels with Gideon. He weren't all bad, no matter what folks thought."

"Take care of my son." Kitty patted the precious bundle one more time. "I'm going to name him John Travis Wright—John after his grandfather, and Travis for his father, and he'll bear my family name until his father returns to give him his rightful name."

"Oh, yo' daddy would like that, Miss Kitty. Pity he ain't here to see his grandson. He'd of loved him just like you do. And when his daddy come home, he gonna be so proud—"

"Hugo, set the tray up for Miss Wright," Corey interrupted, unable to listen to the conversation any longer. "She needs to start getting her strength back."

"Yes, I have more responsibility than ever now," she said, removing the cover of the tray to look down at the hot buttered grits and the slab of juicy fried ham. There were lard biscuits and homemade apple jelly, and a glass of milk. Her stomach rumbled. It had been quite a while since she'd had fare such as this. She looked at Corey appreciatively. "I do thank you. I want you to know that. And I won't burden you any longer than necessary."

"My dear, you will never be a burden." He got to his feet, motioning to Dulcie and Hugo to take their leave. "If you want anything, anything at all, you have only to ask. My servants are at your command. My home is your home."

He was almost to the door when she called out to him, almost reluctantly. He turned to meet the violet eyes. "Corey, what about Nancy? How does she feel about me being here? It's none of my business, of course." Her voice trailed off.

"My dear, Nancy no longer remains in this house. You need not to be worried about her ever again. I don't intend to concern myself with her, so neither should you."

He went out and closed the door behind him. Kitty ate ravenously, then lay back upon the pillows and stared up at the blue canopy over her head. She had never thought she would see the day she would be in Corey McRae's house, but then she had not counted on being burned out of her own. She knew Jerome Danton was responsible, but how could she prove it? Who would believe her, despised as she was in this county?

"Oh, Travis, where are you?" she whispered, tears stinging her eyes. If only he would return. Together, they would rebuild, and Danton and his hooded cowards would not dare ride against them. Travis would stand up to him or anyone else who tried to intimidate them. And when he did return, he would take vengeance on all who had hurt her.

But where was he? It had been months. She would have to send word to General Sherman himself, beg him to find Travis and tell him he now had a son. That would bring him back, she was sure. She would write the letter as soon as she felt up to it, and she would give it to Dulcie.

For all Corey's graciousness, there was still something sinister about him, something she did not trust. For the moment, she was forced to accept his hospitality. But she intended to remain on guard against whatever trickery he might have in mind.

She wanted to see her baby again. She wanted to hold him close and whisper to him how much she loved him. She had to tell him about his grandfather, and about his father. Where was the bell cord to ring for Dulcie? Dulcie would bring little John into her and let her hold him awhile longer. But she was so sleepy, so tired, and her eyes fluttered a few times, then gave way to the deep sleep of exhaustion.

Corey McRae stood outside the door, peeping through the crack, for it was not quite closed all the way. He had heard her anguished whispers, seen the fight and spirit in her beautiful eyes. It would be a real challenge, but he would win. It would take cunning and maneuvering, but by God, he was going to win. Kitty Wright would be his.

Chapter Sixteen

KITTY stood on the veranda that swept across the front of the mansion. The bare trees lining the circular driveway stood like naked sentinels against the cold, bitter wind, fiercely struggling to stand tall against the onslaught. The flat land was barren, stark, but when spring came, the land would burst with growth. There would be cotton, and tobacco, and corn. Corey McRae would make the plantation thrive.

Pulling her robe tighter, Kitty stared down the road until it disappeared over a slight rise. There was not a rider to be seen this morning. But then, few people would be moving about in the chill, especially on Christmas Day. That did not stop Kitty from hoping, and she stood watching and praying as she had every morning for the past ten days. Four of the days had been spent in bed, supposedly to regain her strength after the birth of the baby. She had felt fine and wanted to get up sooner, but neither Dulcie nor Corey would hear of it. So she had spent the time composing a letter to General Sherman, begging him to get in touch with Travis and tell him about the birth of his son. She had given the letter to Dulcie. And she had waited, praying for an answer.

Something must have happened to Travis. He would have returned otherwise. She could not make herself believe that he just did not love her and had mustered out of the service and gone on back to Louisiana. He would have come by one more time to try and talk her into going with him.

Where was he? Dear God, he had left Goldsboro the end of March, and here it was Christmas Day. Was he dead? Somehow, she would have known when his dear heart stopped beating. There would have been a sudden awakening in the middle of the night, or a cold shroud engulfing her during the day. Yes, she would have sensed it if Travis had died. He had to come back. He had to.

Corey had been kind, almost too kind. What was he after? He knew how she felt about her land, that she would never sell, and he knew that she had no intention of marrying him. So far, he had mentioned neither the purchase of her land nor her becoming his wife. He seemed to adore little John. Kitty was frankly puzzled. Corey McRae was not the sort to be nice to anyone without a reason. She remained on guard, knowing that sooner or later she would discover what he was up to.

She knew she had to leave. But where could she go? There were no buildings left standing on her land except the tiny servants' shacks down near the swampy area. She would go home to one of the shacks, she thought, suddenly brightening. There was Jacob. He would remain loyal. He would chop wood to keep a fire going, and he would hunt for food. And always, she would continue to pray for Travis' return.

It had been a long time since she had gone into town, but she knew the gossips were probably having a time talking about how she was living in Corey McRae's house. Nancy would have made sure they all knew about it. They would be saying she was his mistress now, and Kitty could not tolerate that kind of talk. No, she could not remain here any longer.

Tomorrow, the day after Christmas, she would leave, taking the baby and Jacob.

"Missy?"

She whirled around, her face lighting up in a happy smile as she recognized Jacob standing in the doorway to the veranda. "Jacob, Jacob, oh bless you. Why haven't you come sooner?" She ran across the porch to throw her arms around the old Negro. "I've sent messages to you time and again. . . ."

He stood there twisting his old hat in his gnarled hands, staring down as he mumbled, "I tried to come, missy, but they turnt me away at the door, said Mistah McRae didn't want me around. Even Dulcie wouldn't let me in. She say she'd like to, 'cause she knowed you wants to see me, but she say Mistah McRae won't let no field nigger in his house, jest the ones what's trained proper to come inside. I only got in today 'cause Dulcie, she feel sorry fo' me 'cause it's Christmas. I brung somethin' fo' the baby."

He reached in the pocket of his overalls and pulled out a delicately hand-carved wooden dog. Kitty took it from him, turning it over and over in her hands as she stared at it in wonder. "Why, Jacob," she breathed in awe. "It's an exact replica of Killer, Poppa's faithful old hound. Why, you did a beautiful job, and little John will always treasure this. I'll tell him about the old dog, how he went to war with Poppa. Oh, this is wonderful." She kissed his wrinkled old cheek, blinking back tears.

"Next to you, Miss Kitty, I think Mastah John loved that old dog better'n anything."

She shook her head abruptly. There was no need to look back. The past held only pain. There was the future to think about. Forcing a smile, she said, "Jacob, I've decided that it's time for us to leave here and go home."

He jerked his head up. "Home? Miss Kitty, they burnt you out. You ain't got no home."

"I've got my land, Jacob. Remember, Poppa always said as long as you have land, you're never poor. You've always got something. So we're going home. I'll live in one of the shacks till spring, or till Travis returns. We'll get by. I have you to help me. Thank God, I have you."

Slapping his hat against his knee, he stomped his foot and shouted with joy. "We's goin' home. Yes'm, we's goin' home. And you don't have to worry about nothin', 'cause I'll be there to look after you till the captain comes home. Praise the Lord."

"Now come with me." Kitty took his hand and pulled him through the veranda doors and back into the warmth of her bedroom. A fire crackled brightly in the fireplace. The thought of going back to what really belonged to her, no matter how bleak, made her spirits brighter than the flames dancing in the hearth. Home. Her home. She was taking little John and Jacob and going home to wait for Travis.

She ran to the bell cord and gave it a hard yank. "I want you to see the baby, Jacob. I think he looks a little like Poppa, but there's no denying he's Travis' son. He has that look about him, somehow, and you know he's got quiet strength, just like his father. And he's a big baby, too. He's growing every day."

The door opened quietly and Dulcie stood there, looking at the two of them with condemnation in her dark eyes. "Mr. McRae is not going to like you being here, Jacob. You promised you wouldn't stay but a minute."

"Bring in the baby and let me worry about Mr. McRae," Kitty said quickly. "It's Christmas, Dulcie, and I'm very happy. So stop your frowning. Be happy for me, too."

Dulcie looked uncertain, then said haltingly, "Well, the baby was asleep last time I looked in. Mr. McRae wants you to start dressin' for dinner. The turkey's almost done, and—"

"Dulcie, bring in my son." Kitty was growing impatient. She was tired of living under Corey's rules. The baby was hers, and she would see him when she liked. She had put up with a lot, and had bit her tongue in silence when the servants kept the baby from her. But she was going home in just another day. Corey could get angry if he wanted. It did not matter now.

Dulcie whirled around, her long cotton skirt swishing. She disappeared through the doorway, and Jacob whispered, "Maybe I better go, missy. No need to cause trouble now. I ain't got no business here. I can go on over and start choppin' wood and gettin' things ready."

"Where have you been staying?"

"Right here on Mistah McRae's place, in one of the servants' cabins. They're right nice, too. Evah one's got a fireplace. Some even got stoves. Funny how evahbody calls 'em servants' cabins now instead o' slave shacks."

They both looked up as Dulcie came back into the room, holding the baby in her arms. Kitty took him and cradled him against her bosom and stared down in wonder and love at the precious cherub. "You are beautiful," she whispered. "Just like your father."

"He gonna have dark hair, too," Jacob said, peering over her shoulder to stare down at the tiny baby. "My, my, he's a fine 'un, Miss Kitty. You sho got good reason to be proud. And the captain, he gonna be proud, too, when he comes back."

"I wrote General Sherman." Kitty rocked the baby, smiling down at him. "I told him about the baby, and I asked him to either get in touch with

Travis or let me know how I might contact him. Dulcie took the letter to town. We should hear something any day. Don't you think so, Dulcie?"

Dulcie didn't speak, and Kitty looked at her sharply. "You *did* send that letter, didn't you?" She did not like the look on Dulcie's face.

"Oh, yes'm, I did. I give it to somebody who say they take care of it. I did. I sho did."

She was nervous, Kitty noted. She was forgetting to talk in the proper way that Corey required of all his servants. For the first time, she began to suspect that maybe the letter had not been sent, after all. Well, she would take care of that. As soon as Jacob took her and the baby home, she would write another letter, and she could certainly trust Jacob to send it. This time she would have him take it to General Schofield, or whoever was in charge of occupation of Goldsboro. Still, she did not like thinking that Dulcie could not be trusted.

Jacob was still beaming over the baby, and Kitty was laughing with delight because little John was waking up and looking around curiously, his rosebud mouth pursing expectantly.

No one heard Corey McRae enter the room. Only Dulcie saw him, and she retreated quickly, scooting around him to get out the door as she saw the anger flashing in his eyes. "Just what is going on here?" he cracked, teeth gritting at the sight before him.

"Oh, Corey, good morning and merry Christmas." Kitty glanced up to look at him only briefly before returning her gaze to her son. "Jacob came to bring a gift, and he hasn't seen the baby. Oh, look, Jacob, his eyes are closed again, but he's smiling."

"My momma always tol' me when a baby smiles when he's a'sleepin', it's the angels talkin' to 'em," Jacob said, completely captivated by the baby.

"Oh, what a sweet idea." Kitty looked at him in

wonder. "And I can see that it could very well be true. Babies come from heaven, don't they?"

"Kitty, dinner is almost ready." Corey's voice lashed out again, this time stronger, and there was no denying that he was quite angry. "I would appreciate your dressing. We do have the baby on somewhat of a schedule, you know, one that the doctor suggested. It does not call for fondling the child at this hour. I believe he is supposed to be asleep. As for Jacob, I think you both know my rules about field hands coming into my house—"

"Jacob is not your field hand," Kitty replied, resentment moving through her body, making her back stiffen. "He is my friend, and he came here to wish me a merry Christmas. As for your so-called schedule, John is my son, Corey, and while I appreciate all you have done for us, I will make the decisions where he is concerned."

Jacob had moved back, uncomfortable. Kitty noticed and told him he could go. "I will send for you in the morning. You go and make things ready." He nodded and hurried from the room, stepping wide so as not to come close to Corey McRae.

Without turning, Corey kicked his leg out behind him to slam the door shut. "What 'things' is that nigra supposed to make ready, Kitty?"

She walked over to the rocker before the fireplace and sat down, still cradling the baby tightly against her bosom. "I am leaving tomorrow morning, Corey." She made her voice light, airy. "I have imposed upon your hospitality long enough. Jacob is going to get everything ready for us."

Corey chuckled as he walked to stand between her and the fireplace. He wore a red velvet coat and pants of dark blue. His shirt was white and ruffled at the throat and cuffs. Kitty could not deny that he was attractive, dressed so dandily, however personally unappealing she found him.

"And where do you propose to go, my dear?" he asked quietly.

"Well, back home, of course."

"Have you forgotten that your home was burned? You have nowhere to go. We are having a bitter winter, my dear, and you have your baby to consider. Stay here with me, accept my generosity, at least until spring, when the weather will turn warmer."

She shook her head vehemently. "No. I must leave at once, Corey. Please don't think me unappreciative, because I will be in your debt forever. But the time has come for me and little John to leave this house. Everyone will be saying that *I* am your mistress, that I took Nancy's place, and I certainly don't want Travis hearing any gossip like that when he gets back."

Corey ground his teeth together, trying not to lose his temper. "But where will you live?"

"They didn't burn out the cabins at the edge of the swamp. They are small, but livable. John and I will live in one, and Jacob will live in the one next door. We'll get by till spring, and Travis may return any day now."

"Travis is dead."

It was as though a bucket of cold water had been thrown in her face. Kitty almost dropped the baby as she struggled to her feet. "How dare you say such a thing? He's not dead! I would know if he were dead. He's sick or wounded or . . . or he has duty and cannot get away. There is a reason."

"Nine months?" he scoffed, moving to the bell cord and giving it a yank. "Be reasonable, my dear. No soldier has to stay on duty nine months after the war is over. He could have come to you if he had wanted to. Perhaps it is time you faced reality. People are beginning to snicker behind your back. The servants even whisper that you are perhaps tetched. It's becoming a joke, Kitty. Wake up, my dear, and realize what is obvious to everyone else around you. Travis Coltrane is not coming back. You have a baby to worry about, a baby without a father. You have land, but no decent house. The taxes on your property will soon be due. How do you propose to pay them?"

She was staring at him, stunned, open-mouthed. Dulcie appeared. Corey had only to snap his fingers and motion to the baby, and the young girl hurried to take little John from Kitty's limp arms, then left as quickly as she had come.

"Well, have you thought of these things, Kitty?" Corey snapped impatiently. "How can you be so selfish? It's not just you to be considered now, you know. There's a helpless baby involved. He can't help it that he has a mother who is too stubborn to face reality. Are you going to kill him trying to prove a point?"

"*Kill* him?" she echoed, horrified.

"Yes, kill him. Do you think he can survive down there in a shack by the swamp? You have no milk for him, and if you leave, I will certainly not send his wet nurse with him. She's needed here for other infants on the plantation. How will you feed him?"

Her hand touched her breast gingerly. "I had milk. I saw it. Perhaps if I start nursing him now, it will return. . . ." She spoke as though in a trance.

Corey moved to take her in his arms and crush her against his chest. "You don't have to leave here, Kitty," he whispered fervently. "Marry me. I want you for my wife. I will accept your son as my own and give him my name. Everything I have will be yours and his."

"No!" She cried, horrified, using both her hands to

push against his chest. "Travis will return. I know he will. He's the man I love."

"You'll learn to love me," he cried, reaching to entwine his fingers in her long, golden hair. Bending her head back, he pressed his face closer, whispering, "How long since a man's lips burned against yours, my dear? How long since the fires of passion moved through your veins? I can make it all happen."

His lips came down, bruisingly. She struggled but was no match for his strength. She began to beat upon his back with her fists, but he pushed her backwards till her knees buckled and she fell across the bed. His body immediately moved to cover hers.

"Don't try to fight me," he breathed hoarsely, raising his mouth only slightly. She could still feel his lips against hers. "Fight me, and I will only have to hurt you, Kitty, and I don't want it like that. I just want to hold you and touch you and kiss you . . . tell you how much I love you and must have you. I know your body is still sick from birth, and I won't take you, not now. But I can have this much. Oh, God, Kitty, let me love you."

A groan came from deep in his throat as he closed his mouth over hers once again, hungrily, tongue thrusting inside to probe about. She began to struggle and fight, terrified, but he quickly caught both her wrists and held her arms above her head with one hand while his other slipped inside her gown to fasten about her breast. He squeezed gently, then roughly, and she heard his gasping noises as though he were experiencing deep pain.

His fingers moved from her breasts long enough to push the skirt of her robe upwards, baring her thighs. Then he was moving himself against her, and she could feel his swollen organ moving to and fro. His fingertips moved to her nipples, gently, then roughly and painfully, and she could only lie there beneath him helplessly while he kept working his swollen flesh rhythmically against her. He worked his hips faster, faster, and the whimpering sound from deep in his throat grew louder, more agonized.

Suddenly his mouth left hers and he was throwing back his head to scream. He gave several more short jerks against her, then rolled away. Sickened and frightened, Kitty shriveled against the pillows, trying to get as far away from him as possible as she stared in horror at the stain spreading on his pants about the crotch. He had actually brought himself to pleasure by his gyrations. What if she were not still physically incapacitated from childbirth? He would have raped her.

Leaping off the bed, she held her robe together and cried, "I hate you, Corey McRae. You're a monster. You pretended to be kind to me and my baby, and this was what you were after all along. Nothing can prevent me leaving now. I'll never be taken in by your lies again, never."

His breathing had become normal, and he lay there for a moment longer, regaining his composure. Lord, he thought, even if it had been only a poor imitation, it had been good. He had actually thrust himself against that sweet flower between her legs. He had almost tasted the nectar. And those breasts, oh, those wonderful mounds of glory, how good they had felt. He would never tire of the fruits from her basket. He was sure of that.

He stood up, straightened his coat, then saw the stain and realized it would be necessary to change before going downstairs. Undaunted, he faced Kitty and smiled. "I intend to have you, my dear, as my wife. You are trying my patience, I must admit. But all my waiting will be justified."

"You are mad," she cried hoarsely. "I'm leaving here

today, at once. And don't you try to stop me." She looked about wildly, spotted the heavy candlestick beside the bed, and grabbed it and held it above her ominously.

Corey merely laughed. "Oh, you don't have to resort to violence, my sweet. The only violence you and I will ever share will be in our bed, and it will be sweet pain that we enjoy. I promise you this. Now, suppose I go and change, and you put on one of those lovely dresses I ordered for you from Raleigh, and we will have a nice Christmas dinnner. I have an exquisite gift for you, something I think you will really like."

"I am leaving here today, Corey."

He gestured helplessly, shrugging his shoulders, the play of a smile on his lips. "Very well. I will send word to Jacob that you and the baby are leaving this afternoon, and I will have Dulcie pack your things. I will even have one of my carriages take you to your little shack in the swamp."

She stared at him suspiciously, biting the corner of her lower lip as her eyes narrowed thoughtfully. She set the candlestick back down on the bedside table. "Don't try to trick me, Corey."

"You have my word." He bowed graciously. "You are free to go any time you wish. I love your spirit, Kitty, and I live for the day when I'll have that same spirit in my bed for always and always."

"That day will never come." She turned her back on him. "Leave now, please. Send word to Jacob, and send Dulcie in to help me. I won't take anything I did not come with, which were the clothes I wore."

"Those rags?" he scoffed. "I had them burned. No, Kitty, you will take everything I have given you. Burn *them*, if you wish, but you will take them. I will drop by to see you in a few days to see how you are getting along."

"I never want to see you again."

"Is that any way to talk to the man who saved your life and the life of your baby? Is that the kind of gratitude that you Southern ladies have? My, my, Kitty. Your rudeness shocks me."

"I am grateful for your help, but now I see that it was all a trick. You were merely waiting for my body to heal so you could take me at your will."

"If that were true, I would have had you that first night you stumbled onto my porch in town begging for help. Wake up, Kitty, and realize a few things. I could have taken you then. I'll be waiting for you to come to your senses."

She continued to stare at the wall before her, anger boiling. Finally the door closed, and she whipped her head about, relieved to see that he was gone.

Pacing the floor furiously, she kept returning to give the bell cord a vicious yank, silently cursing Dulcie for not answering the call. Now that Corey had shown his true colors, she could not get out of his home fast enough.

There was a hesitant tap on the door. Kitty snapped, "Come in," and Dulcie entered slowly, head down, shoulders slumped.

"Thank goodness you're here," Kitty told her anxiously. "I want to take as little as possible, Dulcie, but I wish to leave here at once."

"Ma'm, please understand." The girl took a deep breath, still not lifting her eyes. "I works for Mistah McRae, and I has to take my orders from him. He say fo' me to take you into the nursery, and a tray o' Christmas dinnah gonna be brung in. He and Gertrude gonna pack yo' things. When the carriage is all a'loaded, we take you and the baby downstairs. Please don't say nothin'. Mistah McRae gonna take it out on me if it ain't done this'a way."

Kitty shook with her anger. She did not want to

take all the clothes that Corey had bought for her. When he had given them to her, she had protested, but he would not listen. She wanted nothing from him. She wished it had not been necessary for her to accept his hospitality in the first place. All she wanted was to take little John and leave, but as she looked at Dulcie, saw the tears slipping down her cheeks, she knew that the young girl was frightened to death of her master.

"All right, Dulcie." Kitty sighed and moved towards the door. "Only because of you will I go along with the way Mr. McRae wants it, but please, don't pack any more than you have to in order to get by. I want nothing from that man."

"He say pack it all," she whispered, starting to move towards the huge pecan wardrobe closet. "I gotta do what he say."

Suddenly Kitty stamped her foot and the young Negro whipped her head about to stare at her with wide, frightened eyes. "Why do you do it? Why do you stay here with a tyrant? He has a fit if you don't talk the way he wants you to. If he had heard the way you've been talking in here just now, he'd be angry. There are surely other places you can go, Dulcie, other jobs. You're free now. The war is over, remember? You never have to be a slave again. Take your freedom and live your life the way you want to live it. A lot of good men died to give you that freedom. Don't abuse it by staying here with a man who treats you as though you're still in chains, fearful of the lash."

Dulcie shook her head slowly from side to side as the tears continued to slide down her brown cheeks. "You don't understand, Miss Kitty. It ain't . . . I mean, it *isn't* all that easy fo' us now. The white folks around here, they hates us 'cause we ain't . . . isn't, I mean . . ." Sobs shook her body as she trembled in her frustration.

"Please, Dulcie, speak the way you want to. It doesn't matter to me. Just tell me what it is you want me to know." Kitty touched her shoulder gently.

"They hates us 'cause we ain't slaves, no mo'. They wants to see us starve and die, so they can sit back and say, 'see there? You wanted to be free. You was tickled to death when the Yankees set you free. Now you a'starvin' and a'dyin', 'cause you too dumb to look after yo'selfs. You was better off as slaves.' And they sit back and laugh at us, Miss Kitty. That's what they do. So I'm a'tryin'. Mistah McRae, he pays better'n anybody about. He might be mean sometimes, but they all mean, all white folks, 'cepting ones like you, and they ain't many of you. I *has* to do what Mistah McRae tells me to do. I *has* to."

Opening her arms, Dulcie threw herself against Kitty's bosom as she sobbed convulsively. "When Captain Coltrane returns, Dulcie," she whispered, close to tears, "we'll have a place for you. He'll make our land prosper, and we'll take you in with us. I promise. I wish I could take you with me now, but I'm not even sure I can feed myself and my son, much less Jacob. I can't ask you to share poverty with me."

Dulcie straightened, embarrassed that she had let herself go to pieces. "I'll be all right, missy," she sniffed, dabbing at her eyes with the hem of her apron. "Don't you fret none about me. I does all right. Mistah McRae, he's fine as long as he ain't crossed, and me and the others make sure he ain't crossed. He's awful mad now 'cause you leavin', so let me go ahead and get you out of here 'fore he really get mad. He scares me when he's mad."

"Well, he doesn't scare me." Kitty gave her what she hoped was a reassuring smile. "And don't let him frighten you, either. Just remember, you'll have a home with me one day. Until then, just endure and keep your chin up. Life will be better for all of us. You'll see. Now, you do what you must do, and I will go in the nursery and wait with John till you are ready for me to go."

Dulcie watched the beautiful golden-haired woman leave the room. She could feel only pity for her. Now she was spirited, confident that her beloved captain would return. Dulcie prayed that Kitty would never find out that Corey McRae, suspecting that Kitty was writing to General Sherman, had ordered Dulcie to give the letter to him. Dulcie had cried silent tears as she watched the letter burning to ashes in the parlor fireplace while Corey stood grinning down triumphantly. If Captain Coltrane lived, he had received no word about the birth of his son. Corey McRae had seen to that.

And Dulcie prayed to God to forgive her for her deceit. But there had been no other way, no way at all. She had to think of her own survival.

Chapter Seventeen

IT was February. The ground was frozen, and the wind beat against the thin walls of the cabin like an unrelenting enemy, determined to penetrate and destroy. Kitty sat before the fireplace holding baby John tightly against her. It was cold, oh, dear Jesus, so very cold. To get out of the range of the fire's warmth meant instant chill. She dared not move.

John sneezed, and Kitty wrapped him tighter in the blankets, snuggling him close. Corey had provided for him well, and her pride took a great blow when she had to accept his gifts. Were it not for his generosity, there would be nothing for the baby—no clothes, no food, nothing. They would have perished.

And still no word from Travis. He was not coming back. That fact became more evident with each passing day. It screamed out at her in the black chill of night. Travis is not returning. He is dead. Or else he never really loved her. She was alone, except for the baby.

John had a cold. She touched her lips to his forehead. It was warm, very warm. Oh, God, she prayed silently, don't let my baby get sick. There's no money for medicine or a doctor. Spring, please hurry and get here. Let the warm sun kiss the lands. Give the earth life to grow food and crops. There had to be a way. There had to be. She had come too far, suffered too much, to be defeated now. Jacob was out in the woods hunting. He had to find food—anything—a rabbit, a squirrel, and how wonderful it would be if he found a fat turkey, or even a deer. The last of the meat from the wild hog he had killed two weeks before was gone. There was nothing left but swamp roots, which, when boiled with water, gave precious little nourishment. Corey had been more than generous to send over a milk cow. The pompous white overseer who delivered it grinned maliciously when he relayed the message: "Mr. McRae says you can be proud and starve if you want to, but he thinks enough of the baby that he don't want *him* to suffer. He says he don't think you're stubborn enough to see your own baby starve."

Corey was right. She would not let her baby starve. She accepted the gift and sent a message of appreciation, adding that as soon as she was able, she would repay him, with *money*, she emphasized. That had brought another snaggle-toothed grin from the overseer.

The baby slept at last, his breathing hoarse and rasping. Reluctantly she laid him in the little wooden cradle Jacob had made. Tucking the blankets about him, making sure he was near the fire, she poured herself a cup of swamp-root tea and sat back down before the crackling flames.

The sound of hoof beats crunching into the frozen earth made Kitty jump from her chair. Gathering her shawl tightly about her shoulders, she went to peer through a crack in the boarded-up window. A rider was approaching, and it was impossible to tell who it was just yet. He came closer, and finally a frown creased her forehead as she recognized Jerome Danton sliding down from his mount. How dare he have the nerve to come here? He was removing a large burlap bag tied to the saddle. She noticed that he walked with a slight limp as he moved towards her door.

She opened it against the wind, almost stumbling, not wanting him to pound and awaken the baby. As she faced him, her eyes were cold. "How dare you come here?" she lashed out. "How dare you come on my land? If Jacob were not out hunting with my father's gun, I'd put you in your grave this minute, you marauding murderer."

"Now, Kitty." He grinned, hazel eyes warm and friendly. "I come in peace. At least let me enter and say what I've come to say, or do you prefer that the shack get cold with all this wind blowing in?"

"I don't want you in here," she hissed, hands on her hips, feet apart, eyes glistening with hate. "It's your fault that I live here in this shack. It's your fault I have no livestock, no chickens, no food. The death of a dear friend of mine is on your soul, too. Gideon's mother. Have you heard by now, or do you even care?"

"Kitty, if I didn't care I wouldn't be here," he spoke softly, his gaze imploring her to hear him out. "May I come inside, please? I have no intentions of harming you. I swear before God."

"I doubt that God puts any more credence in you than I do, but you may come in." She stepped back and reluctantly motioned him inside. "Just make your visit brief, please. I have no need of visitors, particularly one whom I despise. Now, what is it you want?"

He stood there staring at her, then reached out and touched her long, golden hair as though wonderstruck. "You are still as beautiful as ever, Kitty. And your eyes. God, they are the color of the wild iris that bloom by the river in the spring. I have never seen a woman as lovely as you."

She jerked her head away from his touch, bristling with anger. "Don't you touch me. Now what do you want, Jerome Danton? Get to the point."

Without being asked, he sat down in one of the

two chairs before the fireplace. Looking towards the wooden cradle, he murmured, "I heard you had a son. May I see him? I know he must be as handsome as his mother is beautiful."

"No, you may not see him. He is asleep." Kitty sighed impatiently. "Now will you tell me what you want? The last time you came, it was to murder and destroy, but the sun is shining, so I doubt you've come here to do me any harm. I hear your kind rides at night, using the dark as a cloak to hide your cowardice."

His eyes flashed as he snapped, "Yes, we do ride at night, Kitty. Someone has to protect the South from the uppity niggers and the vulturous carpetbaggers. They're out to pick us clean. Thank God I am financially secure, and they can't touch me, but I will certainly do what I can to help others. Including you."

"Me?" she laughed bitterly. "What have I got that anyone could want? You see around you what I have in the way of worldly belongings."

"You have your land." His voice was low, ominous. "And it's some of the finest land in Wayne County. I offered to buy it from you months ago, remember? And you refused to sell."

"And I refuse to sell now."

"But you may have no choice. What about your taxes?"

She blinked, bewildered. "I paid my taxes, with the money the government owed my father. No one can take my land."

"You paid your taxes through 1864, my sweet. It is now 1866. Your taxes are due for 1865. How do you propose to pay them, if this is all you have?" He swept his arm in the air dramatically. "Now will you face reality and sell your land to me before it's taken for taxes?"

"No," she said quietly but firmly. "I'll find a way.

I've always managed before, and I'll manage again. Now, if that's why you have come, you may leave."

He shook his head wearily, stared into the fireplace pensively for a few moments, then lifted his gaze to look at her with misery. "Kitty, I'm truly sorry about what happened that night. You must believe me. I tried to warn you about Gideon coming here, but you wouldn't listen. That nigger was giving everyone fits, stealing and destroying. He had the whole countryside in an uproar. We had to take matters into our own hands."

"You took the law into your hands and killed him."

"He tried to run."

"You meant to hang him."

"Isn't that what they usually do with thieves?"

"Yes, after a fair trial by law, not by a bunch of hooded night riders."

"We had to do something fast, to set an example for these other niggers who have gotten out of line. Don't you see?"

She shook her head. "You murdered that boy. And what about the others who rode with him? Jacob has never heard a word from his son, Luther. Did you round them all up and shoot them, too?"

Jerome sighed, knowing it was going to be quite difficult to make her see things his way. "No, we did not round them up and shoot them. They hightailed it out of the county, we heard, the very next day. Having their leader killed scared the hide off of them, and they took off. Last we heard, they were robbing and plundering in South Carolina. Fine. Let South Carolina worry about them. We still got our problems here."

"Jacob brings me tales he hears from other Negroes. I hear you still handle your problems the same way, riding in the night, with robes. Tell me. Why do you burn crosses?"

"Because it frightens people. Niggers are superstitious fools. We ride in, burn a cross, give them a warning, and most of the time it works. They don't give us any more trouble. We had a nigger in town just last week, and he made a sassy remark to Mrs. Stoner. We rode out to his house that night and drug him outside and laid him beneath that burning cross and gave him ten lashes with a whip, and we won't ever have to worry about him again. He was on the way to being a real troublemaker, and now he's as polite and humble as can be. The way he ought to be."

Kitty gave an unladylike snort. "Is that the way I'm supposed to be, now that you've burned me out? Polite and humble?"

"Kitty, my men did that. They wanted to rape you, remember? And I stopped that, but I didn't have anything to do with them burning you out. They did that as an example to other white people who might hold sympathy for the nigger and give the renegades shelter. I'm sorry it happened."

"So am I."

They stared at each other silently for a few seconds, and then Kitty said, "Well, if that is all you have to say, I would prefer that you leave."

"We call ourselves the Ku Klux Klan." He ignored her remark. "There are groups by the same name spreading all over the South to protect our people. No one knows the identity of the members. If they do, they know better than to expose them."

She got up and walked over to the log bin, picked up a piece of wood, and tossed it onto the fire. New sparks went dancing up the chimney as the fresh wood crackled beneath the flames. "If you are trying to frighten me, you are wasting your time. I have not told anyone that I know who the ringleader was that night. I want no trouble with the townspeople. I want only to be left alone. When Captain Coltrane comes back, he'll settle the score with all of you. I won't have to. But I wish I hadn't missed, that night. Quite frankly, Mr. Jerome Danton"—she turned to glare at him, fists clenched—"I wish I had killed you."

"You almost did." He grinned wryly. He lifted his right leg. "I had just leaped to my horse when you fired. The ball caught me in the bone of my ankle. Had I still been standing on the ground, you would have hit me in the back and probably killed me. As it is, I have a permanent limp. The surgeon said he could not remove the ball. It's in the bone, so I'm partially crippled."

Her expression did not change. "I am sorry you made it to your horse."

Pursing his lips, he folded his hands in his lap and stared into the fire thoughtfully for a moment, then said, "I heard you were living with Corey McRae as his mistress. What happened that you have resorted to this poverty?"

"I was never Corey's mistress," she shouted. "He took me into his home that night you and your friends burned me out. I was in labor, and he found me not too far from this very shack. My baby was born in his house, and I stayed there for two weeks, then left to come here. I was never his mistress. Who would dare to spread such a lie?"

"Nancy Stoner," he laughed shortly. "She said you pushed your way into his life, same as the way you did Nathan Collins. She's something, that Nancy."

"She's a vicious, lying schemer."

"Oh, she has her good points. She works for me now, in my dry goods store. True, she has a nagging tongue, and I tire of listening to her, but there are times when she can be, ah, most enjoyable."

"I can well imagine, but I prefer not to hear about those times, if you please."

"Of course. Gentlemen do not discuss their personal lives, do they? Forgive me. Now, I came here to apologize to you, Kitty, and offer you help."

"I don't need your help. I'll manage fine, thank you."

"Can you pay your taxes?"

"Don't worry about my taxes," she screeched, forgetting once again to keep her voice quiet so as not to wake little John. "My life is no concern of yours."

Slowly he got to his feet and moved to where she stood. Before she realized it, he had pulled her into his arms and was kissing her soundly. Releasing her, he laughed down and murmured, "I want your life to be of much concern to me, Kitty. I've always found you desirable. I would like permission to court you."

She was stunned. He kissed her again, and this time, when he released her, she raised her hand to slap him, but he caught her wrist and held it tightly. "Don't. As lovely as I find you, my dear, I won't stand for a woman slapping me. I would hate to bruise that flawless skin of yours. Now, I know this has come as a surprise, but I am quite sincere. I should like to court you and, after a proper time has passed, I will expect you to marry me. We'll build a fine, fancy house right here on your land, if you so wish. I have plenty of money, as much, I would say, as Corey McRae. You and your baby will never want for anything, and while I fully intend to breed you often with children of my own, I will do my best to accept your son as mine. I think I have made you a generous offer."

He limped over to the burlap bag, and Kitty watched, as if in a trance, as he reached into the bag and started pulling out various foods. A smoked ham, several dozen eggs, some potatoes and dried beans. There was even a new woolen shawl for her and a heavy blanket for John. "This is only the beginning, my dear. I'll return in a few days, after you've had time to think over my generous offer, and I will bring more. Is there anything you particularly need? What about material for dresses? I just received a good shipment from the North."

"No." She shook her head from side to side. "Nothing. I . . . I don't want these things. Take them and go, please." She pressed her hands against her temples.

"I'll go for now, sweet, and give you time to get used to the idea of my courting you. Life will be good to you again, you may be sure. If you should need me for anything before I return, just send Jacob for me and I'll be back as quickly as possible."

He opened the door and a blast of cold air filled the shack. The fire flickered dangerously low against the onslaught. "One more thing," he said against the roar of the wind. "Be glad I hold no hard feelings because you left me crippled, woman. But I'll make you pay for it when I have you in my bed." With a good-natured laugh, he closed the door tightly behind him.

Kitty stood for long moments, staring at the closed door, her mind whirling. Then she sat again before the fire. She was rocking the baby when Jacob's familiar call sounded against the wind. He came in swinging a dead turkey by its feet, crying jubilantly. "We gonna have meat on the table tonight, missy. It took me most of the day to track this old bird down, but I done it. I—" His voice trailed off as he saw her expression. Ordinarily she would have shared his joy. Now it was as though she had not even heard him.

His eyes went to the burlap bag, still lying on the floor, its contents scattered where Jerome Danton had tossed them. "What's this, missy? Was Mistah McRae here? He been botherin' you again? Lord, if he'd just leave you alone." He shook his head wearily.

"It wasn't Corey McRae, Jacob. It was Jerome Danton."

"Danton?" The old Negro's eyes bugged out. "What'd he come here for? How'd he muster up the nerve to come here?" His old body was trembling with anger as he came to the fireplace and bent to stare down into her face. "Missy? What'd he say to make you look like that?"

"He told me that the taxes are due now on my land," she answered in a dull voice, her eyes staring straight into the flames. "He told me how desperate I am, and how he wants to court me and eventually marry me. Why do they torment me this way, Jacob? Why can't they just leave me alone?"

He sat down cross-legged, propping his elbow on the threadbare knees of his overalls, his hands framing his black face. "Miss Kitty, these men what got money, men like Mistah McRae and Mistah Danton, they wants a wife to be mistress of all they got. You's a beautiful woman. I bet you's the most beautiful woman in these parts. I hear the menfolks talking, missy, saying how pretty you are, so don't you look at me like that and shake yo' head like you thinks I'm talkin' foolish. I knows what I'm talkin' about. And fo' all of Mistah Danton's and Mistah McRae's money, they'd be mighty proud to have a fine lookin' woman like you fo' their wife. That's why they keep coming around. But don't you let them worry you none. The captain, he gonna come back. Just you wait and see."

Kitty forced a smile. "I have to start thinking of a life without Travis, Jacob. I must stop living in a dream world. There's not just me to think about now. There's little John. He has only me to look after him, and I have to consider his welfare first."

Jacob rocked back. "You ain't thinkin' about marryin' either one of them two, is you?"

"No, no, of course not. But I do have to start thinking about a life without Travis. I can't lose my land. I'm going to have to go into town and talk to the tax collector and see just how much I owe and what can be worked out. Maybe I can go to the bank and borrow what I need against next year's crop. I'm not going to accomplish anything huddling before this fire. Will you stay with John tomorrow while I make a trip into town?"

"Well, how you think you gonna go? Walk? It's miles to town, and don't tell me you gonna stand on the road and wave some farmer down, 'cause soon as they see it's you, they gonna keep right on goin'."

"I'll get a ride same as you do, Jacob, with your people. Some of the Negroes go into town every day. I'll just stand at the road till someone comes by. I need to go into town because I'm going by General Schofield's office and try once again to get a message to Travis by way of General Sherman."

"It's starting to sleet outside. The weather is gettin' mighty bad. I don't think you'll be able to go for a day or two. You'd catch the fever standing out in the sleet, missy, and then how could you look after John if you's sick in bed? I don't know much about tendin' babies."

"Then I will wait until the weather clears." She started rocking to and fro, intensely, as though the energy and spirit were building inside.

Jacob cleaned the turkey with water boiled in a kettle over the fire, then ran a spit through the bird and watched dutifully as it roasted over the flames. Kitty cooked some of the dried beans. Their dinner was tasty and filling for a change.

Jacob bundled up in his old frayed jacket and went outside to milk the cow before bedtime. They had housed the animal in one of the empty shacks, to keep it from freezing. He returned with only a quarter of a bucket and said, "I guess ol' Betsy's just too cold to worry about giving milk."

"She isn't being fed properly," Kitty commented worriedly. "If I can borrow some money at the bank,

I'll stop by the feed store and get some feed for her. We've got to have that milk for John."

The wind howled through the long night, and the glass in the windows rattled, even though boards were nailed across on the outside. Kitty thought the roof was even shaking. She could hear the pelts of ice hitting the tin above, and she huddled down in the covers, holding little John against her body for warmth. How she wished she had been able to nurse him. Now her milk was long dried up, and they had to depend on the old cow. She stared into the darkness of the barren room, the fire illuminating the sparse furnishings with an eerie red glow.

The baby stirred, and she held him tighter, kissed his forehead. It was warm. She prayed it was from the blankets heaped upon them, the heat of her own body. "Don't let him be sick. Don't let anything happen to my baby," she whispered into the darkness. "He's all I have."

And her tears splashed down onto his head, and she kissed them away, feeling more alone and lost than ever before.

As sleep came, her last whispered murmurings were to Travis. "We need you," she cried softly. "Dear God, Travis, we need you so badly."

Chapter Eighteen

JACOB, his face grimacing with disapproval, sat rocking little John before the cracking fire. His yellowed eyes were watching Kitty as she bundled herself up against the stabbing chill that waited beyond the closed door of the cabin. "Miss Kitty, I just don't think you ought to go. You don't know how long you gonna have to stand on that road before somebody come along, much less how long it gonna be till somebody comes by what will give *you* a ride."

She was tying a shawl tightly about her head and shoulders, and she peered worriedly at the baby. "I have to try, Jacob. It's been almost a week since Mr. Danton came, and I've got to borrow some money from the bank and see about those taxes. And I've also got to have some money to get a doctor out here to look at John. I don't like the way that cold keeps hanging on. He wakes me at night, breathing so raspy, and you've heard him cough. It's turning into a bad cold, and I know he needs medicine and more knowledge than I have."

Jacob sighed, knowing it did no good to argue with his mistress when she had her mind set. He, too, would be very glad to see a doctor walk through that door. Little John was sick. If Nolie were here, he grieved, she would know what to do.

Ready at last, Kitty walked over to where Jacob sat

and bent to kiss the baby's forehead. "He's so warm," she murmured worriedly. "I'll hurry, Jacob. I'll try to be back this afternoon. It shouldn't take me long at the bank, or at the tax office, and then I'll go find a doctor. I'll pay him to drive me back out in his buggy."

"You gonna ask about the captain?" Jacob raised his eyes to meet hers anxiously. "You got another letter ready to send to Gen'ral Sherman?"

"Yes, to both questions." Her smile was forced. "Now I really have to leave, Jacob, so I can get back quickly. I'll stop and buy a few things we need. How is the cow doing? Does she have any feed at all?"

"Mistah McRae sent some hay over last week—"

She was almost to the door, but she whipped her head about. "He did *what*? Jacob, you didn't say anything to me about it."

"I figured you had enough on your mind, what with the baby sick, missy. And I knows how mad you gets whenever Mistah McRae sends anything over."

She bit her lip, decided to be on her way rather than discuss the situation. "I'll be back as soon as I can," she said, opening the door to face the icy blast of wind.

She had wanted to make her trip the day after Jerome Danton had made his visit, but the weather had taken a decided turn for the worse. Sleet continued to fall, covering the world about them with a thin sheet of ice. It was as though an artist had dipped his brush into liquid crystal, to paint everything about them into shimmering glory. Kitty acknowledged that the scene before her was beautiful, but it was also ominous.

Stepping carefully among the icy ruts, she looked at the stark, frozen ground, thinking what a dismal sight it actually was. It was as though the earth had never yielded a living growth of any sort, and never would again. She felt as though the whole world were dead, and she the only survivor.

Finally she reached the edge of the empty, lonely road, and as she stood there waiting, she could feel the cold all the way to her bones. A long time went by, maybe two hours, as she stamped her feet and jumped about, trying to keep her blood warm. At last she heard the welcome clopping sound of hooves breaking against the icy ground, and a carriage came into view. She began to wave frantically, and as it moved closer, she recognized the Frank Thompson family.

He leaned forward to stare down at her with squinted eyes. "Well, Kitty Wright. What in tarnation are you doing out here in the freezing cold, standing by the side of the road?"

"I need a ride into town, Mr. Thompson," Kitty pleaded. "My baby is sick, and I've got to find a doctor."

Frank's wife, Adele, stiffened beside him, her hawk nose turning skyward as she snapped, "I'll not have that white trash ride in our carriage, Frank. Get along now."

Frank rubbed at his beard thoughtfully. "Now, Adele, Kitty ain't never done us no harm, and you heard her say her baby's sick. What would it hurt for her to ride in the back of the wagon?"

"Mrs. Thompson, I don't have a horse or a mule, and I have to get to Goldsboro. Please, just let me ride in the back." She was begging, for she was not too proud to humble herself when it came to her baby.

Adele glared at her, the hate and disgust shimmering so strongly that Kitty took a step backwards, shocked to see such a look in the woman's eyes. "You think we'd ride into Goldsboro with the likes of you in our carriage?" she screamed. "Everyone knows what you are, Kitty Wright. Trash! White trash! If your bastard baby is sick, it's God's punishment on you for your sins. It wasn't enough you got a fine man like Nathan Collins killed, then got yourself in the family way by the man who murdered him. You had to flaunt your sin by staying here, unmarried, and letting everyone know what you are."

Frank touched his wife's arm, gave her a shake. "Adele, that's enough."

She shook free of his hold. "No, that's not enough. She had to give refuge to a nigra outlaw, and the Klan burned her out, and she still didn't learn her lesson. Get along now, Frank. I don't want to be seen talking to the likes of her."

"She helped us once when one of our boys was sick, Adele," Frank said, his voice sympathetic. "Seems the least we could do is give her a ride into town. It's awful cold for her to be standing out here this way."

Adele's face had turned red with rage at Frank's reference to their son. "If she's so smart with helping the sick, let her help her own," she shrieked. "As for helping Paul, she only saved him to go off to war and get killed by a Yankee, maybe even by the hand of her traitorous father, or her Yankee lover. I'll not have it, I say."

She jerked the whip from her husband's hand, catching him off guard. Kitty thought she meant to crack the lash over the horses' backs to speed them on their way, but, just in time, she realized the woman was about to bring it down on her. Stumbling in her haste to get away, Kitty fell to the ground. She felt the flesh ripping from her palms against the ice, just as the zinging leather whip landed only inches from her face.

"Woman, have you gone mad?" Frank Thompson was wrestling with his wife, yanking the whip from her roughly. "When we get back home tonight, you got a beatin' comin', for sure. The very idea, you taking a whip to that poor girl. You crazy or something?"

"I'll not ride with her. I'll get out of this wagon first. What will my friends think? Nancy Stoner is my third cousin, and she told me how this . . . this harlot ruined her engagement to Corey McRae. And don't you threaten me with any beating, Frank Thompson! Now get those horses moving."

Kitty picked herself up from the ground with as much dignity as she could muster. Her hands hurt fiercely, and so did her knees. She knew she must have scraped them also on the ice, but she wasn't about to let either of them know she was injured. Looking into Frank's eyes, she said coolly and evenly, "Thank you for your concern, but you had best ride on. I don't want to cause you any more trouble."

Then her violet eyes glittered with sparks of angry red as she turned them upon his wife. The woman actually shriveled away from her in sudden fright. "I guess I'm particular about who I ride with, anyway." Kitty's voice was as icy as the world about them. "So I prefer to wait for another carriage. As for your cousin, Mrs. Thompson, I think you should know she was never engaged to Corey McRae, and he had no intentions of marrying her. She was his mistress. She lived with him in sin. He told me so himself."

"That's a lie," Adele screamed indignantly, as Frank popped the whip and the horses began moving forward. She turned all the way around in the seat to keep yelling. "White trash like you always try to run down decent folk. I know what you are, Kitty Wright. You're not fit to live among decent folk."

Kitty stood there, shaking her head slowly from side to side, shoulders slumped. She would have liked to say more, maybe do a little name-calling herself, but, by God, she was not going to let them reduce her to their level.

Another hour or so passed while Kitty paced up and down in the cold. If someone didn't come soon, she knew she would have to return to the cabin and try again the next day. And time was so precious. Then, a blessing, the sound of horses clopping along broke the dead silence. This time an old Negro was holding the reins, as he sat on the wooden seat of a rickety old wagon. She recognized him as a worker on the McRae plantation. She waved her arms frantically, and when he stopped, she asked for a ride into town. He held out his brown hand to help her up into the wagon.

On the ride into town they talked about the workers Kitty knew. This one, Ben, told her that everyone was fine. Dulcie, he said, would be happy to have word from her, but she would be upset to hear that the baby was sick. "And so will Mistah McRae. Dulcie say he misses that baby somethin' fierce. I heard her tellin' my missus about it. She say he told her that baby makes him want to get married and start havin' young'uns of his own. She say he got real sad when you took him and went home. She say Mistah McRae miss you, too, Miss Kitty."

"That's kind of him," she murmured, a bit surprised to hear that Corey admitted to missing little John. It touched her, but then, some men, no matter how strong or powerful, were moved by babies. Perhaps Corey McRae was one of these. Maybe there was truly another side to him.

"I'll be comin' back soon's I get some supplies," Ben said as they got nearer to town. "I can wait around and take you back."

"I'm hoping to find a doctor and bring him back with me, Ben. I've got to. I'm worried about John. It's kind of you to offer, though, and if you're still around and if I can't find the doctor, I'll accept your offer gratefully. But don't wait on my account, please. You have your obligations to return to Mr. McRae's as soon as you finish your business in town."

He gave her a big grin, displaying skillfully carved wooden teeth. "The boss man wouldn't mind me waitin' up a bit to help you out, Miss Kitty. Naw, suh, he sho wouldn't." Then he laughed as though he knew a secret.

The old Negro got down off the wagon and moved around to help her. Thanking him once more, she looked about and saw that the town really did look deserted.

It was chilly inside the tax collector's office. A thin, bespectacled little man peered at her with irritation from where he sat huddled before a potbellied stove. "Yes, what do you want?" he asked impatiently, wiping at his runny nose with a soiled handkerchief.

"Are you the tax collector?" she asked, ignoring his rudeness.

"I work for the tax office, yes. What do you want?"

She told him her name. "I want to inquire about the tax on my property, formerly the John Wright farm. Now it is mine. I was in here last spring to pay what was owed."

Without comment, he flung aside the carriage wrap that covered his bony legs, exaggerating every movement to let her know that he resented the intrusion. Let him be annoyed, thought Kitty. He was being paid to do a job, and she was a customer.

Moving through a swinging gate, he stepped behind a high counter, then bent out of sight. Kitty moved to stand beside the warmth of the stove. After a few moments, he straightened, holding a large, thick book, which he dropped on the counter with a loud plop. Licking the tip of his right forefinger, he began to flip through the pages. She wondered who he was. He was not the same man she had dealt with on her previous visit, and she had never seen him in town before.

"Ah, here we are." He was actually smiling, his eyes sparkling. "Yes, yes, indeed. Miss Katherine Wright. Your property is listed as delinquent. I will check the other list to be sure, but from what I see here, you are in arrears for your '65 taxes. . . ."

She had moved to the counter and was about to ask the amount when the little man's eyebrows shot up in surprise. "Oh"—his fingertips flew to his lips. "Your tax certificate has already been sold, Miss Wright."

"Sold?" she cried, trying to twist the book around so she could see the records for herself, but his hands gripped the book tightly. "Let me see. This is my property. Who would dare buy a tax certificate on my land? And why wasn't I notified that the taxes were due?" She was babbling almost hysterically, her heart pounding wildly in her chest.

She slapped her palms down on the countertop in frustration and anger. "Just what does this mean? Has my land been sold out from under me? How can you get away with such a thing when I was not notified and given a chance to pay the taxes myself?"

"Miss Wright . . ." He gave her an indignant glare while blowing his nose again. "Delinquent tax notices were posted on the door of the county courthouse, according to law. After the time limit, as set by law, expired, anyone could come in here and pay your taxes and therefore own your tax certificate."

"But what does this all mean?" She shook her head from side to side, bewildered.

He slammed the book closed with a loud clap. "It means, my good woman, that someone else has the tax lien against your farm now, and not Wayne County. You negotiate with them, or, after a certain period of time, as set by the law, they will be able to take your property from you, just as we could have if someone had not bought the certificate."

"You keep saying 'the law,'" she snapped indignantly. "Why wasn't I notified?"

"We posted the notice on the courthouse door." He

looked at her as though she were simple-minded. "That is all that is required. We don't have to go out and knock on your door, Miss Wright, and beg you for money. If you did not see the notice, then that is your problem, not ours. We followed the legal procedures to the letter. So you have no recourse against this office. If you have the necessary funds to buy your certificate, in addition to whatever interest your certificate holder will require, then you will have your land back, free and clear and unencumbered. Until then, there is a lien against your property. I suggest you get in touch with that person. I can do nothing more for you."

"Jerome Danton." The words escaped her lips in a barely audible whisper.

"What did you say?"

"Jerome Danton," she repeated. "That . . . that carpetbagger from Virgina. *He* bought the tax certificate, didn't he?"

"No. No, it wasn't Mr. Danton. Come to think of it, I believe I do recall him coming in and asking about your property, but the certificate had already been sold. Yes." He nodded vigorously. "I do remember him coming in. Got real mad, he did, when he found out someone had beat him to it. Wanted that land real bad, he did."

"Then who—"

"Corey McRae."

"Corey . . ."

"Yes, Mr. McRae." He smiled. "He's the one you have to see. You and about twenty others. Bought up land right and left, soon as those on the list reached the deadline. Yours was the first. I remember it all clearly now. Wanted your land worse than Mr. Danton did."

Kitty stormed out of the tax office. The nerve of Corey McRae to pay the taxes on her property and not even have the decency to tell her about it! And why wasn't she notified about the list and told about the law? Jerome Danton could have been gentleman enough to explain the situation to her. She had been confined to her little shack with a small, sick baby, unable to get out and tend to such matters. All the while, they had been working against her, conspiring to take her land. Well, they would not succeed, by God. No one was going to take her land.

She entered the small bank with the force of the winter wind. Spying a heavyset man seated behind a desk at the rear, she marched straight through the room, while he watched her with curious interest. "My name is Katherine Wright. I want to borrow money, using my farm as collateral. I need to pay off a tax certificate at once. I need additional money as well, to tide me over until I can get a crop in this spring. I—"

He held up his hand for silence and got to his feet slowly. He had bushy gray eyebrows that wiggled when he spoke. "Miss Wright, let me interrupt you before we continue to waste each other's time. This bank will not loan money on land that has a tax lien against it."

"But that's why I want the money," she sputtered. "To pay off the tax lien so the land will be free and clear!"

He gestured helplessly. "I'm sorry, truly I am, but that is the policy of this bank and all other banks. When property has a lien against it, ownership is not clear. Then we cannot lend money on the land involved."

"Then . . . then what am I to do?" She spoke more to herself than to the bushy eyebrows.

"I would suggest that you deal directly with the person who purchased the tax certificate. There is nothing we can do for you here. I'm sorry."

Kitty did not remember stumbling from the bank. She did not know how long she had been standing outside in the frigid weather. She was unaware of anything for a long time. Finally she came out of her stupor. Her body began to tremble with cold. General Schofield. He would help her. He would send a wire to General Sherman, and they would find Travis. And even if Travis no longer loved her—even if he had *never* loved her—he would help her for the sake of their son. It was the only hope she had.

Sergeant Jesse Brandon nearly fell backward in his chair when Kitty Wright walked through the door. Her face was the color of the ice that covered the world outside, and her eyes were glassy. "I . . . want . . . to see . . . the general," she managed with chattering teeth.

"God almighty, you look awful. You sick?" He leaped to his feet, grabbed a chair, and helped her lower herself into it.

"Please," she whispered, her head weaving. "I must speak to the general . . ."

Jesse hurried to the cot in the corner and grabbed a blanket. Once he had it tucked about her, he went to his desk and got a bottle of whiskey. Pouring some into a tin cup, he handed it to her, watching as she began to sip it.

He started talking, explaining that General Schofield had already left Goldsboro. "And I'm leaving, too, in just a few weeks now. I'm mustering out. Federal marshals will be coming in to see that things run smooth, Miss Wright. But is there anything I can do for you right now? Godawmighty, you look awful sick to me."

She raised a weak hand to wave away his concern. "Do you know that I have a son, Sergeant Brandon? Captain Coltrane and I have a son . . . a son that he doesn't even know about. You've got to help me find him. They . . . they're trying to take my land away from me. They already burned my home. My son is sick. I have no money . . ."

Raising blurry eyes to the anxious face before her, she cried, "*Please* find Captain Coltrane for me, Sergeant."

He looked frightened. "Right now, I'm going to find a doctor—"

"No." She clutched his sleeve. "Just find Travis."

She gulped down the whiskey. It felt good, warming. Jesse quickly refilled the cup, and she began to drink again, mumbling. ". . . find Travis and everything will be all right. He won't let them do this to me and our baby."

She continued to babble while Sergeant Brandon stood by helplessly. Corey McRae had issued strict orders that no wires were to be sent to either Sherman or Coltrane. The order had not been easy to follow, what with General Schofield about, but the few times Miss Wright had sent messages, he had been able to dispose of them safely. He, and a few others who were secretly on McRae's payroll, knew that men had been sent to kill Coltrane. They had not returned. That was months ago.

Jesse knew, also, about the two wires that Coltrane had sent to Kitty. One had asked why Kitty had never written to him. Coltrane's wires had been destroyed, and Kitty did not know he had sent them.

Now Jesse stood staring down at the pitifully ill woman, and he felt ashamed. The two must have loved each other. But Corey McRae had money and plenty of it, and being on his payroll had made Jesse's life a hell of a lot easier. He had enough saved to return to Pennsylvania, buy a nice farm, and make a new life for himself and the family he'd left behind. Besides, he soothed his conscience, this girl would be better off in the hands of a man like McRae, who had plenty of money. She'd live a good life. Why, she should be pleased to live in that fine mansion. The only one around anywhere near as rich was that Danton fellow's. He didn't know too much about him, but there was a strong rumor he was head of the group of night riders called the Ku Klux Klan. Well, that wasn't Jesse's problem. Not now. He, by God, was going home. He'd never give the South another thought.

Kitty looked as though she were going to faint. Corey would want to know that she was here, sick, and demanding a wire be sent to Sherman or Coltrane. He was anxious to get her out before someone came in and heard her. Questions might be asked about why she had not received replies to the messages she claimed had been sent.

He left her there, huddled in her chair, holding the tin cup with both hands as she sipped the whiskey. Stepping out into the gray, cold day, he felt snowflakes touch his cheeks. Staring upwards, he shivered and pulled his coat tighter about him. Those were snow clouds, all right. A good three or four inches would be dumped before nightfall.

How in the heck was he going to get word to Corey McRae? He couldn't leave Kitty alone, and it was a long ride out there to the country. Maybe Corey was in his office in town. Ducking his head against the wind, he moved quickly down the street.

The office was closed and locked. McRae came to town only a few times a week, and on a day like this, Jessie was not surprised that he hadn't bothered. He looked about, scratching at his stubby chin, wondering what to do next. He spied the old Negro again, the one who had been hanging around outside his office. The fellow had obviously followed Jesse down here. "What the hell you doin' following me, nigger?" he snapped, taking out his frustration on the frightened man who stood twisting his hat, shuffling nervously.

"I sorry, but I's worried 'bout Miss Wright. She okay?" Ben asked cautiously.

Jessie appraised him suspiciously. Corey had told him about the loyal old Negro who took care of Kitty, but Jesse had never seen him. If this was the one, he didn't want him to know anything. "She's fine," he said, the anger leaving his voice. "Just fine. You can go home now."

"Yassuh, yassuh, I'll do just that." Ben's head bobbed up and down as he backed off the boardwalk and down the steps into the street. "I told her when I give her a ride into town that I'd be glad to take her home, but she say she gonna try to find a doctor to take her back. Then I see her come out of the bank. She looked mighty upset, so I wanted to make sure ever'thing was all right, befo' I went back to Mistah McRae's."

"Mr. McRae?" Jesse's eyebrows shot up with interest. "You work for Mr. McRae? You aren't the old nigra that works for Miss Wright?"

"Naw, suh, I works for Mistah McRae. My name's Ben. You talkin' 'bout Jacob. Miss Kitty, she say Jacob stayin' home with her baby, little John, and little John he sick, and that's how come she gonna try to find a doctor."

Jesse leaped from the boardwalk to the street, clutched the old Negro's shoulders, and gave him a shake that made his eyes widen. "You listen to me, and listen good. You head for Mr. McRae's now, and you get there as quick as you can. You tell him that Miss Kitty is in Sergeant Brandon's office, and she's bad off sick, and for him to get here as soon as possible. Get somebody here to take her off my hands. You got that straight?"

"Yassuh, yassuh." His cottontop head bobbed up and down. "You gonna get a doctor fo' her now?"

"Let me worry about that," Jesse snapped. "Now be on your way, fast." He watched the old Negro scurry away and hoped he'd get to McRae soon. Damn it, the roads were bad, and it was starting to snow hard. Hell, he couldn't call in a doctor for that woman. She might start rambling about Sherman and Coltrane and how come they hadn't responded to her wires. Then the questions would start. The only thing he could do now was see to her himself and hope McRae showed up soon.

When he returned to his office, he found Kitty sprawled on the floor, unconscious. With a pounding heart, he hurried to kneel beside her and touch her wrists. There was life. She had passed out from either her sickness or the whiskey she'd downed so quickly. Lifting her, he carried her to the cot and covered her with as many blankets as he could find. He threw more wood into the stove, knowing he had to keep the room warm. Then he began to pace up and down beside the cot, his eyes watching her anxiously. Now and then she moaned or tossed restlessly, but for the most part she just lay there as though she were dead.

She was beautiful, he thought, looking at the sweep of her long, silken lashes against her ivory-smooth cheeks. Even with the blankets heaped on her body, he could see the swell of her bosom. She was the loveliest woman he'd ever laid eyes on. Her hair was fanned out on the pillow, the color of a sunset after a storm, all gold and red and angry. He knew the color of her eyes, too, because he had thought of them many times—lavender, almost as deeply purple as the wisteria vines he remembered growing on his grandmother's front porch. Oh, those eyes! He just knew they'd burn with red fire when a man held her in his arms and made her body spark.

Thinking of her naked, spread out beneath him,

made him ache and swell, and, oh, Lord, if she weren't sick and he wasn't afraid of Corey McRae, he'd throw himself on top of her right then and there and rip her clothes off and spread those sweet thighs . . .

He couldn't stand it any longer. He hurried to the empty room in the back, the one that had been General Schofield's office, and undid his belt and yanked down his trousers. And right there in front of the big portrait of General Sherman, Sergeant Brandon relieved himself.

It did not take long. Feeling a little foolish once it was all over, he yanked up his trousers, fastened his belt, and returned to the front room. He always hated having to get it that way. It was a hell of a poor substitute. Jesse sighed, sitting down behind his desk and reaching for his whiskey bottle. He downed the cup of whiskey and poured himself another. Nobody would be coming in the rest of the day, not with all that snow piling up outside. He could sit there and drink all he wanted to. He did not fight the heaviness that bore down upon him after a time, and he never felt himself slide from the chair to the floor.

"What in the hell is going on here, Brandon?"

Jesse shook his head. He didn't know which hurt more, his throbbing temples or the sharp kick he had just received in his side. Struggling to focus, he stared up through a sea of pain. Was that Corey McRae glaring down at him? His face was coming closer. Yes, yes, it was McRae, and he was so close he could feel his angry breath on his face, see the way his nostrils flared. "Did you hear me, you son of a bitch? I asked what the hell is going on here? Kitty is unconscious, burning up with fever. Why haven't you called a doctor?"

"Couldn't . . ." Jesse struggled to sit up. "Too many questions. You said to keep things quiet."

Corey grabbed his shirt and yanked him to his feet. "You goddamn stupid bastard! I could kill you. If that girl dies, so help me, I *will* blow your brains out."

Jesse had a brief glimpse of the hamlike fist coming towards his face. There was an explosion of pain, and then he was out once again.

Corey turned away, cursing as he returned to Kitty's side. Kneeling beside the cot, he held her limp hand. She was burning up with fever, her breathing ragged and strained. Damn it, where was Griggs? He'd been sent to find a doctor as soon as they rode into town. The old nigra didn't know how long it had taken him to get back to the plantation. The stupid fool said he guessed a couple of hours, with the snow and all. He had gotten the horse and carriage bogged down in a snow bank and had to walk the last few miles, and there was no telling how long that had taken.

Just then, the door swung open and Griggs stepped inside, followed by a heavyset man whose white beard hung well below his chin. Underneath his heavy coat, Corey could see the stripes of his nightshirt. Griggs had roused him out of bed.

"Over here, doctor," Corey said crisply, motioning him to where Kitty lay. "I don't know how long she's been like this, but she obviously has the fever."

"Well, if you know so damn much, what in the hell did you get me up for?" the doctor said. He elbowed Corey aside and stared down at Kitty. "Get me a chair," he said as he reached to raise her left eyelid.

He continued to examine Kitty, murmuring to himself while Corey strained to hear what he was saying. Finally he leaned back in his chair and said, "Yep. She's got the fever, all right. It's going to be a while before it breaks, too. I have some medicine in my bag and more in my office. You plan to leave her here or move her to the hotel?" He glanced around the military office distastefully.

"Can she be moved to my plantation?" Corey wanted to know.

"*Plantation?*" The old doctor propped his fist on his knee as he turned to look up at Corey. "I don't believe I know you, mister, but if you have a plantation around here, when everybody else I know is living hand to mouth, then you're either Jerome Danton or Corey McRae. And hell, no, she can't be moved that far till her fever breaks, not unless you want her to die."

Corey bristled. "No, I don't want her to die, you old fool. I will move her to the hotel immediately, and I want you to stay with her until the fever breaks."

The doctor almost choked. "You *what*? I have office hours in the morning. I've got a woman at the edge of town who may deliver tonight. I can't just go sit in a hotel room with a woman who's got the fever."

"You will be paid well, doctor, and you will do it, so there is no point in arguing." He turned to Griggs. "Go to the hotel and have them make their finest room ready. Then come back and help us move Miss Wright. Tell Kincaid to keep an eye on the doctor. He's going to be a part of our little family until Miss Wright is over this."

Dr. Sims continued to protest until Kincaid pulled his gun and pointed it right at him and told him to shut up and look after Miss Wright. His face turned red, but he said no more.

Jesse stirred, moaning. Dr. Sims' head jerked about and he sputtered, "Good God, what's that? Another one?"

"He ran into my fist," Corey said matter-of-factly as he walked over and yanked Jesse up by his collar and propped him against the wall.

The sergeant looked about the room, trying to focus. He knew there were people about, but Corey McRae was the only one he could recognize. "Wh . . . what happened?"

"You son of a bitch, you know what happened. Miss Wright is ill, and you got drunk."

"I sent that nigger for you. I didn't know what else to do. She passed out. All I could do was put blankets on her and wait." He rubbed his sore jaw, wincing. He felt inside his mouth. A tooth was loose. "What'd you hit me for, anyway? I was only doing what you told me to do, keeping things quiet. All I knew to do was send for you and let you handle things."

Corey squatted beside him, his back to the doctor. He lowered his voice and said, "All right now, Brandon. What was she doing here in the first place? I've had someone watching her place at all times, and she hasn't ventured outside in weeks. That old nigra has been doing for her. So what made her come to town? I want to know everything she said to you."

"She wanted to see Schofield. I told her he was gone already, that I'd be leaving in a few weeks myself. Then she said something about how they were taking her land, and about how she and Coltrane had a son he didn't know nothing about, and she was begging me to help her find Coltrane. Said her baby was sick, and she didn't have any money."

Corey chewed his lower lip thoughtfully. So she had found out about him purchasing her tax certificate. He had meant to break that bit of news to her himself. Well, when the fever broke, and she was stronger and rational, he would go ahead with his plan. The baby being sick complicated matters. "Where is the baby?" he asked Brandon.

"I don't know. She didn't say. She didn't have it with her, that's for sure."

"And what did you say to her about Coltrane? You didn't send a wire, did you?" His voice rose ominously.

Jesse shriveled instinctively. "No, sir, I didn't send

no wire. She fainted before I had time to say much of anything, and I decided the thing to do was get word to you. I looked for you at the office, but it was locked, and then that old nigger came creeping up, said he gave her a ride into town and that he worked for you. So I sent him after you, and I came back here." He rubbed his jaw again. "And this is the thanks I get for keeping things quiet."

Corey motioned to Kincaid, who hurried over. "As soon as we have her settled in the hotel, you go out to her place and see if the baby is there with that old nigra Jacob. Take them both to my house. Quarter the nigra with the other servants, and then have Dulcie see to the baby. If he is very sick, come back to town and get the doctor. I don't want anything to happen to that baby. Understand?"

Kincaid nodded. He and the rest of the boys had figured out long ago what McRae was up to. He didn't give a hang about that kid, but he was using him to get to Kitty Wright.

After Kitty was bundled up against the cold, they moved her to the hotel. The lobby was deserted, as everyone was either in bed or next door at the saloon. A fire was roaring in the fireplace, and the room was quite warm. Dr. Sims spooned medicine through Kitty's fever-parched lips, then settled down to wait out the sickness.

Kincaid stationed himself outside the door, and Griggs left to take the baby to the mansion. McRae pulled up a chair to sit next to the bed, watching her pale face anxiously.

"It ain't gonna do no good to sit and stare at her," the doctor said irritably, leaning back in his chair and folding his arms across his chest. "Might as well try to get a nap. No telling how long before that fever will break."

Corey merely frowned. In a few moments, the doctor was asleep and snoring loudly.

Kitty stirred, and he leaned forward. Her eyelashes fluttered, and the violet eyes that peered at him glassily reflected pale shimmers of the heat raging within her body. "My . . . my baby . . ." Her voice was feeble. "Please . . . my baby . . ."

She lifted her hand, and Corey took it and pressed it to his lips. "Kitty, darling, I've sent one of my men to get your baby. He'll be looked after. I promise. Rest now. Get your strength back. The baby is going to be fine. I have a doctor here beside you, and we're both going to be right here until you come out of this."

She stared into his face with desperation. "You . . . you'll take care of my baby?"

He kissed her fingertips, rubbed his cheek against her hand, wishing he could hold her. "Kitty, Kitty, precious Kitty, of course I'll take care of your baby. I'll love him as my own, if you'll let me. Just get well, darling, please."

"Corey . . ." Her eyes widened slightly. She recognized him for the first time. "It is you."

"Yes, yes, now rest, darling, please. I'll take care of everything."

She nodded slightly, her lips curving in a gentle smile as her eyes closed. "Yes," she whispered finally.

He smiled, gave her hand one last kiss, and placed it upon her chest. At last, she was totally vulnerable. Helpless. If it were not for the baby, she would continue to fight him. But now she was going to be his.

Chapter Nineteen

COREY stood before Sergeant Brandon's desk, booted feet spread wide, his right hand holding the leather riding crop that he rhythmically slapped into the gloved palm of his left hand. The sergeant squirmed uncomfortably beneath the powerful man's penetrating gaze.

"Are you quite sure that no one, absolutely no one, is aware of the negotiations that have gone on between the two of us?"

Sergeant Brandon shook his head vigorously from side to side, forcing himself to look straight into the man's eyes. Damn, they were black as soot and sparkled with the fires of hell. "I swear to God, Mr. McRae, I ain't never said a word to anybody about what went on between me and you concerning Miss Wright. It would have meant my neck, for sure, not only with the army, but with you. I never opened my mouth. You paid me well. I did what I was told. And nobody knows anything."

Corey's expression did not change. He continued to slap the riding crop into his open palm. "No one knows that I personally gave you money to give to Miss Wright, making her think that money was her father's wages as a Union soldier?"

"No, sir. I gave her that money and had her sign that false document I fixed up. Then I burned it in the stove, right over there. Nobody saw a thing. And the general, he had so much else on his mind right about then that he never even mentioned her again."

"And the letters she had sent here, to Sherman and Coltrane, you are sure no one saw you burn them?"

"Nobody. I was here alone when one of the letters came in, and I burned it myself. Another soldier was in here when that old nigra of hers brought one in, and I had to wait a while, but then, I burned it, too. I'm clean here, sir, I swear to you. I'm leaving here in a few days and going home, and I'm leaving all this behind me. Won't nobody ever know what went on."

"Very well," Corey murmured, folding his riding crop beneath his arm. "You have done a good job, Brandon. I wish you well in your return home, in building a new life, but rest assured, if you ever whisper one word about our transactions, I'll have you hunted down and killed. Do you understand me?"

The sergeant's Adam's apple bobbed nervously as he swallowed and nodded. "Yes, sir. Yes, sir, I understand. And you don't have to worry about me. I swear it on my mother's grave. Once you walk out that door, I'll find it hard to even remember who you are. Don't ever worry about me, Mr. McRae."

Corey's smile was tight, and he nodded ever so slightly as he said, "Goodbye, Sergeant."

McRae opened the door and stepped outside, closing it tightly behind him.

Sergeant Jesse Brandon watched his departure, much relieved. All he wanted was to get out of Wayne County, and out of North Carolina. Forget the whole thing.

Corey started down the street, bowing his head against the brisk wind. He did not see the tall, medium-built man step out of a doorway to block his path. He saw the booted feet planted squarely in front of him just in time to come to an abrupt halt and not slam into him. Looking up, he saw the eyes of Jerome Danton blazing at him.

"McRae." His voice was tense. "I hear you've got Kitty Wright at your place again. What the hell are you trying to prove? Everybody in town knows she hates your guts."

"Does she now? And what would give you that idea? I saved her life, *and* her baby's, the night you and your hooded cowards burned her out of her home. Now she is ill and I have come to her aid once again. But what does all this have to do with you?"

Danton's fists clenched and unclenched at his sides as he tried to control his rising temper. "You can't prove I had a damn thing to do with those night riders burning her out, and if I was you, I'd watch making accusations."

Corey raised an eyebrow in amusement. "Well, now, who are you to be warning me, Danton? Everyone in town knows you are the leader of the Ku Klux Klan, or whatever you call yourselves. And what business is it of yours if I choose to help a neighbor in distress?"

"Distress? Hell, man, you've caused her as much distress as anybody. I know you bought her tax certificate. Does she know it yet? I'll just bet she does, and I'll bet you're holding her at your place against her will."

"Miss Wright is quite ill." Corey spoke as though conversing with a simpleton. "She is still delirious with fever."

"And how about the taxes? How is she going to feel when she finds out you now own her place? I know how she feels about that land, McRae. *I* did the gentlemanly thing. I rode out to see her a while back and offered to buy her land. I knew she was having money problems. You went behind her back and bought that delinquent tax certificate."

Corey spread his legs and began slapping the riding

crop against his open palm once again. If this were to lead to an open confrontation, then he would face it as he did all opposition. "I still do not see that any of this concerns you, Danton. Now, I have other matters to tend to, if you have nothing more to say."

"I've got a lot more to say, McRae. A hell of a lot. I happen to take a fancy to that filly, too, and I'm not about to sit back and watch you maneuver her into doing what you want."

McRae tried to step around him, but Danton moved to block his path. When he moved, Corey saw the slight limp. He smiled. "She isn't a very good shot in the dark, but if I were you, I would be careful in the daylight."

Danton's face colored. He would always have that limp from the ball Kitty Wright put in his leg, but she would make it all up to him one day—in his bed. He pointed a finger at Corey and snapped, "You hear me out, you pompous bastard, you're not going to get away with what you're doing."

Rance Kincaid seemed to appear from nowhere. He had been standing in a doorway just behind Jerome Danton. The sound of a gun hammer cocking made Danton's head whip around quickly, and his eyes widened at the sight of the man standing behind him, pointing the weapon straight at him.

"I reckon the name-calling about ends the conversation, don't it, boss?" Rance said evenly.

"Yes, Rance, it does. I certainly don't intend to stand out here in the cold and banter with a fool." He tipped his hat with an insolent grin and walked on.

Walking beside him, Rance shivered against the chill of the day, and Corey moved in the direction of the saloon. "I think we can both use a drink. By the way, I want you to alert Martin and the rest of the men to keep an eye on Danton. Double our night guards for a while. He might be fool enough to bring his hooded night riders to shoot up the place and burn one of their crosses and try to scare us. If he does, I want as many of those bastards killed as possible. Is that clear?"

"Oh, yeah, boss. We'll pick 'em off like hogs in a pen at slaughtering time." He spoke casually. Killing came easily to Rance and the others who worked as hired guns for McRae.

After a drink, Corey left the saloon and walked alone down the street to his office. Unlocking the door, he stepped inside and moved quickly to get a fire burning in the stove. There was not a lot he planned to take care of during this brief visit, but while there, he could use some warmth.

The kindling quickly ignited, and he removed his heavy sheepskin coat and stood in front of the stove, rubbing his hands together briskly. Eyeing the papers stacked on his desk, he frowned, wondering where to begin. There were several tax certificates he meant to call in. He had no intention of giving the landowners time to come up with money: he wanted their hand. He would have to go over those so he could send Rance and some of the men out to deliver the news to the farmers. They either came up with the money at once, or they left their property. If they did not leave peacefully, Rance and the others knew how to take care of them.

Sergeant Brandon had told him about the federal marshals that would be coming in, and he wondered how much inconvenience this was going to cause. Some of the marshals might not take too kindly to his method of evicting farmers.

Everyone thought old Micah Pursall had just wandered away with a broken heart when McRae foreclosed on his tax certificate. No one knew that old fool had dared to stand up to Rance and his men, meeting them with an Enfield. Micah and his wife and three children would never be found. Let everyone believe they had left. Their bodies were rotting at the bottom of the Neuse River, weighed down with enough stones to keep them under till the fish and turtles got through picking their bones.

Corey had neither time nor patience to go through the tedious process of eviction through the courts. True, the Northern judges were quite sympathetic to the Northern certificate-holders, but now and then one came along who wanted to give the Rebels extra time to come up with the tax money. Corey found it expedient to handle things his way.

One parcel of land belonged to old Zeb Mooney. Only fifty or so acres were involved, but the land was very flat and the drainage good. A perfect tract for tobacco. It was already cleared of trees and stumps, which would save his field hands time. They could get right to plowing as soon as the ground thawed, and be ready for spring planting as soon as the weather was right.

Corey had offered to buy the old man's land, just as he always offered to purchase everyone's before buying their tax certificates. He preferred that business be pleasant, if possible. Unfortunately, most of the Southerners he dealt with were most indignant, and some of them, like Mooney, were downright rude. He made Mooney a fair offer, and when the old man started yelling and screaming about how his boys died defending his land, and how he would live there till he died and then be buried right alongside of them, Corey made another offer—the same amount of money for the property, but with a special stipulation drawn up in the deed. The Mooney family cemetery would remain untouched, and it would be fenced off and never desecrated. Mooney told him he was crazy and gave him five minutes to get off his property.

Well, Mooney was going to be buried a lot sooner than he had thought, but not in his family cemetery.

It looked as though he would have to end up at the bottom of the Neuse River with old Micah Pursall and his family.

The other piece of land Corey wanted right away adjoined Mooney's and belonged to a feisty little widow named Mattie Glass. A deep, rolling stream from an underground spring on Mattie's land cut through the property, and Corey needed that water for his cattle. The plot was only ten acres, hardly enough to quibble over, but the water was important. He made her an offer higher than anyone else would have made, but Mattie turned him down flat, saying she did not even want to dicker with him. Her husband had deeded the property solely to her before he went off and got himself killed by the Yanks at Shiloh. She had two boys, twelve and thirteen, and she was going to raise them right there on her land. Corey had tried to explain to her that ten acres was hardly enough land to worry about, that the generous sum he was offering was more than enough to purchase a small house in town. Her argument was that the land was all her husband had to leave them, and she could never sell it. "Thurman would turn over in his grave if'n I did," she had said, looking at Corey as though he had to be out of his mind even to suggest such a thing.

He would have to do some thinking on that one, he decided, staring at the tax certificate in his hand. Zeb Mooney was really no problem. Everyone thought he was crazy anyway, the way he sat in the cemetery all day talking to his dead wife and sons. No one would be surprised if he disappeared. They would think he walked into the woods and never came out.

Mattie Glass, however, was a different situation. If she were to disappear, as well as Zeb Mooney, and Corey wound up with both parcels of land, well, he was asking for trouble.

Federal marshals would not be along for a few days. He needed to move quickly.

The door banged open, and Rance swaggered in. "It took you long enough," Corey snapped. "Close the damn door. Can't you see you're letting all that blasted cold air in?"

The smug look left Rance's face. "Something happened I don't know about, boss? You were in a pretty good mood when—"

"I don't have time for chitchat, Rance." He thrust the two tax certificates at his foreman. "I want these papers served at once. Tonight. The time limit is up. If Mooney gives you any trouble, take care of him the way you took care of Pursall. As for that widow woman . . . damn, I don't know what to do about her. I'm going to make a lot of enemies if I evict a war widow and two children."

Rance scratched at his crotch thoughtfully, and Corey swore, "Damn it, man, why are you always digging at yourself down there? Do these trollops you cavort with give you lice?"

"Sorry, boss," Rance mumbled. "Just a habit when I'm thinkin' on something."

"Think about Mattie Glass. I want her property because of that underground stream."

"You know, she ain't a bad-lookin' piece of womanflesh. I've noticed her sometimes in town. She's got a nice body. Why don't you just marry up with her and then you'll have her land with no problem at all. When you get tired of her, you can pass her on to me and the boys . . ." His voice trailed off, and his large frame seemed to wither. "I was only trying to be funny," he said.

"This is no time to be funny. I can't do as I please until I have things under control. I want you to take some men and pay Mattie Glass a visit tonight. Put hoods on so you won't be recognized, should anyone see you.

Rough her up a little and put some fear into her. Tell her to sell her land or something terrible will happen to her boys . . ."

"I get it." Rance smiled. He enjoyed this sort of thing. "You don't want everybody saying you evicted a helpless war widow, so me and the boys scare her into selling, and we make sure she knows that if she dares tell anybody she was pressured, she'll wish she hadn't."

"Exactly."

"And what about old man Mooney?"

"Don't waste your time talking to him. Just go over to his place and kill him and throw him in the river. Weight him down good. Then I'll wait a few weeks and file a claim for his property since I hold the tax certificate. By that time, we'll have Mattie off her land. I'll have both tracts, all nice and legal and respectable."

"You sure got everything figured, boss."

"Just don't louse it up, Rance." Corey eyed him warily. "I've got too much at stake."

Corey straightened a few more papers on his desk, then put on his coat.

"How about Miss Kitty?"

"What about her?"

"I heard one of the niggers say they heard Doc Sims say she was getting better."

"So?"

Rance looked uncomfortable. "Boss, I know you want to marry that woman, and I don't blame you. She's the prettiest filly I ever laid eyes on. I was just wondering how long it would be before you got what you wanted."

"Not long, Rance." Corey smiled. "Not long at all. You just take care of your business, and I'll take care of mine. Everything is going to turn out all right. You'll see."

Chapter Twenty

THE world had stopped spinning. The fog had finally lifted. Kitty could focus and make out people's faces. She could lift her head without the wracking nausea consuming her.

When the fever finally broke, she was dreaming that she was floundering in a choking sea and thousands of groping, clawing fingertips were clutching at her body, trying to pull her down. She fought against it, trying to rise, struggling against the forces seeking to drown her.

She opened her eyes and heard someone gasp, "Praise God, she's coming out of it." There was no sea of clutching fingers. It had been only a nightmare . . . a horrible nightmare. She wanted to stay awake, but her body was too weak. While she had awakened from a terrible dream, something was nagging in the back of her mind that told her another nightmare was beginning . . . and that this one was real.

"Miss Kitty . . ." a voice was calling anxiously from that other world, the world she wondered if she were ready for. "Miss Kitty, you need to wake up and drink this pot likker. It's good and hot, and you need yo' strength."

A gentle hand was touching her shoulder, shaking her.

Kitty looked up into Dulcie's concerned face.

"Thank the Lord you gonna be all right, Miss Kitty. You gave us such a scare. You know you been out of your head with the fever for five days now? Even Dr. Sims said he was afraid. Had us all scared to death, you did. And poor Uncle Jacob, he's been out of his mind. What time he weren't down on his knees a'prayin', he been sittin' outside the back door a'cryin'. Now you drink this pot likker so you'll get well."

"My baby," Kitty cried. "Little John . . ."

"He's just fine." Dulcie smiled, nodding proudly. "Mistah McRae sent some of his men to pick up him and Jacob, and they brought him back here, and the doctor looked after him. He was mighty sick, but he's right pert now. Doin' a lot better than his momma, I can tell you that."

It was all coming back. Little John was sick. She needed money. The walk through the frozen slush to the road, getting a ride with old Ben. The visit to the tax collector and the shocking news that Corey McRae, the damned vulture, had bought the tax certificate. No money could be borrowed on land that had tax liens against it. Vaguely, she remembered going to General Schofield's office, only he hadn't been there, and the man who had given her her father's army pay said something about leaving town. That was all she remembered.

"Miss Kitty, you gonna drink this pot likker and get yo' strength back, or you want to lay there and wither away to nothing?" Dulcie was scolding her.

Kitty sipped. The hot liquid was bitter and greasy, but she knew it would give her strength. How many times had she spooned the juice of cooked collard greens and fatback between the lips of sick people she was nursing? A few more swallows, and she did feel better. "No more, not now, please." She pushed it away.

"Well, Mistah McRae said—"

"Dulcie, why am I here?" Kitty pulled herself up to a sitting position. Dulcie saw that she was still quite weak and quickly set the pot likker aside to prop her up.

"I want to know why I'm here," Kitty repeated. "The last thing I remember, I was in town. Now I wake up here, in this house that belongs to a man I despise."

"Well, I don't rightly know, Miss Kitty," Dulcie said with wide, frightened eyes. She was not anxious to get involved in the situation. "All I know is Mistah McRae and Dr. Sims brought you here a few days after little John and Jacob was brought."

"A few days?"

"They say you took real sick in the army's office in town, and you was too sick to move, so they put you in the hotel till Dr. Sims said you could be brought out here. You been real sick, Miss Kitty, awful sick. Like I said, Dr. Sims wasn't too sure you was gonna make it for a while. I heard him fussin' at the mastah for bringing you out here, but the mastah, he say he know you gonna wake up and wonder where yo' baby was, and he wanted to get you out here so you could be near him. He's been real concerned about you, he has. He'd come in here and sit for hours and hold your hand and talk to you and beg you to live, Miss Kitty. And you should see the way he carries on over little John. He's got that boy a'cooin' and a'laughin'. It's something to see, for sure." She laughed, but her merriment faded quickly as she saw the anger in Kitty's eyes.

"You tell Corey McRae I wish to see him at once."

Dulcie had been sitting on the edge of the bed, and she moved quickly to her feet. "I told him I was bringing you up the pot likker. He said he'd come in to see you after you ate and had time to see little John." She was backing towards the door, looking frightened.

"Dulcie, you tell Mr. McRae that I wish to see him

at once, and then you start getting my baby's things together. Tell Jacob we'll be leaving here in a few hours."

The Negro girl shook her head from side to side. "No, ma'm, you ain't able to leave here no time soon. You still not well. Doc Sims, he's coming by later. You talk to him about that."

"Dulcie, will you do as I say?" Kitty's voice rose. "I won't stay in this house a minute longer than necessary. Now, get John ready and send word to Jacob."

The door opened, bumping Dulcie, and the pot likker went sloshing to the floor. She bent quickly and began wiping at the spill with her apron as Corey McRae stepped inside the room, a grim expression on his face.

"What is all this screaming about?" He glared down at Dulcie. "I could hear you all the way down the hall. And you were talking like a cotton-patch nigra again, Dulcie. Hugo has instructed you all about how to speak. Don't let me hear you forget yourself again or you'll feel the lash. Is that clear?"

"Yassuh." She jerked her head up quickly. "I mean, *yes . . . sir.*"

"Now clean up that mess and get out of here. I want to talk to Miss Kitty."

"And *Miss Kitty* wants to talk to you," Kitty snapped icily.

Corey crossed the room, smiling warmly. "Oh, Kitty, Kitty, it's so good to see you awake. You don't know how worried you have had all of us. You were a sick young woman, do you know that? And little John is anxious to see his mommy. He—"

He touched her shoulder, and she slapped his hand away. "Don't you touch me."

He raised an eyebrow. "Now what's all this about? Are you still delirious? I thought you were coming around, my dear . . ."

"Don't '*my dear*' me, you . . . you vulture!"

"Is that any way to talk to a man who saved your life for the *second* time? *And* your baby's? Kitty, I don't understand you."

Glancing at Dulcie, who was still wiping at the spilled liquid, Corey snapped, "Get the hell out of here, girl."

"Yes . . . yes sir." Dulcie nearly tripped in her haste to get out of the room.

He turned back to Kitty. "Now, what is all this about? Why are you so annoyed with me?"

"Oh, don't put on your act for me, Corey McRae. I know what an unscrupulous thief you really are. I know about your sneaking and buying my tax certificate. Well, if you think you are getting my land, you're crazy. I'll see you dead and in hell before you take my land."

Tears were streaming down her cheeks, and her hands were knotted into fists. Oh, if only she were stronger. Why did she have to be sick? There was so much to be done.

"Kitty, have I tried to take your land?" he asked softly.

"What do you mean?"

"Have I tried to take your land away from you?" he repeated. "Even though I own your tax certificate, have I been beating on your door demanding that you pay me the taxes, plus interest, and told you that if you *didn't* pay, you had to get off your land?"

She stared at him.

"Well, have I, Kitty?"

She shook her head.

"Then how can you say I want to take your land away from you?"

"Why did you buy the certificate?"

"To keep Jerome Danton from buying it, of course. He was going by the tax office every day to ask if you had been in to pay your taxes, just waiting for the deadline so he could pay them and do the very thing you accuse me of wanting to do. I have much influence, Kitty, and I made sure that when the deadline came, I was given the first chance to buy your certificate. And I did. But instead of being grateful, you scream accusations at me. How do you think that makes me feel, after my going to great trouble and expense to nurse you and your son through a raging fever? You would have died if not for me, and instead of gratitude, you give me contempt. Maybe I should throw you off your land and forget about you."

She had been listening quietly. His threat did not faze her. Jutting her chin upwards, she asked, "Well, why don't you?"

He had been gazing out the window, but his head jerked around to stare at her incredulously. "What did you say?"

"I said, why don't you? Throw me off my land, I mean, and forget about me. Why *do* you keep rescuing me and putting me in your debt? What kind of game are you playing, Corey?"

He sat down on the side of the bed, leaning over so that one hand was on each side of her. "You beautiful little fool," he whispered caressingly, his eyes devouring her. "Don't you know? Can't you see that I am in love with you? When I talked of marriage the first time we met, it was a foolish proposal, by a lonely man seeking respectability as well as the companionship of a very desirable woman. You were wise to reject me and run away. But now it's different, Kitty. I have fallen in love with you. I also adore your son. I can't stand to see you groveling for every morsel of food. I can't stand to see that boy of yours want for anything. Marry me, Kitty. Let me take care of you. Forget Travis Coltrane the way he has forgotten you. It's been a year, for God's sake. You would have heard from him by now. Don't you realize that?"

He straightened, ran his fingers through his hair, and shook his head. "I don't know. I don't know what is to be done with you, Kitty. I can't understand you. I offer you my heart, my name, my home, my wealth, and yet you turn from me."

"I don't love you," she said quietly.

He turned misery-filled eyes upon her. "Have I asked you to love me? I will *make* you love me, by God. Give me a chance, Kitty. Don't be a fool and turn down what I offer you."

"I cannot marry a man I do not love. It would not be fair to you or to me, Corey. It would never work out. We couldn't be happy."

He nodded, nostrils flaring angrily. "I see. So you'll take John and go back to that miserable little shack in the swamps and both of you will probably die of disease or starvation. All because of your *goddamn stubborn pride.*"

He leaped to his feet, face red. "Well, you go right ahead, Kitty Wright. Take your son and go now, if you wish. But don't expect any more help from me. And don't expect any charity. I own your tax certificate, and until you can pay me, you can remain on your land and work it as a tenant farmer. I will get sixty percent of the profits."

"That . . . that is absurd," she sputtered in disbelief.

"That is the way tenant farming operates, my dear. Didn't you know that? I get sixty percent and you get forty percent, and that is *after* expenses. So it will take you quite a while to ever pay off your debt to me. I doubt that you ever will. I happen to be a businessman. Do you think I should just wipe the slate clean and tear up the certificate? Maybe send you another cow? Send a load of food over every week? What kind of fool do you take me for?"

"Corey, I—"

"Maybe I should just sell the certificate to Jerome

Danton. Perhaps you would prefer dealing with him instead of me. I doubt that he will ask you to marry him. I am sure he will have another arrangement in mind, without the dignity and respectability of marriage, you may be sure. Shall I send word to him that he may buy your tax lien?"

"No." She all but screamed the word. "Corey, listen to me."

"Listen to you?" he bellowed. "Kitty Wright, I have listened to you since the day we met. I have laid my heart at your feet, only to have you laugh and walk over me—"

"I have done neither."

"I'm through begging." He started towards the door, then whirled about and pointed a shaking finger. "You are not strong enough to leave today, but if you wish, no one will stop you. Rest assured I will not bother you again. Just be sure that when the times comes, I have my sixty percent."

He stormed out. Kitty stared after him, lips parted in amazement. She shook her head. Things were happening too fast. The man professed to love her and her son. Was that possible?

Her legs felt weak as she tried to stand. She fell backwards in tearful frustration. Flinging her arm across her face, she blinked back the tears. Travis. If only Travis had returned. Either he had never truly loved her, or . . . she did not want to think of the possibility. Or he was dead. Either way, it was time to face reality.

She was alone. Her land had a tax lien against it. She had a baby. She had no help, only Jacob, who was very old and could not do hard work. She was desperate.

There was a soft rap on the door. Forcing herself back against the pillows and pulling the covers up to her chin, she made her voice steady. "Yes, who is it?"

The door opened slowly. Dulcie stepped in, holding John. "Miss Kitty, Mistah McRae said you might be leaving. He told me to bring the baby in."

"Yes, oh, yes, let me have my baby." She held out her arms eagerly, letting the tears stream down her cheeks. She cradled him against her bosom. Kissing his forehead, she smoothed back the dark hair. He opened sleepy eyes to look up at her, then wriggled contentedly. The eyes were still blue, but there was a definite touch of gray, Kitty thought, a stab of longing slashing her heart. Those eyes would be the color of gray smoke one day, and the lashes long and thick, just like his father's.

She was still holding him, crooning, when she heard footsteps and glanced up to see Jacob standing next to Dulcie. His eyes were brimming with tears. "Missy, you goin' home?" he asked.

"Yes." She made her voice firm. "We are going home, Jacob. We'll survive somehow. We have to."

"Missy, there's somethin' I think you should know."

Fear shivered up her spine. "Jacob, what is it? Tell me!"

"The cow died. Wandered out and froze to death. Maybe she was sick. I don't know. She just died. We ain't got nothin' left, missy, nothin' at all. What we gonna do, missy? Oh, Lawdy, Miss Kitty, how you gonna take care of the baby? How is me and you gonna live, Miss Kitty?"

He turned away, bent shoulders shuddering. Even Jacob was defeated, Kitty thought wearily. His spirit had finally left his old bones. He was scared. He would remain loyal, starve to death with her if it came to that. But he could no longer hide his fear.

"Leave me," she whispered to the two Negroes. "Leave me alone with my baby, please."

Memories came back, memories from the last time she had been in this room . . . Corey's clutching hands, his moist, seeking mouth. She shuddered. Dear God, the only man she ever wanted to touch her was Travis, and he was gone. Now the future held two roads, and only misery seemed to wait at the end of each.

The baby stirred. She gazed down at him and felt her heart warm. *Her* life was over, but his was just beginning. What must she do for him?

She did not hear the door open, did not know that Corey stood next to the bed until he spoke. "Kitty, I don't want us to part in anger. You mean too much to me. I am a businessman, however, and I can't continue to dole out charity. You and I both know that. I have many people begging me for help, and I can't help them all. I will give you a start, though, if you will let me. Jacob tells me the cow I sent over has died. I'll send you another. I'll loan you the money for your crop this year. I won't take sixty percent of your profit this first year. I won't take anything. We'll wait a while, see how things work out.

"But I wanted to say this: should you change your mind, should you decide you will let me love you and your son and care for you both . . . if you decide you will marry me, I will tear up that tax lien. When we marry, your property will become mine, and I will immediately draw up a deed putting it in trust for your son. No matter how many other children *we* might have, the Wright land will always belong to little John. I swear this to you."

She could not believe what she was hearing. She looked at him, completely bewildered.

"I mean every word, Kitty," he said in a strained voice, gesturing with his arms as though floundering for a way to make her believe him. "I love you. I will not see you suffer. I will not see John suffer. But please, I ask only one thing of you. Don't leave this house now. You are too weak. Rest and get your strength back for a few days, while I send my men over to check out your shack and make sure it's snug and warm for the rest of the winter. I want your pantry stocked, too. I have hams in my smokehouse, and I will see that you have some. While you are here, I won't bother you again, I swear."

"Corey, why?" she gasped. "Why do you offer to do all this?"

He touched the baby's downy hair, smiled at him fondly, then gazed into her eyes and whispered, "Because you are the most beautiful woman I have ever met, Kitty Wright, and I love you and want you for my wife. And maybe someday, if God chooses to smile on me, you will accept my proposal."

"You love me enough to do so much for me and my son?"

"Everything I have is yours, Kitty. I love your son as though he were my own."

"But you know that he was born of the love I hold in my heart for another man."

He nodded soberly. "I realize that. I'm not a complete fool. But had it not been for me, the baby would have died, wouldn't he? So I guess that sort of makes me his father, too, since I saved his life. Dr. Sims says he was in a bad way when I brought him here, so you might say that I saved the little fellow's life twice. How can I not love him as though he were my own?"

"But why do you love me? I have never tried to win your favor. Quite frankly, I have always held you in contempt."

"I know, I know, and that is my fault. I tried to win your heart with my money, my power, but you are too free-willed and independent to be swayed by such things. I was a fool, but that doesn't stop me from loving you all the same. And how can I explain love? How can anyone?"

She nodded. It would be difficult, indeed, for her to

try to explain to anyone why she loved Travis so fiercely.

"Well, I'll go now and let you rest." His smile was forced, she knew. "Would you like me to send in Dulcie to take the baby so you can have a nap? You will stay a few more days, won't you? Let me do that much for you, to make up for being so angry before."

She nodded, and he turned to go. But before he reached the door, she called out in a small voice, "Corey."

He turned, his eyes searching hers.

"Corey, I won't promise that I can love you as a wife should love her husband, but I will promise to be a good and obedient wife. There is John to consider, and I can't jeopardize his future while I live on past dreams."

He was across the room so quickly she hardly saw the movement, gathering both her and the baby in his arms and hugging them as he laughed in delirious delight. "Darling, darling, we'll plan a wedding right away before you change your mind. You will see. Everything is going to be so wonderful. You and John will have everything money can buy."

His lips touched hers, softly at first, then hard and possessive. She forced herself to try and return the kiss. She had taken the first step down the road, and she would have to keep putting one foot before the other.

There would be no turning back. Not now.

Chapter Twenty-one

COREY'S black eyes gleamed. His whole body shook with rage. "You fool! You damned, blundering fool! You were in charge! How could you allow such a thing to happen?" He slammed his palms against the marble mantel, oblivious to the stinging pain.

Rance Kincaid shifted his weight uneasily from one booted foot to the other, then yanked off his hat to sling it onto the floor in a sweeping gesture of disgust. "Hell, I don't know!" He turned completely around in his frustration, eyes rolling upwards, then faced Corey once more. "Boss, I just don't know how it happened. I took three of the men with me, and—"

"Which ones?"

"Jabe Martin, Coot Wiley, and Zeke Musgrave."

"And I suppose they were drunk, as usual."

"Boss, they're our best guns."

"Go on, go on." Corey gestured impatiently.

"I didn't know they'd been drinking that much, boss. I mean, we all had a few drinks in the bunkhouse before we left, you know? Talking about how we were going to work things and all. I told 'em over and over what you said, about how we were going to wear hoods so if anybody saw us, they'd blame the whole thing on Danton's Klan, and how we was supposed to go over to the widow Glass's house and ask her one more time if she was willing to sell out. I told 'em if she said no, then we was supposed to bust up the place a little . . . throw things around . . . scare the kids . . . make her glad to sell and get into town where she'd be safe. Just like you said, boss."

Corey strode over to the mahogany sideboard and poured himself a glass of whiskey. He downed it in one gulp, standing with his back to Rance. Then he whirled about suddenly and sent the glass shattering into the fireplace. "Then you tell me how Mattie Glass got *raped*, damn you! Damn *all* of you! I want to know how this happened!"

Rance shrugged helplessly. "It just happened, boss. I don't know why things got out of hand. But she's a feisty one, she is, and she wasn't a bit scared when she opened the door and saw us standing there with those white hoods over our heads. She had a shotgun pointed right at us, and we could see those boys of hers standing back in a corner. We didn't even get a chance to say nothing, because she was yelling we had till she counted ten to get off her property and then she was going to start shooting. She started counting."

Corey raised an eyebrow. "And?"

"Well"—he hesitated uneasily, then rushed on defensively. "Me and the boys ain't gonna let no female run us off with no gun. Coot just reached out and grabbed that shotgun away from her before she knew what was happening. Then those boys of hers come charging across the room, grabbing chairs and swinging. Coot busted one in the mouth with the gun butt and took care of him right off, and I believe Zeke knocked the other one out."

"And what were *you* doing all this time that you were supposed to be in charge, Kincaid?" Corey's nostrils flared as his glittering eyes raked Rance over, sweeping with contempt.

"I was busting things," he said with a shrug. "That woman kept fightin' and scratchin'. She was like a whirlwind. It got the boys excited, I guess. Next thing I knew, Coot had her down on the bed, and Zeke was holding her arms over her head, and Coot ripped her skirt off and went at it. She didn't quiet down a bit, kept on screaming. Then Zeke got to her, and when he finished, she'd passed out."

"And I suppose you all had a turn." Corey turned his back so Rance would not see that the conversation had aroused him. He was not thinking of Mattie Glass and how it would feel to thrust himself inside her bony little body. He was thinking of the woman upstairs. She was his bride now, and this was his wedding night, and this trouble about that stupid widow was keeping him from something he had dreamed of for almost a year.

"Yeah, we all had a turn. Coot went twice. He's horny, you know. He'll pop a calf in the pasture if he ain't had none in a while."

"Spare me the sordid details," Corey snorted. "I want you to tell me what condition the woman was in when you left her."

"She was still out. Bleeding some. Her face was bruised up from the guys trying to stop her fightin'. We just left her like that, but we knew her and the boys were alive, just shook up a bit."

"And whose idea was it to burn that cross?" Corey jerked his silver brocade coat over his crotch, then folded his hands over the bulge so he could turn and face Rance. "Who burned that cross in front of that woman's house to make it look like the Klan's work?"

"Coot's." Rance looked at his feet miserably. "I see now it was dumb. But at the time, we were sort of scared about the way things turned out, and we wanted to make sure nobody traced it to us—or to you, boss," he added quickly.

"You blundering bastards. So far all Danton's bunch has done is beat up nigras. They've burned many a cross to scare a black boy that got uppity with a white woman. They consider themselves *knights*, you idiot, shining knights, protecting the South and its women. They would *never* rape a white woman. Never! No one believes they were responsible for what happened to Mattie Glass. Everyone can figure out it was deliberately perpetrated to look like the Klan was responsible. The whole county is in an uproar."

"Well, I ain't heard nothing about it."

"And you were hoping *I* wouldn't. That's why you did not report to me this morning."

"It was your wedding day. I didn't figure you wanted to hear about all this on your wedding day."

"I didn't want to be told about it at my wedding, either."

"I figured this was what you wanted when you called me up here, but you could have waited till morning to chew me out." Rance's eyes rolled towards the ceiling, and he smiled suggestively. "Ain't you got something better to be doing?"

"You're damned right I have!" Corey shouted. "And as for 'chewing you out,' as you call it, I ought to have your hide hung on a tree limb for allowing such a thing to happen."

He walked back to the sideboard and poured himself another drink. "Parson Brooks drew me aside after the ceremony, when we were having refreshments, and he told me what had happened. I was horrified and nearly choked on my champagne, trying to keep from letting on that I knew anything. I carried it off, but it was quite difficult, believe me."

"Well, look at it this way, boss. You can go and pay her a visit in a few days and offer your sympathy over such a terrible thing happening, then offer to buy her land again. Maybe you should even offer her a bit more than you'd planned, just out of the goodness of your heart over what happened to her. You know, like you're trying to be a good neighbor and all. She's gonna be glad to sell, and you'll look like a hero, helping her get to town where she'll be safe. See, we didn't say nothing about buying her land. She pointed that gun at us when she opened the door, and nothing was said about land. So she won't connect it with you."

"All right," Corey said finally. "Just tell the men to keep their mouths shut. Maybe it will all blow over in a few days, but I doubt it."

"How come? They can't trace nothing to us. Nobody saw our faces."

"Because the people in this county aren't going to forget what happened any time soon, Rance." Exasperated, Corey downed his drink, then poured another. "You see, the parson says her son woke up sometime during the night to find his brother's face mashed in and bleeding, and he only had to take one look at his mother to see what had happened to her. He ran out and walked to the next house, about a mile or so, and the people living there took him to town to find a doctor. The boy Coot hit in the mouth with the gun butt has a broken jaw. Just about every tooth in his mouth was knocked out. According to the parson, Mattie is badly bruised and torn, and he quotes the doctor as saying she is in some kind of shocked state over what happened. They have her and the boy in the hospital. The one who went for help wasn't badly hurt, though his face is bruised rather badly. So you see, it will be some time before I can approach the woman with my offer. It might make people think."

"I'm sorry, boss," Rance shook his head in dejection. "I really am. I'm going out to the bunkhouse right now and beat the shit out of those guys."

"And start the other hands to talking and wondering

what's going on? Not to mention the nigras and how they'd gossip all over the county. No! I'll say something to them myself and let them know I'm disturbed and angry over the way things were handled. But for now, let's just try to keep things quiet."

"Yeah, you're right. At least we took care of old man Mooney without a fuss. I was in town today and heard somebody in the saloon talking, saying they'd heard he'd disappeared. They figured he just finally went nuts and wandered off. That's the way you said they'd figure it, boss."

"What did you actually do with him?"

"Coot shot him, and then we tied rocks on him and dumped him in the river. Nice and clean. All you got to do now is show up with that tax certificate and claim the property as yours."

"Not for a while I don't. We've got to lay low. Federal marshals are going to be coming in soon, and I imagine the first item of business the good citizens of Goldsboro will place before them will be the rape of the good widow Glass. They won't concern themselves over Mooney. You can bet Danton is going to be furious about the cross-burning. He knows it was meant to put the blame on him, and he'll try to put the marshals on our trail because of the cross. So we have to be extremely careful, Rance. You pass the word along to the boys, and I'll speak to them myself in a few days, like I said. I don't want any of you even going into town. Just lay low. No one will suspect anything if things are at a standstill around here. After all, I have just married, and we have a lavish party coming up in a few weeks. After the party, we'll move back to normal, and I can claim Mooney's land and make the pitch to the widow Glass. She should be all right by then."

"Yeah, sure, boss, anything you say." Rance retrieved his hat from the floor, then flashed a knowing grin. "If that's all for now, I guess you'd like me to leave so you can take care of some, uh, other things."

Corey did not return his smile.

"Good night, Rance." His tone was curt.

When he was finally alone, Corey gazed into the crackling fire and sipped the rest of his drink slowly. Dr. Sims had said it would be several weeks before Kitty was strong enough for the excitement of a large wedding, so there had been a simple ceremony with only the parson and his wife in attendance.

He thought about the huge party that was being planned to celebrate the marriage. Everyone of any wealth or stature, political or social, had been invited. He knew that he and Kitty would be acknowledged quickly as a couple of high station.

A complete orchestra had been engaged from Raleigh. Hugo was, of course, in charge of food and drink, and the spread would be lavish. Corey had ordered expensive silver trays as gifts for each couple, with his and Kitty's names engraved on them and the date of their marriage. It would be a party that people would talk about for months.

Things were going his way, and it was time for the fulfillment of his greatest desire. Now, with the ache of longing, he knew he could wait no longer. She was his—like this house, this land, she belonged to him. She would bend to him. He would be gentle these first nights, not wanting to frighten her. She was still weak. He would be content with tame loving for the time being, and keep that trunk hidden in the back of his closet. There would be time for his treasures later. Lots of time.

Chapter Twenty-two

KITTY stood at the partially opened door leading to the veranda, staring through misty eyes into the somber night. Her nails dug into her clenched hands, but she was not aware of the pain. No, the real agony came from within.

If it weren't for little John, perhaps she would have walked out onto the veranda and hurled herself over the edge. She shook her head from side to side. There had to be some way of coping. Perhaps Corey really did love her.

"Maybe it isn't as terrible as it seems," she whispered, squeezing her eyes shut as tears began to sting. "He professes to love the baby. He swears he loves me. Maybe we will be happy. Maybe one day I won't think of Travis every moment of my life . . ."

"Darling?"

She whirled about to gasp at Corey standing only a few feet away. He had come through the door between their two bedrooms without a sound. Had he heard her anguished whispers? His eyes glittered. Was it anger or desire?

He stepped closer. "Darling, I'm sorry I was detained. One of my men had important business with me, but I cursed every moment that kept us apart. I've dreamed of this moment for so long . . ."

He frowned, eyes raking over her pale blue satin

gown, the one she had chosen for their wedding. "You haven't undressed," he said accusingly.

Her gaze followed his to the crumpled gown on the floor beside the canopied bed. There were delicately lace-edged holes in the bodice, holes through which her breasts were supposed to protrude.

She took a deep breath, searching for the right words. "Corey, that gown looks like something a . . . a woman of the night would wear. How can you ask *me* to wear such a thing?"

His hands touched her shoulders. "Darling, we're married now. Anything we do is quite permissible."

She shook her head. "You don't understand—"

"I *do* understand!" he snapped. "I understand that I have kept up my end of the bargain. I've given your illegitimate child a name. I've deeded your land to him, free and clear, when he comes of legal age. I give you wealth, position . . . everything a poor Southern woman yearns for in these destitute times. But *you*, you have given me nothing, and you refuse me the delight of seeing you in the gown which I bought especially for our wedding night. I should have known you would be ungrateful."

"I will submit to you, Corey," she said tonelessly. "That is my duty."

"It is your duty to do whatever I tell you to do." He was quaking with rage as he pointed to the crumpled gown. "And I order you to put on that gown and model it for me. Show me what I have bargained for. Show me what I have *purchased*!"

"You . . . you didn't *buy* me," she sputtered. "We discussed our arrangement. I told you I would be a dutiful wife, and I will. I said nothing about parading around in the clothes of a *whore*!"

He smirked. "You aren't exactly a blushing virgin, Kitty. You have a child, remember? And I don't think his conception was any divine miracle. And I know there was another man besides your Yankee lover, that Luke Tate who kidnapped you."

"Oh, you throw the past in my face sooner than I'd anticipated," she cried.

"Stop acting like a child. Everyone knows you gave birth out of wedlock, and now I've given you the respectability of marriage *and* given your bastard my name."

"You call my son a bastard?"

"Kitty, Kitty," he laughed ruefully, struggling to hold her. "Will you stop playing the role of an indignant lady? Be yourself. Be the wanton, passionate woman I know you can be. Be the woman in *my* arms that you were for your Yankee lover."

Lavender eyes flashed with purple and golden sparks. Her chin jutted up. "What I shared with Captain Coltrane will never be shared with you, Corey. I said I would be a dutiful wife, and I will submit to you when you want me, but that is *all*."

His hands moved quickly to squeeze her breasts possessively, painfully, but she would not cry out and give him the pleasure of knowing he was hurting her. "You're my wife now, Kitty, and you'll do anything I say. I own you, as I own everything else around here. You will do as I wish."

His breath upon her face was hot, and she could smell whiskey. His fingers tightened their grip. "I can be gentle with you and make you revel in passion that you never dreamed existed, or I can be quite unpleasant. It doesn't matter to me, for I intend to take my pleasure in any manner I choose. Resist me, and you will only suffer."

"And you said you loved me," she spat out, clawing angrily at his hands. "Lies. All lies."

Giving her a vicious shove that sent her sprawling across the bed, he laughed. "Oh, I do love you, sweet, just as I love all my things. And I'll learn to love you even more when you start obeying. Not that I don't like your spirit. Oh, please, my dear, don't ever lose that spirit. But you must learn to unleash it at *my* will, not yours. I want you to let it go when I'm inside you, and then you can go wild with passion and roll your buttocks and thrust that sweet love nest against me and release all the spirit you want."

He was slipping off his coat, removing his cravat, his shirt, eyes riveted upon hers. Kitty could not believe this was happening. He had been so kind, so solicitous, and now he was a madman. And there was no denying that with each word he spoke he was becoming more and more aroused.

And then he was naked, towering over her, his swollen member staring at her. He leaped upon her, ripping at her gown as he covered her face with wet, hungry kisses. He tore the delicate dress quickly from her body. With legs bent, he straddled her, yanking at the filmy undergarments.

She lay naked beneath him.

"Lovely," he breathed hoarsely, squeezing one rosy nipple as though testing the ripeness of fruit. "So lovely. And mine."

He attempted to kiss her lips. When she would not open her mouth, he grasped a handful of golden-red hair in his fingers, twisting until she cried out in pain. Then, with her lips parted, he lowered his mouth, wriggling his tongue inside at the same moment he maneuvered his swollen organ between the silken thighs.

One plunge, one hard, thrusting plunge, and he lifted his head to cry out in anger. "No, no." He muttered a string of curses, then jerked away from her to huddle on the side of the bed, head in his hands as he babbled to himself.

Kitty stared at him in wonder, then reached to pull at a coverlet to cover her nakedness.

He turned wretched, tormented eyes upon her. "I feared this. I feared that once I tasted your sweetness I wouldn't be able to control myself. I wanted it to last for hours—*hours*, do you hear me?" He pounded upon the bed with his fists in frustration, and she cringed.

"Maybe . . . maybe tomorrow night . . ." she whispered hesistantly, secretly grateful that the assault had ended.

His lips curved suddenly into a suggestive leer. "No. The night is just beginning, Kitty. It won't take long for you to prepare me again. And this time I'll last much, much longer." He stretched out beside her, reaching to dig his fingers into her arm and pull her closer as she tried to move away. Guiding her stiffened fingers toward his flaccid organ, he commanded, "You can arouse me, Kitty. You know how to make a man swell with desire. Make me want you, and I'll stay inside you till the sun rises."

"No!" she screamed. "I can't."

"You can and you will, unless you want me to throw you and your child out into the streets tomorrow. I'll tell everyone how I discovered on our wedding night that you had the pox, that you were diseased and filthy. No one will lift a finger to help you. No one. You'll starve, you and your bastard. Now, what is it going to be? Marriage? Or starvation and death? Make up your mind fast, because I have lived for this night, and I intend to enjoy every second."

She thought of her precious baby, sleeping peacefully in the room just across the hall. His own father had not returned, and his life, his future, lay in her hands. All over the South, people were starving among the ruins of the war. But she and little John had a chance to survive.

She forced her fingers to close on his limp organ. She felt him stiffen. His fingers began to massage her breast as his tongue licked up the side of her cheek.

She wanted to gag. "Feel me all over," he commanded huskily. "Yes, that's it. Down there. Squeeze them, too. They like that. Oh yes, oh yes, oh yes . . ." He was crooning.

"Squeeze me back there. Now, up and down. That's it. Oh-oh! On your back. Quickly!"

He slung her over, spreading her thighs roughly as he plunged inside. She held her breath, waiting for his movements to begin, but he lay very still, his breathing ragged as he whispered, "Like velvet. I knew it would feel like hot, sweet, velvet. I want to stay here all night. I want to feel myself inside you all night long. No man has what I have. No man will ever be here but me."

His head rested on her chest, tongue flicking at her nipples. Suddenly his whole body contorted. Once, twice, three times, he thrust inside her, hands moving to grip her buttocks and slam her even tighter against him, and then once more he was cursing, rolling away. "Too good. Too damned good." He leaped to his feet. "We've got to do something about that. We've got to make it last longer."

Kitty blinked back the tears furiously, clawing at the sheets beneath her. Never had she been so desperate. "Please. No more, Corey. Not tonight. Maybe you're just eager because it is our first time."

He dismissed her reasoning with an impatient wave of his hand. "Oh, what do you know? You're just a woman." He paced up and down the room, still naked and making no attempt to cover himself as he folded his hands behind his back. "I have a problem. A problem you cannot understand. I always come quickly with a woman, and the more desirable she is, the faster it happens. I feared it would be even worse with you, because I've wanted you so fiercely. And I was right. Women of the night, the prostitutes and harlots, *they* know how to take care of such a problem. And you, my sweet, are going to have to learn. This is our wedding night, and it has to be special. I must bring you pleasure, too."

He whirled around. "Well?" He looked down at her with dancing black eyes, an expectant smile on his lips. "What do you intend to do for me? You have to arouse me and make me ready for another turn, so that I can take you to the heights of pleasure also."

She turned her face away.

Travis, Travis, where are you?

Trembling fingers twisted in her long hair, painfully yanking her head around. Corey was moving to straddle her naked body. He pushed her globular breasts together, sliding his stiffening member to and fro between them. He gave a low, guttural moan. "Make it good. I know you can, I know you have the spirit in that sweet, hot flesh. Oh, Kitty . . ."

He rocked back and forth between her breasts, head thrown back in wild-eyed ecstasy. Saliva drooled from the corners of his mouth, his whole body shuddered. Thumbnails dug into her reddening nipples, and she could feel his testicles dragging across her belly. "Ahhh, don't let it happen yet, my animal of pleasure. I want it to last forever."

He continued to undulate between her breasts as she tossed her head wildly from side to side, fighting the nausea that was rising in her throat.

Suddenly he gave an outraged cry, squeezing her breasts savagely and rubbing them hard against his member. Then he was whimpering, like a child in pain. It was over. Thank God, it was over once again. He rolled away from her and got to his feet. She watched in numbness as he moved across the room and disappeared through the doorway into his own chambers. All the while, he was cursing her for not making him last longer, admonishing himself for being so eager, swearing that next time would be better.

Kitty lay prostrate for only a few moments. Then, wrapping a sheet around her, she moved to the bell cord and gave it a vicious yank. It seemed hours before Dulcie knocked.

"Please come in here." Kitty fought the hysteria. The wide-eyed girl stepped inside uncertainly, looking about the room.

"Please draw me a bath at once," Kitty said. "A hot bath. A very hot bath."

Never had she felt so soiled. Even during the war, when she traveled with the soldiers and fought the maggots and the lice, she had never felt so unclean. The impulse to scream was like a fierce burning in her throat, and she clenched and unclenched her hands as she waited for the bath.

Finally she was able to step behind the silken screen with its gold-embroidered panels and slip down into the soothing, steaming water. "Leave me," she whispered to Dulcie.

The water had a calming effect, and she began to think clearly once again. So this was what her life was to be. Corey was insatiable, and the future would hold all manner of depravities. And she was helpless. As his wife, she would have to endure whatever he chose to inflict upon her.

There was, however, some comfort in the realization that he was unable to control himself for any great length of time. The acts would be short, and Kitty decided she would make them even shorter.

Endure. That would be the sole thought on which she would concentrate from this time forward. All else would have to be erased from her mind. She would bear children, run the household, tat and sew, and sit with the other women. It was a lifetime ago that she dared to dream of going away to school and studying to be a doctor. Now she could not even farm her own land. Her life was not her own any longer. Nothing she had ever wanted out of life would come to be. Ever. She had stopped living. Dreams were gone.

"Kitty?"

She sat straight up in the tub, sloshing water over the rim onto the floor, her body rigid.

"Oh, you're taking a bath." Corey's voice came from the other side of the silk dressing screen. "A wonderful idea. You'll rest better tonight. Hurry and finish and come see what I asked Hugo to prepare for us. I noticed you didn't eat much at dinner. But then, what bride feels like eating on her wedding day?" He chuckled.

"It was exciting, I know," Corey was saying. "But you must remember that you are recuperating from your illness, and you were a very sick young lady. Dr. Sims says you must take care of yourself or you'll be right back in bed again. We can't have that. Not with our wedding party coming up soon."

Rubbing herself frantically with a towel, Kitty grabbed the thick velvet robe that had been placed beside the tub. Thank goodness it covered her from her neck to her toes, giving little emphasis to the generous curves of her body.

"Hurry, my dear. Your food will get cold." His voice was different, not all husky with desire. "I want you to enjoy yourself and then get right into bed for a good night's rest."

She stepped around the screen to see that Corey was wearing a silk dressing gown, his hair neatly brushed. Smiling, he gestured to the ornate silver tray he had placed upon the bedside table. She saw china cups filled with steaming tea and watched silently as he laced each with honey. A tray of daintily arranged sandwiches looked appealing, despite the feeling in the pit of her stomach.

"Venison," he gestured. "You didn't touch yours at dinner, so I had Hugo slice the meat thinly and place it between bread. It will give you nourishment."

He was seated in one of the exquisite Victorian chairs. Uneasily, Kitty lowered herself to the edge of the bed. Picking up one of the sandwiches, she took a small bite. It was delicious, and if he would just leave her alone, she might be able to fill her empty stomach.

"Tomorrow you must sit down with Hugo and go over the invitation list for the party," he said pleasantly, sipping his tea. "I have invited everyone I think is important, but I want to make sure you include your friends and relatives."

"You know I have neither." It was difficult to swallow, sitting opposite Corey. It was as though he had completely forgotten the words he had screamed at her, calling her son a bastard, taunting her.

"Oh, you do have friends *now*," he snapped. "You're my wife. No one would dare snub Mrs. Corey McRae. So, if there is anyone you wish to have invited, I will see to it that they are here."

Chuckling, he added, "Perhaps there is someone you would like to invite just to lord it over them?"

"No, no one," she murmured, shaking her head from side to side, her expression somber. "I don't want revenge. I just want peace."

Picking up a small frosted cake, he took a bite. "I thought about inviting Nancy Warren Stoner. That would be a much-needed comeuppance for her. She wouldn't dare refuse an invitation to attend such an event, and I would love to see her face. You, the woman she hates more than anyone else in the whole world, are now mistress of the house and hold the position she so coveted. You'll never know how that woman tried to get me to marry her, Kitty."

Her whisper was barely audible. "I don't want to know."

He went on as though she had not protested. "Our last encounter was quite unpleasant, and she made some rather ugly threats. I've also heard that she is getting herself involved with that scoundrel, Jerome Danton. He and those blasted night riders of his. Disgusting. Every one of them should be hung from the highest limb in Wayne County."

"I don't think they had anything to do with what happened to Mattie Glass."

Corey's head jerked up. He swallowed hard. "What did you say?"

Her voice was emotionless, but her lavender eyes sparkled with anger. "I heard about what happened to the widow Mattie Glass. I think it's atrocious, but I do not believe that Jerome Danton and his men had anything to do with it."

"And how did you come by this information? Who have you been talking to?" He was unable to keep the alarmed tone from his voice.

"The parson's wife whispered to me about what happened. She told me that some people think Mr. Danton is responsible. I don't think so."

"Now why do you say that? A cross was burned. This *is* the way Danton and his hoodlums do things."

"No, it is *not* the way they do things. They have never attacked a white woman before, and if they did do such a thing, they would not have left such an obvious calling card. I think someone burned the cross to put the blame on Danton's men."

"You sound quite concerned, my dear. Why?" He gazed at her through narrowed eyes. Before, she had seemed placid, whipped, defeated. Now he saw the anger sparkling, and he could not understand the change.

"I want whoever did it caught. I happen to be

quite fond of Mattie Glass. She was one of the few people who was ever kind to me when I was working at the hospital. She came with other women from her church to minister to the wounded, write letters for them and do what they could. The other women would always go out of their way to hurl insults at me. Nancy did her job well. She had everyone hating me and blaming me for Nathan's death.

"One day, one of the women from the church, who happened to be a cousin of Nathan's, suddenly went into a rage and began calling me all kinds of names. Mattie came to my defense. She reminded her that she professed to be a Christian, and that it was a sin for her to judge me. She took the woman outside, then came back to apologize for her. We talked a bit, and I told her not to bother herself with me, that I was used to the insults."

Kitty blinked hard. It moved her to think of one of the few times anyone had shown her any tenderness in the past year. "Mattie cried. She stood there and looked at me with tears streaming down her face and told me how she hated the way her brothers and sisters in God were treating me. I never forgot her kindness. And each time she visited the hospital, no matter how busy we both were, she always found a moment to come up and whisper to me that she was still remembering me in her prayers. She is a good woman, a Christian woman, and it makes me so angry to think of what happened to her. I want to see the men responsible punished."

Corey would have to make sure that he and Rance did not discuss anything where they might be overheard. There was no telling what Kitty might do if she discovered his men had been responsible.

"In a few days, when Mrs. Glass is feeling better, I intend to pay her a visit and offer to buy her land for a generous sum of money. She can then move into town and raise her sons there. It's too dangerous for a woman to be living out here in the country without a man around for protection."

Kitty's look was suspicious. "Why would you do that? Why should you care?"

"For the same reason you care, because I think a deplorable thing has happened."

"I still don't understand why you would offer to buy her land."

"What kind of a person do you take me for?"

"Corey, I *know* you," she sighed, setting down the tea cup and dabbing at her lips with a linen napkin. "I have found out that when you are nice to people, you always have an ulterior motive."

"That's not a very nice thing to say to your husband, Kitty. I won't stand for it."

"It's true." Her eyes locked with his, blazing. "You are nice to people only when you figure you will get something out of them. Look how you used *me*! You ravished me mercilessly tonight, with no tenderness or affection. You called my child a bastard, ridiculed my helplessness. No, Corey, I see you now for what you really are—selfish, uncaring, unfeeling. So you must have a motive in wanting to help Mattie Glass. What is it? That lovely stream on her property? I visited there with Poppa many times as we made our rounds selling the honey from our hives. I know how lovely her land is. I will wager that you already own her delinquent tax certificate, but are trying to create a respectable image. You don't want it said that Corey McRae threw a helpless widow and her two children off of her land."

He got to his feet so quickly that the teacup went clattering to the floor. "If I would not hate to see that lovely face of yours marred for our party," he said through gritted teeth, fists clenched at his sides, "I'd teach you the price you pay for insulting your husband. I would teach you your place, just as my servants have felt the lash to learn theirs."

She stood up also. "I don't fear you. You can force me to submit to you, and you can beat me at your will, but I will never fear you."

An evil smile crept across his lips, and Kitty fought the impulse to shiver. He could look quite formidable, but she was not about to be intimidated.

His black eyes began to dance with pleasure, and he suddenly laughed. Purple eyes sparkling like fiery red rubies, peach blossom cheeks flushed with her rage—she was beautiful! "My God, Kitty, you are the most delightful creature I have ever met, the loveliest woman I have ever seen, and I will be the envy of every man in the state for having a wife like you. Perhaps you hate me now, but you will come to revel in your new status."

"I *do* hate you," she hissed, not caring if he did take the lash to her. "I had no idea just how selfish and brutal you could be until tonight. I will always hate you."

Amused, he raised an eyebrow. "And I suppose you will always love your dashing cavalry officer, even though he deserted you when you were carrying his child?"

"Yes." She nodded firmly. "I will always love Travis. Nothing you can do will ever change that. And I refuse to discuss him with you."

"Very well." He yawned, touching his fingertips to his open mouth. "It doesn't matter anyway. You're mine now, and you will live your life the way I choose. The past doesn't have any part in our present or our future. Continue to resent me and you will only find misery. This I promise you."

He bent and brushed his lips against hers, but she

turned her face to the side. "Good night, my loving wife," he laughed. "Sleep well."

He left, closing the door.

It was over. For a little while, praise God, it was over.

Chapter Twenty-three

WHEN Dulcie opened the blue velvet drapes that morning, Kitty awakened to ask that her son be brought to her. Fed and bathed, he snuggled in her arms as she marveled once again over his precious cherub's face. He soon fell asleep, and Dulcie returned him to his nursery, then helped Kitty dress.

Another servant brought in her breakfast tray. Kitty forced herself to eat the hoecakes, slathered in molasses and fresh-churned butter, but the slab of fried ham was too greasy for her still weak stomach. After a second cup of tea, she lay back down on the bed Dulcie had freshly made. It was not long before Hugo arrived with the invitation list.

"I have no names to give you," Kitty told him sharply. "I don't care who Mr. McRae has invited."

"But it is your wedding party." Hugo looked annoyed. Kitty didn't like him. There was something about him that she found distasteful. Perhaps it was his profound loyalty to his master.

She dismissed him quickly. "Plan the party the way you and Mr. McRae wish, Hugo. I don't want to be bothered with any of it. I'm tired now, and I'd like to rest."

He bowed slightly. "Whatever you wish, madame, but I should inform you that Mrs. Rivenbark will be here shortly after lunch to take fittings for your gown."

"*What* gown? I have not requested any new clothes."

"You are to be fitted for your ball gown, madame." He sounded exasperated. Before Corey came along and tutored him, Hugo had been a cotton-patch slave. It galled her to see him take such a condescending attitude toward the Negroes around him.

Now she eyed him coolly and said, "All right. Have Mrs. Rivenbark come upstairs when she arrives. I suppose I am expected to be fashionably dressed for the occasion. Dear me, Hugo, what would I do without *you* to coach me?" she added sarcastically.

He frowned, gave his slight bow once again, and left the room with a tight, angry look on his face. Dulcie could not control her giggles. "Miss Kitty, you sure put him in his place. You got no idea how mean he is to the rest of us."

"I can imagine, Dulcie. Life here doesn't seem very pleasant for anyone. It doesn't matter about me. I can cope. But I will not allow my child to suffer."

"Oh, you don't have to worry about that baby. I looks after him real good, ma'm. He's such a cute li'l fellow. I look after him like he was my own."

"I would like his cradle to be brought in here so that I can care for him myself."

Dulcie faced Kitty with a frightened expression. "Miss Kitty, Mistah McRae won't allow that. He say I'm to tend to that young'un, 'cause you gonna have plenty to do."

"Plenty to do?" Kitty echoed. "What does he mean?"

"Oh, I thinks he wants you to have lots of teas and parties and—"

"Well, we'll see about that. I have no intentions of fluttering around serving tea to a lot of old biddies who secretly hate me. I want to spend as much time as possible with my son. He's the only thing in this world that means anything to me. You bring in the cradle like I told you to, and all of his things. I am taking over his care. And when Mrs. Rivenbark leaves this afternoon, I would like you to send for Jacob. I haven't seen him in a while and I want to talk to him."

Dulcie stared down at her feet.

"Well?" Kitty asked impatiently. "What's the matter now?"

Dulcie continued to bow her head as she mumbled, "Mistah McRae ain't gonna allow no field niggers in this house, ma'm. Jacob's come to the back door several times to ask about you, but Fanny, the cook, she would send for me, and I'd have to tell him he couldn't come in. Last time, Hugo told him the next time he showed his face at that door, he'd run him off the place. Told him he better think about that, 'cause he wouldn't have nowhere to go."

"And you let him treat your uncle like that? And what about his grandsons?"

"Fanny, she look after them. Oh, I wanted to stand up and say something, but it'd just make things worse for everybody. Hugo can run those grandboys off with Jacob, and then what would Jacob do? Nobody wants to give an old man a job, Miss Kitty. Jacob knows that."

"Then I'll go into the fields and find him myself. And if you don't bring John and his things into this room, I'll do that myself, too. Honestly, Dulcie, I had hoped that you and I would become close, that I could trust you. After all, I asked you to slip one of my letters to Captain Coltrane out, didn't I? I realize you're frightened of Hugo and Mr. McRae, but I am mistress of this house now, and I should have some say-so."

She stopped as she saw the look on Dulcie's face. Tears were streaming down her cheeks, and her shoulders were trembling. Slowly, realization spread through Kitty like liquid fire. "You never mailed my letter, did you?" she cried. "Dear God in heaven, Dulcie, I trusted you!"

The Negro girl continued to sob, and finally Kitty snapped in disgust, "Never mind. I had Jacob take letters directly into town. I know some messages were mailed. What pains me so is to realize *you* betrayed me. What did you do with the letter I gave you? You might as well tell me the truth now."

"I . . . I gave it to Mistah McRae." Her voice was a low, anguished moan. "And when he finds out I told you, he gonna beat the skin off my back, for sure. He gonna run me off this place. I ain't gonna have no place to go."

"You'll find another job, Dulcie. You're young, strong, efficient. I wish I could keep this confidential between us, but I intend to let Corey know that I have found out about his deception. Oh, damn him!" She leaped off the bed and began to pace up and down the room. "Damn him to hell! I learn more and more about how devious he can be."

Dulcie continued to stand holding the chamber pot, the tears still flowing. With a sudden feeling of pity for the girl, who had done only what she had been told to do, Kitty put her arms around Dulcie's shoulders. "You will find another job if Mr. McRae makes you leave, Dulcie, and you will be better off. Not everyone in this world is as mean as Corey McRae, thank God. I wish I could leave.'

She started to walk away, but Dulcie began to cry even harder, and Kitty whirled around, alarmed. "Whatever is the matter, Dulcie? I won't let him beat you. And if Hugo tries, you run straight for me, do you hear?"

"It ain't that," the girl sobbed. "I can't get no other job, missy, not working in no house. They'll put me in the fields, and I can't work in no fields, not when I'm gonna have a baby."

"A baby?" Kitty gasped. "Whose baby?"

"Hugo!" She spat with contempt. "He got me this way when I first come here, and I lost the baby. I was glad. But he got me this way again, and I come to love little John so much that I wants a baby of my own, even if it is by Hugo. I don't want to lose this 'un, but I will if I get run off from here and put in the fields to grub on my hands and knees in the dirt all day." She hicupped.

"A very touching scene."

They both turned to see Corey standing in the open door between his room and Kitty's. He can move as silently as a cat, Kitty thought, a chill moving up and down her spine.

He stepped closer. "Now, Dulcie, don't you worry about a thing. One day Mrs. McRae will thank you for helping me to save her from herself. She is much better off married to me, as she will come to realize once she gets over her stubbornness."

He slipped his arm about Kitty's waist, and she stiffened as he kissed her cheek. "Good morning, my beautiful bride," he whispered. She did not respond. He turned to Dulcie once again. "You will remain here, and I will see to it that your duties are lightened as the time for your confinement approaches. We don't want to lose this baby. Goodness, no. If you learn to read and write and become efficient and educated enough to take over the duties of the house along with Hugo, I will see that he marries you."

"I don't want to marry him!" she screamed, then cringed as she realized her mistake in contradicting her master.

"Oh, Hugo isn't all bad. He's just trying to do the job I have asked him to do. Now, you run along and empty the chamber pot, then tell Fanny to prepare refreshments for this afternoon. The fitting will take a while, I am sure."

Dulcie started to leave, but he called out to her once again. She stopped walking but did not turn, keeping her head down fearfully as he said, "I also overheard my wife's request about moving the baby in here. It will not be done. I don't want that old fool Jacob coming in the house, either. Now get on with your work." The snap in his voice sent her scurrying.

Kitty whirled on him furiously. "How dare you tell me I cannot move my son into my room with me? And Jacob is a very old, dear friend . . ." She was trembling with rage.

He gripped her shoulders and gave her a violent shake. "Now, you listen to me, woman, and you listen well. You are trying my patience. *I* run things in my house. Is it going to take a sound beating to put that in your mind? I will not tolerate these scenes, especially in front of my servants. That baby is not going to be moved in here because I have other plans for you besides tending to him. You are going to be a social leader, my dear. As for Jacob, I will not have my wife entertaining a field nigra in my house. Is that clear?"

He released her, and she stumbled dizzily, almost falling, but he caught her again, fingers digging into the soft flesh of her shoulders. "I have had about all I intend to take from that spitfire temper of yours, Kitty."

She was coming out of her dazed state and she turned on him furiously. "How dare you talk to me this way, as though I were a slave? I will move my son in here, and I will see Jacob, even if I have to go to the fields myself. And now that I know you kept Dulcie from mailing my letter, I think I hate you even more! If I can find a way, I will leave."

His palm cracked across her face, sending her reeling backwards. Losing her footing, she fell to the floor. Before she could make a move, he was there to yank her back up, entwining his fingers in her hair. Again he slapped her, this time knocking her across the bed. Then he was falling on top of her, pushing up her skirt, ripping at her undergarments. Twisting and moaning, Kitty fought him with every ounce of strength she could muster, but she was easily overpowered. She felt her legs being spread apart roughly, and then he was pummeling inside her, thrusting to and fro savagely, not caring that she cried out with the pain.

After one loud grunt, he moved back and then grinned down at her triumphantly. "Do you like that, my dear? Do you like being slapped around and then taken by force? Of course you do. And don't worry about any bruises on that beautiful face. I'll have Hugo bring in something right away. Now get yourself together. Mrs. Rivenbark will be here soon."

"You bastard!" The words hissed across the silence of the room. "You filthy bastard! I hate you! And I will find a way to leave you."

Never had she seen him so angry. He twisted back around to fall on top of her again. His fingers squeezed down on her throat until she felt herself slipping away into a deep void. "You try to leave me, ever, and I'll kill that brat of yours. Do you hear me? I'll kill him, and then I'll ravish you until you're worn out and useless and no man will ever want you. Don't keep trying my patience, Kitty. I warn you."

His voice came from far, far away, and just when she felt the hands of death reaching out for her, he released his hold. She coughed, choking in the sweet air. Corey stalked to his own room, slamming the door loudly after him.

Kitty was still lying there when Dulcie returned. "Oh, missy." She dropped the chamber pot with a loud clatter as she rushed to the bedside. "That man done hurt you, ain't he? I should of knowed, when you made Hugo mad, he'd run straight to tell him you was riled up, and then he'd be a'standing on the other side of that door a'listening. Oh, Lordy, Lordy," she moaned over and over.

Kitty struggled to sit up, yanking down her skirts self-consciously. It was obvious that she had been raped by her own husband. "Just please get me some brandy, Dulcie," she whispered miserably. "That will help me more than anything else right now."

He would kill John, Kitty thought in terror once she was alone. He's insane. He would do it.

Dulcie returned with the brandy, and Kitty downed the first glass quickly, then asked for another. "Miss Kitty, don't make him mad no more, please. He . . . he's got ways of making a woman suffer," Dulcie whispered.

Kitty looked at her sharply. "What do you mean?"

"That other woman, that Stoner woman . . . when she stayed here, there was nights she screamed. And there were other women, and they screamed." Dulcie lowered her voice, and Kitty had to strain to hear. "Mistah McRae's got another room, on the top floor, and he don't let none of us go in there. Nobody goes in there but him. He keeps it locked all the time. That's where he took those other women. That's where the screaming came from."

Kitty chewed her lower lip worriedly. "Were those women all right later? I mean, the next morning?"

"We left trays outside their door. Sometimes we didn't see 'em come or go. Miss Nancy, though, she looked all right, maybe a bit tired. Even Hugo has said he'd love to know what goes on in that room. Miss Nancy must not have minded too much, though, 'cause she sho did try to get the mastah to marry up with her."

"A pity she didn't succeed," Kitty murmured, then asked, "How is the door locked? Is it opened with a key like the others in this house?"

Dulcie nodded. "But only Mistah McRae got the key."

"Well, we may just have to find another way in there."

The brown-skinned girl shook with fright. "Don't ask me to help you, Miss Kitty, please. I don't want to know what's in that room. You just pray to God you don't never find out, that he don't ever make you go up there."

Kitty tried to rest after Dulcie finally left her, but her mind was whirling. Hugo came in to inspect her face, and she flinched as he touched her. Satisfied there were no bruises, he gave a smug smile and insolent bow and left her. Dulcie returned with a tray at lunch, but Kitty could not eat. Then, all too soon, Mrs. Rivenbark was announced.

She fluttered into the room, a fat, red-cheeked woman with wisps of gray hair flying from the tight bun rolled at the nape of her neck. She was very friendly, and Kitty suppressed a smile as she remembered the woman as one of those who had crossed the street to keep from passing her.

Mrs. Rivenbark was talking incessantly, and Kitty was lost in her own thoughts until she felt a hand on her shoulder. "Mrs. McRae, are you looking at any of these sketches?"

"Yes, yes, that one is fine." She pointed at the one before her, not really seeing it, not caring.

"Ahh, that is one of my most beautiful creations." She was obviously pleased over Kitty's choice. "You will carry the full hoops quite gracefully, I feel sure. This particular design will be lovely in pink silk. We'll start by draping pale pink gauze over a deeper shade of pink. You notice that the neckline is quite low, so

I have designed a shawl to hang in graceful, deep swaths. No ruffles. The dress is stunning with the skirt and shoulder drapes caught up with tiny bouquets of silk roses. White or pink?"

Kitty's mind had drifted once again.

"White or pink silk roses?" Mrs. Rivenbark asked sharply.

"Oh, it doesn't matter. Whatever you think."

"Very well." She sounded dubious. "Mr. McRae told me you were to look stunning, and I feel this will be my greatest creation. May I have permission to do your hair as well? I will come early and dress you myself."

"Yes, yes."

Mrs. Rivenbark clucked about taking Kitty's measurements, commenting on her enviable bosom and tiny waist. "You won't even need a corset."

And then she was saying something that brought Kitty back to the present. "What did you say about Mattie Glass?" Kitty demanded.

"I was saying that the poor woman is miserable. Those animals ripped her apart. It makes me so mad. I talked to Dr. Pope just this morning. I went to the hospital before I came here, and he wouldn't let me see her, but he says that while she'll mend physically, he's worried about how all this is going to affect her mind. She just lies in bed and stares at the ceiling, he says. They have to force food into her mouth and make her swallow. One of her sons has a broken jaw and lost most of his teeth. The other one is pretty badly bruised. It's a terrible situation, and the whole county is up in arms about it."

"Please give her my love," Kitty said. "I know how she feels."

Mrs. Rivenbark lifted her eyebrows, and her apple cheeks turned even redder. "Yes. I—I heard about your misfortunes during the war. I'm sorry."

"Do they have any idea how long she will be in the hospital?"

"Several weeks. Me and the other ladies in the church are going to keep trying to visit her. I just hope they catch the animals who did it. No woman is safe till they do. And I just don't believe the Klan had anything to do with it. I heard from the parson that a message was nailed to the door of the hospital during the night, and whoever wrote it said they were a member of the Klan, and they declared before God that their group was not responsible. They even said the Klan was trying themselves to find out who's responsible and see that they're punished."

Finished with her measuring, she began to tuck her swatches of material and sketches into a large cloth bag. "I, for one, will be glad to see the federal marshals get here. Folks in town plan to demand that their first order of business be to find those men. It's the Lord's blessing that Joe Paul and William Earl were knocked out. It'd be a horrible thing to watch something like that happening to your mother."

"Yes, it certainly would," Kitty agreed. "What about the sheriff? Is he trying to find them?"

Mrs. Rivenbark snorted. "He's got his hands full trying to keep the whites and nigras from killing each other. The town is filled with uppity nigras now, and we just aren't going to put up with it. My man, Josh, he keeps his gun right by the bed. Had to hide it when the Yankees were in town, or they would've taken it away from him. Lord, I was glad to see them go. Still a few around, but they don't do anything but drink at the saloon and mess with those women. They're supposed to be keeping order, but I sure haven't seen any. It's not safe for a woman to even walk the streets in the daylight by herself."

She sighed. "Well, I will be back in a day or so, and

we'll start sewing. We'll have everyone in the county talking about how lovely you are. I hear some very important people have been invited. Is it true the Governor himself has been invited?" she asked excitedly.

"I really don't know," Kitty said, shrugging. "I haven't seen the invitation list. I am leaving all that to Corey."

The woman looked at her curiously.

"I have been ill, you know," she added quickly.

Mrs. Rivenbark nodded. "Oh, yes, that's right. I suppose you aren't up to handling the details. I hear the menu is sumptuous! Roast quails and ducks and pigs and deer. And there will be fruits and vegetables brought in from Raleigh. And the cake! I hear the cake is going to be this tall." She stretched her hands about a yard apart.

"You seem to know more about my wedding party than I do."

Once again the apple cheeks glowed. "Well, it is the talk of the town. Everyone is hoping to be invited. Me, included."

"Well, I'll see what I can do about that."

"Oh, would you?" The dumpy little woman beamed. "My, what a treat it would be for me to be standing at the foot of those stairs when you make your grand entrance wearing *my* dress! It would be a night I would always remember."

Kitty walked downstairs and all the way out to Mrs. Rivenbark's buggy. Her husband was waiting, and he bowed, beaming. Kitty remembered him, too. He was another who had snubbed her. Now, just as Corey had predicted, he was positively obsequious.

Kitty breathed in the fresh air. Spring would soon burst across the land. Already she could taste it. Dogwood trees were threatening to burst into blossom, and she caught the first pungent fragrance of the wild honeysuckle that was beginning to creep along the edge of the veranda.

Just as Josh Rivenbark was helping his wife into the buggy, Corey came walking around the corner with Rance and Coot. Kitty detested his hired guns. They swaggered so cockily when they walked, holsters low, hats tipped forward to shade their ugly, swarthy faces. She disliked Coot most of all, because he reminded her of Luke Tate. And whenever Corey wasn't around or did not happen to be looking, both Coot and Rance leered at her, eyes moving over her body. It made her want to run.

"Oh, Mrs. Rivenbark . . . Mr. Rivenbark," Corey called affably, turning on his charm. "Good afternoon. How did my wife's fitting go? Did she choose a lovely gown, befitting her dazzling beauty?" He gave Kitty an adoring gaze, and she fought the impulse to retch.

"Yes, yes, she did." Already in the buggy, Mrs. Rivenbark was fumbling in her bag, showing Corey the sketch and the swatch of pink silk.

Corey was studying the sketch thoughtfully, then examining the swatch of silk. Kitty looked at Rance and Coot out of the corner of her eye and saw that they were giving her that look again. She tilted her head up and flashed them a withering gaze, and they looked away self-consciously, but not before she saw the flash of anger in Coot's eyes.

"The design is fine."

Mrs. Rivenbark beamed.

"I especially like the décolletage. My wife's generous endowments should be displayed like rare jewels." Kitty felt her face flame, heard the snickers from Coot and Rance, saw Josh Rivenbark's astonishment.

"But the material is all wrong. I want my wife in green silk, Mrs. Rivenbark. An emerald green to match the jewels I plan to give her."

He looked at Kitty for her reaction. He was smiling expectantly. She stared at him. Frowning over her lack of enthusiasm, he turned back to Mrs. Rivenbark. "She will be wearing an emerald necklace, set with diamonds, and matching earrings. Go by Giddens Jewelers in town and see them. I haven't picked them up yet. Make sure the green matches exactly."

"I may have difficulty—" she began.

"Then make a trip to Raleigh," he said, dismissing her protest. "You'll be paid for all your time and effort."

"Yes, of course, whatever you say," she said quickly. "She's going to let me do her hair, too, Mr. McRae. I'll dress her completely."

"Fine. Good day." He reached and grabbed Kitty's arm, pulling her up the steps and across the veranda.

"I wanted to stay outside and enjoy the fresh air, if you don't mind," she snapped.

"Well, I do mind. You are not to wander about unescorted. Not ever, do you understand? And Coot and Rance and I have business to discuss, and we don't have time to walk you about."

"I wouldn't want to walk with any of you anyway. I'd rather sit in my room and rot."

He opened the door for her, and there stood Hugo, waiting to lead her up to her room. "Hugo, make sure Mrs. McRae does not wander about outside unescorted," he said crisply. "I want her to lie down now till dinner."

He gave her a meaningful smile. "Rest for tonight, my dear. I look forward to spending the evening with you."

He turned on his heel and hurried back to his men, while Hugo kept his arm clamped on her elbow. Kitty shook it loose and ran across the entrance foyer. Hoisting her skirts, she ran up the stairs, pausing at the first curve to bend over the polished mahogany railing and scream, "Don't you ever put your hands on me again, Hugo. Never!"

And his laughter echoed behind her as she hurried the rest of the way to her room, tears streaming down her cheeks.

Chapter Twenty-four

THE ride into Goldsboro was tense. Kitty moved as far as possible from Corey, but he only chuckled over her anger. Her protests against the trip were brushed aside.

"The trip will do you a world of good, my dear. You need some fresh air."

"I could get fresh air if you would let me out of this house," she retorted. "I don't need to ride all the way into town with you."

He raised an eyebrow and pulled at one side of his moustache, enjoying her displeasure. He smiled. "Oh? You aren't anxious to walk with me through the town that once spat upon you? You won't relish the bowing and scraping? The invitations to our ball have not been delivered yet, and there's quite a bit of speculation about who will receive one. I think we'll find the obsequious behavior of your former enemies most enjoyable."

"That is not my idea of fun. What am I to do? Parade up and down the streets all day long?"

"No. We'll take a stroll, and then I have business to see to. You may visit some of the shops and enjoy yourself."

They took their leisurely stroll up and down the main street. Corey had been right, the fawning of those who had treated her with contempt was sickening. And all because I married a rich Yankee carpetbagger, she thought with disgust. It doesn't matter how he takes their land from them. It doesn't matter that he's a damn Yankee! He's rich and powerful, so they admire him.

"Run along now, dear," Corey said as they stood in front of his office. He brushed her cheek with his lips after whispering menacingly, "Don't you dare turn away from me here in public."

She stiffened, accepted the kiss. He gave her an adoring smile. Rance had followed their carriage on his horse, and Corey turned to him and reminded him once again to stay close to her. "Don't make yourself obvious, but if anyone says anything out of the way to her, you be ready. I want her protected at all times."

"And *watched*," Kitty snapped, jerking her velvet shawl tighter about her shoulders. "Why don't you just tie me to a hitching post like a horse?"

"That wouldn't be very nice." His mouth turned up in a grin, but his black eyes were deadly. "Rance knows there are other reasons to keep an eye on you, my sweet wife. I don't want you going to any of your nigra friends and begging them to help you run away. Such an attempt would be quite foolish on your part and perhaps disastrous for little John."

"Corey, if you ever hurt John, I'll find a way to kill you. I swear it."

He snapped his fingers and Rance stepped forward. "Get her out of here. Married less than a week and, goddammit, she's already a nag."

Rance snorted. He reached for her elbow, but she snatched it away. "Touch me and I'll make a scene right here that this town will never forget."

She whirled and flounced hooped skirts as she stomped down the boarded walkway. Behind her she heard Corey order Rance once again to stay close. She had been told to go into the shops, but she marched right by them. Rance caught up with her and said worriedly, "The boss said you were supposed to go shopping, Mrs. McRae."

"I know where I'm going," was her snapping reply.

"Mrs. McRae, listen to me . . ." She kept walking, putting one foot in front of the other, chin up, eyes straight ahead. Rance hurried alongside. "I can't let you just take off. Now, I don't want to make a scene, but if you don't turn around and head back to those shops, I'm going to have to pick you up and carry you back to the boss's office."

She turned a corner.

"Mrs. McRae, I hate to do this . . ."

He reached out to grab her, but she started running.

"Hey, come back!"

"Shoot me in the back," she laughed, taunting him, as she turned to run up the steps of the hospital. Looking back over her shoulder, she was not surprised to see how angry he was. But there was something else in his eyes, too. Fear? Why? Rance Kincaid was mean and bullish, and Corey was always bragging about how everyone was scared of Rance because he had such a notorious reputation. So why did he look frightened now, she wondered. His face had turned pale, and he was backing away. "I'll wait at the corner," he yelled, sounding defeated. "And don't be long, either, or I'll come in there and drag you out. So help me."

He stalked away. She watched him for a moment. It *was* there. She had seen it. He looked scared!

She shrugged, hurrying inside. No longer did the hospital corridors echo with the screams and moans of the wounded and dying. The air was no longer thick with the smell of blood and decay. She knew she could look out a rear window and not see a huge pile of severed arms and legs. The wide-plank floors, however, still had many dark bloodstains, probably soaked into the wood for the life of the building.

It was quiet. She stood inside the door for a moment, remembering all the months she had spent here. She did not hear anyone approaching.

"Kitty? What are you doing here?"

"Oh, Dr. Sims," she gasped. "You startled me. I came to visit Mattie Glass. She's still here, isn't she?"

"Unfortunately, yes." He tugged at his beard, sucked in part of his lower lip as he stared at her thoughtfully. "But why have you come?"

"She . . . she was a friend," Kitty answered.

"I doubt that she will see you. She doesn't want to see anyone. I think every woman in the county has been here, and she hasn't seen a one of them."

"Well, will you tell her I'm here and ask if she will see me?"

He nodded. "Just don't be surprised when she refuses. I wonder about the woman's mind. I don't think she'll ever be right in the head again."

I could tell you exactly why, Kitty said to herself as the doctor walked away. I could tell you what it's like to be raped—the degradation and humiliation. It could very easily drive a woman insane. But I won't attempt to tell you, because you could never understand.

Kitty suddenly felt a wave of strength she had forgotten existed. She had been through hell and endured. Corey McRae was no more formidable a foe than Luke Tate had once been, and she had found a way to escape then. All she had to do was wait, endure, and sooner or later her time would come.

"Kitty? I'm surprised, but Mattie wants to see you," Dr. Sims said, returning. "Come with me."

He led her to Mattie's room. Kitty entered and shut the door behind her, then fought the impulse to gasp.

Mattie Glass had always been so vibrant. Even when her husband had been killed in the war, her faith in God had kept her going. But the woman in the bed, staring at her with sunken eyes, the flesh gray and drawn, hair tangled—this was not the Mattie Glass Kitty remembered.

Kitty moved cautiously towards the bed. A smile crept across the woman's thin, white lips. "Kitty Wright. How good of you to come."

Spontaneously, their hands touched. Mattie squeezed Kitty's fingers. Tears filled her eyes and overflowed to trickle down her sunken cheeks. "It was awful . . ." she whispered tremulously. "You just don't know . . ."

"Yes, I do know." Kitty was blinking back the moisture in her own eyes. "That's why I came, Mattie. First of all, because you were a friend to me when I needed one. And to share your pain and sorrow. It happened to me, too, Mattie, many times."

She sat down and told the woman of her own horrors, in graphic detail, sharing secrets she had held in her heart for so long. The words did not come easily, and several times Kitty choked back a sob as she told of the humiliation and pain. "I was used, defiled. Many times it would have been so much easier to seek death. But I didn't, Mattie. I endured. I've found that is the key—endurance."

"God bless you," Mattie said. "Oh, Kitty, God bless you for sharing this with me. You . . . you went through so much more than I. You didn't give in and just want to die, as I have done since that night."

"I didn't have a child then, either. I had only myself. You have your sons to think about."

"Yes, yes that's true," she said, her voice filled with shame. "I've wallowed in self-pity and haven't thought about them at all. They're all I've got now. I have to regain my strength and my will and fight my way back, for their sake."

"You certainly do. And if there is any way I can help, you know I will."

They exchanged smiles. The whole atmosphere in the room had changed, as though a cloud had been dispelled by sunshine. "Now, let's talk about the future," Kitty said brightly. "You still have your home."

"Corey McRae bought my tax certificate." Her eyes stopped shining. "If I lose my home, what am I to do?"

"Corey and I are married now."

Mattie raised her head from the pillow, eyes wide. "No. I don't believe it. I knew you'd given birth to a son. I was hoping your cavalryman would come back and marry you. Oh, Kitty, Kitty, is your own agony ever to end? How could you marry that man? He . . . he's a fiend. He . . ." Her head fell back. She closed her eyes momentarily, then looked up and said, "Forgive me. I've said too much. He's your husband now, and you obviously had a reason for marrying him. If you love him, then that is your concern, not mine."

"No, I don't love him," Kitty said hotly. "I hate him. But I had no other choice. He bought my tax lien, too. My baby and I had been starving—truly starving. I was completely vulnerable. There was no one I could go to for help. You have many friends, Mattie. All of them are eager to help you if you'll let them."

"Oh, how I hate to see that man take my land." There was grit in her voice, and Kitty rejoiced. All was not lost. Mattie was not defeated.

"Then don't let him take it."

"How can I stop him?"

"Talk to your friends. Perhaps enough money can be collected among them to pay your lien and keep him from taking your home away. Fight back, Mattie. Stand up and fight. Get out of that bed and get yourself together and make up your mind that you aren't going to let one nightmare ruin your whole life. Think of your sons. Think of your dead husband and what he would want you to do. Do you think he'd want you to give up?"

"No," she nearly shouted.

"Then fight!"

The women stared at one another, deepening their bond.

Mattie nodded firmly. "I'll do it. I never wanted to impose on my friends before, but I know they'll help me. I'll do it, Kitty."

The door opened and Dr. Sims stepped in, looking sheepish. Before Kitty had time to worry over his expression, Corey followed, lips smiling but eyes blazing. She knew the look well. He was trying to appear pleasant, but inside he was seething. She knew why. He had told her he would pay a visit to Mattie and offer her a substantial sum for her property, and Kitty knew he wanted the land but did not want people saying he took advantage of a helpless widow.

"Kitty, darling," he oozed. "Aren't you thoughtful to visit Mrs. Glass? You should have told me you were coming. We could have come together."

Kitty stood up, winking at Mattie, which neither Corey nor Dr. Sims could see. "Oh, I don't think you would have wanted me along, dear. I believe your visit is not of a social nature." Leaning over, she kissed the woman on the forehead and said, "I'll leave you now, as I have some shopping to do. Perhaps I can get back to see you soon. If not, I hope you will be able to come to our party. I'll see that you receive an invitation."

Corey was frowning.

"Party?" Mattie blinked. "I don't think—"

"Of course you can." Kitty smiled brightly, patting her shoulder. "Remember, you are going to get up out of that bed and go back to living. You're going to try and put what happened out of your mind. You will come to the party if I have to send a carriage for you."

"But even if I were able, I'm still in mourning."

"Then wear black. And if you don't have a black dress, I will see that you get one." She turned to Corey and gave him a smile. "Won't we, dear?"

"Of course, of course," he said brusquely. "Now, if you have shopping to do, you had better go. I plan to start for home shortly."

With one more nod to Mattie, Kitty brushed by Corey and Dr. Sims and hurried from the hospital. Mattie would have her dress, she was thinking furiously as she hurried towards Mrs. Rivenbark's dress shop, ignoring Rance, who was close behind.

She was merrily humming "Dixie" as she opened the door to Nina Rivenbark's dress shop. A bell tinkled as she stepped inside. Within a few seconds, the apple-cheeked woman was swishing her wide hips through a curtained-off partition at the back of the room.

Clapping her hands in delight, the woman said, "Oh, I'm so glad you stopped by. It will save me a trip out for a fitting, and I have the material your husband wanted. You are going to be delighted when you see the way that green silk matches those emeralds. I took a swatch down to Giddens Jewelers, and they took the jewels out of the safe so I could see if they matched. Glory be, it was a sight to behold."

"Oh, I'm not here for a fitting, Mrs. Rivenbark. In fact, I can only stay a moment. I would like to see what you have available in black crepe."

"Black crepe?" She looked aghast. "Unfortunately, I have a large number of dresses on hand in black crepe. Goodness knows, we have enough womenfolk in mourning. But why are you interested?"

Kitty explained.

"I can certainly take care of the poor dear, and I

think it will do her a world of good to be out and around people once again. I hear she's pining away to bones in that hospital. I will go there tomorrow and fit her myself, and then if I don't have her size on hand, I can surely re-stitch something for her."

"Just add the cost onto whatever my bill will be," Kitty instructed.

"Of course. Now, before you run, let me show you the green silk. I know you and Mr. McRae are both going to be quite pleased."

She stepped behind the curtain, then returned with a large bolt of the most beautiful green silk Kitty had ever seen. It was as brilliant as the leaves of a magnolia tree, and just as shiny and lustrous. "It is pretty," she murmured, wishing she could muster some excitement.

The bell tinkled once again, and as Kitty turned, she heard the haughty laughter of Nancy Warren Stoner. "Well, I do declare. It's Mrs. Corey McRae. Now, isn't this a surprise? Am I supposed to curtsy in Madame's presence?"

Kitty thought once again that Nancy could be quite lovely if her nasty disposition did not show. Her head was thrown back, eyes glittering maliciously as her lips twisted sideways in a mocking smirk. She wore a rich blue velvet riding cape with hood, all edged in white fur. She did make a striking picture. Reaching to push back the hood, she gave her head a toss and said, "Well, Kitty. Am I to curtsy or not?"

Kitty chose to ignore her. Turning back to Mrs. Rivenbark, she said, "Yes, this is lovely, and I am sure the dress will be beautiful. May I expect you tomorrow for a fitting?"

"Yes, indeed. I will come out in the morning and we will get right to work."

"Good day, then."

She tried to brush by Nancy, but her path was blocked as her adversary sidestepped quickly. "Aren't you going to speak to me, Kitty?"

"Our conversations never begin or end on a polite note. I see no reason to waste our time."

"Oh, but I do. You see, I was planning on paying you a visit, but running into you this way has saved me the trouble. And I was not coming to congratulate you on maneuvering Corey McRae into marrying you, either."

"I neither expected nor desire your felicitations," Kitty said. "Now if you will excuse me . . ."

Kitty moved to the right, and once again Nancy stepped quickly in her path. "You will hear me out. I won't waste any time, and then you may be on your way. I suppose congratulations are in order. That was quite an accomplishment, marrying a man of wealth to help you achieve some respectability and give your illegitimate child a name."

Kitty was determined not to let Nancy make her angry. "Then I accept your congratulations and ask that you keep your comments to yourself. Now, we have nothing further to say to each other."

"Oh, yes, we do. *I* happen to be married now—"

"You always were. You never found out for certain that David was dead, did you? The last time I saw him, he was quite well."

"David *is* dead." Nancy's voice dripped hatred. "I am now married to Jerome Danton. He is rich, very rich. But thanks to your damned Yankee carpetbagger husband, people look down on him. They blame him for everything that happens around here, things that Corey McRae is actually responsible for, he and those hired hoodlums of his."

Kitty was plainly shocked. She had not heard that Nancy and Jerome had married. Nancy rushed on.

"Now they blame Jerome for what happened to the widow Glass. Jerome would never do anything like that."

"*I* haven't said he did," Kitty pointed out.

"I think your husband's men are the ones responsible for what happened to Mattie Glass, and I think they tried to make it look like the night riders did it. Everyone thinks Jerome is their leader."

"They are no longer called night riders *or* vigilantes. They are called the Ku Klux Klan now, and I happen to *know* your husband is the leader. I was there the night his men shot Gideon. I watched his mother die of a heart attack, and then they burned my home, my barn, destroyed everything I had, and left me lying on the frozen ground, about to give birth. Both of us could have died."

"That's a lie!" Nancy's face was turning red, and Nina Rivenbark rushed forward to try to quiet her.

"No, it is not a lie," Kitty said, quite calmly. "Your husband limps because of a ball *I* put in his leg. Has he ever told you that? I meant to put it in his heart. So if he gets blamed for things, it's his own fault. Not mine, nor my husband's."

"Corey McRae's men raped Mattie."

"You can't prove that, and it's a very serious accusation." Kitty was not defending Corey out of affection. She could not bear the thought of his having any connection with such a horrible thing. Surely even Corey was not fiendish enough to have a defenseless woman ravished.

"It's true. Jerome told me. Corey wants Mattie's land. He bought her tax certificate. Jerome knows for a fact that Corey went to see her and asked her to sell out. He didn't want to mar his image by putting a helpless widow and her children out of her home, and she refused to sell. She told Jerome she'd never sell to him, either, but *he* went away. *He* did not take men and go back and rape her and beat up her children."

Nancy was livid as she continued. "The night after it happened, some men came to our door and were about to drag Jerome out and lynch him. If he hadn't been on guard and had some of his friends watching out for him, ready with guns, he'd be dead now. All this is Corey's fault. He had his men dressed up like the night riders so Jerome would look responsible."

Nina Rivenbark tried again. "Please, Nancy, calm yourself. There's no need for all this."

"Shut up," Nancy screeched at her, deliberately sweeping a display of merchandise to the floor. "Just stay out of it. Maybe you have already forgotten that this trollop caused the death of one of our bravest soldiers?"

"I don't hate you. I pity you," Kitty cut in before Nancy could continue with the story of Nathan. "Oh, Nancy," she whispered. "Let's bury the past. God only knows, it hurts too much to remember. We've both suffered enough."

"Oh!" Both women turned in the direction of Nina Rivenbark, who was looking relieved. She bustled past them towards the front door, where Corey McRae stood.

"Darling, I thought I might find you here." Corey's lips touched her cheek, and she did not turn away. Then he stiffened, aware of the tension in the air. Looking from her to Nancy and then to Nina, a frown creased his forehead. "Is anything wrong?"

"No, everything is fine," Kitty said, perhaps too quickly, for his eyebrows shot up suspiciously. "Nancy and I were just saying that the past should be forgotten. I was about to invite her and her new husband to our party."

A master at disguising his true reactions, Corey was

the perfect gentleman as he smiled and murmured, "I have only this day heard about your marriage to Mr. Danton. I offer you both my congratulations."

Kitty waited. Was Nancy going to hurl her accusations at Corey?

Suddenly Nancy exuded charm. She curtsied slightly and, smiling, said, "Why, thank you, Corey, that's very kind of you. Jerome and I will have the pleasure of extending our felicitations when we attend your party." Turning to Kitty, she held out her hand, which Kitty obligingly touched. "Thank you for your kind invitation, Kitty. We wouldn't miss it for the world, believe me."

Her eyes flashed coldly. Her hand felt clammy. Kitty withdrew from the clasp and murmured that she looked forward to seeing her soon. She knew she had not seen the last of Nancy's attempt at revenge, but at least she had made a gesture towards a truce.

Nancy left, and Corey's eyes swept over the broken glass and scattered fans that covered the floor. Nina Rivenbark opened her mouth to speak, but Kitty silenced her with a look. "I bumped into the counter. Wasn't that silly of me? Mrs. Rivenbark and I were about to clean up the mess when Nancy happened by. Here, let's do it now."

She started to bend over and pick up some of the fans, but Corey's hand snaked out and caught her arm, stopping her. "I am sure Mrs. Rivenbark would not like to see one of her most valued customers doing something so laborious, my dear." His voice was tight, and Kitty realized he was quite upset over something. Then he was turning to Nina, all charm and graciousness once again. "Now that I am here, I would like to see the green silk for my wife's dress. Did you match the color with the emeralds?"

"Oh, yes, sir, Mr. McRae. You are going to be so pleased. I took a swatch right over to Giddens Jewelers and had them get those jewels out of the safe, and, oh, my, they are beautiful! Truly fit for a queen."

Corey slipped his arm around Kitty's waist. "Why, she is a queen, Mrs. Rivenbark, *my* queen, and I want the whole world to know that."

Mrs. Rivenbark displayed the material, and Corey gave his approval. Then he bade her good day and led Kitty outside, his fingers wrapped firmly around her elbow. Once outside, he all but yanked her down the sidewalk in the direction of the buggy. "What is wrong with you? You're hurting me. Let me go."

"I'll let you go when I get you inside the buggy," he said between gritted teeth. "You and I have something to discuss, my dear."

Hugo was hovering nearby to help Kitty up into the carriage. He would sit beside the driver as he had done on the way into town. Kitty settled back against the soft velvet cushioned seats, hating the buggy's design. Its half-cocoon shape, wrapping about her on both sides and above, isolated her from the world. And the view was obstructed by Hugo and the driver.

Corey lowered himself beside her. When she tried to move away from him, as she had done on the ride into town, he grabbed her roughly against him. He yelled at Hugo to start moving at once. "Now you listen to me," he hissed angrily into her face. "Just what did you say to that woman?"

"Nancy?" He was the one who had wanted Nancy at the party, to mock her. She had extended the invitation on the spur of the moment as one last gesture of peacemaking. She started to say as much to Corey, but he cut her off impatiently.

"I'm not talking about her, and you know it. I'm talking about Mattie Glass. She was withering away, defeated, having to be force-fed. Now she's as spunky as though nothing ever happened. I made her a most generous offer to buy her land so she could move into town and be safe, and she laughed! Said she would find a way to pay the tax lien and whatever interest I charged on my holding certificate. She says she won't sell out, no matter what."

"Well, good for her," Kitty laughed, despite the ominous look on his face. "She needs to stay on that land. You know, Corey, to some people, their land is their God. It's their hold on life. Take that away from them, and they have nothing. That land is the one hold on sanity that Mattie has left. I made her see that. Now that thought has given her the strength she needed. I'm proud of her. She's going to make it."

"You think so? We'll see about that. I happen to want that property very much, Kitty, and I get what I want."

"Not *all* the time. This is one time you will fail. Mattie has many friends. They'll rally together and help her, just as she's helped them so many times in the past. You'll see, Corey, that your money won't buy you everything."

"It bought *you*, didn't it?" he sneered.

"You didn't buy me, Corey," she snapped, her fingers arching with the burning desire to send her nails raking down his smug face. "You made me vulnerable, helpless, and you beat me down to a point where I had no choice. And if I hadn't had my son's welfare to consider, you would never have succeeded in your scheme. I would sooner have starved to death than marry you."

The muscles in his jaw twitched, and his chest began to heave. His nostrils flared angrily, and his hands began to move from her shoulders, inching their way towards her throat. But she was unafraid. "Where is your pride?" she goaded him. "Look at all the trouble you went to in order to make me marry you. You brag about the women in your life, yet you had to use trickery to get me. With all your money and power, you have no pride."

His fingers squeezed down upon the delicate flesh, and she began to claw at him, struggling to breathe. "I could kill you right now, my sweet, if I were tired of that body of yours. But I'm not. Watch your step and keep your mouth shut or I *will* tire of you, much sooner than I anticipate. Remember your bastard son. I could just as easily kill him, too. Know your place, Kitty, and stop fighting me, or you'll make me do something I really don't want to do, my sweet. Now you have caused me great inconvenience with Mattie, and you have put me to a lot of extra trouble and expense. But I *will* own her land, no matter what I have to do to get it. Just stop fighting me, do you hear me? As much as I desire you, there is just so much a man can take."

With one last squeeze, he released her, smiling triumphantly as she fell back against the seat. He watched her clutch her throat as she gasped for breath. Very slowly, her blue face began turning pink, then ivory.

She stared at him in wonder, heart pounding. What kind of madman was he that he could take her to the brink of death without batting an eye, and speak so easily of murdering a baby?

"Hugo!" Corey cried, eyes not leaving her face. He was smiling that horrid, triumphant smile she hated so. "Hugo, turn down the next path, wherever it is."

"Yes, Mr. McRae," Hugo called back, not turning around. He gave the order to the driver.

"What . . . what are you going to do?" Kitty whispered, still terrified. Had he decided to go ahead and kill her and get it over with?

"I am going to teach you a lesson, my dear. I want

what is mine. You excite me so when you flash those eyes in anger." She felt a wave of revulsion as he reached out and caught her hand and drew it to his crotch. She felt the swollen organ.

He continued to stare at her, chuckling as the driver reined the horses down a bumpy path, finally stopping a good ways from the main road. "Leave us now," Corey ordered to the two men, and they quickly obeyed.

"Now, he said, eyes riveted upon hers. "Take off all your clothes."

"All my clothes? Corey, please, no, not here. I'll freeze."

"Do you want to return to the house with your dress hanging in shreds? Do as I say. I want you completely naked. Don't argue with me any more today, Kitty. You have exhausted my patience. Start undressing and be quick about it."

It was quite an effort, there in the cramped carriage. He had to help her with the fastenings on the back of her dress. It was pulled over her head. The hoops were unsnapped and tossed outside to the ground. Then off came the pantalets and the chemise.

"Lovely . . ." He cupped her breasts in his hands, leaning to kiss each hungrily. "Oh, Kitty, if you were not so beautiful, I wouldn't tolerate you. But you are an exquisite creature."

Parting her thighs, he gazed hungrily at her most private parts. Her face flamed with humiliation. Fingertips touched, probed, squeezed. Then he was yanking her legs wide apart, pushing her back on the seat. She felt his rough, eager thrust and gritted her teeth, squeezing her hands into tiny fists, praying it would end quickly. In and out he moved, hips thrusting so violently that the carriage rocked. The horses stamped their feet and snorted.

The movements became faster, faster, and his mouth covered hers, tongue plunging inside her mouth as though he wanted to devour her.

Then it happened—that final push and ensuing slump and moan that told her it was over.

"One of these days I will be able to last for hours. I can feel it," he said casually. "Now put your clothes in order. We're going home, and then I have to take care of seeing that you learn a very dear lesson."

"What are you talking about?" she asked fearfully, thinking of the secret locked room on the upper floor.

"You'll find out. It's something I've decided must be done to make you realize, once and for all, that that spirit of yours is going to have to be controlled. You had no damned business going to see Mattie Glass."

"Corey, I only told her that her life wasn't over."

"And I suppose you didn't goad her into trying to keep her land?"

Kitty did not meet his gaze, nor did she respond.

"I thought so," he said with satisfaction. "As soon as she started talking, I knew you had put that idea in her. Well, my dear wife, you're going to learn to stay out of your husband's affairs."

Fear became a tight knot in Kitty's throat as she tried to speak around it. "Corey, what are you planning to do to me?"

But he did not reply.

He refused to speak the rest of the way home, and Kitty did not dare ask any more questions for fear of angering him further.

They arrived at the mansion, and Kitty ran up the steps, across the porch, and did not stop running until she reached John's room. He was sleeping peacefully, but she grabbed him and cradled him against her bosom, holding him tightly. He was the only thing in her life that mattered. Dear God, she loved him so.

He blinked sleepily, then smiled at his mother, cooing happily and snuggling closer. Even though Corey did not approve of her spending so much time with him, Kitty was with him almost every waking moment, doting on him, loving him, clinging to her one hold on sanity.

"I'll find a way for us, my darling," she murmured, nuzzling her lips against the fine hair that grew darker every day.

Mercifully, Corey left her alone that evening. She retired early, falling into a fitful slumber, afraid that he would come to her.

She awoke with a start. Light strained to enter the room around the edges of the heavy velvet drapes, but Dulcie had not come in to awaken her. Pushing back the coverlet, she padded across the carpeted floor to open the curtains herself. Startled to see how bright it was, her eyes went to the mantel clock. It was almost ten! Why, she was always up before eight, to bathe and dress and hurry in to spend the morning with John. What was the matter with Dulcie?

Struggling into her robe, she hurried from the room and crossed the hall. The door to the nursery was closed, and she flung it open, ready to admonish Dulcie for not awakening her.

The room was empty. She ran to the cradle. It, too, lay vacant, and her hand flew to her mouth to stifle the scream that was working its way from the depths of her soul.

And then she saw Corey.

He stood in the doorway, leaning against the frame, arms folded across his chest. "What's wrong, darling? You look upset. And you're still in your robe at this hour! Tsk! tsk!" He gave her a crooked smile, the corner of his mouth turning up in sinister fashion. "You are getting to be quite lazy, aren't you? Or don't you feel well? Would you like me to summon Dr. Sims? Perhaps you're having a relapse."

"Where is my baby?" she whispered hoarsely, stumbling towards him, heart thudding wildly.

"Oh, yes, the baby." he continued to smile. "Well, Kitty, as I told you yesterday, I just can't have you meddling in my affairs, and I can't continue to put up with your rebellion. You have to learn that you have a place, and I expect you to stay in it. So, to teach you a lesson, I have sent Dulcie away with the baby. They will stay with friends of mine in Raleigh, until after the party, at least. You are going to be much too busy to hover over that child the way you do. They may stay away even longer. It all depends on how you conduct yourself. When I am confident that you will give me no more problems and learn to be a dutiful, obedient wife, then you will get your child back. It's all up to you."

Rage ripped through her body like the stab of a lightning bolt through a giant oak. "You bastard!" she screamed, leaping at him with fingers arched, nails ready to rip into his face. "I'll kill you! You can't take my baby away . . ."

He threw his arms out as she reached him, hitting her across her face with enough force to knock her to the floor. She struggled to get up, still screaming and clawing at the air like someone gone mad, but he casually moved to place one booted foot upon her breasts and apply enough pressure to keep her where she lay.

"You are only making matters worse by your behavior, Kitty," he said quietly.

When she continued her tirade, he grew impatient and reached down to wrap his fingers into her long, golden hair, yanking her painfully to her feet. Then, very methodically, he slapped her back and forth across her face until her shrieks quieted to subdued sobs. Releasing her, he allowed her to slump to the floor once again.

"I repeat, my dear. It is up to you, when and if that child returns to this house. Be obedient, give me no cause to become irritated with you, and I shall have Dulcie return with him. Otherwise, who's to say what might happen to the little brat? My friends are wealthy, and also childless. They would be most delighted to adopt him."

"You can't do that to me. For the love of God, Corey, have mercy. Don't take away my baby."

"I already have," he snapped. "And you forced me to do it. I made an agreement with you before we were married, and I kept my end of the bargain. You haven't kept yours. You've fought me every step of the way. You have argued with me, sassed me, treated me with disrespect. I won't have it. Your going to Mattie Glass yesterday was the final blow. You've caused me a great deal of inconvenience. I intend to have her land, and now I have to find another way to get her to sell without my having her legally evicted and looking like a cold-hearted monster. Damn you, Kitty, why in hell didn't you stay out of it?"

"Don't do this to me." She struggled to stand, her cheeks burning. "Corey, I'll do anything you say, but bring John back to me, please. He's all I have."

"Then you will appreciate him more when he does come back, won't you?" He smirked, trailing the back of his fingertips down her reddening cheeks. "I think everything will work out fine for us, Kitty. I think this little lesson is all it will take for you to learn your place and stay in it. Then we won't continue to have these unpleasant scenes. Now, suppose we go into your room, and you can show me just how much you want to please me. Don't hold back anything. Show me what a grateful, loving wife you are, my dear. And remember, I'm going to be taking everything you do into consideration when I decide whether to have Dulcie bring your baby back."

Kitty left the nursery and crossed the hall to enter her bedroom. Corey was right behind her, to close and lock the door behind them.

She stood motionless, staring out the window at the world beyond.

"Turn around," Corey commanded.

She obeyed, saw him lying on the bed, naked.

"Show me," he laughed. "Show me how much you want me and desire me, my loving wife. I'm waiting." He wrapped his fingers around his swollen organ.

With stiff, cold fingers Kitty removed her robe, and let it fall to the floor. Then she pulled her gown over her head and stood before him naked. He gasped with delight.

"Make it last a long time, my darling . . ." He opened his arms to her, eyes glassy. "Show me how much you respect me."

With an ache in her heart so deep she nearly fainted, Kitty moved to the bed.

She knew what she had to do.

Chapter Twenty-five

NINA Rivenbark stood back in appraisal, then gasped. "Oh! Mrs. McRae, you're lovely. I don't think I've ever seen anyone so lovely. That dress, the emeralds, your hair! Look! Look in the mirror, my dear. It's like seeing a fairy princess come to life." She clapped her hands with delight, body jiggling as she bounced up and down.

Yards and yards of the lovely dark green silk were draped over hoops. Deep swaths cut down like a shawl to shape the tantalizing décolletage, exposing the barest hint of pink nipples. Her breasts seemed to pour out of the dress. At her throat she wore the emerald necklace Corey had presented with his usual flair. The jewels were exquisitely beautiful, and their fiery green hues danced in the light from the chandelier above.

Kitty stared at her golden-red hair piled upon her head in a pyramid of poufs and dips, a single cluster of curls twisting provocatively upon her left shoulder. The coiffure, like the dress, was embellished with the first blossoms of the dogwood tree. The white, four-petaled flowers accented the drape of the skirt. A few were placed in the swath of silk below her shoulders, and perhaps a dozen had been placed in her hair. The effect was breathtaking, and Kitty's violet eyes picked up the luster of green.

"Oh, your cheeks are flushed. You don't even need

to pinch them to make them rosy," Nina cried, walking around Kitty to further admire her creation. "Mr. McRae is going to be so pleased. Now, if you would just smile—"

"I have no reason to."

The beaming woman laughed nervously. It had been difficult working with someone who stood like a dead statue, and Nina had wondered many times why Kitty Wright McRae seemed so miserable. The world lay at her feet, yet she was the picture of dejection.

"You should see the crowd downstairs," Nina rushed on, tucking the dress here and there, adjusting a curl or a flower. "I heard Hugo tell one of the other servants that everyone who received an invitation accepted, except the Governor, and he had another commitment. There must be over three hundred people down there! I don't know where Hugo will put them all. He's doing a splendid job, though. The last time I peeked over the railing, he had the servants on their toes, serving champagne and little dainties. And the orchestra was starting to set up their instruments."

She chattered on, but Kitty was not listening. She was thinking about little John, wondering how he was. Dulcie was with him. She had that much for which to be thankful. Dulcie seemed to love him, and she would see that he was taken care of. But did he miss his mother? Did he cry for her? No, he was probably too small, even at five months, but who could say what went on in the minds of infants? This very moment he might be sobbing for the snuggling comfort of her arms.

She blinked back the tears, shook herself. This was Corey's night. It had to be special. She had to do what he expected or he would not bring John back any time soon. He would continue to torture her. Everything had to go perfectly. She would paste on her most gracious smile, say and do the right things.

"Oh, I almost forgot," Nina said, snapping her fingers. "The widow Glass, I passed her when I came in."

Kitty looked at her strangely. "You mean she was here *that* early? My heavens, you arrived over an hour ago."

"She was the first guest, and Hugo complained to me about it as he brought me up here. He said he didn't know why she came so early, or what he was supposed to do with her. The champagne wasn't even opened yet. He seemed quite annoyed. Anyway, as I came in, she grabbed my arm, and she had this wild look on her face. She said she had to talk to you right away, that Hugo wouldn't let her come up, because Mr. McRae left strict orders that no one was to see you except me. He wants you to make a grand entrance down the stairway, after all the guests have arrived. I can't blame him. It is going to make quite a sight. I want to make sure I'm down there to see it myself. I told her I'd tell you she was down there. She was wringing her hands."

"I don't understand," Kitty said, more to herself than to the chattering woman. She looked at her sharply. "Did you provide her with a proper dress, as I requested?"

"Oh, yes, yes. A very simple black crepe. Tasteful, but elegant. She was wearing it. Had her hair pulled back in a bun, and she would have looked halfway attractive if she hadn't been tearing at that handkerchief in her hand and crying. Well, who's to say what makes her behave as she does? What that woman's been through was enough to drive her crazy, I guess. Hugo said he hoped Mr. McRae just asked her to go home, since she obviously wasn't feeling well."

Kitty chewed on her lower lip thoughtfully. "No. No, he wouldn't do that," she said.

"I want you to go downstairs and find Mattie and

bring her up here. Don't let Corey see you searching for her. If Hugo says anything, you tell him I refuse to go downstairs until after I see Mattie. Do you understand?"

Nina was hesitant. "I . . . I don't know, Mrs. McRae. I don't want your husband mad with me."

Kitty stamped her foot in exasperation. "If you don't do as I say, I'll tell my husband that I find your work unsatisfactory. He'll never do business with you again. Now go downstairs and find Mattie and bring her up here. Take the back stairs and slip in among the crowd. If you're careful, no one will notice you. Now go on."

Shaking her head in dismay, Nina backed slowly towards the door, then turned and hurried out. Kitty pressed her fingertips against her temples. Something was very wrong. Had Corey frightened Mattie? More and more, lately, she found herself wondering if what Nancy had told her were true. Had Corey had anything to do with Mattie being attacked and raped? Oh, God, she prayed not. Surely he drew the line *somewhere*?

Finally there was a soft tap on the door. "Come in," she all but screamed.

The door opened. Nina stepped inside, looking quite upset, followed by a teary-eyed, trembling woman dressed in black. "I'm going now. If anyone asks, I had no part in this," Nina said quickly, pushing Mattie Glass into the room, then moving outside and closing the door behind her.

"Mattie, whatever is the matter?" Kitty began.

"Oh, Kitty, Kitty, you're going to hate me for what I've done to you." Mattie burst into hysterical sobs, burrowing her face in her hands.

Kitty flew to her side, placing an arm about her shoulder, leading her to the velvet sofa in front of the fireplace. Mattie collapsed in a sitting position, but

Kitty was forced to stand. She could not crush the floral blossoms on the back of her hooped skirt.

"Now tell me what this is all about." Her voice was gentle, and she kept a reassuring hand on Mattie's shoulder. "I would never hate you, Mattie. Just tell me what has happened to upset you so."

"The marshals, they came to see me about . . ." She sniffed, coughed, sobbed once more, then cleared her throat, fighting for composure.

"Yes, go on. The marshals came to see you about what happened to you. I hope you were able to tell them something that will help them find out who was responsible."

"I'm afraid I have."

"Afraid?" Kitty raised an eyebrow. "What do you mean?"

Mattie shook her head from side to side. "I just didn't know what it would mean when I gave them . . ." She began sobbing wildly once more.

Exasperated, Kitty dug her fingers into the woman's shoulders. "Now stop crying, Mattie. Get hold of yourself. Any minute now Hugo is going to pound on that door and tell me it's time for me to make my entrance. Tell me what it is you are so upset about. I am not going to hate you, and I don't know why you dare think I would."

The woman turned mournful eyes upon her. "Kitty, when that first man attacked me . . ." she swallowed hard, fighting for composure ". . . I was not yet unconscious. I was still struggling. I've told no one, not even the sheriff, because I didn't trust him, that I was able to tear something from that man's shirt. It was a button, a button with 'CSA' on it."

"That means the man was wearing an old Confederate uniform shirt," Kitty gasped. "That may help some, Mattie, but a lot of our soldiers still wear the shirts now and then."

Mattie lowered her eyes, knotting a wet lace handkerchief in her trembling hands. "There was something else. I tore at his hair. I ripped a lock of his hair, and when I returned home from the hospital, I remembered that. I found it, between the bed and the wall. It was red, fiery red."

"So the man had red hair and wore an old Confederate uniform shirt. Those are two good clues, Mattie. You gave these to the marshals? That's fine. They have something to go on at least."

Mattie shook her head in short, quick jerks. "You don't understand what I'm saying, Kitty. Don't you remember I said those men wore hoods over their heads? How do you think I tore that lock of hair from that man?"

Kitty stared at her, puzzled. Then she snapped her fingers triumphantly. "Oh, Mattie, I know what you mean now. You were able to struggle and get that hood up to where you could tear at his hair. Then you must have seen his face. You can identify at least one of the attackers. That's wonderful. And I don't blame you for not telling anyone until the federal marshals came . . ."

Her voice trailed off as she saw the look on Mattie's face. "Why do you look so upset? Mattie, I don't understand. You should be glad. You may be able to identify that man. Isn't that what you want?"

"The marshals took the button and the lock of hair," she whispered tremulously. "They said they were going to investigate. They did, and they came back to see me and told me they had found out about a red-haired man who wears an old Confederate shirt. They want me to identify him."

"Then by all means, do so. What's the matter? Are you afraid of him? You certainly have no reason to be. Once you have fingered him as the responsible party, the others will be easier to find. The law will take care of all of them. You have no reason to be afraid."

Mattie took a deep breath, let it out slowly, then spoke the words that sent chilling fingers up and down Kitty's spine. "The man they want me to identify works for your husband, Kitty. His name is Coot Wiley."

"Wiley?" Kitty felt her eyes bulging. She swayed. Grasping the back of the sofa for support, she whispered, "Yes, yes, of course. Coot does wear an old Rebel shirt most of the time. He's so dirty and filthy, probably never bathes. I don't think I've ever seen him without that shirt. And he does have red hair. If it was Coot, and you can identify him, then that means Corey was behind it all. He wanted to frighten you into selling your land."

"Exactly." Mattie nodded. "Oh, Kitty, please don't hate me. I didn't mean to cause you grief."

"Cause *me* grief?" Kitty blinked, confused. "Mattie, I don't understand. How can you cause *me* any grief? Corey is the one in trouble, not me."

"But he's your husband, and he will be in deep trouble if this is all brought out."

"Mattie, I told you that day I visited you in the hospital that I don't love Corey. He found me in a desperate situation, and I had no other path to choose except to become his wife. I had my son to think about. I hate Corey McRae, now more than ever, because I believe he *did* have something to do with what happened to you. He probably masterminded the whole thing. I hope he gets what's coming to him. So please, don't think you have caused me any grief."

"But they're coming here tonight."

"Who's coming?"

"The marshals. I didn't know anything about what they had found out until just before I started getting dressed to come here. They came to my house and said they wanted me to identify that . . . that man." She shuddered with revulsion, memories of the horror washing over her. "I told them about the party, Kitty. I asked them couldn't they wait until tomorrow, but they couldn't."

"Well, it's best to get it over with," Kitty sighed. "Don't worry, Mattie. If Coot Wiley is one of the men responsible, and Corey was behind it all, the marshals will deal with them."

Kitty was trying not to show the sudden burst of hope that was flowing through her veins. If the marshals could prove Corey was responsible, then it would probably mean he would go to prison. Then she would be free!

"Kitty, there's something else." Mattie had gotten to her feet, reached out to clutch her arms.

There was a sudden, loud pounding on the door, and Hugo was calling. "The master is ready for you, madam. Now."

"What is it?" Kitty whispered anxiously, frightened by the look in Mattie's eyes. Somehow she sensed that what the woman was about to say would be the most astonishing news yet. "Tell me quickly."

"The marshals. They . . . one of them—"

The door opened and Hugo stepped into the room, eyes flashing with anger at the sight of Mattie. "What are you doing here?" he demanded. "How did you slip up here? I told you Mr. McRae said no one was to see Mrs. McRae until after she made her entrance. Get out of here at once."

"Now, you wait a minute, Hugo," Kitty flared, matching his anger. "Who do you think you are to burst into my room and tell my guest to get out? I think you overestimate your importance and position in this house."

"I think you underestimate your husband's authority." He gave her the insolent sneer she hated. "Now, shall I call him up here or will you have your guest leave and make your entrance? Everyone is waiting at the bottom of the stairway, and the orchestra is playing."

Kitty looked at Mattie, burning with the desire to hear what she had been about to say. "Give us one more moment, Hugo, please."

"No!" He snapped. "Come with me now. I am not going to have the master angry with me. I follow orders."

"Oh, Kitty, I . . ." Mattie shook her head, then lifted the skirts of her black crepe dress and ran across the room, swishing by Hugo to disappear into the hallway.

Kitty had no choice but to make her entrance. Whatever Mattie was going to tell her would have to wait until later. She moved by Hugo. He continued his insolent smirk.

When she appeared at the top of the curving stairway, her hand lightly touching the banister, she tilted her chin upwards, forced a smile upon her lips. A wave of sighs and gasps of stunned reaction swept across the faces. Slowly, she made her descent. She caught sight of Corey waiting at the bottom with outstretched hand, pride and triumph gleaming in his black eyes. This was his moment. The king awaits his queen. She prayed fervently that it would all be over soon. The king would be exiled—the queen freed.

She tucked her hand in the crook of his arm. The crowd moved back, making a path for the two as they walked towards the ballroom to the left of the entrance foyer. People continued to murmur. "You are the loveliest woman I have ever seen, my darling," Corey whispered in a tone filled with awe. "And to think you are mine, all mine. Oh, my darling, you do me proud tonight."

She kept the forced smile on her lips as they began

to dance in the middle of the room, the crowd forming a circle about them. It was a waltz, and Kitty held out her skirt with one hand, making the swoops and swirls, and Corey expertly maneuvered her on the floor. Others began to dance. And finally, the music ended. People descended upon her, complimenting her on her marriage, her loveliness. Men bowed and kissed her hand. Women who had spat at her before now curtsied as though she were reigning royalty.

"Enjoy it, my dear," Corey whispered, lips so close to her ear she could feel the warmth of his breath. "This is your moment of glory. Those who scorned you now bow and scrape. I want you to remember that it was *I* who gave you all this. *I* took you from the gutter and made you the empress you are now. I have given you the world."

"Then give me my baby," she turned her head slightly to hiss, as someone she had never seen before kissed her outstretched hand.

"Ahh, you shall have him quite soon." He turned to acknowledge a greeting, accept words of congratulations, then moved his lips back to her ear. "I think you should bear my child as soon as possible, darling. It's not good to dote on John so much."

Shivering with revulsion, she wondered if she could possibly love a being created from his degrading lust. But soon she might be free, she remembered, and the smile she gave her next admirer was genuine. Soon, all this could be over.

Her eyes searched the throng for Mattie, but she was nowhere to be seen. What if Hugo had thrown her out of the house? Finally she was able to move away from the crowd in the ballroom and find Hugo with a tray of champagne. Stepping close so no one could overhear, she murmured, "Hugo, have you seen Mrs. Glass? I wish to talk with her."

"I have no idea, Mrs. McRae," he responded in a

bored tone, making no effort to lower his voice. "She ran down the back stairway, and I do hope she kept right on going. Her kind has no business at this party."

Kitty's fiery temper got the best of her. "Who are you to say who does or does not belong here, Hugo? Corey took you in and gave you a bath and taught you how to speak properly, and now you look down on everyone around you! I will not have it."

Whipping his head about, he snapped, "You're a fine one to talk. I know what you were before Mr. McRae picked you up and wiped the dirt off, and so does everyone else. You always did love the shiftless trash niggers, didn't you? Jacob and his kind. You can't stand to see some of my people have the backbone to rise up and better themselves."

Guests who could hear what was being said backed away in astonishment. For a few seconds, Kitty could only stand there, shocked, unable to believe what she had just heard. Then, before she realized what she was doing, her hand cracked across Hugo's face. Startled, he dropped the tray and the crystal glasses filled with champagne went crashing to the floor.

"How dare you speak to me that way?" she cried. "How dare you?"

The orchestra had ceased playing, its members distracted by the scene. Guests began moving closer, filled with curiosity. Suddenly Corey was pushing his way through to stare incredulously at the mess of broken glass and champagne spilled upon the floor, and at the angry faces of Hugo and Kitty.

But his presence did not quell Kitty's fury.

"How dare you speak of Jacob in such a way?" she lashed out. "You aren't fit to wash his feet."

"Stop it!" Corey's fingers wrapped around her arm, digging into the tender flesh. She winced with pain but continued to stand there rigidly glaring at the negro.

"It doesn't matter about him anymore, anyway,"

Hugo said with a short laugh, eyes gleaming. "Nobody will be bothered with that old fool again."

"Hugo, I will have you soundly thrashed for this," Corey said between gritted teeth. "Go out to the kitchen and stay there until you hear from me."

His eyes taking on a look of fright, Hugo turned and all but ran from the room, pushing aside the guests roughly in his haste to escape his master's wrath.

Corey released his hold on Kitty long enough to wave his hands in the air. "Please forgive this little scene. You all know our nigras are getting uppity. I've been having trouble with this one, and I apologize for your having to witness such a thing. Please . . ." He gestured to the orchestra frantically to start playing once again. "Let's all dance and enjoy ourselves. This is a festive occasion."

With the music filling the air, people began moving away, but their heads were close together, buzzing. "Now, you, my dear," Corey turned on Kitty furiously, when no one was close enough to hear. "I want you to go to your room and get hold of yourself. I'm going to see to Hugo, and then I will be up to get you. This is a disgrace!"

She turned a frosty gaze upon him, unmoved by his anger. "What did he mean when he said no one would be bothered with Jacob again? Where is Jacob? What have you done with him?"

"I told you to go to your room."

"And I'm not going anywhere till I find out what has happened to the dearest friend I have in this world. If you don't want me to make a scene your guests will not forget, you had better tell me, Corey."

"Who do you think you are? Giving me an ultimatum! You want that brat of yours to stay in Raleigh forever? Now you do as I say, or, believe me, you will regret your disobedience."

She did not move.

Another servant appeared, looking uncertain as to whether or not to speak.

"Well, Lidas, what is it?" Corey demanded impatiently.

"The food. It's ready," the Negro said nervously, tugging at the tightly buttoned shirt and cravat.

"Good, good. Tell the orchestra leader. Have him make the announcement. I have other things to tend to." He turned to Kitty. "I will take you to your room, since you refuse to obey me."

"If you want to avoid a scene," she said, very quietly, a slight smile on her lips so those watching would not think them arguing, "tell me what you have done with Jacob."

"Oh, all right, but you'll pay later for this rebellion. I promise you that. I sent Jacob away, with his grandsons. He is well taken care of, living on a farm I own down in South Carolina. I did not want him around. I did not like your friendship with a cotton-patch nigra. He left three days ago."

She clenched and unclenched her fists, fighting the impulse to send her hand cracking across his face. "You have just given me one more reason to hate you, Corey."

"That doesn't bother me in the least. I never asked you to love me, you little fool, just obey me. All right. Stay here and keep that smile on that beautiful face of yours. Pretend that nothing is wrong. Mingle with our guests. Everyone thinks Hugo was just being uppity. These people are used to the Negroes' rebelling. We can carry this off with a minimum of embarrassment. Later tonight, you and I will settle this latest riff, because I cannot have you—"

"Mr. McRae."

It was Hugo, and his eyes were wide with fright as he tugged at his master's sleeve.

"I told you to get the hell out of here."

For a moment Kitty thought Corey was going to strike him. She could tell he was fighting for control.

"Sir, this is important. Come with me, please. There . . . there are . . ." he leaned over and whispered, but Kitty heard the words ". . . federal marshals on the grounds. One of the guards just told me. They're headed for the front door this very minute."

Corey looked shaken. He turned to say something to Kitty, but loud banging on the front door drowned out the sound of the orchestra, and everything and everyone became silent.

Straightening his coat, mustering every ounce of dignity and control, Corey murmured, "Go to the door, Hugo."

Hugo obeyed, and when he opened it, two men stepped inside. The guests were once more gathering around, and Kitty stood on tiptoe, trying to see what was going on. She caught a glimpse of two men, both bearded, and she could see shining gold stars on their suede vests.

And then she felt herself swaying. No. It couldn't be. *It couldn't.*

"We're federal marshals, and we're here to see Corey McRae," the familiar voice rang out loud and crisp, clearly audible over the curious murmurs of the crowd.

Kitty fought the buzzing in her ears. A dark shroud was trying to close down around her, and she fought against it. It was only a dream . . . like all the others. She would awake in the night to sob hysterically because it was not real. Travis had not come back. She only thought she heard his voice. Her mind was playing tricks on her, because she wanted him so desperately. She only thought she saw the steel gray eyes. None of it was really happening.

"I am Corey McRae."

She was dimly aware of Corey moving towards the door.

"If you have business with me, go around back, to the kitchen. We will discuss it there. As you can see, I have guests."

More words were exchanged. Kitty could not make them out. Suddenly she knew what she must do. She had to make sure. With a pounding heart, she shoved someone aside and fought her way from the foyer and into the hallway that led to the rear of the house and the outside door that would take her down the porch steps and around to the building that housed the kitchen.

She was almost to the door when someone stepped out of the shadows . . . someone who had seen her making her way and knew the house well enough to know she could cut her off by going through the library.

Nancy stood there, her face glowing triumphantly in the soft glow of the candles. She wore a stunning gown of peach-colored satin, and she looked quite poised as she laughed and said, "Yes, Kitty, it's who you think it is. I have known for over a week now, and so has Corey. Travis Coltrane is one of our new federal marshals."

"Travis." Kitty could only whisper his name as her heart leaped. It was real. He had returned. "Travis . . . I have to see him."

She tried to push by her, but Nancy shoved her roughly against the wall and cried, "I told you my husband would not take the blame for what happened to Mattie Glass. I happen to know that she gave Travis the evidence he needed to find out who was really responsible. Now he's here to implicate Corey. Everyone is going to know, at long last, just what a scoundrel he really is."

"I don't care," Kitty laughed, close to hysteria, still struggling to get around her. "Don't you see, Nancy?

I don't *care* about Corey. I never did. I must go to Travis."

"Oh, I don't think your Yankee lover is going to be very happy to see you." Her eyes glittered maliciously in the candlelight.

"Of course he'll be glad. We have a son . . . we'll be together at last, the three of us." Tears were stinging her eyes.

"You and Travis have a son? That's interesting. No one has told him that."

"I will tell him."

"I have already talked to him at length about you, Kitty."

Kitty stopped struggling and met her foe's triumphant gaze. "What do you mean?"

"He really wasn't interested in hearing, but once I started telling him that you were married to the very man he was after, he became quite an avid listener. Now he understands why you never answered his letters. He knows all about how you schemed and connived and plotted to marry the richest and most powerful man in Wayne County, how you got yourself pregnant so Corey would do the honorable thing and give his son a name."

"*His* son? Are you crazy? Everyone knows that Travis is John's father."

"Do they?" Kitty had stopped struggling, so Nancy released her hold and began patting the curls that layered her head. "Who do you think people in Wayne County listen to and believe? You or me? I've told them all that Corey is your baby's father, and that was how you maneuvered him into marrying you instead of me. They know you for the sneaky little trollop you are, just as Travis does."

"Travis will never believe that."

"Go to him, Kitty, and find out for yourself. I think . . ." she paused to smile and take a deep breath, her bosom swelling with victory, ". . . that I have revenged Nathan's death once and for all. I think he sleeps peacefully in his grave at last."

Kitty pushed her aside and ran from the house, the girl's laughter echoing behind her. Bounding down the steps, she reached the path just as Travis came around from the front. He was only a shadowy blur in the faint moonlight that filtered through silver clouds, but there was no mistaking the dear face. Sam Bucher walked beside him, she noted joyfully, giving thanks that he, too, was alive and well.

Travis saw her and stopped short.

Overcome with emotion, she tried to speak, but the words could not get past the lump in her throat. Finally she was able to choke out his name, then whisper, "Travis, darling, it *is* you. Oh, thank God, thank God."

She flung herself at him.

Rough hands clasped her shoulders and threw her to the ground. "Get away from me. Don't you ever come near me."

"Travis! You'll hurt her." Sam's voice came through the fog that was settling over her.

"I don't give a damn."

He started to move on by, but she reached out and clutched at his booted foot. "Travis, you must listen to me," she begged. "Please, please hear me out. I love you. I never stopped loving you."

He tried to yank his foot free of her grasp, but she held tightly. He kept moving, and she was being dragged along behind him in the dirt. Sam was bending over, trying to unwrap her fingers, while Travis swore and shoved at her head with rough hands.

"Kitty, let go. Let him go," Sam was saying gently. "This isn't the time—"

With an anguished moan, she released Travis' foot and flung herself on the ground, sobbing wildly, then she lifted her head and screamed after him: "If you don't love me, so be it. But at least acknowledge your son."

"That does it!"

Travis turned and stalked back to where she lay. Sam was right beside him, trying to grab him, but he brushed him away. "Travis, don't do anything you'll regret. You're mad right now—"

"Goddamn right, I'm mad. I come back here and find out what the bitch has been up to, and then she has the nerve to try and pin her bastard on me."

With one powerful scoop he lifted Kitty to her feet. In the moonlight she saw the smoky eyes spitting fire. "Just what kind of trick are you trying to play now? Don't you ever call that bastard's kid mine, you hear me? I know the truth, Kitty. I know all about you and what you did to hang onto your precious goddamn land. I hope you choke on it. I sent you messages, but now I know why you never answered them. You were after someone with the money to help you keep your land. Well, you've got him, and your land, so stay the hell away from me or so help me, I'll kill you."

"Take your hands off my wife or I'll shoot you where you stand."

Corey stood there, gun drawn. Sam, standing back, saw and moved with lightning quickness to knock the weapon from his outstretched hand. "We'll have none of that," he said gruffly. "I think you're in enough trouble already, McRae, without shooting a federal marshal."

"Then tell him to take his hands off my wife," Corey sputtered. "And what do you mean, *I* am in trouble? I have done nothing."

"We'll see about that. Travis! Let her go. This is not the time for you two to settle things."

"Settle what things? That woman is my wife. Tonight is our wedding celebration. How dare you touch her?"

"I don't want her!" Travis flung her away. She would have fallen if Corey had not caught her and held her upright. "Not now. Not ever. She worked hard enough to land you, mister, so I reckon you deserve each other. Now can we get on with the business at hand? I don't want to hang around here any longer than necessary. I have a job to do."

"Yes, of course." Corey's voice was evidence that he once again had control of himself. "Kitty, go into the house. Go to your room."

"I won't," she screamed, not about to give up. The man she loved with all her heart and soul stood there staring at her in the moonlight, hatred pouring from every fiber of his being. He had to know, dear God, he had to know that everything he had heard about her had been lies. She married Corey out of desperation to save their child. And she had never received any messages from him.

"Travis, Travis," she begged in anguish, unable to keep the tears from streaming down her cheeks. "Please listen."

Travis pointed his finger at her, his whole body shuddering. "I don't want to hear anything you have to say, Kitty. Don't you have any self-respect left? That man standing there is your husband. Don't humiliate him by making him look like a fool."

"Travis, you have to hear me out. I love you! And you loved me when you left here. That's why I fought so hard to survive, because of your love, because of the baby you left inside me."

Travis shook his head.

"You can't say you never loved me!"

"What we had was no different from what bulls and cows do," he said viciously. "Love you? Hell, no, I could never love something like you."

"See here, this is my wife," Corey interrupted.

Travis sighed, passing his hand over his face. "I know. I know she's your wife. I'm sorry. Take her away. I didn't come here for this. Let's take care of the business we have with each other and get it over with."

Hugo had been standing behind Corey, and now at the snap of his master's fingers he stepped forward. "Take her to her room," Corey shouted. "Pick her up and take her to her room. Lock the door. Stand guard outside. Keep her there. She has had too much to drink. I can't let our guests see her like this. The party is over. Tell everyone to go home."

Hugo lifted Kitty as she kicked and screamed and beat at him. Corey and Travis both glared at her. Only Sam Bucher showed pity.

And then she saw Mattie coming out of the kitchen, and she called out to her, "Please help me. Please make them see that I'm telling the truth, Mattie."

"Kitty, I was trying to tell you Travis was one of the marshals." Mattie ran forward, but Corey grabbed her and held her back. "I wanted to let you know, to prepare you, but there wasn't time."

"Tell him," Kitty screamed from the very depths of her soul. "For the love of God, tell him the truth."

Travis reached out and took Mattie by the arm and started walking in the direction of the kitchen. "I'm sorry, ma'm, but we've got to get to the business at hand. That woman is drunk."

"Travis . . . Travis . . ." Kitty kept screaming his name over and over as Hugo struggled to get her inside the house. The door banged shut, and she slumped against the big Negro's chest in defeat, sobbing quietly.

He took her to her room and dumped her roughly on her bed. "You are going to be in for it with the master." He towered over her, laughing. "When he gets through with those marshals, he's going to come in here and beat you half to death."

"I don't care." She burrowed her face in the satin pillows. "I just don't care."

He walked out. She heard the click of a key and knew she was locked in.

There had to be a way. There had to be. Mattie would help her!

She sat up in bed and dabbed at her eyes. Now was not the time to be hysterical. She must be strong, gather all her wits about her. Mattie would talk to Travis and make him see that she was telling the truth.

She kept hearing the sounds of carriages leaving, knew the party had broken up. Corey was going to be in a rage. She hoped Travis had taken him back to town and locked him up. Coot would not take all the blame for what had happened.

Her head jerked up at the sound of the key turning. The door opened. Corey seemed to fill the room as he entered, and her eyes went to the leather strap he held in his right hand, slapping it rhythmically against the open palm of his left, all the while riveting his gaze on her, his lids narrowed to slits.

Hugo stood behind him, grinning.

"Is everyone gone now, Hugo?" Corey asked, not taking his eyes off Kitty.

"Yes, sir. The orchestra just packed up and left. I sent all the house servants out to sleep in other quarters. No one is in the house now but the three of us."

"Very good. Now you go downstairs and keep an eye out. Make sure no one comes nosing around. I've posted Rance and some of the men outside, as well."

"Yes sir," he grinned, and, with one final look of triumph in Kitty's direction, stepped outside and closed the door.

"You might be interested in knowing that I am not implicated in any way in the attack upon Mattie Glass," Corey said evenly, still popping the leather strap in a steady rhythm against his open palm. "It seems that Coot and some of my men got drunk and decided to rape the widow, and they have all confessed and will take their punishment. I could not afford to lose one of my most prized men, one who was actually involved, so another took his place and gave a false confession. But, there was no hesitancy. They had been instructed for quite some time as to what they were to do if the truth came out. They were willing to do as I said, for they knew my wrath would be much greater than the law's. They all denied that I had any prior knowledge of their actions."

"Oh, you are clever, aren't you?" Kitty snarled. "You can buy men's souls with your damned money, can't you? You can frighten them into doing *anything*! Yet you can't intimidate me—a helpless woman—and that just tears you apart. Doesn't it, Corey?"

His eyebrows shot up, and for a moment he could only stand there and look at her in wonder. Then the anger returned. "Kitty, you have tried my patience for the last time. Everyone will gossip for weeks about what happened tonight. I know some of our guests are bound to have heard you groveling at Coltrane's feet. Have you no pride? Can't you see that he wants no part of you? You are mine now, and it makes no difference that he has returned, because it's obvious that Coltrane doesn't want you."

"He will, when he learns the truth. I'll see to it that he hears my side."

He laughed, black eyes glittering. "And when do you propose to talk to him, my dear? You are going to be a prisoner here for quite some time. I will see to it that you talk to no one. Your precious baby will not be brought back for a long, long time. Maybe never. I am going to break that spirit of yours, once and for all. After I am through with you tonight, you won't dare speak the name of Travis Coltrane in my presence ever again."

He came towards her menacingly, but she did not move. She was terrified but determined not to show it. Holding the strap in one hand, his other snaked out to lock his fingers in the bodice of her dress, ripping it to the waist in one quick movement. Her breasts were bared before him.

A glassy look came over his eyes as he continued to tear at the delicate green silk until she was naked.

"Lie down on the bed," he said hoarsely. "I don't want to mar that beautiful face, no matter how angry you have made me."

She did not move. She prayed that all the hatred she felt for him was mirrored in her eyes.

He twisted her around, flung her across the bed, and she felt the first stinging slap of the leather across her tender buttocks. Sucking a mouthful of the satin coverlet between her teeth, Kitty bit down, determined that she would not scream, would not let him have the pleasure of hearing her cry out.

The blows became harder, faster. She felt her own blood running, the flesh split and torn across her back and thighs. Her tongue got in the way of the fabric in her mouth, and her teeth clamped down and she tasted blood. But she would not cry out.

"Scream, goddamn you," he commanded, his breath coming in short, quick gasps. There was no other sound except for the constant slap-slap-slap of the leather strap above his own grunts of pleasure. Through the sea of pain that engulfed her, she knew he was enjoying inflicting the agony upon her, but she did not realize to what depths his ecstasy went until he fell across her bloodied black, parting her buttocks with rough, eager hands. Thrusting his swollen member into her, he screamed with joy.

His sound mingled with the only cry she gave—for the pain of him tearing inside her was more agonizing than the slicing blows of the strap.

"Mine," he grunted, pushing into her. "Mine . . . mine . . . mine . . ."

Mercifully, it was over. He stood up, towering above her, commanding her to turn and look at him. He walked around the bed, knelt in front of her so that her dazed eyes were upon his face.

"Your spirit is broken, Kitty. I have conquered your soul." And with a smile of complete satisfaction and triumph, he went to his own room.

Kitty lay motionless, body throbbing inside and out. "No," she whispered. "No, you haven't."

Then she gave way to the force that lifted her to oblivion.

Chapter Twenty-six

KITTY would not move from her bed. For several days her body was only pain, pain from head to toe, back and buttocks raw from the welts left by the leather strap. It was only with great effort that she was able to move from where she lay on her belly to the chamber pot.

The morning after, she was grateful to see a familiar face. Addie, one of the Negroes who had left her to work for Corey, took one look at her and could not suppress the cry of outrage. "Oh, dear God. That man, he did this to you? Oh, Miss Kitty, Miss Kitty," she moaned. "I knowed he was the devil hisself, but I thought he loved you."

Kitty did not speak. It did not matter about the pain. It would go away. The bruises would fade, on the surface, at least. The wounds would heal in the same manner. She could only lie there and think about Travis, the way he had scorned her. Kitty knew her heart was broken forever.

Addie brought salve to rub into the wounds. "Hugo say Mistah McRae won't call the doctor 'cause he don't want nobody to know what he had to do to his wife to make her behave. Hugo say Mistah McRae is just furious over the way that party turned out. He had to ride into town first thing this morning to try and straighten out that mess about what some of his men did to the widow Glass. She come by to see you, by the way, but Hugo wouldn't let her in. He say you ain't allowed to have no visitors. You can't even leave yo' room. He got a man right outside the door what's goin' to see you don't leave."

Kitty moaned. It was hopeless. She would never be able to slip out and find Travis and try to make him listen. If only Jacob were here, or Dulcie. She could trust them, she knew. Jacob would tell Travis that he had known she was going to have a baby before she even met Corey McRae, that her condition was the reason she was discharged from the hospital. Dulcie would tell him that she had been forced to give Kitty's letters to Corey, who had destroyed them. There was no telling what happened to the ones Jacob took to town. Corey probably had someone there who made sure they were not mailed.

Mattie would help her, too, she thought wildly. But no one would let Mattie in. Kitty was a prisoner. She also knew that Corey was too devious to allow Travis to remain around for very long. He would be afraid she would find a way to get to him. Corey would arrange to have him killed. Travis had to be warned.

"Addie, do you know where in South Carolina Jacob and his grandsons were sent?" Kitty lowered her voice, should the guard outside be listening.

"No ma'm, I sho don't. Fact is, I didn't even know he was gone till after he done took those boys and left. Me and my man, Will, was talking about it. Mistah McRae sho got rid of him quick."

She rubbed in the salve as gently as possible, but Kitty still winced with pain.

"Is there anyone else who would know? Can you ask around for me? You have to help me, Addie. There's no one else I can turn to," she said desperately, reaching out to clutch the old woman's arm. "Jacob is gone. Dulcie took my baby to Raleigh. I have no one left I can trust. And I'm sure you heard Captain Coltrane is back. He's a federal marshal here, and he believes the worst of me. I have to get to him, Addie. I have to talk to him."

Addie had stopped smoothing the salve on the torn flesh and backed away from the bed, eyes wide with fright as she shook her head from side to side. "No, ma'm. I ain't gonna get myself in trouble. Mistah McRae would kill me and my man, too, if either of us did anything to help you. Hugo watches all of us, just like a vulture waits on sump'n dyin'. I ain't gonna get myself kilt. No, ma'm. I feels sorry fo' you, and I pray fo' you, but I ain't gettin' kilt."

Addie left. Kitty lay there and cried, then hated herself for giving in to weakness. She would find a way.

Corey came in late that afternoon, gloating again over the Mattie Glass incident. He was still left with his best gunman, Rance Kincaid.

He taunted Kitty. "Your lover came back, and he all but spit in your face," he laughed down at her. "Now, perhaps you will have the good sense to give up your foolish dreams and realize you are mine. And don't get any dangerous notions about finding a way to see him. I have guards posted all around, my dear. There is no way out for you."

He lit a cigar and positioned himself in front of her, grinning, black eyes glittering with delight. "I regret that you're feeling so poorly, Kitty. I really do. It grieves me to see that lovely flesh bruised. I also miss our lovemaking. A few more days of rest, however, is all I'm going to allow you. I know how long it takes to get over a beating such as the one I gave you. I've inflicted enough upon my servants to know just how long it keeps them out of service. So you can lie there and pretend all you want, but I will know when to come to your bed."

He reached down and scratched at his crotch. Kitty closed her eyes, not wanting to see the swelling there. He talked of letting her recuperate, but she knew him well enough to realize that his lust might get the best of him. Then he would take her.

To get his mind on something else, even at the risk of angering him, she said quietly, "Travis loves me. Sooner or later he will get over his anger and want to find out the truth. He'll talk to other people in town. He'll find out I was discharged from the hospital because of the baby I was carrying. He'll find out when my son was born. He'll start counting the months. And *he* will come to *me*."

"I thought of that possibility, my love. I sent two of my best men to kill him."

Ignoring the pain, she pulled herself up from the bed and screamed, "You bastard! I'll tell! So help me, no matter how you beat me, I'll tell that you were responsible."

He gave her a rough shove that sent her sprawling back on the bed.

"I'm not talking about now, you little fool. I sent two men to kill him some time ago, right after I decided it was you I wanted for my wife. I had your messages to him destroyed, just as I had someone take care of the ones he sent you. But my men weren't smart enough to get the job done. I have since found out that they did track Coltrane down, and there was a shootout. My men were killed, and Travis was only wounded. I understand he was laid up for quite a while. Now I have to carefully plot a way to get rid of him. The situation is a bit more difficult now, since he is a federal marshal, but there are ways. It will work out. I want things to calm down a bit, first. It might look suspicious if he were suddenly killed right after I was the central figure in his first investigation.

"All in good time, my dear." He smiled. "All in good

time. But what do you care? He's made it obvious that he wants no part of you. I have Nancy to thank for that. She did her job well. As much as she hates me, she did me a great service."

Kitty could only lie there, mind whirling. There had to be a way out of all this.

"I tried the gentle approach with you, Kitty." His voice was suddenly soft, coaxing, and she opened her eyes to stare suspiciously. "I tried to make you love me. I really did. You know the money you supposedly got from your father's pay as a Union soldier? There was no money from him. *I* put up that generous sum out of my own pocket. It was all arranged with that sergeant working under General Schofield. I wanted to see you have the money to try to make it on your own, to show you that you couldn't, that you needed me. But you were doing a good job, so I was forced to use other means to make you bend. I hired your negroes away from you. I took advantage of your maternal state. I tried every way possible to make you need me, but no, you had to continue being obstinate. But you see, Kitty, sweet, I always get what I want. So it didn't bother me in the least to break you. It didn't bother me to give you the thrashing you deserved last night. I intend to keep you, for the rest of your life. The sooner you realize that, the better it will be for all of us. Now, if you cooperate, I'll bring little John back after Travis Coltrane is taken care of. I can't risk his seeing the brat. I'm not blind. I know he looks like his father."

Kitty shut his words out. Travis had to be warned. And one puzzling thought remained. Why had he come back? Why hadn't he gone back to his beloved bayou country? Why did he return to Wayne County, where she was? Because he *did* love her? Only now, that feeling may have been destroyed by Nancy's lies.

* * *

It had been five days since the beating when Kitty once again begged Addie to help her. "You are my only hope, Addie. You are the only person who comes in here besides Corey. You are my only contact with the outside world."

"Miss Kitty, you know I likes you and always have," the old Negro said gently, as though speaking to a child. "But I can't do nothing fo' you. I gots my own hide to think about. Mistah McRae would either kick me out or kill me. And he sho would have me beaten worse'n what he beat you, before he did either one. Lord knows, I wish I could help you, 'cause you were good to me when I was a'starvin'."

"Yes, I was," Kitty snapped, suddenly furious. She had never been one to throw up past favors, but she was desperate. "I did help you," she reminded her woman. "I shared what little I had, but when that was gone, when everyone on my land was suffering, you and your husband walked out on me. Corey has admitted to me he deliberately took my friends from me, so I would become weaker and weaker. Have I hated you? No. Even now, if you came to me and asked me for something, if I had it in my power, I'd do whatever you asked. Look what that man has done to me! You see my body, how he beat me. You see how he keeps me a prisoner. He even took away the one thing on this earth that gave me a reason for living, my baby. Now he's told me he plans to have Travis murdered. Oh, my God, Addie, I appeal to your Christian goodness. Help me, please." Her voice broke.

"Oh, Miss Kitty." Addie's eyes were filled with tears. "When you talk like that, what can I say? You make me feel so guilty. But I got my own hide to think about, too."

Kitty reached out and clutched at her desperately. "Listen to me and do as I say and you won't be in any danger. You can send word to Luther, can't you? He's

Jacob's son, and he'll help me. I know you and your people keep up with each other. Luther is bound to be somewhere around the countryside. Send word to him that I need his help. I've known him all his life. He'll help me. I know he will. Tell him everything that has happened, and he'll protect you. And Luther is smart. He'll know how to help me escape from here and get to town and find Travis. You two are the only hope I have left."

Addie sucked in her breath, rolled her eyes upwards as her whole body trembled. Finally she lowered her gaze to meet Kitty's anxious face. "All right," she whispered, "I'll do it. I'll get word to Luther. But if he don't help, then there's nothing else I can do. I'm sorry. I hope the Lord will forgive me if I'm doing wrong. But Miss Kitty, I is scared of Mistah McRae. All us niggers is scared to death of him."

"And you have reason to be. I would sooner face the devil. He has to be stopped. Now, please, get word to Luther, somehow, as soon as possible."

Addie left, shaken. Kitty hoped that the guard stationed at the door would not notice and become suspicious. She did not know the woman all that well, and she could only pray that she would follow through on her promise without looking guilty.

Towards morning, as dawn filtered around the edges of the heavy velvet drapes, she opened heavy lids to see Corey's shadowy figure standing at the side of her bed. Dear God, don't let him want me now, she prayed. Not now, please.

"Sorry to awaken you," he murmured, "especially at such an early hour, but I have made a decision I thought might brighten your day."

Apprehensively, she sat up in bed, careful to keep the covers up about her chin.

He sat down and she cringed, shrinking away from him. "Now, is that any way for a loving, dutiful wife to treat her husband?" It was hard to make out his face in the shadows, but she knew he was smirking. "You should never move away from me, my darling. You should want to be close, very close."

His fingertips brushed her cheeks. She fought the impulse to shudder.

"I am leaving this morning for Raleigh to take care of some business. I probably won't be back for several days. Hugo is going with me, but the guards will still be posted outside your door. Addie will bring you your trays and see to your personal needs, but I'm sure you understand I have to be certain that you don't leave this room. By the way, your friend Mattie Glass has called to see you twice. Hugo told her you were ill and not up to receiving guests. She's a stubborn one, especially since you helped her. Oh, Kitty, Kitty," he sighed. "You and that defiant spirit. You've caused so many people so much grief."

"If you came here to tell me that you will be away for a few days, then it is indeed good news," she snapped. "I may have to stay in this room, but at least I won't be bothered by your coming around to gloat over me."

"I like to think I'm protecting you from yourself, from making an even bigger fool of yourself than you already have. I've told people you really weren't over the fever, that the party was too much for you and you suffered a relapse. If I let you go wandering around, chasing after your old lover, people will only gossip. He's made it plain he doesn't want you." Corey took a deep breath.

"I do have one last thing to say. I have decided to bring your baby back, Kitty."

Her body stiffened. This was another cruel joke.

"Well, aren't you going to bounce up and down with joy?" he laughed.

"If I could believe you, I would," she said quietly.

"Well, I have thought it over and decided that I may have been a bit rough with you, Kitty. Now, don't get me wrong, I don't regret the beating. You deserved that, and if you give me cause, it will happen again, and again, until you learn to be the obedient wife I intend you to be. Taking your son away might make Coltrane curious. If the baby isn't here, he might become suspicious. So I will bring *our* son home from Raleigh, and you and I will appear to the world as a happily married, loving couple. You will play the role to the hilt, because I don't have to tell you what will happen if you don't."

Her mind was whirling.

"Didn't you hear a word I said, Kitty?" He was brushing his hand down her cheek again.

"Yes, yes, I heard you."

"Then I shall be on my way. In a very few days you'll have your son back, and we'll go on with our lives. You'll have everything a woman could want, wealth, position, a child, and a husband who—despite what you might think—loves you very deeply. Now, give me a kiss of gratitude. Show me some affection."

He lowered his lips, pressing her close to him by placing his hand on the back of her head. His lips mashed down, and she fought the impulse to gag as he thrust his tongue inside her mouth. She would not allow her body to stiffen. She must not make him angry now.

At last the kiss was over. "Ahh, I knew you would see things my way, Kitty." He squeezed her breast possessively. "I wish I had the time," he whispered huskily. "I'd like to strip you naked and kiss every inch of that beautiful body, feel myself inside you, knowing all that loveliness belongs only to me."

She held back the sigh of relief as he reluctantly got to his feet. "There isn't time, but I promise I will make it up to you later. You can show me how grateful you are when I return. Until then, my darling, just rest your body for the lovemaking to come."

After he'd gone, Kitty sprang from the bed, shaking with excitement. She waited for perhaps a half hour, until she could be sure Corey and Hugo had left the plantation, then she went to the door and pounded on it impatiently.

"Yeah, what do you want?" A sleepy, irritated voice wafted through the thick pine. She recognized Rance. It figured that Corey would leave his most trusted man on guard duty during the night hours.

"Have Addie come to me at once," she called to him.

"Miz McRae, it's too early. She'll be asleep," he protested. "The cook ain't even started up the fire in the kitchen yet."

"Have her come to me," Kitty all but screamed. "I . . . I have personal problems."

She heard the snicker, the shuffle of a tilted chair being thumped to the floor, boots scraping. "All right. All right. I'll get her."

Pressing her ear to the door, she heard him walking away, clunking down the steps. Knowing in advance it was useless, she turned the knob. Of course it would be locked. There was nothing to do but wait. She did not want to leave, anyway, until John was back. But she had to make sure that all plans were made so she could get away as soon as she had him.

After what seemed an eternity, she heard movement in the hall, a key turning in the lock. The door opened, Addie was shoved inside, then the key clanked once again. "What on earth is wrong, Miss Kitty?" Addie looked at her, eyes drooping sleepily.

She grabbed the Negro woman's arm and pulled her as far from the door as possible. Despite the chilly spring morning, Kitty opened the door to the veranda, and the two stepped outside. In the shadows below she could see the other guard. He was asleep.

"Now, listen to me." She turned to Addie, whispering so low the servant had to bend her ear to almost touch her lips. "Corey has gone to Raleigh for several days, but he'll be bringing John back with him when he returns. That is when I want to escape, the first night he's back. Will must find Luther and make the arrangements."

"He found Luther," Addie said quickly, and Kitty's heart pounded with hope. "He says Luther's got to lay low, too. The law and that Klan is after him. He says he'll help what he can, though, 'cause of the way you and your pa always treated him and his daddy. He told Will for me to find out what you wanted him to do, and he'd see if he can do it. He says he ain't sure where his daddy is, though, and it'd take a long time for him to find out. How big a hurry you in, Miss Kitty, and what you want Luther to do?"

Kitty told her. Luther would have to find a way to get her and the baby out of the house the night Corey returned from Raleigh. He would need to find out where Travis would be so that she could go straight to him. They could not waste a moment.

"Miss Kitty, you done tol' me how that man don't believe that young'un of yours is his," Addie said worriedly. "If Luther does get you out of here and gets you into town, and that man of yours turns his back on you the way he did the night of the ball, you gonna be in one heap o' trouble. Mistah McRae, he liable to take that boy away from you fo' good. He's liable to beat you to death, he gonna be so mad."

Kitty took a deep breath, shivering. "It's the chance I must take, Addie. It's the only hope I have. Corey is going to have Travis killed. I have to warn him. I also have to let him see his son. He'll look at him and *know* he's his."

"Well, you can't look at a baby that young and tell nothin' about who the daddy is," the old Negro scoffed.

"I knows lots of women who got babies by other men, and they passes 'em off as belongin' to the one they happens to be married to. He ain't gonna be able to tell just by looking."

Kitty felt tears of frustration stinging her eyes. "But I have to *try*, Addie. Don't you see? I can't just give up. And if Travis won't believe me, at least I'll be out of this house. I'll have a chance to run. I'll take John and leave North Carolina and go North, anywhere to escape Corey. Now you stay with me long enough for Rance to believe you are helping me with my 'personal problems,' and then go back to your cabin and tell Will exactly what I've told you. Have him find Luther again and explain what I want him to do. Tell him where the guards are posted. The day Corey returns with John, Will can have a prearranged signal with Luther to let him know that as soon as it's dark we're going to make our move. Corey always has his brandy and cigars after dinner. We'll move quickly. You'll make sure his brandy bottle is laced with enough opium to make him fall asleep and stay asleep until morning."

"Lawdy, Miss Kitty, I might give him too much and kill him," she said fearfully. Kitty motioned her to calm down, and Addie whispered, "I don't know nothing about putting stuff in folks' drinks. I might put in too much or too little. He might wake up before you wants him to."

"I know quite a bit about drugs, remember? I will tell you exactly how much to put in the bottle, and when he's passed out, you'll pour out what's left and replace ordinary brandy so he won't find out later what happened. Just go and tell Will everything I have told you. Leave everything else up to me and don't worry. I won't let you get in trouble, I promise. The risk will be mine."

They went back inside. Addie's worried look did not

leave her eyes. Kitty finally admonished her by saying, "Quit looking that way. You'll make someone suspicious. Now, you've been in here long enough that Rance will think you were doing something, so go do what I told you to do, then bring me my breakfast tray at the usual time. Tell Will to be extremely careful, but I want him to get the message to Luther as soon as possible."

Kitty tapped on the door, lightly this time. Rance turned the key, and then Addie was stepping outside, moving by him and down the hall quickly. But he did not close the door and relock it immediately, as he usually did. Instead, he leaned against the side and looked at her with half-closed eyes, smiling.

"You know, the boss did himself proud when he got a pretty little filly like you. I envy him. Me and all the boys. We talk about you a lot, 'bout how you look, how lucky the boss is to have something like you to crawl into bed with at night."

Kitty bristled angrily. "How dare you speak to me this way? I'll tell my husband."

"Aw, he won't believe nothing you say." He grinned. "I'll just tell him you tried to proposition me so you could escape. He'll believe me, and then he'll beat that pretty bee-hind of yours again, so you just keep your mouth shut, if you're smart. He don't trust you. So how's about you and me being friends? I might could make things easier for you."

"How?"

"Oh, I'll tell him you were real good while he was gone, didn't give none of the boys any trouble."

"I hadn't planned to give anyone any trouble."

"Well, if I tell him you did, he'll believe me, now won't he?" He sucked a tooth loudly, stuck his finger in his mouth and dug something out of a cavity, then wiped it on the leg of his pants. "You don't want me telling him nothing bad, do you? So why don't you just loosen up that robe and let me have a peek at those teats of yours. Me and the boys, we've talked about those teats, how big they are. I want to see how pretty they really are."

He took a step closer, as she moved back inside the room clutching her robe even tighter about her throat.

"Aw, come on, Kitty, let me have a peek. I ain't gonna make you give me nothing you don't want me to have. All I want to do is look. Who knows? You and me might get to be real good friends." He licked his lips hungrily, and she saw the trickle of saliva drooling from the corner of his mouth. "See, I know a secret about the boss, something he don't know I know about. I've bedded up with some of the gals in town that he's bedded with, and they've told me about this little problem he has. You know what I'm talking about, how he can't last so long, you know? And they told me how it just wasn't good for them, that he always got his before they got theirs. That's a bad feeling, being left empty like that.

"Now, the ladies like me. I can go for hours. I can make them get theirs over and over. I always leave 'em worn out, and they love me. I'll fill you up, honey, all you want."

He kept walking into the room, and she continued to retreat until her back was against the door to the veranda. "If you don't get out of here I'll scream. Servants will come. They'll tell my husband you were trying to force yourself on me. He'll kill you."

He held up his hands. "All right, all right. Let's don't make trouble for each other, okay? I won't fill your glass till you ask me to, but for now, you're gonna open that robe and show me those teats or I'm gonna tell the boss something you ain't gonna want him to hear when he gets back."

He moved quickly back to the door, stepped out into

the hall. She stared at him incredulously as he hissed, "Now you get that goddamned robe open and show me what you got, and don't start screaming, 'cause I'll start yelling for the guard downstairs the minute you do, saying you tricked me in your room to try and escape. Now do it, damn it. I'm tired of begging."

Kitty knew she had no choice. But it came to her that this might work to her advantage when the time came for her to make her move. There was a guard directly below her veranda. He could easily be taken care of in the dark, as could the others stationed about the mansion—all by Luther and his men. But Rance, positioned outside her door, could be a problem. Unless she seduced him, gave him a drink, and drugged him.

Slowly Kitty's hands moved from their clutching grip at her throat, allowing the robe to fall open.

"Shit, pull it open," he whispered hoarsely, eyes bulging. "I can't see nothing."

She pulled open the robe and stood there in her long, flowing gown. It gathered just below her bosom, exposing much cleavage, her body clearly visible beneath the thin fabric.

"Scoop 'em out." Rance's nostrils flared excitedly. "I want a good look, damn it."

She riveted her eyes on his face, hating him. She reached to yank down the bodice abruptly, allowing her large breasts to tumble forth.

"Ohhh, just look at that." Rance was all but dancing. "My Lord, I ain't never seen nothing so danged pretty."

His tongue flicking out like a snake, he began to stagger forward, arms outstretched, hands opening and closing. "Got to kiss 'em and touch 'em one time, Kitty," he mumbled.

The sudden sound of footsteps made him stiffen, then whisper, "Somebody's coming. Fix yourself."

Yanking up her gown, closing her robe, Kitty turned away just before Rance stepped back into the hall.

"It's about time you got here," she heard him say in a jovial voice. "It's all I can do to stay awake."

"What's the door doin' open?" she heard another guard grumble. "You know the boss said it's supposed to stay locked all the time."

"Oh, we was talking. She's complaining about not getting to go for a walk, what with the weather so nice and all." He closed the door, turned the key abruptly.

Kitty did not realize she had been holding her breath until she let it out. She had been spared. Another few moments and he would have grabbed her. A shudder moved over her body.

Soon. It would have to happen soon. And now she felt sure she could handle Rance.

Chapter Twenty-seven

"YOU sure this ain't gonna kill 'em?" Addie asked nervously as Kitty measured the opium into two bottles. One contained Corey's favorite brandy. The other, the wine Dulcie said Hugo favored.

"I know what I'm doing," Kitty told her.

Dulcie hovered nearby, looking as anxious as Addie did. "She knows, all right. Don't you fret. She knows 'zactly what she doing. She gonna give 'em just enough to put 'em to sleep till morning, and they won't know what happened. They might figure they was drugged, when they find out Miss Kitty done run away, but we'll swear we didn't know nothing about it. They know we ain't got no opium."

"That's right," Kitty said. "I told Dr. Sims I was having cramps and headaches and couldn't sleep at night, so he gave me a bottle."

"Humph," Addie snorted. "I been knowing how to make that stuff from poppy flowers all my life. Used to give it to my chillun, I did. Mistah McRae gonna think we did it, me and you, Dulcie, and we gonna get our hides tore plumb off by that strap of his. You just wait and see."

Kitty shot her a quieting glance. "I told the two of you to put the blame entirely on me. If anyone asks you any questions, tell them you saw me meddling about the liquor cabinet. I've been allowed to move about inside the house this afternoon for the first time. Corey thinks now that he's back and has brought my baby to me that I am wrapped up in him completely, with no other thoughts on my mind. Tell them you thought I was just taking something to drink to my room. The two of you have helped me so much already that I don't want you to be beaten on my account. If my escape isn't successful, I will swear no one was involved in this except me.

"Addie, you are sure that Luther will be here tonight?"

Addie nodded. "Will said he got the signal to him soon as he could after he saw Mistah McRae's carriage coming down the drive. Soon as I sits a lantern on the kitchen steps, Luther will know that Mistah McRae done passed out from his brandy, and Hugo passed out from his wine, and all that's left for him to do is have his men move in and take care of the guards."

"And what about the other servants? Do any of them suspect? The fewer who know, the safer we are."

"Me and Dulcie and Will have been real quiet. I don't think they suspect nothing. They'll be in their cabins by then anyway. And soon's I'm done, I'm leavin' here too," Addie finished.

"I'm going to pretend I passed out with Hugo," Dulcie spoke up quickly. "When he wakes up, I'm going to be laying there right beside him, playing like I'm just as groggy as he is. I'll undress him if he ain't already, and I'll be naked myself, and I'll giggle and tease him 'bout how good it was, and he won't know no different. I just hope he passes out before he . . . you know . . ." Her voice trailed off, misery mirrored in her eyes.

"Don't you worry." Kitty patted her shoulder. "Get him to drink one glass of wine and he won't be awake long enough to undress. You'll have to get his clothes off. Now, be sure you have John's things packed in a bag and hidden behind the drapes. I want to be able to walk across the hall and pick him up and leave at once. Oh, I hope he doesn't wake up and start crying."

Dulcie told her he had been sleeping pretty soundly after being fed his supper.

"All right. Now all we do is wait. Put the bottles back where they belong. Somehow, I'll get through dinner. Honestly, I feel as though bumblebees are flying around in here." She patted her tummy, and the two women laughed stiffly.

Kitty wore one of her simpler dresses that night, a pale pink muslin with a scooped neck, long sleeves, and a flowing skirt without ruffles, or hoops. Luther would undoubtedly have a horse for her, and she did not want to be hindered by clothing. She brushed her hair down about her face. Tonight she would see Travis, show him their son. Beyond that, she didn't know.

Tapping on the door, she informed the guard she was ready to go downstairs for dinner. He turned the key, opened the door, and she brushed by him, moving swiftly down the long hallway towards the stairs.

Corey met her in the entrance foyer with glittering eyes that told her he was anxious to bed her. The thought went stabbing through her. What if he passed up his cigars and brandy? What if he wanted to take her straight up to bed? Luther might be so disgusted that he would not try another night. No, she couldn't let it happen.

Stepping forward, she obediently accepted his kiss. "Are you happy to have your son back, darling?" he murmured as he led her into the dining room. "Are you as grateful as I thought you would be?"

"Oh, yes, Corey." She made her eyes meet his and flashed him a fawning smile. "You've been very kind to me, and I've had much time to think of the problems I have caused you. Perhaps things can be different."

He frowned and she panicked. Had she gone too far in appearing so eager? He touched the tip of his moustache, eyes squinting as he pondered this change in her. He held out her chair, and she sat down primly. Moving to seat himself at the other end of the long, polished table, he gazed at her studiously in the glow of the flickering tapers. "I think I know what you are up to," he said without emotion.

Her heart leaped. She had been about to lift the goblet of water to her lips but instead moved her hands to her lap, for they were trembling. "Whatever do you mean?" She made her voice steady.

He snorted. "You have your baby back. Now you are ready to play the role of dutiful, obedient wife. Then, when you think you have me under your spell, you will plead for the life of your lover. You waste your breath, my darling. I cannot risk having him around. He will have to be disposed of."

Hugo appeared with a tray of roast chicken. Addie followed with a bowl of yams, then returned with another filled with collard greens and fatback. With the servants' departure, Corey snapped, "Well, am I right? You do plan to plead for Coltrane's life, don't you?"

She lifted a slice of chicken onto her plate, praying silently that she could carry on this conversation without giving her true feelings away. "Corey, you are not being fair with me. I agree to be the wife you want me to be. I admit I have rebelled and shown you great disrespect. You made me see that my most important concern right now is the welfare of my son. True, I thought I loved Travis, but he humiliated me. I threw myself at his feet. He rejected me. Perhaps he would have done so even if Nancy had not gone to him with her lies. You see, Corey, I have no way of knowing."

She continued to put food on her plate, stomach lurching in rebellion. "Perhaps Travis came here merely out of duty. He always was one to obey orders. If he mustered out of the army and became a federal marshal, he would go wherever they sent him."

"Let me tell you something," Corey said eagerly, shaking his ornate silver fork at her. "You are absolutely correct, my dear. I know why he was sent here. The government is concerned about the activities of that Klan, and they are also concerned about what they consider a land war between Jerome Danton and myself. I found all this out when I went to Raleigh. I talked to one of the Governor's aides, and I went to see a federal army officer, and both told me what I have just told you. But I imagine Coltrane was only too glad to be sent here, if only out of curiosity to see what became of his wartime mistress. You are ravishing, Kitty, and any man who did not desire you would be insane. The man probably thought he would come back and find you working as a saloon girl. You would make a pleasant diversion for him when he was not working on his assignment. He was probably furious to learn that you were married to one of the men he is here to investigate, and also frustrated to find that he won't have the pleasure of knowing that glorious body of yours again."

She bowed her head, concentrating on cutting the slice of meat she did not want. "I suppose everything you say makes sense," she murmured. "I know you don't believe me, but more and more I come to be grateful for what you have given me, Corey. You saved my life twice. I suppose I've deserved your mistreatment of me. I will make up for it, and whatever you do with Travis Coltrane is your affair. I do not intend to meddle in my husband's business."

A wide grin split his face. For a moment she thought he was going to leap from his chair and run to her.

"My darling," he whispered. "I've longed to hear you say these words. And tonight, after I finish some business, you and I will go to my special room on the third floor, where no one will hear us. All night, all day tomorrow, we'll make passionate love."

He glanced about the large, empty room. Then, with a conspiring gleam in his eyes, he whispered, "If I didn't have to see some people after dinner, we would go to bed as soon as we finish eating." He gave an exaggerated moan. "Oh, let's talk of something else, darling. I won't be able to stand it."

Change the subject, she thought quickly. "Perhaps we can have another ball later, one that will be successful. I'll be stronger. There will be no interruptions."

"Of course we will. This time we won't invite so many people." His appetite had suddenly become huge. He chewed and swallowed with gusto, enjoying himself.

"By the way—" he paused to sip his wine, dabbed at his lips with a linen napkin—"we have been invited to a ball at the Governor's mansion in Raleigh next month. You will have a new dress, new jewels, diamonds this time. You will look even more beautiful than you did the other night. We'll have Mrs. Rivenbark come out next week to begin the fittings."

He frowned. "The bruises, my darling. Have they disappeared?"

"No." It was hard to keep the coldness, the hatred, from her voice as she remembered the pain and humiliation of that night. "It will be a while yet, I'm afraid."

"Well, when we do get her started, she will just have to work quickly. Let me know when you think you are ready." Cocking his head to one side, he looked at her thoughtfully and murmured, "I regret having to beat you, Kitty, but the time had come."

"Can't we try and forget all that?" Again she reached

for her wine glass, her voice shrill. She wondered how long she could continue this charade. Every nerve in her body screamed with anticipation of what was about to happen. And here they sat, eating and drinking and chatting as though there had been a reconciliation.

He nodded. He continued making small talk, asking how she had found little John. Was he delighted to see her? She nodded, said the appropriate things.

She held back a sigh of relief when the meal finally ended. Corey escorted her to the bottom of the stairway. She could hear two men conversing behind the closed doors to the library that served as his private office.

Just as she was about to start upstairs, Corey suddenly reached out to pull her into his arms, his lips pressing down on her. She forced herself to return the kiss. When at last he released her, he smiled, eyes glazed with his passion. "I'll be counting the minutes, my darling. I want you so desperately. Kitty, I know you think me a power-mad fool, and I know you still harbor resentment for the way I connived to make you marry me. But in my own way, I do love you."

He kissed her again briefly. Then, adjusting his coat, smoothing his hair, he turned and walked swiftly towards the library.

Rance was standing in the upstairs hall, and he gave her a yellow-toothed grin. "Boss told me to lock you back in, Kitty. I imagine he'll be along soon, though. Bet you can't hardly wait."

"I want to say good night to my baby."

He shrugged. "Just make it fast. The boss still don't want you wandering around a whole lot, you know. Don't none of us quite trust you after that scene at the party."

Oh, how she wanted to hurl something insulting in reply, but now was not the time. She went to the nursery door, entered, and closed it behind her. Dulcie was leaning over John's cradle, and she looked up with fearful eyes. "Is everything all right?" she whispered anxiously.

"I hope so. Do you have his things ready?"

"Yes'm. They're over yonder behind the drapes, just like you told me."

"Good." She bent and kissed the sleeping baby, crooning to him so quietly that even Dulcie could not make out the words. Soon they would be happy.

"Miss Kitty, there's two men down there with Mistah McRae," Dulcie said worriedly, fear etched in her expression. "Addie say all three of them might drink that brandy and pass out together. And what if one of them don't? What if he drinks from another bottle, and he's still awake and the others pass out, and he yells about it? It's going to ruin everything."

"I've thought about that." Kitty chewed her lower lip. "I hope Addie had the good sense to offer them brandy while they were waiting."

"Yes, she did, and she said they took it, and she was smart enough to give them a drink from a bottle what wasn't poisoned, so they wouldn't pass out before Mistah McRae got in there. She hid the first bottle, figuring by the time Mistah McRae went in, they'd be ready for another drink, and he'd pour it from the poisoned bottle."

"Dulcie, it is not *poison*," Kitty hissed. "I put laudanum in that bottle . . . opium . . . do you understand? I put enough in it that after two drinks, they're going to pass out. Now stop using that word 'poison.' It sounds so vicious."

Kitty turned towards the door to return to her room, but Dulcie called out to her. She turned, saw the tears streaming down the chocolate-colored skin and was moved. "Good luck, Miss Kitty. God bless us both, Miss Kitty . . ."

"Thank you," Kitty murmured, blinking back her own tears. If it weren't for Dulcie and the other Negroes, there would never have been a way to escape. She hoped someday she could repay them.

Rance was leaning against the open door to her bedroom, picking his teeth with a knife. "It's a shame the boss is back. Me and you, we get along real good, don't we?"

"Yes, yes, we do." Kitty lowered her lashes demurely, missing the surprise in his eyes.

She moved by him, deliberately brushing her breasts against his arm, felt the quick intake of his breath. It would be no problem coaxing him inside. She had no worries about that.

She sat on the side of the bed, hands clasped together tightly. She wanted to pace up and down the room to pass the time. It was difficult to remain still. But if Rance heard any sounds of anxiety, he might become suspicious. The minutes passed with agonizing slowness. A half hour—she would wait half an hour. Hugo should be asleep by then, as well as Corey and his friends. Addie would place the lantern on the steps at the back of the house. Luther would have the signal to make his move.

Finally, eyes riveted on the mantel clock, Kitty took a deep breath and stood up. The time had come. It was now or never. She went to the fireplace and picked up the log she had laid aside for the purpose of knocking Rance unconscious. It would have to be a good blow. If she did not hit him hard enough, there would not be a second chance.

Rumpling the covers all the way down to the foot of the bed, she tucked the log beneath. Then she walked quietly to the door, and made her voice low and husky. "Rance? Rance, may I speak with you a moment?"

"Sure." He spoke pleasantly, almost anxiously. The

key turned, and the door opened. They faced each other. Her smile was inviting.

"I'm afraid my husband has been detained with his friends. I suppose they got to drinking and he just forgot all about me." She gave a mock pout, then gestured about the empty room. "It . . . it's rather lonesome in here. Do you suppose you could keep me company?"

He was almost gasping. "Kitty, I'd sure like to, but what if the boss comes upstairs? I mean, if he caught me in here, he'd kill me."

"Couldn't you step out on the veranda and ask the guard to throw a pebble against the window when Corey's friends leave? That would give you ample time to get back into the hallway while Corey is saying good night."

She moved closer, once again brushing her breasts against him. That was all the persuasion he needed. Licking his lips hungrily, he all but ran across the room, shoving open the doors. She watched with satisfaction as he leaned over the wooden railing and called down in a low voice: "Bart. Hey, Bart. How about throwing a stone against the window when the boss lets his friends out the front door?"

She could not hear the man's response, but he obviously asked what was going on because Rance snapped, "None of your goddamned business. Just do what I tell you."

He stepped back inside, smiling broadly. "Kitty, I knew you was hungering for a real man, and you got one now. I'm gonna give it to you like you ain't never had it before."

"I know," she whispered, backing toward the bed, lowering herself invitingly. She held open her arms. "Come show me. Now."

He was unfastening his pants, yanking them down. She closed her eyes, unable to bear the sight of his nakedness even in the dim glow of the lantern. She felt him shoving up her dress, his breath coming in rasping gasps. "It won't be as good this time, Kitty, honey. We ain't got long. I'll arrange it next time, though, so we can really be together for awhile. I'll make it good, I promise . . ."

Her hand was snaking slowly along the sheets towards the pile of bed covers.

She felt for the log, fingers closing about it. She brought her weapon down, hitting him soundly on the back of his head. Instantly, he slumped into unconsciousness.

Quickly she shoved his repulsive body off her, leaped to her feet, and adjusted her clothing. Without so much as a glance, she left him there and hurried out of the room, across the hall, and into the nursery. John was sleeping peacefully. Wrapping the blankets tightly about him, she lifted him in her arms, cradling him against her bosom as she seized the bundle Dulcie had left behind the drapes. Then she made her way swiftly down the hall, down the stairs, her footsteps and ragged breathing the only sound echoing in the deathly silent house.

Please let everything be taken care of, she prayed anxiously, heart pounding so loudly she feared it would awaken John. Luther has to be waiting right outside. Everything has to have gone according to plan.

Pausing outside the closed library doors, she strained for any sound. All was silent. She fought the impulse to run the rest of the way as she forced herself to tiptoe past, moving towards the front door.

Her hand was on the knob, but suddenly the door flew open. Her lips parted to scream, and then she recognized Luther's face, anxious, excited, smiling triumphantly. He took the bundle from beneath her arm, allowing her to hold the baby tighter. Guiding her out onto the porch with his free hand, he whispered,

"Everything is all right. It's all taken care of. I've got horses waiting down the drive a piece, and my men and I will take you into town on a back road."

She waited till they were away from the house, and then she burst into tears of joy. "Thank you, Luther. Thank you and God bless you. I don't know what I would've done without you."

"Don't thank me yet. I had somebody find out where Coltrane spends most of his time, when he ain't working—one of the saloons. All I can do is take you as close to that place as I think is safe for me and my men. Then you're on your own, Miss Kitty. I wants to help you all I can, but I got my own hide to look after. If I'm seen in town, my neck will be stretched from the tallest tree they can find by sunrise. I wish I could stay and see it through, but you got to know how it is with me."

She agreed, grateful for everything he had done and not about to ask for further help. Once in town, she felt sure she could handle the situation herself.

They reached the pecan grove, and Kitty saw eight Negroes already mounted on their horses. Luther took her arm and walked her quickly towards a mount and, motioning to the baby in her arms, asked worriedly, "You think you can ride and hold onto that, too?"

"Yes, I'm an expert rider, Luther. I can manage. I know you're anxious to get there and be on your way, and I'll ride as fast as I can."

"Good." He took John from her arms and held him while she swung up into the saddle. Then she reached down and took the still-sleeping infant. Luther got on his horse, then motioned towards his men and cried, "Let's go."

They rode through the night, cantering the horses at a speed Kitty found awkward. But she managed to keep up. Once John awoke and began to cry. She held him tighter, crooned to him over the sounds of the horses' thundering hooves. Mercifully, he closed his eyes after a while.

The night was dark. A cool spring wind whipped about her face. The road was rough, unfamiliar. The Negroes had been forced to make their own back paths, and she was caught up in a world of thick, shadowy trees. Several times a low branch would slap against her and she would fight to remain in the saddle, holding the reins with one hand, her baby with the other.

They did not take the old wooden bridge into Goldsboro. Luther knew of a shallow crossing in the Neuse River, where they waded the horses through the dark, flowing waters. When they had worked their way up the steep bank on the other side, the road fanned out a bit, and Kitty did not feel quite so smothered.

Finally the town loomed ahead. At the edge of the woods Luther stopped his men, then rode back to where Kitty had reined her horse in. "I've got to leave my men here. I'll take you the rest of the way. Stay close and move slow."

When they reached a dark alley behind a row of buildings, Luther said anxiously, "Okay, Miss Kitty. This is as far as I go, and I got to get out of here fast. I'll take your horse. Hate to do it, but we needs all the horses we got. Had to steal these. You go down that alley, and when you get to the third building, there'll be a man waiting for you. He's supposed to have found out exactly where Coltrane is right now. He'll hold the baby for you while you go in, if you wants him to. He ain't no part of us, so nobody will suspect him of anything. His name's Willy Joe, and you can trust him. I told him to do what you wanted or I'd cut his throat. I hope everything turns out all right for you. And if you ever need me again, I'll do what I can."

She got down from the horse. "Luther, I can't thank you enough. But how will I be able to get in touch with you?"

"I know everything that goes on. I got folks keeping me up on things. You run along now."

He turned swiftly, disappearing into the night.

Shivering with the night chill and the creeping fear that moved over her body, Kitty made her way down the alley. She had not gone far when a shadowy figure loomed up from behind a trash barrel. Her throat constricted with terror. The voice drawled, "Don't be scairt, ma'm. I's Willy Joe."

"Thank God," she murmured.

He quickly told her that he had peeked in a window and watched Marshal Coltrane off and on for the past few hours. "I got a friend who works in there, cleans up and all. I got him to follow the marshal when he went upstairs. He's in room twelve. You can go through the back door and up the steps to the side. They's carryin' on something fierce out front—piano a'goin' and folks a'singin'. Nobody gonna see you, I hope. You want me to take that baby and keep him for you while you go up?"

"No. I'll take him with me." She did not dare part with John. What if someone came along and questioned a black man holding a white baby in the alley behind a saloon? And she wanted Travis to see his son, the sooner the better.

"Then I'll be getting along." He sounded relieved.

She thanked him for his help, then watched him scurry away. As she turned towards the rear door of the saloon, the sound of raucous music and laughter reached her ears. The moment of reckoning had come. Taking a deep breath, pausing to kiss little John on his forehead, she opened the door and stepped inside.

The hallway was dark, illuminated only by the lanterns that glowed through the archway leading to the saloon. She could see men laughing and drinking, women dressed in bright, flashy colors. They sat in men's laps, on the bar, on tables, skirts hiked up above their knees to display shapely legs. Their breasts were almost completely bare. Many of the women were adorned with feathers, some even had them tucked into their hair. Even from where she stood, she could see their brightly painted lips. *This* was where Travis spent his time? She shuddered.

The hallway had only one lantern, at the far end, but she could make out the numbers on the door. Her heart was thundering as she saw 12. Now. Balancing the baby in the crook of her left arm, she knocked softly.

There was no sound from the other side, and she felt a wave of panic begin to wash over her. What if Willy Joe had been wrong? She knocked a second time, louder.

"Yeah, who is it?"

She trembled at the sound of the dear, familiar voice. She knocked again, so loudly she feared someone in another room might hear.

She heard him swearing, the shuffling of feet. Then the door flew open, and she found herself staring down the barrel of a pointed gun. "What the hell is it," he snarled angrily, then lowered the gun as his face became a mask of shock and bewilderment.

"Travis, I have to talk to you. Please. . . ." Catching him off guard, Kitty shoved past him and into the room.

And then she saw her—lying naked upon the bed—Nancy Warren Danton.

"What are you doing here?" Travis was quickly regaining his composure and his anger. "Get out of here, Kitty."

"What are *you* doing here?" Kitty ignored him and addressed herself to Nancy, who was staring back at her insolently, making no move to cover herself.

A loud buzzing began in her ears, and her whole body began to tremble with a mixture of shock and anguish. Nancy, here, naked, in bed with Travis.

"I might ask you the same thing." Nancy sat up in bed.

"I have every right to be here," Kitty snapped. "I brought my son to his father—"

"Oh, Kitty, are you still trying to pass that kid off as Travis'? Everyone in town knows the truth. Goodness knows you worked hard enough to trap Corey into marrying you. The least you could do is be faithful to him." Nancy's hair hung loose and wild about her face, and she gave it a toss. "You know, that's a rotten trick, even for you, taking Corey's kid and telling another guy it's his. What do you want from Travis, anyway? Corey's given you the world and everything in it."

Kitty kept her voice even. "I'm telling the truth when I say this is Travis' son! *You* have spread your lies, just as you did about Nathan's death. The only reason you haven't turned the town against Travis and had him shot in the back is because you saw a chance to use him to hurt me. Tell me, Nancy, where does Jerome think you are tonight?"

Nancy's eyes narrowed. "That's none of your damned business."

"All right, you two, that's enough." Travis stepped forward, grabbing Kitty's arm. "Take that baby and get out of here, woman. I made it clear the other night I want no part of you and your scheming. I don't know what you're after now, but you aren't going to get me involved."

"No, I'm not leaving. Nancy is leaving, because you and I are going to talk, alone. And if she doesn't leave, then I'm going to run down those steps, screaming at the top of my lungs, that Jerome Danton's wife is up here naked in bed with the marshal. Do either of you want that? I think not. Nancy, you have exactly one minute to get your clothes on and get out of here."

Nancy looked to Travis, her face red, body trembling in rage. He scratched at his beard thoughtfully, realizing Kitty was not one to make false threats. "Do as she said, Nancy. I'll hear her out and be done with her. She wants a big scene, so she'll get it, but we don't want trouble with your husband. So go."

Nancy dressed quickly, but as she reached the door she turned and gave Kitty one final, hating glare. "I'll fix you for this, you little bitch. I'll fix you for all time."

With the door closed, Travis turned to Kitty and sighed wearily. "All right. Say what you've come to say and then get the hell out of here."

"Travis, there is so much to say." She blinked back tears, fighting back the emotions quivering from the depths of her soul. How she had longed for this moment, prayed for it. Now it was here. But she had wanted him to look upon her with love and longing, not loathing.

She pulled the blankets back from their son. "Look at him," she said tenderly. "Travis, look at him. Is this the son of Corey McRae? I see you every time I look at him. If he were awake, if you could see the way his eyes are turning from baby blue to the color of your own, you would know. You should know in your own heart. Doesn't it stir something within you to gaze upon your own son? He was born in December, Travis. December! Think back to those last precious hours we had together at the end of March, just before you left. He was conceived then. You left your seed in my body. This is the product of that seed. I didn't even know Corey McRae at that time. I was fired from the hospital because everyone knew I was carrying your child, and Nancy had everyone hating both of us because of the lies she told. I had no place to go."

She swallowed hard, but the tears would no longer be held back. "It's such a long story, Travis, but you have to believe me. *This is your son.*"

He turned away, his expression stony. "Why are you doing this, Kitty? The man is rich. He gave you what you wanted. So what do you want of me?"

"I want you to acknowledge your son!" she screamed, unable to keep her voice down any longer. "Here, take him. Hold him in your arms. He's your flesh and blood, Travis. Yours!"

He whirled around to face her, fists clenched at his sides. "You expect me to believe you? You never wrote to me! That goddamned land of yours meant everything to you. I meant nothing. I tried to get you to go with me, but no, you had to stay here, to hang on to your precious land. You latched on to McRae because he had something I didn't—money. I know how the Southerners were losing their land right and left, once the war was over. I should have known you would stoop to anything to keep yours. But, fool that I was, I kept on writing to you, sending messages, explaining why I was delayed. You got scared that I just might come back and mess up your little tea party, so you even had men sent to kill me. They almost succeeded."

He ripped open his shirt with one quick yank, and she winced at the scar below his left rib cage. "They almost did me in. Me and Sam got them, all right, but nobody to this day can figure out how I managed to live. Sam got it out of one of them before he died, how a man named McRae sent them. I didn't connect it all with you till I got back here and pieced the story together."

"Yes, you pieced it together from the lies that Nancy was so anxious to tell you, and you believed her. Why didn't you come to *me*? You not only believed her, you took her to bed."

"I didn't come to you because you happen to be another man's wife now. And who I take to bed, and when, is my business. I see yours didn't stay empty for very long." He threw a sneering look at the baby. "Hell, I always knew you were made of grit and hell, Kitty, but this beats everything. I know Corey is a son of a bitch. I know he was behind the attack and rape of that Glass woman, but I can't prove it. I know he and Danton's Klan bunch are responsible for every bit of trouble in this part of the country, but damn it, you're McRae's wife, you're the mother of his child, so why don't you get the hell out of this room and out of my life before something else happens?"

"This is *your* son, Travis! Yours! Corey sent those men to kill you, not me. I swear on my father's grave that I knew nothing about it. I wrote you letters, and Dulcie, my maid, admitted to me that she was forced to turn them over to Corey. He destroyed them. What do I have to do to make you believe me?"

He had been standing with his back to her, drinking slowly from the bottle of whiskey on the bedside table. The room was small and dirty, and the air was fetid. He turned slowly, and his eyes were filled with misery as he whispered hoarsely, "Kitty, I'll never believe anything you say, ever again. If you had really loved me, the way you swore you did, you would have left here with me last year."

"You *know* why I had to stay."

He sent the bottle hurling across the room to smash against the wall. "You stayed because of your goddamned land! Well, you've got it. So why are you here trying to make me believe I'm the father of that baby? Why? When Corey McRae finds out you've pulled this stunt, he's going to be madder than hell, and I don't blame him."

The glass shattering had awakened John, and he began to cry lustily. Kitty moved him to her shoulder, patting his back soothingly. He continued to cry. Travis covered his ears and stumbled away. "Get him out of here, will you? And don't ever come back. I just want to finish what I came to do and then get the hell out of North Carolina and go home. I wish I'd never come back."

Kitty was not about to give up. Walking over to the mussed bed, she laid her crying son down. His arms and legs flailed the air with fright, hunger, and anger, all mingled together in his lusty wails. "Look at your son. Just look at him, Travis."

He stormed over to the bed, stared down at the infant. "There are thousands of men who are fooled into thinking they've fathered babies that aren't really theirs. You think by looking at him I'm supposed to suddenly claim him as my son? Wake up. What we had, or might have had, is in the past, over, finished, forever. Go home to your husband. You have your life to live and I have mine. For God's sake, woman, where is your pride?"

Her spine stiffened as she met the icy glare of the man she had loved with all her heart. "I only came because I love you, Travis, but I suppose I was a fool. What we had never meant anything to you. And you're right. I have no pride, or I would never have come here."

"Hell, I know why you came here. . . ." He reached out and pulled her into his arms, his lips bruising against hers. Just as quickly, he released her. "For this. You want me now as you wanted me when we were together. You always were a hot-blooded woman. Oh, sure, you tried to hide it, didn't you? But when I took you in my arms and held you like this, you couldn't hide your passion. No more than you can now."

He crushed her against him, kissing her again, his tongue thrusting inside her mouth. She beat upon his back with her fists, her body trembling with the sobs that ached for release.

He maneuvered her down on the bed, beside the baby, who continued to cry. Ripping at her dress, he forced her thighs apart and jerked at his own clothes until she felt him shoving inside her roughly. "This is what you wanted," he said. "This is all you ever wanted from me. Well, I'll give it to you, and then you can go home to your husband."

The baby stopped crying, staring about the room vacantly. The rocking of the bed had soothed him. Kitty lay helpless beneath Travis, allowing him to have his way with her. She refused to struggle. He could take her body, take what he wanted, but she would not return his passion. Everything within her had died.

The past danced before her closed eyes in slow motion—hours of laughter and love, moments spent dreaming of a lifetime of happiness together. Never did she think it would come to this degradation. She had loved him. She had tried her best to find him. She had given him a son. All was in vain. She was no more to him than a harlot, a woman in red feathers.

With one final thrust, it was over. He lay on top of her, gasping. She smelled the whiskey, realized how drunk he was as he finally moved away, lurching to his feet. "Now get out of here," he said in a rasping voice. "And take that baby with you. Go home to your husband. Get the hell out of my life."

She could not move. Perhaps, she thought, she had died. Maybe her heart had broken, and life had truly left her body, and this was the way it felt to be dead.

"I said get out of here!" Travis reached down and grabbed her arm, yanking her to her feet so roughly that she stumbled and fell to the floor. "You got what you came for. Now go! I never want to see you again.

And you can tell that husband of yours that I won't stop till I see him in prison. I know what he's done. I'll find a way to prove it."

She was struggling to stand, holding onto the brass railing of the bed for support. "You won't live that long," she whispered hoarsely.

"Oh, so now you threaten to kill me?" he laughed, voice slurred. "How do you plan to do it? Shoot me? No, you have wealth now, don't you? You can hire men to do the job for you, and maybe this time they'll succeed."

"No. Corey will try to have you killed, Travis. Not me. You underestimate his ruthlessness and his power. I visited Mattie Glass in the hospital and made her realize that she had to regain her spirit and go on with her life. Corey was after her property. He was furious when he went to the hospital and found she was ready to fight back to hang on to her land. To punish me, he took my baby away and threatened to get rid of him if I did not bend to his will. After the party, he beat me and kept me locked in my room with a guard posted outside my door day and night so I could not come to you. He vowed he would get rid of you so you would be out of my life forever."

She began tugging at her dress, yanking it down about her waist. His eyebrows shot up. "What are you doing? I've had my fill of you for one night. I don't want to see your body."

Ignoring his protest, she turned about so he could see the bruises still laced across her back from the leather strap Corey had used. When she faced him once again, there was no denying the flash of anger in the smoky gray eyes. "You can see what he did to me," she said quietly. "Believe me when I say he will kill you if you don't leave town. I came here tonight praying that you would believe me and acknowledge John as your son. I wanted us to leave together, to make a new life. The only thing that mattered to me was you, Travis, you and our son. But now it's all over. I should have known you would never believe me, because you never really loved me, anyway."

She reached down and wrapped the blankets around the baby and picked him up.

Travis stood watching, running his fingers through his hair. His mind was buzzing from so much to drink. It was hard to think.

"No, I don't believe you," he said with finality. "If that baby were mine, you would never have married Corey McRae."

"I married Corey because I had no other choice. Jerome Danton and his men burned down the little house I was able to build on my land. They left me on the frozen ground, about to give birth. Corey came and took me to his house and saved my life *and* the baby's. He asked me to marry him then, but I refused. I tried once more, with Jacob, to make it on my own. I still had hopes you would return. Then the baby got sick, and I became sick, and I was in town, trying to borrow money for food. We were starving. I passed out. Corey took me to his home, had a doctor care for me and John. By then, I was ready to do anything to keep my baby from dying. And all that time, Travis, I wondered where you were, why you did not come for me—for us."

She turned towards the door.

"Where are you going?" he asked.

"I don't know. I'll try to find Jacob. Corey had him sent to South Carolina so he couldn't help me. I couldn't have gotten here tonight if it hadn't been for his son. I'm sure you've heard of Luther . . . you and the Klansmen are looking for him and his band of men. I hope you never catch them. Even though I failed with you and realize I made a complete fool of myself, at least I'm free of Corey. I'll never go back to that house. I'll be better off dead, and perhaps my son will be also."

"Kitty, do you really expect me to believe all this?" He threw up his hands in frustration. "I know you, woman. I know the kind of grit you've got. You'd never have given in to marry a man you didn't love unless it was to keep your land."

"Or save my son's *life*," she said wearily. "I'm leaving now. We have nothing more to say to each other. There is a thin line between love and hate, Travis, and I have just crossed over."

Kitty was only a few feet from the door when there was a sudden crash and the splintering of wood. Travis had his gun in a flash and was about to fire when he recognized Corey McRae shoving into the room along with several of his men. He kept the gun pointed at them, eyes narrowed threateningly as Corey looked from him to Kitty, who stared back with terrified eyes, her baby clutched tightly against her bosom.

"So! This is how you betray me!" Corey barked at her. He looked at Travis coldly. "You can put your gun away, Coltrane. I have no quarrel with you. I'm afraid my wife is not content with the bed of only one man. This has happened before."

"You lie!" Kitty screamed. "You know why I came here—to tell Travis the truth!"

"Kitty, Kitty." Corey shook his head. "Don't make a scene. Let's keep this as quiet as possible for appearance's sake, shall we? Now you just come along."

"No!" She took a step backwards, towards the window, her face ashen. "I know what you'll do. You'll take my baby. You'll beat me. I'd rather die."

Nancy swished into the room, mock sympathy in her voice as she cried, "Oh, dear me, I should have minded my own business. I didn't *mean* to cause any trouble."

"You!" Kitty blazed. "You sent for him!"

"No, she didn't." Jerome Danton stepped in behind her. "She came home from visiting a sick friend and told me she happened to see you slipping into the alley behind the saloon. I didn't have to do much figuring to see what you were up to, Kitty. I was at the party, remember? I heard about the way you threw yourself at this man's feet and made a fool of yourself. And as much as I despise your husband, I did what any man would do. I sent my men riding to let him know his wife was making a fool of him."

"How noble!" Kitty laughed caustically. "Perhaps I should have sent for you when I came in here and found your wife naked in bed. Instead, I told her to get out and let me speak to the father of my child, or I'd scream for all the world to hear that she was up here making love with him. So she runs to you so you'll send for Corey."

She flashed a venomous look at Nancy, who stood confidently smirking, sure that everyone would think Kitty was lying to save her own skin. "You just don't give up, do you?" Kitty was able to laugh again, despite the desperate situation she found herself in. "You won't be satisfied until I'm in my grave, will you? You'll go right on hating and hurting. Oh, Nancy, there has to be a special place in hell for bitches like you."

"Jerome, I don't have to listen to such things," Nancy whined, turning her face against her husband's chest. "Take me away from all this."

Jerome's jaw twitched as he put his arm stiffly about his wife to lead her from the room. He continued to stare at Kitty, a puzzled expression on his face.

"Go on, get out," Corey snapped. "Both of you. Go tell the whole damned town. I'll bet you don't even wait till morning."

Jerome turned back angrily, about to say something, when Travis moved between them. "All right. That's it.

You two want to fight, you do it someplace else. Danton, get the hell out of here. McRae, take your wife and go."

Kitty shook her head again. "I'm not leaving with him. I won't—"

"Oh, yes, you will." Travis crossed the room and grabbed her roughly, shoving her into Corey's arms. "You're getting out of here with your lies. Go make some other man miserable. I've had my fill of you, woman."

Corey pushed her into Rance Kincaid's grasping hands. "My head still hurts from that blow you gave me," Rance hissed at her angrily.

"Shut up," Corey snapped.

But Travis had overheard. "It seems your wife went to a great deal of trouble to come here tonight, McRae," he said, a curious note in his voice. "Obviously, she isn't very happy with you, for some reason."

"The reason is you, Marshal Coltrane," Corey stiffened indignantly. "I'm afraid my dear wife still has fantasies about the lurid life she led as your mistress. I have forgiven her past, since she has borne me a son. I suggest you do the same."

"I don't need any advice from you, McRae. I couldn't care less about your marital problems. But you and I both know what dealings I *do* have with you, and our day of reckoning will come."

The two men stared at each other with hatred.

"Yes, that day will come." Corey bowed slightly. "Until then, I bid you good night and offer my apologies for any inconvenience and embarrassment my wife has caused you this night."

Rance half-dragged, half-carried Kitty down the hall, and she struggled to hold onto John, fearing he would slip from her. Then, just as they started down the steps, she saw Sam Bucher walking up, and she called out to him frantically, "Sam, Sam, help me, please. Don't let them take me away. Please."

"What's going on?" Sam bristled, his hand going to his holstered gun, eyes flashing.

"Stay out of it, Sam," Travis yelled from the splintered doorway. "It's over now. Let them go."

Kitty's pleas echoed down the stairway, disappearing as she was taken out the rear door by Rance, with Corey and two of his men following close behind.

"What in hell went on here?" Sam stared at the door wide-eyed. "What did Kitty come here for? How come she's screaming?"

"She tried to make me think that baby is mine," Travis snorted. "And to think I actually loved that woman at one time. Just goes to show, you can't trust a damned woman."

"Did you ever stop to think she just might be telling the truth?"

Travis looked at his longtime friend incredulously.

"You heard me right," Sam said soberly. "She just might be telling the truth. I've asked a few questions. The boy was born almost nine months to the day after we left this town. I found out she was discharged from the hospital because the holier-than-thou ladies around here demanded that she not be allowed to stay there, pregnant with a Union soldier's baby. Feelings were running high against her, what with that bastard you killed being built up to be such a big hero, and her getting the blame for what happened to him."

"Oh, shit, you don't believe that," Travis scoffed. "That's the story *she* spread. She wanted to keep her land, and she had to have a rich husband to make that possible. So she got herself in the family way by McRae, and he married her. She's still a fine-looking woman. I don't imagine she had to do much persuading."

"No, I don't imagine she would, but I don't think that's the way it happened."

"Have you gone soft, Sam? The woman is conniving—"

"You see it a different way, because you love her. I can look at it in another light, because I love the girl like my own daughter. I know she really and truly loved you, and I don't believe she's lying. I think that boy is yours, and I think she married McRae because she was desperate. You better do some serious thinking, Travis. I know about Nancy Danton, and how she's been slipping up here to your room, and it's easy to figure out what she's up to. She knows her husband is mixed up in the Klan, and she knows he and McRae are going to wind up killing each other if their feud isn't stopped. If she can get to you, she figures you'll get McRae out of the way and make life easier for her husband. I heard a few other things, too. She chased McRae, but it was Kitty he wanted."

"Well, you've been busy nosing in my business, haven't you?" Travis said.

"Somebody has to look after you, you're so god-durned stubborn. Always were. I'm going to find that nigra Jacob. I trust him, because John Wright did. If he tells me that baby is yours, then I won't have any doubts and you shouldn't either."

"Kitty is married to McRae now. Let it be, Sam. Just stay out of it. We came here with a job to do. Let's do it and get the hell out of here and head back to the bayou. There's peace there."

He walked over and picked up a new bottle of whiskey, uncapped it, and took a deep swallow.

"You know, you drink more now than you ever did before," Sam said quietly. Are you trying to forget something?"

"Yes. Everything. I wish you'd do the same."

"Tell me one thing. What would you do if you believed that boy was yours?"

Travis did not have to think. "I'd take him away from McRae, you can believe that."

"And what about Kitty?"

"To hell with her."

"Damn it, Travis, you aren't being fair to the girl. Who knows what hell she went through when we left here a year ago last March?"

"She did all right for herself," he sneered, tipping the bottle to his lips again. "She married the richest man around. She got what she wanted. If she'd really loved me, she would've gone with me like I asked her to."

Sam watched silently as Travis took several more long swigs from the bottle, then said, "All right. You're going to continue to be stubborn, so it's up to me to prove that you're wrong. That boy is yours, and you and Kitty still love each other."

"Forget it!" Travis sent that bottle smashing against the wall, then fell across the bed in a stupor. "Forget all of it. I wish to hell I'd never come to this goddamned town. I wish to hell I'd never seen those damned purple eyes." Travis fell asleep.

"You, my drunken friend, are going to learn the truth," Sam said with determination. "And tomorrow, you'll love those eyes. Just as you loved them yesterday. Just as you love them now. Only you're too goddamned stubborn to admit it."

He hurried from the room. There was a lot to do and little time.

Chapter Twenty-eight

KITTY opened heavy, swollen eyes to stare dizzily into the semidarkness of the room. Everything was hazy, spinning. Something was wrong, terribly wrong. The pain in her body began throbbing.

Her breasts was burning. She started to move her hand to touch the tenderness there, and that is when she felt the shackles at each of her wrists. Gasping in terror, she tossed her head from side to side. Yes, her arms were stretched high above her head and shackled to the bed posts.

She gazed downwards, eyes moving along her naked body to her thighs, spread wide apart, and on down her limbs to see that her ankles were also fastened to the posts at the end of the bed.

It had not been a nightmare. Corey had brought her here, to this wretched room, and he had thrown her upon the bed and stripped her naked, all the while cursing her for what she had done.

"You have humiliated me in front of the whole town," he had shrieked. "Everyone will know that Corey McRae's wife went to Marshal Coltrane's room and threw herself at him. But your scheme didn't work, did it? He still won't believe the brat is his, will he?

"And I was so foolish as to let you betray me," he had ranted on. "Where would you have been by the time I awoke this morning if Danton's men hadn't come to tell me my wife was in another man's hotel room? You drugged me and my men, and then you persuaded Dulcie to help you get Hugo out of the way. Oh, you were clever, my darling, very clever, and it almost worked."

Kitty had been unable to speak. Staring up at him, seeing his angry eyes on fire and bulging, his whole body trembling with rage, she knew of no words to save her. It was done. Now she could only lie and watch and listen. And pray that no harm would come to her son. Hugo had snatched him from her as they'd entered the house, and she had heard his wails from the second floor as Corey dragged her on up to the third, to this torture chamber.

"Dulcie has been taken away," Corey had said as he rummaged in a wardrobe closet, returning with a small chest and a triumphant grin on his face. "I can't have her around, now that I know she cannot be trusted. I told Hugo to get rid of Addie, as well. I don't know how you got into town, but I figure that outlaw Luther had a hand in it. Rance tells me all my guards were knocked out about the same time. Addie played a hand in it somewhere. So they're gone now, my dear. All your nigra friends. It's just you and me."

"My baby," she had cried then, straining against the shackles that held her. "For God's sake, Corey, do with me what you will but don't harm my baby."

"Harm your baby?" He stopped unfastening his shirt to stare down at her incredulously. "Why, my sweet, loving wife, do you think I would harm *our* baby? He's mine, too, you know. You have nothing to fear about him, as long as you don't try anything foolish again. But that is nothing to worry about. You won't have the opportunity. I won't make the same mistake again. I think I will keep you right here, forever. I will spread the word, with Dr. Sims' confirmation, of course, that you have suffered a nervous collapse. You have not been 'just right' since the birth of our son. You will be confined to bed, with someone to watch you at all times. Later, when I've taken care of Coltrane, and Danton and his men, you will have had time to realize how well off you are."

His laughter had been frightening. "Ah, my sweet, when you recover from your little nervous collapse, I will be the most powerful man in this state. And what a lovely portrait we will present to everyone, a man and his wife and his son, so loving and happy. And who knows? By then my own seed may be growing inside you. Then our family will be complete, won't it?"

Kitty had watched in horror as he opened the chest and began pulling out all sorts of devices she had never dreamed existed. "See this?" He held up a feathered object. "Nancy used to love this one. She said it drove her insane. I have every size you can imagine. I found these lovelies in a little shop in Paris that I had heard about. I became so captivated that I ordered everything they had to offer. Oh, you may find that a few will cause you a bit of distress, but you won't mind. The overall ecstasy will more than compensate for any minor little discomfort. And quite frankly, my dear, I really don't care if you do suffer this night. I intend to make you scream, as punishment for what you tried to do this night—what you *did* do! It will take a while for me to live down your antics this time, but people will understand when they hear you are tetched."

He was naked, standing before her, wearing a horrendous object over his manhood. He moved to get on the bed, straddling her. She could only lay there helplessly as he violated her brutally and mercilessly. Her cries of protest and pain only served to excite him more, and she was grateful when the blackness finally took over, and sweet oblivion carried her away.

The minutes passed. She tried to sleep but could not. Where was John? Was he being cared for as he should be? And what of Dulcie and Addie? She prayed they would not suffer.

If only Travis had believed her. But he had thrown her back into the arms of the man she feared. He had rejected his own son. Dear God, hadn't he *ever* loved me? Why was it so easy for him to believe the worst?

Slowly, she began to seethe. Travis was to blame for all of this. Had he not gone away with the troops, they would have married. He had left her behind, carrying his child, alone, no one to turn to.

And the love in her heart began turning to hate.

Suddenly she heard footsteps coming down the hall. Her body tensed. There was the sound of a key scraping in the lock, and she threw her head quickly to one side and pretended to be asleep. Perhaps he would go away.

The door clicked shut. She held her breath. Was he there in the room with her, staring at her naked body, becoming aroused and trying to decide which of those despicable toys he would use now?

"She's still asleep."

Corey's voice was very faint. Her eyes flashed open. The room was empty. She was about to murmur a prayer of thanksgiving when she heard Rance's guttural laugh from the other side of the door.

"Really worked on her good, huh, boss? When you get your women in this room, they always get fixed up, don't they? What do you have in there, anyway? I'd love to know what's behind that door—"

"None of your damn business," Corey snapped. "Now, you listen to me. I want that widow taken care of tonight. I want her scared out of her wits. This time we'll make sure Danton's men look responsible, and you'd better not mess up. Do you understand?"

"Right. I've already got two men in ambush for

Frank Dawson. Everybody knows he rides with Danton. When we get through with that woman, we'll fire her shotgun once, make it look like she killed one of her attackers. When the marshals get there, they'll find Dawson dead, and that will connect Danton in a way he can't get out of."

Kitty's mouth opened in a silent scream. What were they planning to do to poor Mattie Glass now?

"I don't want that woman killed. You make sure of it," Corey barked. "But I do want those boys of hers hurt bad enough that she'll be willing to sell out and go where it's safe, to make sure they don't get killed next time. You make that clear to her, understand?"

"Yeah, I know. The more land you get, the more power you've got. We'll eventually run Danton and his bunch out of this county."

"Exactly. With every parcel I take over, he becomes weaker and weaker. I want him out of the way. I intend to be the power in these parts, with no competition. I've worked too hard and planned too long for anything to go wrong now."

"What if Danton won't clear out? Have you ever thought about that? What if he just sits back and holds on to what he's already got?"

There was a pause. Kitty strained to hear, knowing it was very important that she know everything that was said.

"We'll have to kill him," Corey said with finality. "I don't want him around. He controls too many men. And that whole damned Klan group is growing. Not just here, but all over. I won't have it here. I'm going to stop it before it gets any bigger."

"Look, boss, I'm not taking up for Danton or the Klan, and we both know I fought for the North, so I ain't got much sympathy for Johnny Rebs in the first place. But if I was in their boots, I'd probably want to get an underground movement going, too. I'd never admit the war was over and the South was whipped. And the South ain't going to admit it. Not a hundred years from now. So they've got to do something to strike back at the landgrabbers and carpetbaggers. No offense!" He paused to chuckle. "And at the 'uppity niggers,' as they call 'em. So what I'm saying is that you're smart, real smart, to stop the Klan from getting any stronger here. Get 'em out. All of 'em. You be the power in this part of the country. You got enough money for us to hire the best guns around, haven't you?"

"You know I have."

"Then we'll hire them. We'll have an army all our own. Who knows? You may be Governor of this damn state one day. Now don't you worry about a thing. My men will be back any time now saying Frank Dawson is dead. Just as soon as they do, we'll ride on the widow Glass. It's almost dark now."

Almost dark, Kitty thought in panic. She had slept through the day. Where was John? Oh, God, if she could only free herself and find a way to warn Mattie. At least, she thought with a fierce wave of pride, she still had the will to fight back.

She looked about the room. It was becoming darker. Besides the bed, the only furnishings were a wardrobe closet and a bedside commode. The drapes were very thick, to keep out the light and muffle the screams that echoed in the dismal place.

Without realizing it, Kitty had been straining at her bonds, and only when she felt the smarting and the slow oozing of blood trickling down her arms did she realize just how fiercely she had been struggling.

More voices. Lifting her head from the pillow, Kitty could barely make out Rance's excited whisper. "Did you get him? Is he dead?"

"No problem." A strange monotone, unfamiliar. The man speaking sounded amused. "We just waylaid him, and bang! He's dead, all right. We got him out at the bunkhouse, putting one of those white Klan outfits on him."

"Good." It was Corey's voice, and she could almost see him smiling and sighing with relief. She fought the impulse to retch. They had murdered someone. Next, they would do something terrible to Mattie and her sons. And she was helpless to stop it.

"We'd better get moving now," Rance was saying. "Boss, soon as we get back, I'll report straight to you. It shouldn't take long. Not over an hour. Two at the most."

"I'll be in here."

Kitty winced.

Feet scurried down the hall. Again the key turned in the lock and though her eyes were closed, she could feel him staring down at her. Through her lids, the room became brighter. He had lit the lantern that sat on top of the wardrobe closet.

She felt seeking fingertips trail up her belly, pinch one nipple almost painfully. Then he said, "Wake up, my darling. I'm going to unshackle you for a short while so you can attend to your personal needs. I have a robe for you. Hugo will be bringing a supper tray shortly. You need nourishment. We have a long night of pleasure ahead. I have so many toys yet to show you."

He removed a key from his vest pocket and inserted it into the lock of the shackle on her left wrist. "Ahh, you've been struggling. I see you've cut yourself. You shouldn't resist me, Kitty, and all this wouldn't be necessary." He unlocked her right wrist. "There. Now doesn't that feel much better?"

She rubbed her arms, grimacing at the touch of the tender flesh. He was unlocking her ankles. When she was free, she grabbed at a quilt to cover her nakedness, drawing herself up against the headboard, knees against her chest.

"Now get up and move around. Stretch a bit. I'll get your robe for you, and then I'll leave you alone, if you wish. I can't allow you to leave this room, however, not for many, many weeks. I'm sure you understand why."

"I want to see my baby," she said in a short, clipped voice. "I want to make sure he's all right."

"Oh, he's fine." He waved his hand fliply. "I have a new servant looking after him. He cries for his mommy, because you have spoiled him terribly, but that is more punishment for your behavior last night, Kitty. Knowing your child cries out for you, and you cannot answer."

Her teeth were gritting together, upper lip curled back in a snarl, her voice guttural and thick. "I loathe you, Corey McRae. I loathe and despise you and long for the day I can spit on your grave."

A flash went through his eyes, then disappeared as he smiled, shaking his head from side to side as though mustering the patience to deal with a wayward child. "Kitty, Kitty, why must you continue to fight me? Don't you know I have won? What must I do? Take the lash to your sweet, tender flesh? I don't want to do that. And I don't like to think I am the sort to vent my anger upon a helpless child. So don't force me to do anything unpleasant to little John."

Her heart was pounding. He would do it. She knew he would. Any man who would have a helpless widow raped, her children beaten, had no conscience. She had to hold her temper.

"Good. I see in your eyes that you realize you have no other choice except to bend to my will." He nodded his approval. "Now, you get up and tend to your needs, and I'll get you a lovely robe, so that when Hugo brings in your supper tray you will be all right."

She did not move. "When may I see my baby to know he is all right?"

He sucked in his lower lip, studied her between narrowed lids. After several moments of silence, he said, "Tomorrow. I can understand your anxiety. So, if you behave yourself tonight and show me pleasure, I promise you that tomorrow I will have your son brought in to you for a short while. You can see for yourself that he is being well cared for. And, if you continue to cooperate, you will see him again soon."

He touched her cheek with his fingertips, and this time she did not flinch in revulsion. "You're an intelligent woman, Kitty. Foolish, yes, but you do have superior intelligence. I feel quite confident that you are going to come around."

He stepped away, towards the wardrobe closet. Kitty was about to step from the bed, the quilt still wrapped about her, when the air was split with the sound of gunfire.

"What the hell." Corey twisted away from the closet, sprang to the drapes, and flung them open. "That's here! On my land."

He was almost to the door when someone began pounding on it. "Mr. McRae, you better come quick." That was Hugo's frightened, anxious voice. "There's trouble, big trouble."

Corey flung the door open, and the Negro stood there in the illuminated hall, eyes milky white and bulging with terror. They could still hear guns firing steadily, and now and then the anguished screams of men hit.

"It's Danton's men. Bound to be," Hugo was saying. "Rance and the others haven't had time to leave. They must have been waiting."

Kitty was forgotten as Corey ran from the room, yelling at Hugo to get his guns, round up the servants, anyone who could shoot. "What in the hell went wrong?" He was cursing as his voice disappeared down the stairway along with their thundering footsteps.

Kitty leaped from the bed, flinging open the doors to the closet. A robe hung there, and she grabbed it, pulling it on her trembling body. Then she fled from the room, plunging down the hall, hands sliding along the railing as her feet moved rapidly down the stairs to the second floor. She ran all the way to the nursery and pushed the door open, only to scream at the sight of the empty cradle. John was not there!

Up and down the hall she ran, from room to room. Where was everyone? Where in God's name was her son?

The gunfire was getting closer. Hysteria bubbling in her throat, she covered her hands with her ears and stood in the middle of the wide hallway, rocking to and fro, trying to think. Where could Corey have sent the baby? Where would he be? She did not know what was going on outside, but with so many guns firing, she had to make sure John was safe.

A window shattered. Then another. Men were shouting. Hoofbeats thundered by. Someone screamed in agony. Another window shattering, this time in the nursery! Dear God, she had to find John!

She made her way to the first floor, where she ran into the parlor to find the brocade sofa in flames. A lantern had been hit by gunfire, spilling onto the fabric. Grabbing a small rug, she began to beat at the hungry fire hysterically. Let the house burn later. Later, she would thrill to see it in rubble and ashes, but not now, not when she could not find her baby. He was here somewhere, he had to be. If Corey had taken him away to Raleigh again, he would have told her.

The front door crashed open, and she whirled towards the entrance foyer to see Jerome Danton towering there, face flushed with anger and eyes gleaming murderously. He was pointing a gun at her, but she did not tremble.

"Where is he?" Jerome snarled. "Where's McRae?"

Several more of his men ran in behind him and were told to search the house.

"Please, don't harm my baby," Kitty cried. "I had nothing to do with any of Corey's plans. You must believe me. But he's hidden my baby. That's all I care about. I promise you, Jerome, I don't know where Corey went. He and Hugo ran out a while ago, with guns. Just don't harm my son, please."

"Beating up on kids is Corey's way, Kitty, not mine. I believe you. And if my men find your baby, I promise you he won't be harmed. But do you know what your husband did tonight? Do you know?" His voice rose to a scream.

"Yes, I know!" She screamed back at him, suddenly coming out of her stupor to be angry. Gone was the fear, and in its place, the fighting spirit that always shone through any crisis. "I know, because I overheard him talking to Rance Kincaid about the murder of your man Dawson, the plot to attack Mattie Glass and beat up her sons—all of it. But I could do nothing! Do you understand me? I was *shackled!* And now God only knows where my baby is."

She fought the impulse to cry, to sink beneath that giant invisible web that would smother her like some enormous spider's nest. No, this was not the time to wilt. This was the time to fight back.

They stood facing each other, eyes locked in a gaze that questioned whether the other could be trusted. Finally Jerome spoke. "All right, Kitty, I believe you. I think I've believed you all along. I'll try to help you find your baby, but I warn you, I came here to end this feud. Those idiot gunmen of his didn't capture Frank's horse. He came back to his corral, and there was blood on the saddle. We rode back the way we figure he'd come, and we found more blood. It didn't take much more figuring to know Corey was behind it all. Now I know why. He wanted to get Mattie Glass so scared she'd sell him her damned land, and this time he'd make me and the boys look responsible for sure, by leaving Frank behind dead."

"Exactly! Now, are we going to stand here talking about it, or are you going to find my baby?"

"Kitty, I have no idea where your baby is. The thing I need to do right now is find Corey. You stay here. Take cover, because there's going to be more shooting. When it's over, I'll help you. I promise. Now do as I say."

"You expect me to just sit here and wait?"

Just then another window exploded, and they both fell to the floor.

"Yes, I do," he said with strange calmness. "Unless you want your head blown off. Now there's a lot of places out there where Corey and his men can be holed up. Anything can happen. So you just creep around and put out all the lanterns so there won't be more danger of fires." He looked at the scorched sofa, then crawled on his hands and knees to put out the last remaining lantern in the room. Except for the softly glowing chandelier in the entrance foyer, they were in darkness.

"Jerome?" a voice Kitty did not recognize called out from the hallway. "We've looked all through this house and we ain't found nothing. Let's go."

"Put out those lights in the hall," Jerome snapped. "I don't want to be a perfect target for those bastards. No telling where they are."

He moved his feet, stealthily as a stalking cat. His man did as he was told, and they were surrounded by the dark. Kitty could barely hear their feet moving across the polished mahogany floors. Then she was alone.

For long moments, she crouched in the darkness. Where was John? In one of the old slave cabins out back? Had Corey had him taken there so she would not hear him crying for her?

Each time gunfire split the air, she covered her ears and gritted her teeth to keep from screaming. It was like the war all over again. The cries, the thuds of falling bodies, the smell of sulphur. There, staring into the void about her, she could see the battlefields again. The nightmare was returning.

Dear God, in all of this, where was her baby?

Chapter Twenty-nine

TRAVIS sat in his room alone. By the light whispering through the open window he could see the bottle in his hand. Lifting it slowly to his lips, he took a long swallow. Damn the burning. The warmth was what counted—that sweet, sedating heat that spread through his body. It took away his pain.

To think that Kitty Wright could love him was ridiculous. She had used him. But in the back of his mind was the nagging question that even the burning whiskey could not dull. *Why* was she trying to pass her son off as his? Corey was rich and powerful. What did Kitty think she could gain?

Damn it, he would never get over her. Never. And if he didn't need those last few drinks left in the bottle, he would send it crashing against the wall. He'd done that a lot lately. Made a lot of messes and wasted plenty of good booze, too. No, this time he would finish the whiskey. Then he could send it smashing against the wall.

Sam Bucher did not bother to knock. He opened the door so swiftly that it banged back against the wall, and he found himself looking down the barrel of the gun Travis was pointing at him.

"You're damn lucky there's a lantern in that hall, or you'd be dead by now," Travis said in a slurred voice, the hammer clicking back in place as he shoved the weapon down into his holster.

"And you're damn lucky you're still sober enough to pull that thing out so quick." Sam kicked the door shut and walked over to light the lantern beside the bed.

"Where the hell have you been all day?" Travis lifted the bottle to his lips, then cried out in angry protest as Sam knocked it from his hand.

"You've had enough. Now you sober up and listen." His face was red, his eyes glowing. "I'll tell you where I've been—out doing the checking I said I was going to do. You know who brought Kitty into town last night?"

"I don't care."

"You will care. About a whole hell of a lot of things when I tell you what I found out. It was that nigra Luther."

Travis showed signs of interest. "The outlaw we've been looking for?"

"Right. I got hold of a nigra that hangs around the saloon downstairs and put the fear of God in him. I've had him pegged all along, figuring he kept Luther and his gang informed as to what goes on around town. I was right, and he broke down and told me it was Luther and his boys who helped Kitty escape by slipping onto the McRae place and taking care of all the guards. Then Luther brought Kitty to town."

Sam wiped perspiration from his brow. It had been a busy day, and he'd been up since way before dawn, determined to get to the bottom of things. "The Negroes were the only friends Kitty had after she got kicked out of the hospital, Travis. She stayed with them awhile, then moved back to a shack on her daddy's land. Danton and his gang burned her out. They left Kitty in labor, and McRae took her in."

"Why shouldn't he?" Travis snapped. "She was having his baby."

Sam threw his hat down on the floor and stomped on it. "Goddammit, man, why do you have to be so blamed stubborn? I'm trying to tell you. That's not Corey McRae's baby. Kitty is telling the truth! I've asked enough questions that there's no doubt in my mind. That's why they kicked her out of the hospital, because the pious, hypocrite women around here wouldn't stand for her working there in the family way. That black boy told me a hell of a lot, how he saw her almost attacked the night she left the hospital because she was wandering around with no place to go. McRae came to her rescue. She'd never met him before that night. I even know the date the baby was born. The kid is yours."

Travis sucked in his breath, a cold chill moving up and down his spine. His son. No, it couldn't be. Yet Sam had obviously done a lot of checking and believed everything he had learned. Sam was not easily fooled.

"Well, aren't you going to say anything?" Sam was fuming. "The girl had your baby. You went off and *left* her. She had no place to go, and McRae took advantage of her. And there's more. I found out Jacob was shipped off with his two grandsons to some farm down in South Carolina, right after me and you hit town. It's like McRae wanted to make real sure we couldn't talk to him. You understand? Kitty is telling the truth, and there's no telling what kind of nightmare you've sent her and your son back to live in."

He sat down on the side of the bed, eyes searching Travis' face. "There's still more. I rode out to that Glass woman's cabin today and talked to her. She's about the only woman in town that didn't snub Kitty, and she says that girl worked day and night at the hospital and never left, not till she was thrown out. She says everybody in town was condemning her for carrying a Yankee soldier's baby in her belly. So how can you deny what's so? Damn it, man, how can you deny your own son?"

"All right." Travis' voice was quiet, ominous. "So the boy is mine. That still doesn't change anything where Kitty is concerned. You and I both know how I begged her to go with us."

"Hell, I can see why she wanted to stay. She'd had enough of war, Coltrane. Hadn't we all? She'd just lost her father, and this was her home."

"It doesn't matter. There's too much that points in the other direction. What about those hired guns that came after us? They almost got me, remember?" His eyes flashed with remembrance. "She's got a damn good setup, Sam, married to a rich bastard like McRae. She'll still have it good when the son of a bitch is behind bars."

Sam leaped to his feet and began pacing the drably furnished room, running nervous fingers through his graying hair. Finally he whirled around and spread his hands and cried, "Well, if you believe the boy is yours, what do you intend to do about it?"

But before Travis could answer, there was a loud pounding on the door. Both men reached for their guns as Sam yelled for them to come in.

The Negro Sam had questioned opened the door and stood there, twisting his old straw hat in gnarled hands. His eyes were bulging, and his lips were trembling. "I . . . I thoughts you lawmen would wants to know . . . they is big trouble out at the McRae place. Leastways, they's gonna be, soon's Danton and his men get there."

Travis was already off the bed and pulling on his boots.

"What the hell are you talking about?" Sam demanded.

"I seen 'em ride out of town, that's all." He started backing towards the door.

Sam reached out and clamped a burly hand on the Negro's scrawny shoulder. "No, hell, that ain't all. Just what do you know?"

The black man cringed, looked from Sam's glaring eyes to Travis', then said, "I gonna get killed if'n anybody hears me tellin' this—"

"You're gonna get killed if you *don't* start telling it," Sam snarled. "Now hurry it up."

"One of Danton's men, man named Dawson, got hisself killed tonight. Danton figured McRae had a hand in it, so he rounded up his men, and they done gone to settle things once and for all. I seen 'em riding out about five minutes ago, and I figured you'uns bein' the law and all, you'd want to know."

"You were right." Sam gave him a reassuring pat. "Now get the hell out of here and keep your mouth shut. Don't repeat what you've told us to anybody else."

Travis was on his feet. "Let's go."

Within minutes they were riding their horses out of town and towards the McRae plantation, pushing their mounts as fast as they would go. Neither man spoke.

Travis was thinking about his son, rolling the words around in his mouth, his mind, his heart. *My son!* He actually had a son. Damn Kitty to hell for not waiting for him, he thought fiercely. But she no longer mattered. Let her have her wealth and her fine house and her daddy's land. By God, he was going to have his son. He was going to take him and go back to Louisiana and the peace and quiet and beauty of the bayou. The war and its painful memories would fade away. He and his boy would find happiness.

The horses' thundering hoofbeats broke the night silence. *Faster*, Travis spurred his horse, and Sam saw and did likewise, *Faster, damn it, faster.*

It seemed an eternity before they heard the sounds of gunfire and knew they were close. "You gonna just ride in there?" Sam yelled over the cannonade. "We'll get our heads blowed off."

Travis did not answer. Only when they reached the gates to the plantation itself did he rein in his horse and stop. Dismounting, he said, "We go the rest of the way on foot. The shooting is coming in spurts now. I think the war is over. There's just a few hanging on to keep it going."

They moved down the curving driveway. Sam stumbled over something and looked down to make out a body. A few feet further on another man lay dying. He didn't pause to give him aid, because he knew he had to keep up with Travis.

"All right, hold it!" Travis yelled, sighting Jerome Danton standing in the moonlight. Pointing his gun, he walked forward. "Make one move, Danton, and I'll blow your guts open."

Jerome dropped his gun, raised his hands, and limped forward. "Okay," he said. "It's all over. I got what I came after."

"Tell your men to throw down their guns," Sam ordered. Jerome obeyed and, one by one, men began stepping from behind trees, shrubs, out of nowhere.

"They killed one of my men. Frank Dawson," Jerome said in a quiet, subdued voice. "I came here to settle this fight once and for all, and I did. Most of McRae's men are dead. We caught them by surprise."

"You're all under arrest," Travis said coldly. "Where is McRae?"

"I want to tell you something, Marshal." For the first time since he began talking, Danton displayed anger. "I found out from Kitty what McRae had planned. He killed Dawson to haul his body along to the widow Glass's. He was going to work her over again, have her boys beaten, so's to scare her into wanting to sell her land and move to town, where she'd be safe. He holds the tax lien on her property, but he didn't want it said he kicked a poor widow woman off her land. He wanted to make things look nice. He was going to leave Dawson behind, to link him to me and my men so I'd get the blame."

"Where is he?" Travis repeated coldly. "And where is his wife and the boy?"

"McRae's around back. I shot him. If he ain't dead, he soon will be. Nobody knows where the boy is. Kitty was hysterical when I talked to her. She can't find the boy either."

Travis was already walking in the direction Danton was pointing. Sam watched him anxiously, wishing he could go along but knowing he had to stay behind to cover Danton and his men.

Rounding the big mansion, Travis could make out the grim scene a little distance ahead. A Negro servant held a lantern over Corey McRae, and Kitty was kneeling beside him, sobbing. Very touching, Travis thought bitterly, and drew closer with stealth, hoping to overhear what was said.

He did not arrive in time to hear Corey's dying words. "In my own way, Kitty . . ." he whispered into her anxious face, "I did love you. I've left it all, everything I had . . . to you."

"Corey, please, just tell me what you did with my baby," she pleaded, her hands clasped against her bosom as she knelt beside him. Even at his death she could feel only loathing, and even that was overpowered by the anguish of not knowing where little John had been taken. "Just tell me where my son is, Corey, please."

He gave one last guttural moan, and the blood that gurgled from his mouth was a thick, muddy red in the lantern's yellow glow. He coughed and the blood gushed forth in one final spurt. Then his head slumped to the side, eyes pinpointed toward the stars.

Travis got within earshot just as the servant said,

"Miss Kitty, don't you fret. That boy is down in one of the cabins. Mistah McRae had him taken there 'cause he got tired of hearing him cry. He's just fine. You know Lottie? She lookin' after him since Dulcie and Addie got sent away."

Kitty had not noticed Travis standing nearby. Breathing a sigh of relief, she murmured, "All right. Just so I know he's safe. The shooting seems to be over now. Get a blanket from the house to cover Mr. McRae."

The servant slowly set the lantern down on the ground beside his mistress and the body of his master, but his eyes were watching the taut, grim lines on the face of the tall man standing nearby. A shimmer of light caught on his chest. A star. The man was the law. Everything would be all right now.

The Negro scurried by Travis Coltrane to disappear into the darkness.

Kitty tried to feel something as she looked down at Corey's body. She did not want to hate, yet she could not deny the passion of pure loathing. He had tricked her, abused and tormented her. Yes, yes, she was glad he was dead. Even if Travis were lost to her forever, she had her son. She had her life again. No longer would she suffer from Corey McRae.

It was over. Praise God, her suffering was over.

With a trembling hand she reached out to dig into the soft earth, scooping up a handful. Swaying slightly, she let it trickle through her fingers and fall silently to the ground. "This is mine now," she whispered. "Whatever else is over and done with, this land is mine."

She did not see Travis steal slowly away in the shadows, moving toward the row of old slave cottages.

Suddenly a man approached from the front of the house. Kitty glanced up sharply, hearing the steady, determined thud of boots. When he reached the circle of light where she knelt, her head shook slightly. She gasped his name, then held her arms open and was drawn up against his broad chest.

Sam Bucher patted her back. "It's going to be all right, Kitty. It's over now. I deputized one of the servants to keep an eye on those varmints out front. Can't find Travis. He just disappeared."

"Travis is here?" She raised her head back to search his face hopefully. "Travis?"

"Yes." He was able to give her a slight smile. "Yes, he's here, Kitty, and I think he believes now that your baby is his son. I did some checking today, and we were talking about all I'd found out when we got word about the trouble here. We came right away. I don't know where he's gone, but he knows that little one is his now."

She moved from his arms, tucked her small hand into his large one. "Come with me, Sam. Let's go down to the cabins. That's where John was being kept. Then we'll find Travis. Oh, Sam, Sam, I have so much to tell him, so much to explain. And he'll listen to me now. I know he will."

Kitty reached the row of cottages. "Lottie? Lottie? Where are you?" she called anxiously into the night. She could feel dozens of pairs of eyes upon her even though she could not see them. She knew they were frightened and watching. "Lottie, I want my baby! Answer me, please." Her voice broke.

Sam caught up with her. "Relax, Kitty. They're frightened. There's been a lot of shooting, and they don't know what's happened and they're scared. We'll find your boy. Don't you fret.

"Someone answer us!" Sam's voice boomed with authority. "We want Mrs. McRae's baby."

Finally, when Kitty thought she would surely

scream if someone didn't answer, a hesitant voice called to her out of the shadows. "Miss Kitty, it's me, Lottie."

"Oh, thank heavens!" Kitty whirled in the direction of the voice. Sam held up the lantern, and a plump Negro woman with a colorful bandanna wrapped about her head stepped into the light. Her hands were clasped together over her white apron, and her head was bowed, eyes fixed on the ground. Kitty rushed forward to clutch her shoulders. "Lottie, tell me. Where is my baby? I must have him! Now!"

Sam took a step forward. "Kitty, easy now. I told you. These folks are frightened." He looked at the woman and made his voice gentle, coaxing. "It's all right, Lottie. You can give the baby to Mrs. McRae now. There's been some trouble, but it's all over now. I'm the law, and we've got everything under control. You give the lady her baby, just like she says."

The Negro broke into tears, covering her face in her hands. "He's gone."

Kitty's heart leaped into her throat. "Gone? What do you mean he's gone? You were caring for him, weren't you?"

"Yes'm, yes'm, I was. Takin' good care of him, too, just like Mistah McRae told me to. But a little while ago, just before you come, another man come. He had a star on his chest, and he was mad, and he say he gonna shoot somebody if'n he don't find his boy. I ain't wantin' to die, Miss Kitty. You gotta understand. He was like a madman. Went around kickin' on doors. My man went outside with a lantern, and that's when we saw he was the law. He say if'n he don't get that boy, somebody gonna die. What was I to do? I wrapped that baby up in a blanket, and I give him to him, and he took off like the devil hisself was on his heels."

Kitty would have fallen if Sam's arm had not been

about her. Her anguished cry wrenched his heart. He held her tightly against him.

"It's all right. Travis came and got the boy, and we'll find them at the house. Let's go."

They ran all the way. Someone had the house aglow with lanterns, and Danton's men were milling about inside, quiet now, satisfied. Their work was over and they were willing to face whatever consequences lay ahead.

As Kitty and Sam rushed in the front door, Jerome was waiting for them. "Marshal, there won't be any more trouble, I promise you. And I'm sure a judge is going to realize we were justified in what we did. Especially when Kitty gets up and tells why Dawson was killed, what McRae had in mind. I mean, when you think that he was going to have a helpless widow attacked *again*."

Sam shoved Kitty into a nearby chair and faced Jerome. "Have you seen Marshal Coltrane?"

"I did!" one of Danton's men said from where he stood leaning against the mantel above the fireplace. He held a bottle of brandy in his hand and took a sip. Sam moved closer, and the man said, "He came tearing around the other side of the house, carrying something. He got on a horse and went galloping off!"

Sam Bucher did not trust himself to speak. He knew what had happened. There was no point in lying to Kitty now, no use saying everything would work out. Travis and little John would not be back at the hotel. Without a doubt, Travis Coltrane had taken his son back to his beloved bayou, to the peace he believed they would find there.

Chapter Thirty

KITTY stood at her bedroom window, staring out but seeing nothing. How could Travis have done such a thing? She bit down on her lip viciously and whirled around to glare at the empty room. How could he have taken a helpless baby who needed constant care? How could Travis hope to provide for him? Louisiana was a long way from North Carolina. Did he plan to travel that distance on horseback, holding a six-month-old baby in his arms? How was he going to feed him? Did he even know what a baby that small was supposed to eat? It had been a week since that night. Were they in Louisiana by now?

Pressing trembling fingertips to her throbbing temples, Kitty tried to think. Corey had been buried three days ago in a simple service with no one in attendance except a reluctant minister and a few servants who felt obliged to be there. Hugo had been killed that night, also. And Rance. The matter of cleaning up after the massacre had been left to the servants. She had spent all her time in her room, alternately praying and cursing.

There was money. Oh, yes, there was plenty of money now. It was all hers. Corey's dying words had not been lies. The wormy-faced lawyer from Goldsboro had paid her a visit the day of the funeral to tell her that she had inherited all of her husband's holdings. She was extremely wealthy now. But nothing mattered except Louisiana and getting John back from there.

She began to pace up and down, picturing in her mind Travis and her son living in Travis' family home deep in the Louisiana bayou. Travis had often described to her the crude cottage built on tall poles on the river bank, with swamps and marshes surrounding them for miles around. Travis and his family had lived off the bayou, fishing, selling alligator hides to traders, trapping animals.

Her deep concentration was interrupted by a hesitant rap on the door. "Yes?" she snapped. "Who is it?"

"It's me, Miss Kitty," Lottie's voice filtered through the pine wood. "You got a guest downstairs. I told him you left strict orders you wasn't to be disturbed, but he said if I didn't come up here and tell you he was downstairs, he'd come right on up here himself. I didn't know what to do."

Sighing with exasperation, Kitty marched over to the door, flinging it open. Lottie stood there with bowed head, twisting her apron in her chubby hands. Kitty was instantly contrite and made her voice gentle. "Who is downstairs, Lottie? Who is demanding to see me?"

"That man." The Negro woman's voice broke, and she raised moist eyes to her mistress. "That man what kilt Mistah McRae. He got the nerve to come to this house aftah what he did, and say he gonna see you no matter what."

"Are you talking about Mr. Danton?" Kitty asked incredulously. "*He* is here? In this house?"

"Yes'm."

Kitty sucked in her breath. "All right," she said, curiosity bubbling. "I'll go downstairs and see what brings that man to this house. I thought he was in jail."

With a swish of her skirt, she moved by Lottie and

walked swiftly down the hall, moving on down the stairway to where Jerome Danton stood, just inside the front door. She spoke no greeting, just stood on the bottom step, her hand resting on the round banister head. She stared at him.

"Kitty, I had to talk to you," he began, then paused to glance around at two of the servants who hovered nearby, eyes round with wonder. "Is there somewhere we can talk . . . in private?"

"In the parlor," she said crisply, lifting her skirts and stepping down to lead the way.

Once inside, with the double doors closed behind them, Kitty whipped about to face him. "All right. Get to the point. Why are you here?"

"You sound angry." A smile played on his lips. "Kitty, you and I both know I did you a favor by killing your husband. You never loved him. He was cruel to you. You said so yourself. He was a vicious man who needed killing."

"Then you did not come to pay your respects to the bereaved widow?"

He chuckled. "You are no bereaved widow, and I regret nothing. My reasons for visiting are quite personal."

"I don't see that we have anything to discuss, personal or business. And why aren't you in jail?" She walked to the sideboard and poured wine into two crystal goblets and handed one to him.

He took a sip, then sat down on the sofa and crossed his legs. "I am not in jail because there was a hearing and in view of all the facts, the judge did not find me or my men guilty of murder. It was a land war, a range war, a grudge fight, whatever you want to call it. It's over. It's that simple." He downed the rest of his wine in one gulp.

"Kitty, you wanted financial security for yourself and your son, but now you have no son. You have nothing but this house and all your late husband's land. I am truly sorry, and that is why I have come. To offer my help."

"How can you help me?"

"Well, let me start at the beginning. Remember the night that Nancy pretended to just happen to see you enter the hotel and sent word to Corey where you were?"

Kitty nodded.

"I'm no fool," he snorted. "I knew what Nancy was when I married her, but I needed a wife. I hoped she would change, but she didn't. For the time being, I was more interested in settling a score with Corey. I admit I am the leader of the local Klan group, but we deal with money-hungry, land-grabbing carpetbaggers and uppity niggers—not helpless widows. When he pinned that on me, the rape of Mattie Glass, I vowed I'd go to my grave before I let him get away with it. Why, we've beaten the flesh off niggers' backs all the way to their backbone for just looking at a white woman the wrong way. Do you think we'd go out and rape one?"

"Get to the point, Jerome."

"The point is, I kicked Nancy out after all this was over with. Don't ask me where she went, because I don't give a damn. She's gone for good. It's just me now, me and my money and my men. And I want to help you get your son back."

Her heart skipped a beat. "How do you propose to do that?"

"Well, are you going to sit back and let him get away with kidnapping your baby?" He got up and went to the sideboard and poured himself another glass of wine.

He turned to give her a probing look. "Do you think he's going to bring him back? Hell, no. That boy is gone for good unless you go after him."

"I have wanted to find him, but I haven't yet been able to figure out how."

"I'll take you to Louisiana to find your son and bring him back."

He said it so matter-of-factly!

"Are you mad?" she cried. "I have no idea where Travis took John. I wouldn't know where to start looking."

"Let me handle that part. We'll go to Louisiana, and we'll set up a headquarters in New Orleans. I'll hire detectives to inquire around. I'll send scouts into the bayou. Oh, we'll find where Travis Coltrane lives, all right. Then I'll hire enough guns to go in there and bring your son out. It may take a while, but I'm willing to take that time."

She moved to the window and stared out at the morning glory vines twisting about the white columns of the porch. The sweet fragrance of wisteria blooming along the railing touched her nostrils. The lawn was a carpet of green velvet. Roses bloomed in carefully planned patterns among the magnolia and pecan trees. The world was alive again. It was time for a new life.

"What is in all this for you?" she asked, a bit startled to find him so close, and there was a strange, dazzled look in his hazel eyes. "Why should you want to help me get my baby back? You walk with a limp because of a ball I put in your leg, one that I intended for your heart. We have always been enemies. So why do you come here and offer to put yourself out so? Is there to be some sort of bribery?"

"Bribery?" His smile was soft, his breath warm on her face. He was standing too close. She tried to move back but found herself pinned against the window.

"No, Kitty. We have never been enemies except in your mind. I came to you once, remember? I gave you fair warning about that nigger Gideon slipping onto your place at night to see his mother. I came for another reason, also."

"Yes, you certainly did. You said I would see the day I would beg you to buy my land. Well, that day is not going to come. I can hire others to take me to Louisiana. I surely don't intend to be bribed—"

His hands moved to clasp her shoulders. "No, Kitty, you didn't let me finish, just as you wouldn't let me say all I came to say that day. It's you I want."

"Me?" she gasped, reaching to yank his hands from her body. "How dare you?"

"I dare because you are the most beautiful woman I have ever seen. I mean you no harm. I only ask for a chance to court you. I know you've been through a lot, Kitty, and it may be years before you can open your heart to another man. I ask only that you give me a chance when the time comes. Now will you let me take you to Louisiana to find your son?"

Kitty tried to see inside him. Was it a trick? Was he going to be like the other men in her life?

Kitty managed to smile. "All right, Jerome. I won't promise you anything, and do not ask me for anything. I accept your kind offer to help me. And I thank you."

With eyes shining brightly, he bent his head slightly, lips eager, but Kitty ducked beneath his outstretched arms and bobbed around to move away. "I said not to ask me for anything, Jerome."

"Not even a kiss to seal the bargain?"

"We have no bargain. You offered to help. I accepted that offer. No more. We'll let the future take care of itself. For the present, I want no man."

"Ahh, you still carry a torch for that Yankee, don't you?" He sounded bitter. "Kitty, where is your pride? He doesn't want you. What kind of man would take a baby from his mother? Coltrane kidnapped that boy. That's a crime. We'll have the law in Louisiana to help flush him out of that swamp he's gone to. The man is as conniving as Corey McRae, and you're better off without him."

"That's not true!"

They both whirled about to see Sam Bucher standing in the doorway. Neither had heard him come in, and while he stood glowering, Lottie pushed her way in to say, "I tried to tell him you was busy, Miss Kitty, but he wouldn't listen. He just barged right on in here."

Kitty nodded. "It's all right, Lottie. Go and leave us alone." When the door was closed, she walked over and clasped Sam's hand, startled to find it cold and unyielding. "Sam, whatever is the matter with you? Why are you so angry?"

"I don't like hearing that kind of talk about Travis. Few people know him like I do, that's true, but it still gets my dander up to hear him cut. He isn't conniving, and while I don't know his reasons for doing what he did, I'm sure he thinks they were pretty good or he wouldn't have done it. Now what's this I heard him talking about?" He gave Jerome a look of contempt. "What did he mean when he said he'd have the Louisiana law flush Travis out of the swamp?"

"We're going to Louisiana," she told him, ignoring the angry furrow of his brow. "Mr. Danton has kindly offered to escort me there. We're going to set up a headquarters in Louisiana and hire detectives to find Travis and get my baby back. I can't live without my baby, Sam. He's all I've got."

Her voice broke, and when Sam reached out to pat her back with a burly hand, she fell against his broad chest for comfort, as she had done so many times in the past. "I reckon I didn't expect you to just sit back and let him get by with it, Kitty," he said gruffly, eyes warily locked with Jerome's. "That's why I came, to tell you I'm going there myself to try and reason with him. Like I said, I'm sure he thinks he had a good reason. I'll try to make him listen, though."

She pulled back to give him the stubborn look he knew so well. "I'm going, too. I don't care how far away it is, or how long it takes to get there. I'll walk, if need be, but I intend to get my son back."

Sighing, Sam said, "All right, but Danton stays."

"Danton does *not* stay!" Jerome exploded. "Kitty agreed to let me take her. We'll get the job done. You plan to go in and plead, and Travis Coltrane doesn't understand that kind of language. He'll understand *my* kind, believe me."

Sam threw his head back and laughed. "And you'll wind up as dead as all the others who thought they could face up to Travis Coltrane. He's a hell of a man anywhere, but down in that bayou he's king, and he knows it. You'll do well to take your butt back to town and stay out of this, mister."

Jerome crossed the room and put his hand on Kitty's arm. "We have an agreement. I am going with Kitty."

Sam laughed again. "Oh, another one."

"What do you mean by that?" Jerome snapped, moustache quivering.

Sam stopped laughing. Kitty had never seen him look quite so ominous. "I mean you're another man after the prettiest woman God ever set on this earth. But I got news for you, mister. There's only one man for her, and she knows it. You're wasting your time."

Cocking his head to one side, Jerome said quietly, "But does *he* know it, Marshal? Does he want her? I think not. I think one day very soon Kitty will realize that fact and open her heart to someone who can give her the love she deserves."

"Well, it won't be you."

"You don't know that."

Kitty stepped between them, hands pressed against

her ears. "Stop it, both of you! You sound like children. *I* will be the judge of what goes on in my heart, not you two. So stop it, please."

A strained silence fell over the room.

Kitty pulled her hands down. "All right." She spoke very quietly. "Jerome, you go back to town and make the necessary arrangements. How soon do you think we can leave?"

"Tomorrow. It'll take me the rest of the day and most of the night, but I'll have everything ready and be here to pick you up shortly after sunrise." He shot Sam a triumphant look.

Sam was undaunted. "I'll be here, too."

"Nobody said anything about you tagging along."

Ignoring Danton, Sam put his arms across Kitty's shoulders. "You will let me go along and try to reason with Travis, won't you? Remember, I know where he's gone. No one else does. And it is a long trip. You want to be alone with this scalawag all that time?"

"Bucher, you're pushing your luck."

"You've already pushed yours."

Kitty cried out once again. "I said stop it! I'm not going to have this quarreling. Yes, Sam, you may come along. If you can go into the bayou and reason with Travis, it may save us all a lot of trouble." She looked at Jerome. "And I am sure you can understand that it would be best if we weren't alone for such a long journey. What if one of us got sick or something? We need all the help we can get, and Sam knows the way."

Jerome sucked in his lower lip petulantly. "All right, but he'd better stay out of *my* way."

"Boy . . ." Sam pointed a shaking finger, his face reddening.

Kitty held up her hands, moving her head from side to side in disgust. "That's enough for today. Please, both of you leave me now. I've much to do to make ready for the trip."

"Kitty, I need to talk to you. It won't take long," Sam said quietly.

"All right." She nodded to Jerome. "I will see you tomorrow."

With one last glare at Sam Bucher, Danton opened the door and stepped outside.

Sam turned to Kitty with misery-filled eyes. "I don't blame you for making this trip, honey. I'm glad that your mind is made up. But there's something I want you to bear in mind. Whatever his reasons were, Travis thought he was doing the right thing when he took that boy of his and rode away from here. He left me behind in a mess, and he knew it, and look what good friends we are. He felt he had a damned good reason. When I find out what it is, I'll know how to deal with him."

"He did it to hurt me," Kitty said bitterly, walking to the sideboard to pour herself another glass of wine. "He hates me, Sam. He never really loved me. He just wanted to hurt me, because he blames me for so many things. Why couldn't he just leave me alone?"

"*You* didn't leave *him* alone. You wanted him to believe that boy was his. You obviously still loved him."

"I did then. I don't anymore."

"Kitty, you'll never make me believe that. I know you and I know Travis, and you're two of the most stubborn people I ever saw, but you love each other. I saw it before either of you did. I'm the one that pointed out that fact to Travis, and he called me a fool."

She sighed with exasperation. "That was *then*, Sam. This is now. What's in the past no longer matters. He hates me now, and he took John to try and hurt me."

She brushed a tear away, turned her back so Sam wouldn't see.

"You do still love each other, Kitty. A lot of things have happened, I agree, but I believe, with all my heart, that you two will get together. I *know*. Now, I want you to promise me that when we get there, you'll let me try to talk to Travis before you let that hothead Danton do anything foolish."

"I promise," she murmured.

Sam gave her a fatherly peck on the cheek and left quietly.

Chapter Thirty-one

PULLING an ornate silk rope, Kitty opened the heavy, full-length drapes of gold velvet. She could see the city of New Orleans through wide, multi-paned glass doors which led onto the balcony. Pushing these open, she stepped outside. A cool breeze drifted across her face, and she wrinkled her nose at the smell. Sea air, Sam had called it.

The St. Louis Cathedral loomed up out of the darkness. Sam had pointed out landmarks early that morning, before he left on his mission. She knew the place called Jackson Square was somewhere beyond the cathedral, the busiest section in the daytime. The sound of laughter and voices drifted through the night, and she supposed the sound came from people leaving the Paris Opera after an evening's entertainment.

Kitty was growing more anxious with each passing moment. Sam had said he would do his best to return by dark. "I just don't know how things are going to go," he had told her, a somber expression on his leathery face. "Travis ain't the kind you just walk right up to and start telling what's on your mind. You got to feel him out, see what kind of mood he's in, and go from there."

"I don't care what kind of mood he's in," she had wailed impatiently. "Just tell him if he doesn't give my baby back, I'm going to send hired guns into those swamps. I'm not bluffing, Sam. I mean it."

Seated in the hotel dining room that morning at breakfast, Sam and Jerome had eaten ravenously. Kitty could not touch a bite.

Jerome had given Sam a contemptuous glare and said, "Money talks, my good man. Wait and see. If you return without that boy, I will have men ready to go into the bayou by sunrise tomorrow. I promise you that."

"Oh, you're out of your mind."

"Stop it!" Kitty had slapped her palms on the table, sending the dishes into a brief dance. People turned to stare, and she lowered her voice, staring at the two men alternately. "I listened to your quarreling for two weeks. It was bad enough riding bumpy stage coaches and dirty trains, and wondering if we'd ever get here. All the while, I had to listen to you two sniping at each other."

Sam had replied, "You should have left him at home. He ain't good for a damn thing. Travis is just gonna kill him."

Jerome had paled slightly at that, but recovered to snap, "I consider myself quite accurate with a gun. I killed my share of Yanks."

"You ain't no match for Travis Coltrane." With that, Sam rose. "Now I'll get back soon's I can," he had said with finality. "You're just going to have to sit tight and be patient."

Kitty had spent the rest of that endless day fighting off Jerome's advances. He was most determined, but she was damned if she'd ever love another man.

After a fretful dinner, during which Sam did not appear, she had retired to her room. Now, standing on the balcony, from the corner of her eye she saw a man's shadow in the room behind her. Kitty managed to stifle her scream just in time: it was Sam.

She ran to him.

"I didn't mean to frighten you," he said. "I figured you were downstairs eating, so I just let myself in."

She studied his face. "You have bad news," she whispered.

He lowered himself into one of the ornate chairs beside the fireplace, not looking at her. "Yes, I'm afraid I do."

She moved on stiff legs to seat herself opposite him, leaning forward anxiously. "You talked to Travis? Did you see John? Is he all right?" Her heart was pounding.

Sam stared into the fireplace as intensely as if flames actually crackled in the empty grate. With great difficulty, he forced himself to speak. "Kitty, I found Travis right where I figured he'd be, at his cabin in the bayou, up on them stilts. He didn't seem at all surprised to see me. In fact, he seemed kind of glad I was there."

"The baby," she said intensely, reaching across to clutch his knee. "Tell me about my baby. Was he all right?"

"Little John?" He met her eyes for the first time, and a grin made his moustache and beard quiver. "Ahh, that boy's fine, just fine. He's his granddaddy and his daddy all rolled into one, and you couldn't ask for a better combination. Travis has got an old Creole woman there looking after him while he's out trapping and fishing during the day. The boy is just fine, Kitty. You ain't got a worry in the world about that. It shows in Travis' face how much he loves the boy."

"But did you tell him I'm here?" she asked, feeling a wave of desperation. "Did you tell him we came for John?"

"Well, I'm getting to that. Right away, Travis wanted to know had I turned in my badge and come home to stay, and when I told him I'd only come for a visit, on business, he looked at me in that way of his, you know, like he can see right through to your brain and know what you're thinking?"

She nodded. He had looked at her that way many times.

"I just came right out and told him why I'd come, and that you was with me. I reminded him he was breaking a law by taking that boy, because he had no legal claim on him. He just looked at me like I was tetched and then laughed and said the law of the bayou said otherwise, and if I thought I was going to touch that boy, I'd better just go ahead and draw on him and be done with it, because I'd have to take him out over his dead body. He meant it, too, and that's what really got to me, Kitty. Me and Travis, we been together a mighty long time. Been through hell and back together. And there he sits, telling me to draw a gun on him. Now, he knew I couldn't draw on him."

"But you did tell him I would not return without my son?" she cried.

"Yeah, I told him all that and a lot more, too, about how you and him really love each other, but you're both too proud and stubborn to admit it. Well, it seems that when Corey McRae was dying, you didn't know it, but Travis was standing right behind you. He said you took up a handful of dirt in your hand and said, 'This is mine now. Whatever else is over and done with, this land is mine. . . .' "

He gave her a long, searching look. "Did you do that, Kitty? Did you pick up a handful of dirt and say all that?"

"Well, something like that, yes," she said, perplexed that Travis had made something of it. "What I meant was that even though I'd lost my father, and Travis, and had lived in hell with Corey, the land was now mine—mine and John's. I was reaching out to touch the only thing that was real to me."

He nodded. "Yeah, I can understand that, but you have to understand that Travis took it another way. He always did feel that your land meant more to you than he did, and he resented it. So when he saw you clutching that dirt, he said something just popped inside him.

"All along, he didn't know it, but he was clinging to the hope that maybe you did love him. But right then, he knew there was no hope. He'd already decided the boy was really his, so he just did what came natural. He went and got his son and he came back here. And here is where he plans to stay."

"Oh, God," Kitty moaned, swaying to and fro, her hands wrapped around her knees. "I didn't mean it the way Travis took it, Sam. I swear to you on my father's grave."

"Well, me believing you don't matter. It's what Travis believes. I spent all day arguing with him, trying to make him see things the way they really are. But he's stubborn. He don't want no part of you, and the boy stays where he is."

She gave a short, bitter laugh. "And you said you thought he loved me. You were going to make him see that. You were a fool, Sam, a fool! And so was I, to ever get mixed up with such a villain!"

She got to her feet and began pacing up and down anxiously. "I'm not going back without my baby, Sam. I won't leave without him. If I have to go into those swamps by myself and crawl on my hands and knees, I won't go without him."

"Oh, I told him all that," he said matter-of-factly. "He just laughed. He said he reckoned you had so much money now you thought you could do anything, but the one thing you couldn't buy was that boy. He says as ruthless as you are, he don't want you for the mother of his son. I'm sorry, Kitty, but that's what he said, and I have to shoot straight with you. It's over."

She stared at him incredulously. "You mean you think I should just leave and go back to North Carolina without John? I won't do it, Sam."

Sam got up and walked to where she stood, putting his strong arms about her. "Honey, I love you like you was my own daughter, and I ache inside because I know you're aching. But believe me when I say that I know Travis better'n you or anybody else. And he ain't going to give up that boy. You're wasting your time."

She shoved him away. "So you're scared of him. Well, I'm not. I'll fight him with my bare hands if I have to."

"Oh, Kitty, Kitty." He shook his head from side to side, and she could see that his eyes were moist. "I wish I could help you. I honestly do. But there's nothing anybody can do. Maybe, in time to come, he'll change. But for now, there's just nothing we can do."

"I'm not giving up my child, Sam."

They faced each other silently for several moments, and then Sam sighed and said, "Well, I guess I never figured you would, Kitty, and hard as it is for me to say this, I have to be honest and say I won't help you any more. I did what I could. I brought you here. I went into the bayou and found Travis and talked till I was blue in the face, trying to get him to change his mind. Now I've done all I can do, and I won't take up arms against my best friend. I'm going back to North Carolina and finish the job I've got to do up there. Then I'll probably come back here and head into the bayou, too. It's my home. Just like North Carolina is your home. That's where you belong."

"And I won't go there without my baby."

"Well, dang it, girl, how do you expect to get that baby?" His eyes flashed. "I done told you, Travis ain't giving him up. Are you going to march in there with a gun? Hell, you wouldn't get past the first swamp before a snake or a gator had you."

She pursed her lips, and up went that stubborn chin, and Sam knew Travis was in for a fight. "I'll find a way." Her voice was clipped. "Don't you fret about me any more, Sam. Believe me, I'll find a way."

"Travis will figure you don't aim to give up easy. He'll be on his guard."

"I don't care. I won't go home without my baby."

Sighing, Sam shook his head. Shoulders slumped in defeat, he walked to the door. "Kitty, there's a stage heading east tomorrow at noon. I plan to be on it. I wish you'd give up and come back with me."

Her fists were clenched, her lower lip trembling. "How can you ask me to leave here, Sam? That's my baby out there in that . . . that damned swamp! You know I can't go off and leave him. God knows, he's all I've got."

Sam stood looking at her a long time. Then he turned away once again. "Goodbye Kitty. God bless you," he said quietly.

And then he was gone.

Chapter Thirty-two

JEROME Danton waved his arms in the air wildly. "I tell you, woman, it simply cannot be done. I've spent a small fortune trying. Two men are dead, and six have refused to go back in there. The word is out. There isn't enough money in the world to hire anybody to go back and try again. You've got to face the facts. It cannot be done! Travis Coltrane is in the bayou with your son, and you are never going to get him back."

He stopped his frantic pacing to stare down at Kitty seated in a chair by the fireplace, watching him.

"I still refuse to give up."

"It's been two weeks, Kitty! I've been trying for two weeks. I even went to the federal marshals here and asked for help, but they're not going to get involved. Oh, no, you aren't going to get them to take any men in there. 'It's your problem,' they said. 'We've got enough to worry about in the city without getting into a family fight.' That's what they said. And I don't blame them. I thought I could buy the necessary men to get the job done, but the word has spread. No one else will go in there."

"I will go there," she said matter-of-factly. "I'm not afraid."

He stared at her incredulously. Then he fell on his knees before her and clutched her hands desperately.

"No, Kitty. You can't. I won't let you. He'd kill you. You must face reality. Travis has us beaten. There is nothing more we can do. Let's go back home. We'll be married. We'll have other babies. We'll make a new life and forget the misery and pain of the past."

She jerked her hands from his grasp. "I don't intend to leave New Orleans without my son. You can leave whenever you like."

His pleading expression turned to cold anger. "It isn't your baby you're after, is it?"

For a moment she could only stare at him, bewildered. Then she murmured, "I don't understand what you mean, Jerome."

"Oh, the hell you don't. It isn't that baby at all. I should have figured it out before now, but I was so blinded by you that everything else was blotted out. It's Coltrane you want. And you've been using me to get to him. You knew if we got the baby back here, Travis would come after him, and you'd be waiting with open arms to beg him to take you back."

Kitty was fighting to remain composed. "That is not true, Jerome. I'm through with Travis for all time. As for me using you—if you will recall, you are the one who offered your help. I did not go to you. Now you make me think this was all a scheme for you to make me love you."

"There's a stage east leaving at noon today, and I plan to be on it. You're going back with me."

"I'm not leaving without my baby. You go ahead. And if you will figure out how much money all this has cost you, I will see that you are reimbursed."

"Just like that?" He laughed bitterly. "You pay me off? Damn you, woman, I want more than that."

He reached down and yanked her into his arms, his lips mashing down to bruise hers. Caught off guard, Kitty found herself pinned, but she quickly recovered and began to struggle. He had a tight hold, and one of his hands was mauling at her breast. His tongue was forcing its way into her mouth, and when she felt it enter, she bit down.

With a yelp, he leaped back. "You vixen! I'm going to take what I've got coming to me." His face was purple with rage as he advanced towards her. "I'm going to show you I'm every bit the man Travis Coltrane is. I'll make you beg for it. I'll make you whimper and moan and call *my* name."

Kitty's fingers closed around a heavy figurine that sat on the table next to her. Raising it above her head, she cried, "Jerome, don't make me do this."

He looked from her face to the ominous figurine. Then his shoulders slumped. The anger left his face. "All right. I guess I've got sense enough to know when I'm beaten, even if you don't. You can put that thing down. I won't try again."

She held onto it. "I don't trust you, Jerome. I never did. Despite your offer of friendship, I never forgot the way you let your men burn my home and left me in the snow to die giving birth."

"I didn't know you were about to give birth," he snapped.

"You didn't care."

"Hell, you had just tried to kill me. I was wounded, you know."

"You had just helped murder a young boy in cold blood."

"An outlaw!"

"You weren't the law. It wasn't your place to judge him."

"He was a worthless, no-account nigger who deserved to die."

"That was not for you to decide. You took the law into your own hands, just as you did the night you attacked Corey's place and killed him and a lot of his men."

"I'm not going to argue with you." He snatched up his hat. "I'm going to my room and finish packing my things, and I intend to be on that stage. You do whatever you want to."

She nodded curtly.

He paused at the door to turn and ask if there were anything she wanted done when he got back to North Carolina. "I'll still be a friend to you, if you'll let me."

"I have written to Corey's attorney. He is handling all my affairs for me until I get back. Prepare a bill for your services and submit it to him, and he will see that you are paid. I do appreciate your trying to help, Jerome, even though I suspected all along you had an ulterior motive. I wish you a pleasant journey, and I will see you when I return. With my baby." She added firmly.

After he had gone, Kitty paced the room nervously. First Sam, now Jerome. There was no one left but her. By God, she was going to get John or die trying.

Tying on a bonnet and taking a lace shawl from her wardrobe trunk, she left her room and went down the back stairs of the hotel. One of the maids saw her and looked astonished to see her in the service section. "Mrs. McRae, whatever are you doing back here? If you need anything, the desk will be glad to get it."

"What I need, the desk can't help me with." Kitty reached into her bag and brought out a gold piece. It glimmered in the overhead lantern. "This is yours if you will direct me to a person who is for hire."

The maid did not take her eyes off the gold piece. "For hire to do what?"

"Anything. There is always someone around who is for hire to do anything, if you have enough money. I have enough. Direct me to him and this is yours."

"Of course. Wait right here while I tell someone I'm going to be away for a little while."

She disappeared, and Kitty tapped her foot impatiently. A few moments later, the young girl reappeared, motioning Kitty to follow her.

They went out the back door, stepping into a cobblestoned alley. Pools of slime and filth littered the way. Several stray cats gave them wary looks as they passed, hovering possessively over rotting fish carcasses.

They reached the crowded street. The girl extended her hand to Kitty, guiding her through the throng. Jostled and pushed, they made their way to another alley, this one as filthy and odious as the one they had just left. They had not gone far when the girl stopped in front of a thick wooden door. "This is the back door to Billy Jack's place. It's a very rough place, not fit for a lady. Don't go inside. Just knock and ask to speak to Billy Jack himself. He'll either do what you want or help you find someone who will."

She held her palm open for the gold piece. Kitty gave it to her, and she quickly scampered away.

Turning to the door, Kitty knocked. A moment passed, but there was no response. She knocked again, this time so hard that her fist stung. She heard the shuffling of feet, then there was a loud creak as the door rattled open. A heavyset man with a craggy face and yellowed teeth stared down at her. His shirt was covered with greasy stains, and he had a terrible odor.

Swaying slightly, Kitty held onto the doorway to support her weakening knees as she said, "I want to see Billy Jack."

"I'm Billy Jack."

She turned her head as his whiskey breath hit her face.

"Well, what do you want?" he snarled, noting her revulsion. "I ain't got time to stand here all day."

She took a deep breath, stiffened her spine, and forced herself to face him. "I am told you are for hire."

"For hire to do what?"

"Anything, if the price is right."

"Well, what is it you want done? Don't beat around the bush."

"Are you familiar with the bayou?"

He nodded. "I was born and bred there. I know it inside out."

"And you know of a man named Coltrane? Travis Coltrane?"

His eyes sparkled, but only momentarily. "Yeah, I know him. Why? What do you want him for?"

"That is my concern," she said crisply. "All I'm asking you to do is take me to him. I have business with him. Personal business."

He put his hands on his hips and leaned over to eye level, meeting her gaze. "You want me to take you into the bayou to where Coltrane lives? Lady, do you know how much that will cost you? A thousand in gold. And I ain't gonna take you right there to his place. I've heard how somebody is out to get him, and how he's already shot two of 'em. I ain't aiming to get shot. I'll take you to within spittin' distance, and then you can go the rest of the way alone."

"Just point me in the right direction, and that will be fine. I'll have the money with me when we leave."

He reached up and scratched at his nose, then dug into his buttocks anxiously as he said, "Okay. You got a deal. When you aim to leave?"

"As soon as possible. I don't want to have to make my way alone in the dark."

"Then be back here in half an hour—with the money. Lady, you got yourself a guided tour into the bayou. And put on something besides that fancy gown. That won't last five minutes there."

He closed the door in her face, and she turned and ran all the way back to the hotel. Once in her room, she dug into her wardrobe trunk and brought out the old, faded Confederate uniform she had worn in the hospital. She had had a hunch it would come in handy.

Stripping off her green taffeta gown, she stepped into the gray pants and shirt. Tying her hair back, she jammed a cap down on her head. Her face void of any rouge, she looked like a young Rebel soldier. She'd seen some of the men on the streets wearing pants or shirts they'd had during the war. No one thought anything about it.

Wrapping the gold in her handkerchief, she stuffed it inside her shirt. Then she slipped out of the hotel once again, heart pounding.

Billy Jack was waiting in the alley with two horses. His eyes bulged when he saw her. "Now, that was a complete change." She said nothing, and when he offered to help her mount her horse, she brushed him aside and climbed right on.

"I gotta respect a woman who knows how to take care of herself like you do," he laughed. "What I can't figure out, though, is how come you got to go to Coltrane. A pretty thing like you, why, he oughta come crawling outa that boggy land and find you, 'stead of the other way around."

"May we be on our way, please?" Kitty urged him. "I do want to take advantage of the daylight."

"Sure, sure." He mounted his horse. "We won't be riding long, lady. Once we get in the bayou country, we're gonna have to go on foot. You understand this ain't no picnic."

"I understand." She nodded. "Just lead the way."

As they rode through town, a few curious eyes looking their way, Kitty felt the cold steel of the small derringer against her bare skin. She had tucked it inside the waist of the uniform trousers. She prayed she would not need it, but if it came to Travis' life or taking her son back, then she would have no choice. She just hoped he would listen to reason.

No, she corrected herself. There would be no begging and pleading. She would surprise him and catch him unawares. Then she would hold the gun on him and take the baby, and there would be nothing he could do about it. That was the way to handle it. Sam had tried reasoning, and had even done some pleading on her behalf. Jerome had sent hired gunmen charging in to try and flush Travis out. Well, she would use cunning and catch him unawares. No conversation, no arguing. Just take the baby and go. It would be simple. It had to be.

Soon they were out of the city. The woods on each side of the road looked dense and ominous. Billy Jack reined his horse down a path, and Kitty followed. Snakelike vines hung all about them, and they swatted at the stinging deerflies and mosquitoes. The horses protested as their hooves began to sink into the muck.

"It's almost as dark as night in here," Kitty called out to Billy Jack. "I had no idea it was like this."

"Few people do." He was stopping his horse, dismounting. "It ain't the kind of place people like to visit just for fun, missy. Now, we're going to have to walk the rest of the way. You follow me and watch what I do and where I stop. There's quicksand around here. You know what that is?"

She nodded, but he wasn't looking and went on to explain the deadly substance to her. "You step in quicksand and it's going to suck you under. It looks like solid ground, some of it, so you gotta be extra careful. Try to step close to the tree trunks. Walk on the roots of these cypresses sticking up like little knees, see? But you've got to watch out for snakes, too. Damned cottonmouths are everywhere, and if they bite you, you're done for."

Kitty shivered. She had been in swamps and dense woods from time to time during the war but never anything as quietly frightening as this place. They seemed lost in a world of gray and green foliage, vines wrapping clutching fingers around everything in sight. Now and then a strange sound would split the air. Billy Jack would identify its source. "An owl . . . that one's a bull gator . . . just a bird." They all sounded terrifying to her ears, but she was determined to keep her composure. Somewhere in all this dismal isolation was her child, and she intended to get him out of here at any cost. Oh, what could Travis be thinking? How could he bring a *baby* here?

Suddenly, as though a curtain had been drawn, they stepped onto a river bank. Kitty sucked in her breath at the beauty of the scene before her. Moss-draped trees lined the bank. A pink-feathered bird with incredibly long legs stood in the water. Billy Jack said it was a flamingo.

"There is beauty here, isn't there?"

"Oh, yes ma'm." He nodded. "There sure is beauty in the bayou. Oh, there's ugly places, too, and there's danger. But there's beauty. That's why folks like to live here. They find a peace they don't find back there in that other world, I reckon. I grew up in a little shack at the edge. Fishing off the river for the rest of my life didn't shake my britches up, so as soon as I was old enough, I went to the city. I can see why some would rather stay here, though. I guess it all depends on what you want out of life. Too much quiet would run me crazy."

They made their way along the river bank. Kitty spied a few of the stilted cottages Travis had told her about. "Coltrane lives in a house like that, doesn't he?"

"Yeah. It ain't too far from here. We go around the next bend, and the river forks off into a slough that winds back into the Blue Bayou for a couple of miles. His place is back up in there. No other houses around his. His family laid claim to the Blue. They didn't want nobody else building around them."

"And what is the Blue Bayou?"

"Oh, that's just a name somebody gave it a long time ago. I hear that just before the sun sets over the treetops in the evening, and just before it rises in the morning, the whole world in that slough turns blue. Like a piece of the sky just drifted down and covered everything. The water, the trees, the air—everything is blue. So they call it Blue Bayou. It's said to be the prettiest place in the swamps. I've heard more than one say that, so it must be true."

They rounded a bend, and Kitty could see the river forking. "Up there. Just follow this bank." Billy Jack pointed.

"You aren't going with me?" she asked, frightened now for the first time.

"Me?" He laughed. "No, ma'm. Not me. I ain't got no business with Travis Coltrane and don't want none. He ain't bothered me, and I ain't plannin' on botherin' him. I'll be heading back to town now, if you'll just give me my money."

Kitty sputtered, "Back to town? Well, how will I find my way out of here?"

"There's a notch in that cypress where we stepped out of the woods. Just follow the river bank back, then you'll see the path. It ain't hard. Believe me, ma'm, I took a chance on even bringing you this far. He's liable to get mad over me doing this much, so I'd appreciate it if you'd not tell him who brung you in. Now, can I have that money? The bargain was for me to take you within hollering distance. I didn't say nothing about waiting around to get shot at."

Turning her back, she reached inside her shirt and brought out the little pouch with the money inside. Handing it to him, she murmured, "I'd pay you an equal sum to wait here for me."

He laughed nervously. "You ain't got enough money to pay me to hang around here, lady. Now, good luck to you. I don't know what your business is with Coltrane, and I don't want to know. But for your sake, I hope you're a friend of his, or the gators gonna be eating you for breakfast."

With a wink and a flash of yellowed teeth, he waved, turned, and broke into a run as he weaved his way along the river bank.

Kitty had never felt more alone. Casting a wary eye skywards, she figured she had about an hour or so until sundown. She would pick her way carefully, find Travis' cabin, then hide out through the night. Just before dawn she would creep into his house and take him by surprise. Perhaps he would be sleeping so soundly that she would not even have a confrontation with him at all. She could take John and be on her way, and by the time he awoke she would be safely back in town. She had already decided the first thing she would do would be to hire bodyguards in case Travis came after her. Once she was on the stage, started for home, it was doubtful he would pursue her. But Travis was unpredictable, and she wanted to be ready for any possibility.

Threading her way along the river bank, she paused several times to wonder at the magical beauty of her surroundings. Despite the mission before her, she found herself bathed in the first tranquility she had known in a long, long time. It was easy to see why Travis loved this bayou country.

So far there had been no alligators or snakes or anything threatening. An annoyed turtle had rolled off a log, making a loud splash as he disappeared into the water. An owl cried out, startling her momentarily.

She had to be getting close. She slowed her pace, peering above reeds and bushes before stepping into a clearing. She paused to listen for human sounds.

Then, like an invisible hand passing overhead, the air about her turned from clear to a pale, pale blue.

Gasping, Kitty froze where she stood, watching as everything around became bathed in the azure color. Blue Bayou. It was true. In that moment between daylight and darkness, the world had turned blue. It took her breath away.

Slowly the light paled and the world grew dark. She moved faster, wanting to sight the cabin before seeking refuge for the night.

Rounding one more bend, she saw it, not a hundred yards away. There was no sound. Squatting down behind a rotted tree trunk, Kitty stared at the cabin sitting up on stilts. That had to be Travis' home. There she would find her precious baby. It was all she could do to keep from breaking into a run. She had to find shelter for the night. Eyes darting about, she could see nothing but swamp. She could not crouch where she was all night. Snakes and alligators would be roaming.

The sound of voices snapped her head up. Travis was standing on the porch talking to a plump old woman, her head wrapped in a bright bandanna. Kitty could not hear what they were saying, but it was obvious the woman was leaving. Travis waved to her, and she began to descend the ladder leaning against the porch. Would she come this way? Kitty's heart was in her throat. If she did, there was nothing for Kitty to do but crawl on her stomach into the swamp itself, lest she be discovered.

A sigh of relief escaped her lips as the woman went beyond the cabin and into the woods behind it, disappearing. Travis went inside. It was nearly dark. Alone again, she made her way forward steadily. She reached the ladder and inched her way up.

She crouched on the porch. Inside she could hear Travis talking to John, lovingly, adoringly, and the answering coos and gurgles of her son. Oh, dear God, she thought frantically, clenching her fists, don't let me ruin it now. Don't let me run in there and ruin it all.

She crawled to the farthest end of the porch, sinking down into the shadows. There she would spend the night, trying not to fall asleep.

With the dawn, Kitty would be ready. She would creep inside and take her baby. And, God willing, by the time Travis awoke she would be safely back in New Orleans.

The night air turned chilly, and Kitty hugged her knees to her chest, wrapping her arms tightly about her legs. It would be the longest night of her life.

Chapter Thirty-three

KITTY opened her eyes slowly. Shivering in the early morning chill, she wrapped her arms about her shoulders. And then she saw it again—Blue Bayou. The foggy mist rising up from the river, the moss-draped trees, the reverent stillness of the silent woods and swamps, all shrouded in a soft blue haze. It was ethereal. Kitty was awed.

But then she was wide awake. She knew it was time to move. There was no time to lose. Dear God, she had not meant to fall asleep.

"Hello, Kitty."

He was sitting on the porch railing, knees apart, hands folded between. A blue man, she thought dizzily. A handsome, strangely smiling, blue man. "Oh, no . . ." Her hand flew to her throat.

"Oh, yes." He continued to smile. "Did you really think you could slip up on me, Kitty? You seem to have forgotten a lot of things. I have instincts about people. I can smell them around me. It's a special sense I have, and if I didn't have it, I would've been dead long ago. I'm surprised you didn't remember that. And don't reach for that gun you had tucked in your trousers. I've already relieved you of it."

She began to tremble. "How long have you known I was here?"

"I knew when you first came up the ladder. When

you didn't come on inside, I figured you were going to wait till just before dawn. How do you like Blue Bayou? Beautiful, isn't it? Few people ever experience such a sight. Now you can see why this place can crawl right into your heart and stay. It's another world, untouched by all the ugliness in the one you came from."

Slowly she got to her feet, anger giving her the strength she needed. "Travis, I came to take my baby home. You had no right to kidnap him."

"No?" He raised an eyebrow, one corner of his mouth turning up in that insolent smile. "I had every right, lovely lady. He's my son."

"I brought him to you and tried to tell you that, but you wouldn't listen."

"After all you had done? Why should I believe anything you tell me? But now I've got my son. So you can go back to North Carolina and sucker some other man. Sam told me you had Jerome Danton with you."

"He's gone. So is Sam. There's no one left but me, and I don't intend to leave without John."

"You're in my territory now, Kitty. Your hired guns found out they didn't have a chance against me, so how do you think you're going to fare? I won't shoot you. I've killed a lot of men, but never a woman. But I promise you this, you won't take my boy away from me. Now, I'll do the hospitable thing and invite you inside for a cup of coffee, and then I'll take you to the main road myself, to make sure a gator or a moccasin doesn't get you. It's dangerous in these parts when you don't know your way around. It's dangerous even when you do. So let's go inside. We'll be on our way as soon as Malah gets here."

"Malah?" she echoed, stunned by his calm certainty.

"The old Creole woman who looks after John while I'm off fishing. She'll be here in about an hour or so."

He moved lithely from the railing, his feet not making a sound as they touched the floor. His fingers closed in a steely grip around her elbow. As she looked up into his eyes, she was startled to see that in the strange predawn light they, too, were blue, instead of the smoky gray color she had once loved.

Roughly, he jerked her down the side and around to the front porch, all the way to the door. She was flung inside. Looking about, Kitty took in the crude but comfortable furnishings. There was one corner for cooking and eating, with a small wood stove and a handmade table. The floor was covered with a woven reed matting. Her gaze took in the wide bed, the roughhewn tables and chairs. And then she saw the wooden box in a corner, and she yanked out of Travis' grasp to run quickly across the floor.

John lay on his side, sleeping soundly, his thumb in his mouth. Tears stung her eyes. Except for being a bit chubbier, he was the same. "My baby," she whispered, arms reaching out for him.

"No," Travis said harshly in a low voice, grabbing her and spinning her about to face him. "Don't wake him up, Kitty. Not now. You'll only make things worse when you leave without him."

"He cries for me, doesn't he?" she said accusingly. "I know he does. That's why Corey had him taken to one of the slave cabins, so I wouldn't hear him crying for me. And even after all this time, he hasn't stopped, has he? Oh, Travis, how can you *be* so cruel? It doesn't matter if you hate me, but don't take that hatred out on our child. Can't you see what you're doing to him? Do you despise me so much you would let an innocent baby suffer because of it?"

He had been staring at her intensely, his jaw twitching. Suddenly he was scooping her into his arms and walking towards the bed.

"Travis, what do you think you are doing?" she protested, stunned. "Put me down."

He laid her gently on the bed, then lowered himself to pin her body beneath his. Brushing her hair from her face with a tenderness she found surprising, he whispered, "Kitty, I want to tell you something. I never wanted a woman like I wanted you. From the first time I saw you, I knew I had to have you. Oh, I fought it. You'll never know how damned hard I did fight it. I refused to believe I could love any woman. Sam saw it before I did, and he tried to tell me, but I laughed at him. But he was right. I did love you. Maybe I still do, but you've done too much, Kitty, for me to ever trust you again. I'd be scared to turn my back on you."

Wriggling in his arms, she snapped, "I don't want you to love me, you pompous ass! All I want is to take my baby and get out of here."

"You aren't going to take that boy, Kitty. You can just get that out of your head right now. He's here, and he's going to stay here."

"You think this is any place to raise a child?"

"I was raised here."

"Yes, and look how you turned out! An animal, a savage! You think I want that for my son? I want him to have the best. I can give it to him now. Can't you see that? You're selfish, Travis. You don't care about him. You never cared about me."

He laughed, a deep, husky laugh, and his gaze upon her was warm. The blue was not here in the cabin, Kitty realized, and his eyes were smoky gray, still fringed with thick, dusty lashes. Her body was starting to tingle, and she hated it for betraying her. He always did have this effect on her. She was weak, and he knew it.

His lips were so close she could feel them brushing against hers as he spoke. "We had some good times together, whether we loved each other or not, didn't we? Seeing you in that old Reb uniform"—he chuckled —"brings back a lot of memories, Kitty. Nights spent on pine needle beds, hours when we were locked together as tight as a man and woman can get."

He was pressed tightly against her, and the familiar longing began to burn in her. She cursed herself.

"Oh, honey, it was good," he murmured. And then his lips were closing over hers, warm, possessive, his big hand cupping her face, holding her still as his mouth worked hungrily. His tongue darted between her lips, touching hers, and she could not suppress the satisfied sigh that rippled through her body. His hand moved to cup her breast gently, squeezing possessively.

Kitty told herself this was wrong, but her body was crying out for the familiar passion that it knew only Travis could satisfy. Nimble fingers worked at the buttons of her shirt, and then her breasts were tumbling forth into his eager hands. As he lowered his face, she caressed his soft, dark hair, moaning out loud as his teeth bit gently into one taut nipple. He began to suck hungrily, at the same time she felt her trousers being worked down over her writhing hips.

She could only succumb to the hot fever that was consuming her body. Powerless, helpless, she could do nothing but moan as he worked on her body, igniting fires that had never entirely burned out, but had been smoldering all this time.

"It was always good, wasn't it, Kitty?" He lifted his eyes to stare into her face. "God, you're beautiful. If only you hadn't been such a conniving little—" And then he trembled, clamping teeth upon her breast once again, this time so fiercely she cried out in pain. At the same time, he was moving on top of her, spreading her thighs with his knee, then mounting her.

She wanted to fight back but could not. Her body was betraying her now just as it had so many times in the past. Travis possessed this strange hold over her, and she was powerless to control the gnawing hunger that stripped her of her will.

He filled her with himself. "You can stay here," he whispered against her breast, lying very still, all of him inside her now. "You can stay here and tend to John like Malah does, only you'll be my woman. I'll satisfy you every night of your life, Kitty."

"No," she whimpered, twisting beneath him, struggling for the self-control she knew would not come. "Never that way, Travis. Never."

Almost viciously, he began to move his hips to and fro, plunging in and out, slamming her against the bed. "Then we'll just have it this one last time to remember for always," he ground out as he raised up to press a thumb into each side of her pelvis, fingers gripping her backside to hold her firmly beneath his assaulting thrusts. Again and again he pummeled into her.

Kitty felt the rising cry of her body as her nails dug instinctively into the strong, firm muscles of his back. It was coming, that strange, wonderful feeling that only Travis could make happen. It was coming, and she could not stop it, and suddenly it was there, and she was clinging to him, sobbing aloud with the wonder and joy of it all. The cry of ecstacy could not be suppressed as the wild sweetness engulfed her. She felt him reach his own height, the moans of pleasure escaping his lips.

And then he was gathering her close, rolling on his side once again, holding her tightly against his body. "It could never be this good with anyone else," he said quietly. "There were women before and after, but never one like you, Kitty."

She lay motionless, the passion subsiding and being replaced once again by cold anger. Even now, she thought indignantly, he could speak of others.

"I hate you, Travis," she said, quietly and simply. "And if you are through with me, I would like to take my baby and go."

He raised his head, that crooked smile on his lips once again. "You aren't taking the boy, Kitty. Now, you can just get that through that pretty head of yours once and for all. You can stay and be my woman, and tend to my son. I'd like having you in my bed every night."

"You go to hell." She tried to slap his smugly smiling face, but he caught her wrist, gripping it so painfully she winced.

"I told you once, Kitty, you'll never slap me again. Now don't make me be rough with you. If you won't accept my terms, then the thing for you to do is just get the hell out of here."

She chewed her lower lip thoughtfully. There had to be a way. She had come too far to fail now, and there would never be another chance. "All right," she said finally, deciding to go along and play his little game until she could work out a plan. "May I have that cup of coffee first?"

"Of course." He moved from the bed, straightening his clothes. "I always like to oblige my ladies, especially you, Kitty. You're the best."

She bit her tongue. Now was not the time to quarrel. And his lovemaking had been good, even though she still cursed her body for its betrayal. She would always remember this time, and all the other times when he had made her glory in her womanhood.

He moved to the stove, and she watched as he got a fire going, then set a kettle to boiling. Her eyes darted around the room. Her heart leaped into her throat as she saw it—the rifle propped beside the door. No, she wouldn't shoot him in the back. She could never do that. But she could bring the rifle butt crashing down over his head, to knock him unconscious while she took John and made her getaway. And once she was back in New Orleans, she would hire her bodyguards. He would no longer be a threat.

Quietly, she moved from the bed. His back was turned, and he was talking about the coffee, saying something about how he hoped it would not be too strong for her, but she should remember the strange concoctions they'd been forced to drink during the war.

Without making a sound, Kitty picked up the rifle by the barrel, butt end up. Travis never suspected a thing, for he was intent on making coffee. She was able to sneak right up behind him, then, with every ounce of strength she had in her, she brought the rifle down in a slanted arch, striking him across the back of his head. His knees buckled forward, and he crumpled silently to the floor.

She did not pause to see how badly he was hurt. It did not matter. She would not *let* it matter. What was done was done. She could not stop now.

Turning, she ran to the makeshift crib and reached down to scoop John into her arms. His eyes flashed open, startled, and he began to cry with fright. "Shhhhh, darling." She held him tightly. "It's all over now. Mommy has you, and we'll never be apart again."

She was almost out the door when she remembered the rifle she had dropped after striking Travis. The swamp was dangerous, and she was alone now. She might need a weapon. Quickly, she hurried to retrieve it. Juggling John with one arm, she maneuvered the rifle and made her way out and down the ladder.

Her feet touched the ground. The Bayou was no longer blue. It lay before her, gray and ominous, and she knew the path ahead would be dangerous. She would have to watch herself every step of the way. John was still crying, and she crooned to him as she began to walk quickly.

Something caught her eye, and she turned to see a bright bandanna—then the startled expression on the face of the woman who wore it. Malah. She cried out to Kitty, but Kitty turned and fled.

Threading her way gingerly along the river bank, she found the first bend. How much farther to where she would enter the swamp? Dear God, she did not know. She had to watch carefully for the sign of the path. If she missed it, she could wind up wandering along the river until Travis awoke and came after her.

Something bellowed to her right, and she suppressed a scream as she realized she had passed within a few feet of a slant-eyed alligator lying on the river bank. He opened his mouth, displaying dozens of long, razor-sharp teeth. Bile rose in her throat, and she stumbled over a piece of driftwood, almost falling. Righting herself, she began to run, leaping over debris in her path. Move . . . run . . . fast . . . faster . . . her heart was pounding, its thundering beats echoing above John's frantic shrieks.

The path! Thank God, the path was there. She cut from the river bank to enter the vine-covered world of the swamp, knowing instinctively that from this point on she could not move fast. She had to be on guard against quicksand, snakes, the slapping branches and ripping thorns. And it was almost dark. No sunlight penetrated the thick growth above.

How long had she been gone from the cabin? She had no way of knowing. An hour? John had fallen into an exhausted half-sleep, and he snuggled against her weary, aching shoulder, his thumb in his mouth. Picking her way along, she continued to croon to him, telling him that soon they would be safe. Soon he would have warm, dry clothing and food.

Then she heard it, and her blood turned to ice.

"Kitty? *Kitty, where are you?*"

Travis. She could hear him crashing somewhere behind her, and not too far behind, either. Oh, God, how could he be so close? He knew this place, of course. Now she had to move even faster.

"Kitty, you're crazy! You'll never make it out of here. You're putting John's life in danger as well as your own. Answer me, damn it."

Something slapped against her face, something sticky and grabbing, and she fought the scream bubbling in her throat as she realized she had stumbled into a giant spider web. And there it was, the ugly gray thing, as big as her hand, and she slapped out with the rifle, knocking it away as she twisted and turned, stumbling, falling, dropping John to the ground with a soft thud.

She scrambled to her feet, holding the gun under her arm as she covered the baby's mouth with her hand. He was awake once more, about to cry. "Forgive me, darling, but I can't let you make a sound," she whispered frantically.

Whipping about, she realized with panic that she had somehow gotten off the path. There were no weeds trampled down, no defined trail, nothing—just brush and vines and trees and swampy patches that might be quicksand. Oh, where was the trail? How could she have been so careless? Because she was frightened, that's how, she cursed. There had to be a way out of this place . . . had to be . . . had to be . . . the silent chant thundered in rhythm to her heartbeat.

And then she heard the loud, agonizing cry. She froze where she stood.

"*Quicksand!*"

The tortured cry was Travis'.

"Quicksand! I'm in quicksand! Kitty, help me!"

"It's a trick!" she said out loud, angry that he would stoop so low. It had to be a trick. He *knew* these swamps, every inch. He would never be so foolish as to stumble into quicksand.

"Help me, *please.*"

She continued to move forward, and then something made her stop. She looked at John. His eyes were turning from a baby blue to a smoky gray, and he was staring at her intently, as though he knew, somehow, what was going on, and he was asking her how she could walk away from his daddy and leave him to die.

"This is ridiculous," she hissed. "You can't know what's going on. You're just a baby. And it doesn't matter. He was going to take you from me, can't you see that?" Tears were streaming down her cheeks. But John continued to watch her steadily.

Closing her eyes, she remembered the kisses and the fury, everything that had ever transpired between them. God, she had loved him once, and she loved him still, even though she hated admitting it. She could not turn back.

"Kitty, for God's sake!"

The voice sounded weaker. He was not moving forward.

John continued to stare at her, and suddenly she screamed at him, "You're just a baby! You can't condemn me. You can't really know."

She turned back slowly, woodenly.

With a raging heart, she plunged back the way she had come, running when possible, thorns ripping at her body, fighting the brush. She reached the clearing, and froze. Travis was in quicksand up to his waist. She could see it sucking at him, pulling him under. He was only a few feet away, and her toes stood at the edge of what must have been the beginning of the treacherous mire.

"Help me, Kitty." His eyes mirrored the terror he was feeling. "I've only got another few minutes if you don't."

She shook her head, choking back the sobs. "I don't know what to do."

"Put the baby down. Then unload the gun quickly. It might accidentally go off. Hand it to me butt end, and you hang onto the barrel with one hand, brace yourself with the other to that tree there. Just hang on and let me pull myself out."

John did not make a sound as she laid him safely out of the way. Then she unloaded the gun and gripped one hand tightly against the tree, digging in to brace her feet. She extended the butt end towards Travis, leaning forward as far as she dared.

Slowly, very slowly, he lifted his arm up and out of the quicksand. Inches separated his fingers from the gun. "Not close enough," he whispered in agony. "It won't work."

Kitty moved instinctively. Yanking off her shirt, she paid no mind to her bare breasts as she wrapped the garment around the treetrunk, then gripped a dangling sleeve with shaking fingers. It gave her the span she needed to lean out a bit more. This time, Travis was able to close his hand around the butt.

"Good girl. Now hang on," he panted. "I'm going to have to work my way out slow. You're going to have to brace yourself, honey, and use every muscle you've got!"

The first pull came harder than she had expected. Kitty's foot slipped, and Travis sank another inch. "Kitty, you've got to hold on," he cried, his face twisted in anguish. "For God's sake, hold on!"

She was ready for the next tug. He moved up and forward, slowly, very slowly, working his fingers up on the butt of the gun. He was almost to the trigger, his chest free now, moving his grip ever so carefully. Kitty could feel the flesh tearing in her hands as Travis' strength pulled against her, causing the material of the shirt to cut tautly into her hand. She did not move.

Her teeth dug into her lower lip, and she tasted blood. Her head was swimming dizzily as she stood frozen, hardly daring to breathe. One slip and he could go sliding back down into the gray-green mire, out of reach, and she would have to stand there and watch him, helpless, as he sank to his death.

Her eyes squeezed shut. If he slipped, she did not want to see it. She could not bear to see the slime close over those smoky eyes that had haunted her day and night for so long. Could it end like this? It would have been better had she died on the battlefield. This hour would haunt her forever.

Suddenly there was a tug so strong that Kitty felt her bloodied hand slipping from its grip on the shirt. "I can't hold on!" she cried, feeling herself tumbling forward.

Her eyes flashed open. She was falling straight into Travis' outstretched arms. Folding her against his chest, he gasped, "It's all right, Kitty. It's over. You got me out."

They clung together in silence for long moments, hearts pounding, and then he was tilting her face upwards to meet his probing gaze. "Why did you do it? You could have let me die. You would never have had me to worry about ever again."

"I couldn't leave you," she said quietly, clinging to him. "Not again. Travis, you won't believe me when I tell you I never stopped loving you. Everything I did was for John, so he wouldn't suffer. But you won't believe that. And I can't make you.

"But that doesn't mean I want you dead. I'll fight you till I die for my baby, but I don't want you dead." Her voice broke, and she tried to pull back, but he held her tightly.

With her golden-red hair nestled beneath his chin, Travis moved his hands up and down her back. Her closeness was all he had wanted. It was time he understood that. "We've been through hell, girl. You know that? And it's over, all of it. We've got a lifetime before us, and by God, we're going to make up for all the hell."

She pulled back to look at him cautiously.

"Yes." He smiled his crooked smile. "I love you, Kitty, and I'm not going to let you go again. Now let's take our boy and get to New Orleans. We've got a long ride ahead of us to North Carolina, and I imagine I've got a lot of work waiting for me when I get there."

"Travis, you mean it?" she whispered, swaying against him.

He held her tightly. "Hell, yes, I mean it. Any woman who did what you just did has to be in love. And that's all I ever wanted, Kitty, was to know you really love me."

"Travis, I do. And I always have."

Their lips met. It was a strangely gentle kiss, a kiss of promise.

John cried out indignantly, and they drew apart. "We've got a hungry boy on our hands," Travis laughed, scooping him up tenderly. "Let's go."

Holding his son in one arm, Travis put his other around his beloved. He led them out of the swamp. Their hearts, at long last, were at peace: Kitty and Travis were nearly home.

Across a landscape consumed by the scorching emotions of Civil War, comes an epic tale of love and conflict, desire and hate, of beautiful, rebellious Katherine Wright who was abducted, ravished, and torn between two men:

Nathan Collins, the Rebel, who dreamed of making Katherine his wife, but would never accept her craving for a life of her own.

Travis Coltrane, the Yankee, who made her wild with fury one moment, and delirious with passion the next.

Two loyalties. Two loves. One triumphant saga that rips across war-torn lands and the embattled terrains of the heart!

Avon 47704 $2.50 LW 10/79

"In the best tradition of Scarlett O'Hara"
Publisher's Weekly

BARBARA FERRY JOHNSON

DELTA BLOOD

Leah had always known what it was to be a woman, to want as women want. And now, on the night of New Orlean's most dazzling ball, a lifetime of smoldering passions drew her into the deepening twilight, into the bayous that echoed still with drum-beats and Voodoo chants . . .

in an unforgettable saga of the Civil War, as throbbing with life as the splendorous South it portrays.

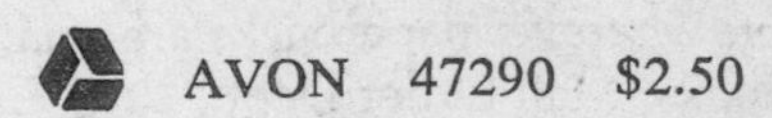

DELTA 7-79